JOHANN LAESECKE

Road Trip Blues

The Roaring Road Series Book 3

I0629134

ROAD TRIP DOG
PUBLISHING

To Lori,
The love of my life, who told me to stop talking about writing a book and start writing it.

The Roaring Road is a work of historical fiction. Names, characters, organizations, places, events, dialogue and incidents portrayed in this novel are products of the author's imagination or used fictitiously.

THE ROARING ROAD
Book 3 of The Roaring Road Series
Copyright © 2017-2019 by Johann C.M. Laesecke
For more information contact: johann@roadtripdogpublishing.com

Road Trip Dog Publishing
An imprint of The LaureDan Company

The Roaring Road website: www.theroaringroad.com

Cover design and illustration by Don Henderson
Henderson Graphic Design & Illustration www.hendersongdi.com

Print ISBN   978-0-9964861-6-3
Epub ISBN   978-0-9964861-7-0

A YOUNG GIRL'S JOURNEY

Location: The Prussian Partition of Poland

She played quietly in the children's day room in the family quarters of the citadel while her six-year-old brother napped in his day bed, supervised by a young nanny. The little girl was very intelligent and at eight years of age spoke French almost as well as her native Polish. Her father, Count Stefan Czarnecki, was a *szlachta*, a member of the nobility class. Kaiser Frederick-Wilhelm IV of Prussia granted Count Stefan's title on October 30, 1854. At the time, Poland was not a sovereign country since Prussia, Russia and Austria partitioned it, but many held on to their Polish identity. A member of the Polish nobility class typically controlled one or more villages. Count Stefan was lord over a large area with many villages.

Shattering the peacefulness of the children's playroom, several armed soldiers and household staff burst into the room and swept up the children and the nanny. The soldiers brought them to the large ballroom in the castle where she saw her father and mother. The household servants began to sort through the books and playthings.

The ballroom was a scene of chaos. Count Stefan was issuing orders to his soldiers, giving them instructions and sending them on missions. Servants were taking down the large paintings and portraits from the walls and carrying them down to underground storage vaults. Other house servants were packing trunks of clothing and household goods under the direction of the butler. Footmen were bringing large trunks in and carrying full trunks out to load into wagons in the courtyard. Horsemen bearing messages came and departed every few minutes. Coachmen hitched and unhitched teams of horses as wagons and carriages came in empty and left the courtyard loaded. Everything was moving faster than she had ever seen anything happen in her young years, yet her father and mother maintained calm and order.

The girl went to a window that overlooked the village. She smelled smoke in the air and it gave her the feeling that something terrible was happening, but the little girl did not cry. She took her strength from her mother, the Countess Magdalena, who calmly issued orders to the household staff for preparation of provisions for a long journey. The girl did not understand at first, but listened and learned that there was a great danger coming, and the family would have to leave even though her father had many soldiers.

Still, she felt confident with her father's soldiers because they were always protective and kind to her and her brother. Captain Gregorz was Count Stefan's second in command and had given long and loyal service to his lordship. She liked Gregorz, he taught her how to ride a horse and he often brought her and her brother out with his grandchildren to watch the soldiers training and marching around the countryside, and they would cheer the soldiers practicing their shooting at the gun range. When she told her father she and her brother wanted to learn to shoot like the soldiers, he gave them small rifles and the soldiers taught them how to shoot. They carved small wood toys as prizes for her and her brother when they had a good shooting practice and sang songs to them as they presented the toys. It all seemed so exciting then, but today their faces were grim. There was none of the usual casual banter among the men.

Early the next morning a caravan of fourteen wagons was ready to depart. Count Stefan was staying at the citadel with a company of soldiers. The little girl, her brother, the nanny and Countess Magdalena were to ride in the third wagon. The feeling of danger and adventure was in the air and she was excited. Nothing like this had ever happened before in her life, and now they were preparing to travel on a great journey. She felt safe, trusting her father's soldiers would not let anything happen to them.

Count Stefan came to the wagon train to say good-bye to his family. Magdalena held herself with dignity but the girl could see tears in the corners of her eyes. Her husband put his arms around her and whispered in her ear, reassuring her that all would be well, as it was in earlier times, and Magdalena recovered her calm demeanor.

It was the first time the little girl had ever seen her mother cry, and she and her brother began to cry too. The count hugged his son. He took his son aside for a short walk to tell him he must be brave and help the soldiers protect and take care of his sister and mother.

Count Stefan turned to the little girl. Although he loved all his family, she was the apple of his eye. "Vera, my *księżniczka*, my princess, I expect you to be brave like your mother. My trusted friend Gregorz is commanding the soldiers I have assigned to escort you, your mother and your brother to France for safekeeping. I will come for you when it is peaceful again. Now, young lady, pay attention and learn your lessons. Follow your mother's instructions precisely. This is important so you will grow up to be a beautiful and intelligent countess, worthy of being addressed as Lady Vera." He gave her a cloth bag, saying "Here is your favorite doll that went missing yesterday. I found it in your playroom and Nanny made this cloth bag to protect it from the dust on the road. Take good care of it on your adventure. I want you to show it to me when I come to bring my family back home when all is safe again. I want you to know that I love each of you very much, and I will miss you until we are reunited."

The count gave each of his family a last hug and kiss. Then just as quickly as he had arrived he left, turning away from his family so they could not see the tears welling up in his own eyes.

Count Stefan gave final instructions to Gregorz and his soldiers who were traveling with the caravan, some in the wagons and others riding horses alongside the column.

Vera watched her handsome, strong father as he walked with military precision like the general he was before becoming a nobleman as a reward for his success on the battlefields. She waved to him when he turned to wave as the caravan began to move out of the courtyard. The shadow of a storm cloud fell over them, and by this omen she knew she would never see her father again.

The first days were exciting as they traveled through the countryside and she saw things she had never seen before. Several times during the first two days they saw small groups of soldiers marching toward her father's citadel to join the soldiers there. Magdalena set aside the pain of leaving her husband, and by showing her stoic resolve she kept up the spirits of her children along with the servants, soldiers and the families in the caravan. Vera noticed the soldiers with the caravan were mostly older men, retired soldiers, and soldiers with large families, along with a few of the younger soldiers. The soldiers were all heavily armed and somber, but when they were near the family they always smiled and seemed confident.

Countess Magdalena and her children changed into peasant clothes so they would not be recognized as nobility. "We must be very careful" Magdalena told her children "Some peasants do not like the nobility. Until we cross the border into France, do not leave the wagon unless Gregorz or I tell you to do so and always stay close."

Tension filled the air one afternoon as they came to a halt at a place where soldiers in different uniforms were guarding a gate across the road. Gregorz went ahead to talk to the officer in charge of the gate. It seemed that they were not to be allowed to pass, but Gregorz and the other officer went inside a small building. When they came out, the officer told his soldiers to allow the caravan to pass.

This proved to be true, as several times over the next few days people threw rocks at the wagons as they passed through the towns and villages. Some of the children in the larger towns ran alongside to hit the wagons with sticks. At night the caravan would camp away from the towns, the wagons formed in a square with soldiers stationed to watch the countryside around the wagons at night. The first casualty occurred on a morning five days later when one of the older soldiers was found stabbed to death, his rifle and uniform stolen. It was the first time Vera had seen a dead person and she stared at him, thinking he was only asleep and would wake up. Magdalena pulled her away as soldiers prepared to bury him. The journey now ceased to be exciting and Vera began to know fear. She wanted her father to ride up and tell them it was safe to go home, but in her heart she knew he might already be dead.

The caravan made its way slowly and they began to see farmers out in the fields planting their crops. The next few days passed without incident but Countess Magdalena and Gregorz were grim because the caravan's food supply was dwindling. One afternoon the caravan had to stop when a wagon's axle broke. It was late in the day as the soldiers went to cut down a straight tree to make a new axle. While they were away a band of gypsies fell upon the caravan, guarded at the time by the young and inexperienced soldiers and the mothers and wives of the caravan who could shoot. The gypsy band surprised them and with knives, spears and clubs they drove the travelers away from the disabled wagon. The gypsies took the broken wagon, replaced the axle and departed swiftly. When Gregorz returned he surmised that the gypsies had been watching and pounced when the opportunity presented itself, bringing their own replacement axle.

During the brief skirmish, one of the young soldiers was severely wounded and a young woman was killed. Gregorz ordered the caravan to wait while they buried the woman. The young man died an hour later and the caravan stayed overnight to bury him next to the woman's grave. It was a very somber group of travelers who took to the road the next morning. Gregorz sent scouts ahead and they returned to report a band of gypsies was traveling just ahead of the caravan, waiting and watching for another opportunity to raid. Worse yet, the caravan now had very little food for themselves and for their animals because Gregorz had not been able to talk any farmers into selling, and Count Stefan had given strict orders that they were not to steal food from the poor farmers. The scouts said that the gypsies appeared to have even less food, so they saw the caravan's wagons as rich plunder.

Two days later the caravan awakened to the sounds of a battle ahead. Gregorz sent a young soldier to the top of a hill to observe, and he returned to report that the gypsy camp was under attack by a large group of men. The attackers appeared to be townspeople, not soldiers in uniform. Gypsies were often despised by local townspeople even though at night the men would go to a gypsy camp to buy women for pleasure, and the women would go there to buy cooking spices and potions to treat ills and injuries. Sometimes a friendly town would invite the gypsies in to sell their potions and put on shows of dance and magic.

Even though the gypsies had previously attacked their caravan, Magdalena told Gregorz to advance his soldiers to help the gypsies. However, as they came over the rise Gregorz saw the attack was almost finished, the attackers slaughtering the few survivors as they ransacked and burned the gypsy wagons. When the attackers saw Gregorz and his uniformed soldiers coming they ran, not wanting to face armed soldiers, but the carnage already visited upon the gypsy band was brutal. Cautiously the soldiers approached followed by the caravan wagons. Countess Magdalena told Vera and her brother to stay in the back of the wagon. Magdalena ordered Gregorz and his soldiers to see if there were any wounded, but very few of the gypsies were brought to the caravan for the women to tend to their injuries. Against orders, Vera and her brother slipped out of their wagon to look. Vera stopped in horror when she saw a young gypsy girl about the same age as herself lying on her back off to the side of the road. The gypsy girl's brightly colored dress was bloody and she had a nasty looking gash on her head.

Vera heard the gypsy girl whimpering and crying so she sent her brother to get their mother. She sat on the ground next to the gypsy girl and gently took the gypsy girl's hand to comfort her, softly telling the girl that she had sent her brother to get help. The gypsy girl looked at her and said something in a language Vera did not understand, but she instinctively knew that the gypsy girl was dying. Vera pointed at herself and said "Vera". The gypsy girl put her hand over her heart and said "Charani". She was clutching a battered and torn cloth doll in her arms. Charani said something in her language and put the doll in Vera's hands, making motions to indicate she wanted Vera to take the doll and bring it back to health. Just as Magdalena arrived, the gypsy girl laid back and cried for a minute before she died. Magdalena was angry that Vera disobeyed orders not to leave the wagon, but secretly pleased to see her daughter had compassion to care for the dying girl. Vera told her mother that the girl who had given her the doll was named Charani, and she promised the dying girl that she would take care of it. Even Magdalena's inner strength could not overcome the sadness her daughter felt, and she cried as she held her daughter. Vera was sad that she was not able to help the gypsy girl, so she decided to help the doll and name it Charani in the gypsy girl's memory.

A young soldier sent out to scout reported that a company of Prussian soldiers was on the way, so Gregorz ordered everyone to get in the wagons and go back over the hill to turn down another road, afraid that they could be blamed for the attack. They escaped only because the slaughter of the gypsies was so horrific it slowed down even the battle hardened Prussian soldiers.

Later that night in camp, Vera and her mother carefully inspected the doll and cleaned it as best they could, patching and sewing up the damage to the fabric. Vera took her own doll from its cloth bag and used the bag as a blanket for the injured doll, getting some straw to make a bed for it. Magdalena was proud of Vera because she showed the grace and compassion of a *szlachcianka*, a noblewoman.

A week later, out of food because they were unable to get anyone to sell to them, the caravan crossed the border into France. Magdalena spoke French and found they were a little kinder to the caravan travelers and were able to purchase small amounts of food in some of the towns.

Gregorz knew their destination and guided the caravan to a chateau in Bordeaux owned by an English baron who had married a beautiful French countess. The baron was a successful merchant and owner of a fleet of trading ships. They made their home in France, visiting England twice a year for the baron to conduct business. Gregorz found the chateau but he did not speak French and heard the chateau's guards shouting the alarm as the caravan approached. The travelers looked so ragged the soldiers suspected them of being bandits. The baron's soldiers closed the gate and took up shooting positions behind the chateau walls.

Gregorz sent for Magdalena, but before the messenger found her, Vera, who had been allowed to ride her pony with Gregorz in France, got off and bravely walked up to the chateau's gate. At least one of the French soldiers eyed her suspiciously, as if she might be part of a ruse to get them to open the gate. He lowered his rifle and fired but missed because a sergeant grabbed the rifle at the last second. The French sergeant pulled the soldier from the wall and berated him, saying that they were honorable men who did not shoot unarmed little girls. Upon hearing the shot, the lord of the chateau, Baron Peel, rushed to the gate to see about the commotion. He climbed the stairs to the wall just as Vera, bravely standing alone in front of the gate, began to tell his soldiers who she was. Magdalena was running to her daughter but after he heard the shot, Gregorz held her back to protect her. He had sworn an oath to Count Stefan that he would protect the family. Vera had gotten past him, but he was not going to let Magdalena come to harm if he could prevent it. Gregorz knew he was courting danger by ignoring Countess Magdalena's shouted orders to let her go, but he considered his oath to his Count to be of a higher order.

Baron Peel heard the girl say her father was Count Stefan Czarnecki and then heard Countess Magdalena shouting at Gregorz. Count Czarnecki and Baron Peel met years before when they began trading for luxury items rarely found in Poland. The count and the baron became friends and trusted business partners. The baron ordered his soldiers to stand down and open the gate. Baron Peel sent a footman to ask the baroness to have servants bring food to the dining hall, having seen some of the caravan's people with gaunt figures. When Lady Lorraine heard who was at the gate, she came quickly, her servants running to keep up with her. Lorraine embraced her dear friend Magdalena and sent her servants to bring the caravan people into the dining hall and summon the village doctor to see to anyone who needed medical care.

Magdalena cried tears of joy for they had arrived and were safe at last. Vera had not eaten for two days and almost fainted as she climbed the steps to the dining hall. Baron Peel saw her stumble and personally carried the brave little Polish girl who had stood up to his soldiers inside and gently set her in a chair at the table.

When everyone was seated at the table, a young girl asked to change places so she could sit next to Vera, who was so hungry all she could do at first was eat, but soon the girls were talking in French and giggling together. After dinner the girls were excused and Lady Lorraine's daughter brought her new friend to her quarters. She had her maid prepare a hot bath for Vera and bring out some clothes since they were about the same size and Vera's clothing was filthy and torn. Vera showed the gypsy doll to her new friend and told her the story of how she had come to receive it and name it Charani.

Countess Magdalena and Lady Lorraine came in, and seeing everything going splendidly they formally introduced Magdalena's daughter Vera to Lorraine's daughter Marie-Laure. They also discovered that the two girls were the same age.

A few weeks later came the news that Count Stefan Czarnecki and his remaining soldiers had died as they fought to buy time for his family and old friends to escape. The peasant uprising was quelled, but the Czarnecki citadel was in ruins and everything of value looted. Baron Peel sent an agent to Poland to investigate, and he came back to report that there was no hope for Magdalena to safely return as there were threats of further conflict.

Baron Peel and Lady Lorraine would not take no for an answer when they invited everyone in the caravan to live in the village. In time, the Polish soldiers became friends with the French soldiers and went into Baron Peel's service or found work in the village. The baron invited Magdalena and her children to live in an apartment in the baron's large chateau. Magdalena was determined find a way to return his kindness and began teaching French to her soldiers, and Polish and German to Baron Peel's French soldiers. Magdalena also helped tutor their daughters and the children of the village.

As the years went by Vera and Marie-Laure became lifelong best friends. Magdalena and Vera traveled to England with Baron Peel, Lady Lorraine and Marie-Laure on their frequent visits, and Vera learned the English language.

On one of their trips to London, an English lord invited the Baron, Lady Lorraine and Countess Magdalena to a ball at his manor. The invitation included Marie-Laure and Vera, both of whom were now lovely young women and quite sought after by eligible bachelors in both France and England. At the ball, Vera met and danced with a tall, handsome Polish man named Jakob Winiarzski. Several years before, he arrived in London on one of Baron Peel's ships after escaping from a peasant uprising in Poland. Jakob went to work as a trader for the English nobleman and on his own started a small shop to work on machinery. Vera fell in love with the dashing and resourceful Jakob but it took another year before they succumbed to the inevitable and were married. They decided to emigrate to the United States because they heard that America was the land of opportunity.

"Even back then, my father had a talent for machinery and became interested in automobiles when they were still seen as toys for the wealthy. The rest is history. He met your father Marvin and because of that, you met me!" I told Dan.

"Laure, that is an incredible story and what an adventure! We could make a movie about it and you could play Magdalena or the grown-up Vera. But one thing I don't understand, why did your mother name you Laure-Marie instead of Marie-Laure?"

"When my mother became pregnant, she wrote to Marie-Laure that if she had a girl she was going to name her Marie-Laure. Her friend replied in a letter that she was honored, but requested Vera to reverse the order of the names. Vera did not know why, but that was Marie-Laure's request and as her best friend, Vera complied, and that is how I became Laure-Marie. Jake eventually found out that Baron Peel had named one of his new merchant ships the *Marie-Laure* and it sank with the loss of all hands in a terrible typhoon near the Philippines. Maybe Marie-Laure did not want to bring bad luck on her best friend's daughter, but whatever the reason I am very happy being Laure-Marie Winiarszki Lindner. I have never met Marie-Laure, but my mother told me she invited Marie-Laure and her family to visit the U.S. and they plan to come over this summer. I said that if they wanted to come out to

California they can stay with us. I want to ask Marie-Laure to tell me stories about my mother as a young girl. Stories that my Uncle Viktor will only hint at, stories that my mother won't tell me, like how hot Vera and Jake were for each other before they got married."

"That sounds a lot like us. You know, it's a good thing your mother named you Laure because that's what everyone calls you" Dan said with a straight face. Dan must have been taking lessons from our friend W.C. Fields on how to slip little jokes in the conversation before anyone realized what he was up to, and he was getting rather good at it.

"Oh, it must be time for a new one" I laughed. "But you are always fun to be with so I'll forgive you this time." I had been telling Dan my mother's story over breakfast at our small table that overlooked Napa Valley.

"Laure, you're such a gal, a lovely, intelligent lady, and a helluva beautiful wife. And now that I know you are a descendant of nobility, I will have to call you Lady Laure."

"You handsome silver tongued devil, and I mean that in the very best way, especially the part about your tongue. I'm so glad I decided not to shoot you the day we met" I said.

"I'm kind of glad about that as well" Dan replied.

THE LAUREDAN LOCOMOTIVE

"You're buying what?" I asked in amazement. "Have you been smoking the mud pipe? Why do we need a railroad locomotive?"

"We need it for the movie" Dan replied. "The studio accountants don't understand why we need to rent a locomotive for as much time as I estimated, and you know a big part of *Road Trip Blues* takes place on the rails. As it turns out, the Santa Fe is not happy with us after all the mayhem of last summer, even though they acknowledge that most of it was not our doing. The cost they quoted us to rent a locomotive and crew was sky high, so I asked Scott to make the request for us to purchase a Pacific 4-6-2 like the one we borrowed, because Pacific locomotives are known to be fast and reliable."

Our chef Sunny brought the morning mail to our office with coffee and brioche. Dan opened a letter from the Santa Fe railroad and began to laugh as he handed it to me. "This is even better – the Santa Fe is offering to sell us the locomotive we used last summer. Number 3447 is still in Kansas. The district manager thought it might have been abused from our activities, so they are offering to sell it to us at a low price. We know Big Al and the Swedes took good care of it, and Big Al says #3447 is in first class condition."

"And" Dan kept going before I could say anything. "Big Al told me he sent money to his ex-wife to come to Chicago. Turns out she's tired of the cold and snow up in 'Sota and they are talking about moving to California. He wants to play himself in the movie. Sven and Ole said they would play themselves if Big Al engineered the locomotive. So now we have a crew, and they will be paid out of the movie budget since they are cast members. Besides, who else could play those guys? Oh, and Sweetie? Sven and Ole are requesting that you be in the speakeasy fight. I told them you're not playing yourself, but we decided maybe you could be a stuntwoman."

"You guys are really funny and it's nice of you to let me know what you have decided for me. But I'm getting jingle-brained about this locomotive" I replied. "Where do we operate it? Do we have to lay our own railroad tracks? And I was thinking that if we could get Buster Keaton he would be perfect for the engineer role, with him keeping a poker face despite everything that happens around him."

"If we didn't already have Buster Collier I think Buster Keaton should play me" Dan laughed. "Bill can get permission from the railroads to run our executive train over their rails as long as we comply with their schedules and don't shoot up any more railcars. That's how the swells with their private railroad cars do it. The studios have some abandoned track in California and Nevada where we will film our railroad chase and shootout scenes, so there are no railroad schedules to worry about for that. We can borrow a couple of railroad coaches and boxcars for the equipment, the studio budget will cover that" Dan was excited about this and it did start to make sense.

"We talked about hiring Bill for the movie, did Lasky go along with that?" I asked.

"Bill is doubling as our security manager so he will earn it, like he did on our last adventure. I can't complain, Lasky is giving us just about all we asked for except the locomotive, and it's the studio's accountants that are blocking that. Remember, we decided Bill would be an associate producer as well as a cast member, so his cost is covered. Hey Sweetie, I am a fast learner on how to work the Hollywood scene. Douglas Fairbanks has been an excellent teacher. In a way, we owe a lot of this to Douglas, backing the prank that got me in as a producer and mentoring me. Bill will handle all the machinery logistics and knows how to deal with the railroad district managers, and that is a big job for this movie.

We need security staff and Bill knows people all over the railroads and at Pinkerton's, and he is an excellent shooter. Meghan and Frank recently left for a secret government assignment in Europe so they will not be available. Dawn left this morning for another secret government mission. Jake needs to spend more time with his aeroplane business and Vera does not want him to be in so much danger again. He said he would help us out as much as possible" Dan said "but we will need more help."

I began to catch some of Dan's excitement. He does that to me. "Hold your horses! I have been trying to get Uncle Viktor and Evelyn to join us – They can play themselves. She's had theater acting experience, she can dance, she is gorgeous and knows how to handle guns. Those two are looking to work together, and they sure do complement each other. I will call Viktor today. They want to get into something safe and legal instead of speakeasy work."

We went on planning into the late hours as the puzzle pieces of the movie came together when I asked Dan "Do you know if Claire is OK? I called her and Scott will only tell me that she is away on a project, but she's been gone for over a week."

"I don't know, but Scott doesn't seem concerned about it. Those two are devoted to each other, I can't imagine that they are having problems. Knowing Claire, when she gets an idea she runs with it. She is a lot like you that way."

Rather than slowing down, the pace of our lives became busier. Dan was finishing the screenplay and we read it to each other over breakfast. Reading it aloud helped to smooth out the scenes. Dan's writing improved by leaps and bounds and he was enjoying it more as his confidence grew. I was anxious to get back to our LaureDan Company business, even though Josefina had brought the books and contracts with her when my father Jake flew Luigi, Josefina and her parents to Long Grove for our wedding. Jake's aircraft business had grown so fast that he was looking to hire two technicians and he had talked Dorothy and Vera into managing the administrative and accounting side.

Jake would not be able to fly the Montanaris back right away and since they had a rough flight out they were quite happy when I suggested they return by train. Luigi and Josefina amazingly obtained permission from Josefina's parents to drive our Chrysler B70 back to Napa. The Road Trip Dog would ride with them. It would have been scandalous for an unmarried young couple to do that but Josefina told them how Dan and I had done the same thing. Bettina knew that her daughter and Luigi were lovers and by giving his permission Vincenzo accepted it too. He took it calmly when Josefina and Luigi took a long private walk with him to explain their feelings.

Luigi and Josefina convinced her parents that they wanted to get married sooner instead of waiting another year as they had originally planned. It helped that Josefina's parents adored Luigi and gave their approval. Luigi's enlistment in the Marines was up at the end of June 1927, and he was learning winemaking and vineyard management from Vincenzo Montanari, who was happy to know that his legacy winery business would continue with his daughter and son-in-law. The winery had a license to produce sacramental wine during Prohibition, and along with their new coffee business and fruit orchards, the Montanaris were busier than ever.

Col. Mosby had hoped to keep Luigi in the Marines because he was a natural leader and they needed to keep good non-commissioned officers. But even Col. Mosby was happy for them. Josefina told me that the colonel had flirted with her just as he had with me. Josefina was so lively and lovely that any man would try to flirt with her, but her heart was only for Luigi.

THE MURDER

Dan and I settled into our seats on the *San Francisco Overland Limited* where we had booked a first class compartment. The journey began on the Chicago & North Western at the North Western station in downtown Chicago, then the UP took over and it finished in San Francisco 63 hours later.

Our Duesenberg Model X was now a guest at the Duesenberg factory in Indianapolis. Frederick and August wanted to go over the automobile again to update or replace anything worn, and they asked to have it for three or four months while they analyzed the automobile and performed the work. They were very thorough craftsmen and as it was no charge to us, we agreed. They had learned a lot from our well-kept diaries chronicling everything that happened to the Duesenberg, even the bullet holes we got in Kansas. Dan made them promise not to fix the bullet holes, even though the Duesenbergs thought we were crazy to want to keep them.

Despite the comfortable railcar interior and features, we were glad to see San Francisco. At the ferry terminal we boarded the steamer *General Frisbee* to Vallejo where Josefina had arranged for Luigi to meet us and bring us home. I was on top of the world with excitement and thoughts of building our lives together in beautiful Napa Valley.

We talked by phone to Jesse Lasky who was anxious to see our screenplay and final budget. Since there was a great deal of LaureDan Company business needing attention, we decided that I would stay and work with Josefina while Dan went to Hollywood. The next afternoon I kissed Danny and we touched each other with lovers' pleasure, wishing we could spend another hour together but he had to catch the ferryboat to the city. He would spend the night at a hotel, then take the Southern Pacific's *Daylight Limited* to Los Angeles early the next morning. It was a 12 hour trip, two hours faster than any of the competition. In Los Angeles, Lasky arranged a limo and driver for Dan. He was rolling out all the perks for his hot new producer at Famous Players-Lasky Studios.

I was up early the next morning. Josefina was due to arrive for work at 8:30 AM. I was feeling lonely, missing my morning screenplay reading with Dan, and Raider needed exercise. I recently took up running for exercise and decided that Raider, our faithful German Shepherd Dog and I should put the early morning to good use. There was a narrow dirt road leading down to the Napa River to get to the trails along the riverbank. I was not worried about running alone because Raider was with me and I put my Colt M1908 .380 Hammerless Pocket Pistol in a small belt pack. It was a beautiful October morning, crisp and perfect for running. Raider liked to run with me, sometimes going ahead, sometimes running next to or behind me but he never let me out of his sight. On one occasion two bums jumped out of the trees to grab me on the river trail, but when they saw Raider's teeth and my Colt, they ran away.

About an hour later I slowed as we returned to the large home on our rented property. In the kitchen, I put an excellent Montanari blend coffee on the stove, noticing there was another pot of coffee made but it had cooled. I didn't think twice about that, it could have been left by Sunny last night. I went upstairs to freshen up and change clothes when I heard the front door open and Josefina called out her cheerful greeting. I called back to tell her there would be fresh coffee ready in a few minutes.

I was in good spirits after the run and I came down to the kitchen to wait for the coffee to finish percolating. I had just sat down to look over the morning newspaper when Josefina let out a bloodcurdling scream. I grabbed my Colt, pushed the kitchen door open and the dog and I burst through, Colt at the ready and Raider on full alert. When we got to the hallway, Josefina was sitting on the floor outside the dining room, crying with her head in her hands.

Raider and I went into the dining room and I wanted to scream and cry too. Josefina regained her composure and went to the office to call the sheriff. She also called Luigi to come as fast as he could. I looked in horror at our dear friend Colonel Mosby, dressed in his Marine uniform, motionless on the floor. A chair was overturned and a coffee cup shattered, likely when the colonel fell and struck the wall. There were coffee stains all over the wall, floor and his uniform. But what was Col. Mosby doing here? He had not told us he was coming. I went to check for a pulse even though he appeared to be dead. "Luigi said we should not touch anything until he arrives" Josefina said. I felt shaken and we went outside to wait.

Sheriff Harris and two deputies arrived shortly and we told them what we had found. He ordered a deputy to stay with us while he and the other deputy went inside. Harris called out to us that he was using our telephone to call the coroner.

In a little over a half hour the house was filled with deputies, the coroner and his assistants and a reporter from the *Napa Register*. Luigi arrived but the sheriff rudely refused to let him enter the house. He had to go to the neighbors next door to use the telephone to call Major Griffin at Mare Island.

After Col. Mosby's body was removed, Sheriff Harris separated Josefina, Luigi and me to interview us. Raider kept growling at the sheriff. Smart dog. We did not have a very good history with this sheriff. Harris told me to lock Raider up somewhere or he would shoot the dog. I told Harris that if he shot my dog I would shoot him, but I led Raider over to a nearby guest cottage. The dog was unhappy at being separated from me. I was not happy about it either.

We were still being held separately when Major Griffin arrived with Sgt. Reilly and his MP squad, along with a Navy Captain, the deputy commander of the Mare Island base. There ensued a lengthy argument and I feared that the normally calm Major Griffin was going to shoot the sheriff. They backed down only after Harris finally agreed to let Griffin and the Navy captain into the house. When they came out, Griffin talked privately with Sgt. Reilly when Vincenzo Montanari drove up in his pickup truck, having heard what happened. He was enraged when Harris tried to keep him from seeing his daughter and Griffin tried to calm both him and Luigi. He would not calm until Harris agreed to allow Josefina to come out of the house. Vincenzo just about went berserk at the sight of his daughter in handcuffs.

Worried that he was losing control of the situation, Harris ordered a deputy to put handcuffs on me, but when he ordered the deputy to handcuff Luigi, Griffin told him that was not going to happen and Reilly's Marine squad formed up in low rifle ready position. Harris told the Marines to put down their rifles and Reilly responded by ordering to his squad to cover Harris and the deputies. The Navy captain interceded, telling the Marines to stand down, but told Harris that Luigi was not a danger and if deemed necessary he would be taken into Marine custody.

Over an hour later, we still had not been allowed to have food, despite the fact that the deputies made breakfast for themselves in our kitchen. I was enraged and made the demand to call my attorney. Harris laughed and said I had to wait until he was ready to make an arrest. He was clearly enjoying his control and my fury was building to a dangerous level.

Another half hour passed before the coroner and Sheriff Harris came out and announced to everyone "I accuse Laure Lindner of murdering Col. Mosby in the dining room with poisoned coffee. The coroner concurs with the evidence."

Everyone began talking at once. The *Napa Register* reporter was rapidly scribbling in his notebook. I yelled for everyone to shut up and they must have heard the anger in my voice, because they did shut up. "What is this evidence you have that I killed Col. Mosby and why would I do that? Col. Mosby was a good friend to all of us, a man of good character and a respected Marine officer."

"Yeah, we know what a great officer he was, helping you get your hooch shipped out of Napa. I'm taking you down to the jail and you can call a lawyer from there. For the time being, Josefina and Luigi are not under arrest, but I advise them to remain in Napa County until further notice."

Major Griffin bristled at this and said "Sgt. Maranello is a United States Marine and is not under arrest, therefore his commanders may order him anywhere at any time in the performance of his assigned duties. This is not up to you, Sheriff Harris. You have taken liberties with the law and this has been duly noted. Military regulations require a Board of Inquiry be convened after an officer dies under suspicious circumstances, and you will be required to cooperate. Interfering with a military investigation is a Federal offense. You could serve prison time, sheriff or not." Harris showed a glimpse of worry but quickly regained his arrogance.

"I have already spoken to the district attorney and Mrs. Lindner is under arrest on suspicion of the charge of murder in the first degree" Harris replied. "Her fingerprints were all over the coffee cup, and there was poison residue in the cup. The same poison was found in a coffee pot on the stove in the kitchen, with her fingerprints all over that too. She and her husband knew Col. Mosby and we believe she called him here to kill him, possibly related to their contraband booze running operation. We believe that the criminals may have been cheating one another and Laure decided to dispose of Col. Mosby. We have sufficient evidence to convict her for the murder."

Harris glared at me and said "We hang murderers in California, and I look forward to the day when I put the noose around your pretty neck. You have been a thorn in the side of law-abiding Napa residents since you arrived and now you will get your comeuppance. Take her away and book her. If and when her husband returns – although it looks like he has fled and left her to take the fall – we'll book Dan as well."

"You are a moron. Of course my fingerprints are on the coffee cup. They are our coffee cups and coffee pot that we use every day. Did you find any other fingerprints?" I shouted.

The sheriff ignored me. Almost everyone, including most of the deputies was shocked by the sheriff's accusations. Vincenzo and Josefina were outraged, and she whispered to me that they would not let Harris get away with this. When the sheriff noticed Josefina whispering to me, he told her to get away from me or she would be arrested too. Vincenzo had enough and moved to confront the sheriff but Luigi wisely held him back, telling him that would not help and would surely get himself arrested. Vincenzo was loyal to his friends, and he counted us among his best friends in Napa. Major Griffin nodded and I understood his intent, which was to say that this outrage would not stand. Even so, I felt more scared than when I was kidnapped by the Cranston gang when Josefina and I had taken the fight to the goons. I felt angry and helpless at the false accusation of murder, but I knew that my friends and my husband would be tearing this apart as fast as they could.

As I was rudely put in the back seat of a deputy's car Raider began barking and howling from the guest house. I had never heard him howl before and it was a chilling, eerie sound. Josefina called out for me not to worry, she would take care of Raider. Sheriff Harris sneered "That's right little lady, she won't have a worry in the world after we have her body swinging by her neck on the gallows" as he got into his car.

I was rudely shoved into a filthy jail cell that contained two smelly, evil looking women. Even before the jailer left, one of the women said "Oooo, lookee here, a rich flapper type. About time they started jailing them. Let's show her who's in charge here." She came up to me and told me I had to give her my food when it arrived. I grabbed her and threw her hard against the cell door bars and she slumped down, rubbing the bump rising up on her head. The other woman took a step toward me but backed off when she saw what happened to her cellmate. Later, when the food arrived, I gave it to her anyway because it looked and smelled inedible.

The sheriff did not allow me to make a telephone call. I had to keep myself awake as much as possible because my cellmates were giving me the evil eye and mumbling threats. Several times the two came at me and I was glad that Dawn had given me self-defense training. The last time they came at me I broke the nose of one of them and slammed the other to the floor before the sheriff and jail guards arrived. Harris told me I would now be facing two charges of assaulting an inmate.

I am normally a happy flapper, but bad things were piling up and with no visitors or communication to the outside world I was beginning to get concerned that they would not admit that I was here. This was starting to stink real bad.

The morning of the fifth day of my incarceration I was filthy and hungry and was almost ready to eat the swill that passed for inmate food when the cell door was unlocked. The jail warden looked unhappy as he called my name. Behind him stood Major Griffin, Sgt. Reilly and two jail guards holding handcuffs and ankle chains. Griffin had served the sheriff with a federal court order for me to be handed over to the United States Marines Military Police, of which he was the area commander.

The warden told the guards to handcuff and shackle me, then bring me to his office. The warden said I had to stay shackled until formal custody was turned over to the Marines, and there was a lot of paperwork to be filled out, even though I saw no one working on any paperwork. We found out later that was a sham to give the assistant district attorney time to find a judge to overturn Major Griffin's court order, but it was a federal order and no county judge in Napa could overturn it. It took most of the morning before the sheriff grudgingly told the warden to release me into the custody of the United States Marines Military Police detachment at Mare Island.

MARE ISLAND DETENTION

Since the sheriff threatened to arrest Dan, he did not go inside the jail but waited down the road with Luigi in a Marine staff car. Dan looked beyond angry but under control and I marveled at his ability to stay calm. I loved that about him, that when everything was falling apart he steadily and relentlessly worked until things got better. I took strength from his calm and resolve, which was funny because he always said I did the same for him. Once we were both in Maj. Griffin's military Dodge sedan I was unshackled and the handcuffs removed. For the first time in five days I breathed air that didn't stink like urine and vomit. I hugged Dan and allowed myself to cry. He held me gently until I calmed down.

"Dan, I didn't kill . . ." but he stopped me.

"Everyone but Harris knows you didn't murder the colonel. Major Griffin says it appears that someone went through a lot of trouble to set you up for it. I paid a visit to the assistant district attorney who has your case and he talked in circles, so he is in on it. I'm afraid that I got angry and pushed him up against the wall and punched him in the gut so hard he slumped to the floor." At this I laughed, remembering how I had so recently thought about his ability to remain calm.

I thought that someday Harris would do something to us and he fulfilled my expectations. Dan said "Sgt. Reilly was with me and he whispered something in the guy's ear. I don't know what Reilly said but it must have been convincing because I wasn't arrested. The sheriff, coroner and the district attorney are in cahoots and there would be no help from them. Getting you out of jail was our first order of business so Major Griffin and I went to the Federal Court in San Francisco to get the court order. That took a whole day and I've been on pins and needles thinking about you languishing in jail. Major Griffin provided the influence to get a Federal judge to order your release into custody of the Marines, since technically you are charged with murdering a military officer. I arrived home the day after your arrest and they were not allowing anyone to see you. The sheriff said you were a flight risk and they could hold you without visitors. It's outrageous but borderline within the law. Sgt. Reilly offered to break you out of jail and I almost went along with it, but that would just add problems. I'm sorry it took so long, but they threw roadblocks at us every step of the way" Dan told me. "Major Griffin did an outstanding job to get you out of the Napa jail."

"Thank you, Major Griffin. I don't know what this is all about and I am grateful for your help" I told him.

"You're welcome Laure. I knew the charge that you murdered the colonel was ridiculous. You and Dan were good friends of the colonel. Col. Mosby was the best commanding officer I have ever served, and I am determined to clear you and find the real murderer."

"I'm so happy to see you" I turned to Dan. "It was terrible in there and I had to defend myself from two deranged women inmates. I'm supposed to be charged with two counts of assault for defending myself but they attacked me several times."

"We will deal with it if it comes up and it is fortunate that the sheriff didn't remember or he might have tried to keep you in jail on that charge until it was tried in court."

We arrived at Mare Island and got out of the military police sedan. Major Griffin had the decency to give us a moment to hug and kiss. I smelled awful, but Dan did not let that stop him. I even felt a thrill when Dan gave me a quick grab. "Mmm, that feels good. I've missed you so much" I said.

Major Griffin said "Everyone on the base is mourning Col. Mosby's death, he was a respected officer. I have a top-shelf military legal team on the way from Washington D.C. I'm sorry but for now I must abide by the court order to keep you in custody on the Mare Island base. However,

I guarantee that it will not be a filthy jail cell and the only person you might have to fight off is Dan, because I'm putting both of you in the same quarters you stayed in during the Marine Ball. Dan can come and go but Laure, you must stay on the base. Please do not try to leave, it will cause immense complications if you do and it will give Sheriff Harris an excuse to get you back into his custody. We will get to the bottom of this but it could take anywhere from a few days to several weeks. I won't know until the legal team from D.C. gets here. They will have a Federal judge to contact if need be, and I'm arranging and investigation by a military Board of Inquiry, and the sheriff will have to testify."

"Thank you Major Griffin, I won't try to escape after you've put yourself on the line for me. I give you my promise to stay on the base. Can your wife Carole visit me?"

"Yes Laure, in fact she will be at the quarters to greet you and make sure everything is safe and clean. And I'm allowing Dan to stay with you 24 hours a day with no one else in the quarters. Should Dan leave the base I am required to have a guard stay with you to meet the terms of the court order. Regulations require the guard to be armed, and Dan has his 1911. Under the regulations I have to order him to shoot you if you try to escape." Major Griffin let a rare grin appear on his face. "My wife Carole has a temporary appointment as a detention guard and she is a qualified shooter. Carole will be with you when Dan is away" Griffin said.

"That is agreeable, especially compared to where I was. OK my sexy jailer Dan, are you going to tie me to the bed to make sure I don't escape?" Major Griffin appeared to be embarrassed but quickly returned to his military bearing, while Dan said something about having me right where he wanted me.

After a long soak in the bath followed by a rinse under a hot shower, the clean clothes Josefina sent over and a good meal, I was almost back to my normal self. Josefina made party plans and that night our base quarters overflowed with guests. Josefina, her parents, Luigi, Sgt. Reilly, Major Griffin, his wife Carole and several other guests came for dinner prepared on an outdoor grille by a Navy cook who had been a restaurant chef until he beat up a man for insulting his girlfriend. The judge's sentence was that he could join the military or go to jail. Josefina brought Raider, who was overjoyed to see me. Dan said he had been sad and depressed while I was in jail.

That night I told Dan to tie me to the bed to make sure I could not escape, but he said he would take his chances. I told him to tie me to the bed anyway, and I did not have to tell him again.

The next morning Dan told me about his meeting with Lasky. It had not taken very long, Lasky examined the budget numbers I developed and signed off, keeping the copy of the screenplay to read, although after scanning some of it he said he was pleased. He did not learn about my arrest until after the meeting. He first called Griffin and found the major was already on the case.

Dan and I were devastated by Col. Mosby's murder. He had authorized the raid to rescue me and the other girls from the Cranston gang kidnappers. He had even flirted with me in fun. He was a nice older man, an officer and a gentleman who had done more for us than we ever could have asked. We were surprised that Harris had learned the colonel had helped us behind the scenes with transporting our booze and wine. How had Harris found out about that? Luigi said he was investigating to find the source of the leak.

Someone tricked Mosby into coming to our house and gave him the poisoned coffee, but who? Dan and I reviewed everything that happened that morning, but we could not find any clues. I realized how lucky Josefina and I were to have not drank the coffee, or was that the killer's plan? If we drank it and died, Harris would have called it an open and shut case.

The next day Jesse Lasky's secretary sent Dan a telegram to return for a final green light meeting for *Road Trip Blues*, but he thought that if Lasky found out I was charged with murder he might close down the project. Dan decided to go to Hollywood a day early to talk to our friends and get their advice. He made plans to visit Douglas Fairbanks and Billie Dove, who had become trusted advisers. Fairbanks and his wife Mary Pickford were co-founders of United Artists Corporation in 1919, along with Charlie Chaplin and director D.W. Griffith. In fact, Douglas had sealed the story of the prank devised by Louise Brooks that got me set up as a Hollywood producer by letting it be known that he wanted to sign me to UA, and told me that he would if Lasky did not jump to sign me.

Billie Dove loved us because we brought fun and excitement into her life. She was a smart lady and although she had a similar disdain as Louise Brooks had about how Hollywood did business, she was a gifted actress and played along with the studio to become a leading star. Wallace Reid's widow Dorothy Davenport was also an advisor, and she was a producer and director as well. Dorothy continued to be an activist to prevent or treat the morphine addiction that had taken her husband Wallace Reid's life. Under her direction, the Wallace Reid Addiction Treatment clinic had achieved an excellent reputation for discretion and their modern, effective addiction rehabilitation programs.

Although my Mare Island quarters were not the Napa jail, I soon became restless. The assistant district attorney had taken the charges to a grand jury and secured a county indictment to put me on trial, but I was technically in custody of the Marines who would not hand me over to the sheriff unless forced to do so by a federal court.

Probably because the evidence was flimsy despite their big talk, Harris and the deputy district attorney did not move to reclaim custody, and for the time being the case was in stalemate while investigations continued.

Then we found out that the Washington D.C. legal team never arrived at Mare Island. The Navy captain, now appointed acting base commander, had the lawyers recalled and refused any further help. He had chewed out Major Griffin for getting involved in the case without his approval. He said that defending a civilian murderess would besmirch his pristine career and slow his promotion progress. The Marine personnel on the base were outraged, and there were rumblings that Col. Mosby would not have been so cowardly.

Dan reluctantly departed for Hollywood and the next morning I went out for a run on the roads of the Mare Island base. I had pledged on my honor not to escape from the base and last night I stayed at the Griffin home. I was not allowed to carry a gun but Raider ran close by my side. It was a beautiful morning to run, but as we rounded a curve behind a vacant warehouse I almost ran into a group of men. They blocked the road and circled around, taunting and calling me names. A few rocks were thrown and I was able to evade them but was surrounded.

I heard one shout "She's the whore who murdered the colonel, and before that she killed her former husband in Kansas and got away with it." One man brought a noose and others were shouting "Justice for Col. Mosby". One of them had a brick tied to an eight foot length of rope and was swinging it over his head, looking for an opportunity to hit me with it. "Get her" someone shouted and they began to close in. Raider stayed by my side. I tried to feint one way and run the other, but they were too close and blocked me. The man with the brick-on-a-rope came at me next. He could swing it from beyond my reach and if it hit me I could be killed or seriously injured. When he began spinning the brick over his head Raider charged him. The brick was up too high to hit the dog and ninety-five pounds of solid German Shepherd Dog slammed into him and bowled him over. Raider stood over his face, teeth bared and growling, daring the man to get up.

Someone in the crowd yelled "Grab her, pull her down" and they closed in on me again. A man ran up and tried to grab me but I put him down like Dawn had taught me. But there were too many, too close, and hands began to pull at my clothes, angry voices threatening to break all my bones and do worse to me before they hanged me. Raider tried to come to my aid but when he moved away from the man he was guarding, the man got up, picked up the brick and threw it at the dog. Raider lunged at the man but this time the goon pulled a knife and tried to cut the dog. Now many hands were grasping at me, trying to pull me to the ground and I knew that if they got me down they would begin kicking and stomping. I saw the grinning man with the noose moving closer. I thought of Dan just as one of them rolled into my legs behind me and I went down. Suddenly Raider was there, circling and snapping. We were inside a small circle but the goons were wary of the big dog, and he forced them back a step or two, which was enough for me to get up. Two men lunged. Raider bit hard and fast at one and I knocked the other man back, his nose smashed and bleeding.

The others rushed me, and this time I knew my options were running out. Raider did not stop, his teeth snapping at those who put their hands toward me. The man with the brick on a rope got close enough to let it fly at me. I turned and ducked almost in time but the brick struck my shoulder and it hurt to move my arm. Managing to grab the rope in my other hand before it hit the ground, I swung the brick around and up, clipping an attacker in the face but I didn't get enough force behind it. Raider bit another man but we were losing the standoff with the angry mob. With cries of "She's hurt! Get the noose on the fuckin' whore's neck!" they all surged toward me except the creepy guy with the noose, who was throwing the rope end over a tree limb.

A hand pulled on my hurt shoulder and wrestled me roughly to the ground. The creep with the noose put it over my head and laughed as he tightened it around my neck. With my shoulder in pain and body held in the grip of three or four men I was helpless, but Raider never gave up. He was growling and biting the entire time. I saw knives flashing and all I could do was pray he would not be killed or injured.

In my helpless state I wondered who was behind this? Who framed me for murder? Who bribed the district attorney to go along with it? Who incited this mob? Who was so filled with hatred for me?

The other end of the rope was over a tree limb and the rope began to tighten. Raider had run away but I could hear him barking in the distance. I hoped he got away. Raider bravely tried to help me, but there were too many attackers.

The creepy man pulled hard on the rope and I was lifted to stand up. The mob was not going to sit me on a horse and have it run out from under me to break my neck. They were going to tighten the noose and pull me up by the neck so it would take a long time for me to be strangled and die painfully. Another man joined the creepy man, pulling the rope and my feet started to come off the ground.

The familiar crack of an M1911 automatic sounded behind me and Major Griffin arrived from another direction, firing short bursts from a Tommygun. The hangman and his helper were shot and I fell to the ground when they let go of the rope. Carole Griffin appeared next to me with her smoking 1911 pistol and fired at a man who foolishly tried to grab the rope and pull me up. He went down with a bullet in his leg, screaming about being brutalized. I asked Carole if I could borrow her 1911 to show the man what real brutal treatment was, but she smiled and said no but she agreed with my idea. The crowd began to run when a truck roared up with Sgt. Reilly and his MP squad, who jumped off to chase down my assailants.

Wanting to have something in my hand I picked up the brick on a rope, but my shoulder hurt too much and I couldn't spin it around. There was Raider next to me and I sat down and hugged him, then saw he was bleeding. Carole stayed next to me to make sure none of the attackers came back to harm me while her husband and Reilly's MPs captured most of the mob.

The doctor at the base hospital treated my cuts and bruises and I asked him to take care of Raider's wound. He said he was not a veterinarian but I was not in the mood for him to decline. Before I could say anything Carole ordered him to "Take care of the dog", sounding more like a Marine drill sergeant than her usual sweet self. I watched as the doctor carefully shaved the fur from around the wound and upon close inspection it turned out to be a surface cut and not a stab wound, but it took a few stitches to close. I stayed by Raider's head to soothe him and he looked at me with his brown eyes as if to say "We sure took care of that bunch, didn't we?" I promised him the biggest, meatiest bone I could get from the Marine cooks.

Carole told me "Your dog came running barking to me, and you weren't with him so I knew that meant trouble. I sent the landscaper to tell my husband which way I was going, got my gun and followed your dog back to you. He deserves that bone" and called the chief cook. He heard what happened and personally delivered a big meaty bone.

The military police incident report disclosed the names of several base civilian employees, not Marines or Navy personnel. The report went on to say that three men had broken noses and others had been struck on their heads by a heavy object. Three had been shot but would live. Several attackers claimed they were bitten by a vicious dog. One required surgery, and that turned out to be the man who brought the brick on a rope, which I kept.

Major Griffin began the process to terminate the employment of the base employees involved in the attack but the temporary base commander would not sign the orders, saying that would be helping the murderess.

I went back to the Griffins' quarters and placed a call to the telephone number that Dan had given me to tell him what happened. When Louise Brooks answered I was surprised. I trusted Dan but today I lacked patience. "Louise, I thought you promised not to seduce Dan. I'm not having a very good day and I want the straight truth from you."

"Dan told us of your arrest and I am sorry that happened to you. Yes, Dan is here, but he is not alone with me. My husband Eddie is here along with Douglas, Billie, Bill Fields, Mary, Alice, Dorothy and some others."

"Mary? Alice? Who are they?" I asked.

Louise laughed and said "Mary Pickford and Alice White. My friend Peggy Fears is also here." Then to someone else she said "It's Laure, come say hello to her" and before I could reply a male voice took over.

"Hello cousin-in-law! I saw your dancing in the Gatsby film rushes my dear, and you were exquisite. How'd you like to be in one of my films?"

"Who are you?" I was full of dumb questions.

"Eddie. Eddie Sutherland, Louise's husband. Louise and I have not been together much since we got married and I'm making up for that by spending time with my wife. Had to kick Buster out, but that's tough bananas for him."

"You kicked Buster Collier out of your house?" I asked, intrigued.

"No, Buster Keaton. I'm sure Louise's habits are no surprise to you my dear, in fact it seems you are similar in nature" Eddie said.

"We are not similar that way. I am happily married and I don't jump into bed with anyone else" I said hotly.

"OK, hold on. Don't want to get you mad at me. I'll give the phone back to Louise, and I am serious about wanting you to be in one of my films."

Instead of Louise, the voice of Bill Fields was next. He was very nice, as he always was to me. Dan and I really liked the man and his sense of humor. He sounded sincerely sorry about our plight and graciously said he would help in any way he could and that he hoped Dan and I would have dinner with him soon. Then Billie Dove came on. By now I calmed down, knowing that Dan in fact was in a meeting with our friends in Hollywood and not alone with Louise. I loved Louise, but I also knew she had a case of the vapors for Dan. In the next few minutes I talked to Dorothy Davenport, met Peggy Fears on the phone, then Douglas Fairbanks came on to tell me that Dan was boldly doing everything exactly right, under his guidance of course. Then he introduced me on the phone to his wife Mary Pickford, who had been filming on location so Dan and I had not met her when we were there. She sounded wonderful and I realized that although I was talking to Hollywood royalty, she made it seem as if we were everyday friends. Then I talked with Myrna Loy, who I didn't quite remember at first but she was very sweet, then had a quick chat with Alice White who was charming and I remembered that she and Dan had an affair before I met him. Finally, my love got on the line.

"I haven't been able to get close to the telephone, everyone here is clamoring to talk to you. You've made quite an impression on a lot of people in Hollywood, especially after they saw you dance in the Gatsby flicker. Oh, and did I mention that I love you?"

I choked down my tears as I wished with all my heart that I could be there with him. I told him to sit down while I gave him the details about the attack, and how Raider had helped hold off an angry mob and went to bring the Marines. Dan became upset as he heard the story and demanded "Wait, stop. How are you? Are you hurt? Do you feel like you will be safe at Mare Island?"

I assured him that I was OK with just some cuts and bruises and my shoulder hurt but nothing was broken or separated. Then I told him about Raider's injury. "Laure, I know you don't want me telling you what to do, but please, please don't go anywhere without an armed guard. I'm coming home on the next train and I'll go back to meet with Lasky later. You're more important to me than any movie in the world and..."

I interrupted him. "Don't rush home Sweetie, get your business done with Lasky, no need to waste time with extra travel. I am not going anywhere alone until all this is over. I want you here beside me, but don't worry, I'm staying at the Griffin house now and Sgt. Reilly has Marines patrolling the area around the clock. Sgt. Reilly says I can go for a run with him and his squad in the morning if I'm up for it. Luigi is staying at our house with Josefina for her protection. Major Griffin informed me that some of my attackers were later found seriously beaten, and they nervously refused to name those who had done it. I had a suspicion and asked Sgt. Reilly but he just smiled, so I think we can guess what happened. I'm OK and I feel safe with Reilly's men here. They took it personally that I was attacked on their base. The men assured me it will not happen again. I love you so much Sweetie. If you want to put a smile back on my face, bring Champagne and strawberries home with you."

He laughed, told me he loved me and gave the phone to Louise and I apologized to her. "Not necessary Laure. I want you to know I did kiss Dan once, just a sisterly little kiss. He tried to turn away but I'm quick, you know. I'm serious Laure, I told you that I would not go after Dan unless you dumped him. It's tempting to think about, but I consider you a friend and I promised." We said our good nights and I went to the Griffin's guest room to rest. Raider stayed close to me wherever I went. It was comforting that Raider would not leave me except for quick relief breaks, and stayed in my room all night. We were getting to be quite a team.

I had forgotten to ask Dan about Claire. I called the S Bar C Ranch and the butler said she was not home. I hoped there was no problem between Scott and Claire. It made my mind uneasy and with that, along with the events of the day, I did not sleep well that night. When I got up the next morning, Carole said Sgt. Reilly asked me to call him by 7AM if I wanted to go for a run with his squad. I decided a good run would help settle me down. I left Raider with Carole and when Sgt. Reilly knocked on the door, he had over thirty Marines waiting behind him. He said men from other squads for some reason volunteered to run with his squad that morning. Surrounded by Marines, I had a good run.

The men were very polite and no one whistled or made catcalls, but I noticed they often changed positions from running in front, to the sides, to running behind me, but I did feel safe. Afterwards, cameras appeared and I had my photo taken with each runner. They asked if I would autograph the photos when they came back, and I agreed. That afternoon, Carole answered the phone and said we should go to the outside table. Sgt. Reilly and thirty Marines were there, each with a photograph for me to sign. The men had gone directly to the film development shop on the base to demand immediate film processing.

I told Dan about it when he called that evening, and he laughed. "Sweetie, if all it takes to guarantee your safety is having Marines watch you run and you're OK with it, that is just fine with me." I told him I was OK with it, but made him promise to run with me when this was all over. Then he asked if I would promise him a signed photograph, I told him he would get the photograph and a lot more.

MYSTERIOUS VISITOR

I wanted to be with him I but told Dan to stay as long as he needed to get the green light from Jesse Lasky for our movie production. It did not make sense for him to return and go back a few days later. Seeing that I was feeling lonesome, Carole arranged an officers' wives event, with chilled Sonoma white wine and a delicious lunch.

The next day the gate guard called Carole and told her there was someone asking to see me. Since we had no advance notice of a visitor and Dan was still in Hollywood, Carole decided it could be trouble so she called the on-duty MP squad, which was Gunnery Sgt. Gunther Streicher's squad. He and two of his men went to the gate to interrogate the visitor. Sgt. Streicher called to tell Carole that the man's name was Giuseppe and said a mutual friend had sent him. Carole asked Sgt. Streicher to advise Major Griffin, who ordered the sergeant to bring Giuseppe to his office. Carole drove us there, wearing her 1911 pistol in a holster.

Major Griffin, Carole and I had a cup of coffee and the Marine MPs brought Giuseppe into his office after searching Giuseppe for weapons. Giuseppe was a dapper and handsome young man with the continental manners of an educated gentleman.

Giuseppe asked if he could talk to me privately but Major Griffin said no. Giuseppe introduced himself and gave me his card, printed with the name Giuseppe Giordano and no further information except for a Chicago telephone number. Major Griffin asked if I wanted to talk to Giuseppe and I was curious. Sgt. Streicher sat behind Giuseppe with his pistol. Giuseppe seemed like a nice young man and besides, why would an assassin come on a Marine base? "OK Giuseppe, let's talk" I said.

"Thank you Mrs. Lindner" Giuseppe answered politely. At first I wondered who Mrs. Lindner was because I was not used to being called that, and I smiled. Giuseppe smiled back.

Giuseppe began "In the presence of others I must necessarily be discreet and not mention names. I have been asked to offer condolences on your being held under a false charge of murder. I am instructed to tell you that there are things in motion to get this cleared up. I do not know the details. My employer wanted you to know that this particular problem will be solved but at this time we do not know who is perpetrating this fraud. We will advise you and Dan when we know. Until then, please take precautions because whoever did this has significant political influence and may try to cause more trouble. Please take this seriously, and advise Dan to use extreme caution. Under the circumstances that is all I can say. May I advise my employer that you are well and being treated respectfully?" I nodded yes. "Thank you Mrs. Lindner. Major Griffin, may I be escorted back to my automobile?" Giuseppe slowly stood up, not wanting to make any sudden motions that would provoke Sgt. Streicher into shooting him.

I said "Thank you, Giuseppe. I am pleased to hear that a conclusion to this matter is at hand, and I will pass your words of caution to my husband. I feel like I know you from somewhere, have we met before?" I asked.

"Alas, I cannot answer that Mrs. Lindner, but please be assured that I am on your side" Giuseppe responded.

"Thank you for coming to see me" I said, and I moved to shake hands with him. Sgt. Streicher stood up quickly and raised his gun, causing Giuseppe to hold his hands up to show he had nothing in them. I reached up and took Giuseppe's hand to shake it anyway. He raised my hand to his lips and kissed it, and I thought of the day that I met Dan because he tried to kiss my hand too. Sgt. Streicher took a step closer and warned Giuseppe that he would die instantly if he did not let go of my hand.

Giuseppe let go and thanked Major Griffin for allowing him to see me. He turned to me and tapped the side of his nose as Sgt. Streicher escorted Giuseppe from the office.

"I have no idea who this Giuseppe is, but I don't sense that he is an enemy. The news that this will be resolved soon is interesting but I do not know who his mysterious employer is. I will ask Dan next time I speak with him. Thank you for your caution, Major Griffin" I said. Carole and I returned to her home, both of us mystified about my enigmatic caller.

Dan returned two days later. I asked if we could go to our old quarters, but because of the attack on me Major Griffin wanted to keep us close and declined. I did not want to offend or cause any alarm so I agreed that if Dan could spend the night with me in their guest room that would be fine.

I did not want to say anything to Dan if there were devices to listen in on our discussion. It did not feel right to keep information from our best ally, but my idea was speculative and revealing it could cause problems, even if I was wrong. That night, if anyone was listening, they would have only heard the sounds of our lovemaking. We were both very greedy for each other and I wondered what listeners might think. But Dan, as always, was very perceptive of the shift in my state of mind.

"Laure, you seem like a great weight that has been upon you has lifted. What happened?" he whispered.

I replied softly in his ear that it was only because he was back with me again, and that I missed him very much, which was true. I also put my finger beside my nose to let him know there was more I could not say at this time.

Dan whispered to me that Lasky green-lighted *Road Trip Blues*, so we could go forward and as long as everything went well the production's budget would cover us. Lasky asked Dan not to say anything until the studio publicity people set up an announcement event.

In the morning we came downstairs to breakfast just as Major Griffin was picking up his newspaper out of the front flowerbed where the delivery boy usually threw it. He set it aside, being polite and not looking at the newspaper over breakfast in front of guests. After we ate, he picked up the paper and opened it to scan the headlines. Finding nothing of immediate interest he set the newspaper aside and left for his office. While Major Griffin scanned the paper I noticed something of interest. I asked Carole if Dan and I could sit outside at the garden table with our coffee and the newspaper because we liked to read to each other. Carole said go ahead and she would bring out fresh coffee in a few minutes.

As soon as we got to the table I opened the paper and Dan's eyes opened wide as he read the news story I was pointing at, datelined October 11, 1926 from Chicago.

Yesterday at about 4 in the afternoon Hymie Weiss, notorious leader of the North Side Gang and his bodyguards were returning from a day in court. They parked their car by Holy Name Cathedral across the street from Weiss' office in the flower shop where his partner Dion O'Banion was killed in November 1924. As Weiss and his bodyguards crossed the street, Thompson machine gun fire erupted from an upper window of a rooming house next to the flower shop. Weiss took ten rounds in his body and fell next to a light pole near the flower shop. The nearest bodyguard was hit with seven rounds and died on the spot. Sam Pellar, another bodyguard was wounded but he, along with two other bodyguards ran to a nearby doctor's office to receive treatment for their wounds.

Weiss was alive when police arrived on the scene but died on the way to the hospital. His killers escaped out a back door of the rooming house, throwing a Thompson on the roof of a nearby building. It had jammed on the 39th bullet fired in the assassination. The hit on Weiss is thought to be retaliation for the North Side Gang's spectacular ten-

car raid and failed attempted assassination of Al Capone on
September 20.

I whispered in Dan's ear about the visit from Giuseppe Giordano. When we had the meeting with Al Capone, he hinted that Weiss was going to be taken down but warned us not to say anything. Did Al finally decide to pull the trigger – as Dan punned, making me groan – on Weiss because of the assassination attempt? Was it Weiss who was framing me? Was Giuseppe a messenger from Capone? Dan and I decided that we could not tell anyone of this until we knew for sure, and in any event we could not tell anyone we knew what was foretold or we could be charged with being accessories to murder.

Carole came out with more coffee and we stifled our excitement. Before Carole poured the coffee she produced a flask from a strap around her upper leg, poured some whiskey in each of our coffee cups, and topped it with a spoonful of whipped cream. It tasted posilutely wonderful. We drank toasts to each other's happy marriages, and by the time Major Griffin came home for lunch the three of us were in a merry condition. Carole offered to pour whiskey for her husband but he turned it down as he had a meeting with the temporary base commander after lunch. He requested that we stay at the house for the afternoon, and after he left Carole refilled the flask. The three of us got thoroughly soused. That night Carole refilled the flask for us to take to our bedroom. We put it to good use during our private celebration of the death of the man who helped Pádraigh orchestrate so much trouble for us.

Giuseppe was a prophet. My ordeal was over the next day when Major Griffin received a Federal court order freeing me of the charge of Col. Mosby's murder for lack of evidence, along with a Napa County court order quashing the indictment. This seemed to confirm that Weiss might have been behind the frame job. But how did

Giuseppe's boss make it happen, and why were Harris, the coroner and the assistant district attorney in on it? Weiss did have serious political muscle in Chicago and we took Giuseppe's warning to heart about watching out for trouble. I was free to leave Mare Island and thanked the Griffins for all they had done. Without them, I might have spent the entire time in that filthy jail cell with those two psychotic women.

We had a joyous reunion at our home, even Raider seemed happy to be back in familiar surroundings. Josefina wanted to have a celebration dinner so Bettina, Sunny and Josefina worked all afternoon in our kitchen and in the evening a huge party gathered. All our friends from Napa and Sonoma and anyone who could get leave from Mare Island came. We were even more surprised when two special guests arrived.

The first was Giuseppe Giordano, who I introduced to Dan. He thanked Giuseppe for whatever his role had been, which could not be revealed. He had been like an angel when he appeared to tell me my murder charge would be cleared. This time he brought a case of Moët & Chandon Champagne, saying that Gina had told him to bring it as a welcome home gift. Dan and I looked at each other. Gina? Al Capone was her godfather, and that told us who Giuseppe's employer was.

Soon after Giuseppe arrived I was even more surprised when I saw our next guest. It was none other than our beloved Elsie. Dan and I hugged and danced with her for several minutes until Dan asked where her fiancé Dr. Collins was. That almost brought Elsie to tears as she told us that Dr. Collins had been called to Ireland and she had not wanted him to go because it was a very dangerous mission for the Irish Republican Brotherhood. He had gone anyway and was killed in a gun battle with the police. Elsie decided that she wanted return to be our maid. Before he left for Ireland, Dr. Collins had left her some money so she bought a train ticket to Napa and called

Josefina to ask her not to tell us because she wanted her return to be a surprise, which it certainly was.

I don't know how we held up that week, getting sozzled so many times. Dan and I drank, but usually not to excess every night and the next morning we were really feeling our hangovers. But there was Elsie to the rescue, bringing us something really noxious that she claimed was an Irish remedy that would kill us or cure us. What was annoying was that Elsie, who drank more than we did was sharp as a tack, seemingly without any after-sozzling hangover.

Elsie would not tell us what it was, and it tasted so awful that I hoped to never need it again. We got it down and our hangovers disappeared in an hour.

Elsie asked if she could have her job back and I instantly said yes, but asked if that was what she really wanted. It was just a maid's job and there was a good share of hard work involved. Elsie replied that she was a simple Irish peasant girl and that she missed the work, loved us for our love of life, and wanted to be in on our next adventure. I assured her that we were not going to have another such adventure. Dan offered her a role in the movie, but she said she did not want to be in the flickers because if it was shown in Ireland there were people who would come to find her. She was willing to help in any way as long as she was not in front of a camera.

I gave Josefina a bonus, for I had found that she had done a superb job running the LaureDan Company in our absence. Everything was in order and accounted for properly, and she had signed two lucrative new accounts. Dan and I decided to make Josefina a junior partner.

That night Elsie's old boyfriend Darcy Moynihan, the waiter at one of our favorite Napa restaurants was her date. The waiter stayed the night in Elsie's room and I gave Giuseppe a guest room. Over the recent year, since Bettina and Vincenzo had stayed at our house so often to help Josefina we had given them a small apartment in our huge house, so they stayed too. However, even though her parents knew that Josefina and Luigi were lovers, Vincenzo did not want them sleeping together in the next room, so I slipped Josefina the key to one of the guest cottages. The smiles on their faces were thanks enough.

Dan and I took it easy on the panther sweat, not because of fear of a hangover but because we did not want to take Elsie's Irish hangover cure ever again.

That night we lay in bed, enjoying the peacefulness. I laid my head on Dan's shoulder and his hand was gently massaging my back, neck and shoulders. It was one of those times when we shared our thoughts without saying a word. We each knew what the other was thinking. But Dan put it in words when he said "We now have a chance for a normal life. What could possibly go wrong?"

"Dan, every time you say that, something goes wrong."

"Rhatz! Laure, you're right. I'll never say that again."

Later, Dan looked up and said "You're the perfect partner, wife, best friend and lover a guy could ever hope for. I don't know what I did to deserve you, but I'm going to find out and keep on doing it" and put his head back down.

I moaned "Oh Dan, don't stop – you're already doing it."

KNICKERS AND KICKERS

A few days later, after enjoying a lazy breakfast and reading the *Napa Register* to each other, Dan and I sat comfortably together holding hands on our outdoor loveseat, Raider taking a dog nap nearby. It was another time we did not need to talk as we enjoyed each other's company. Elsie saw how happy we were and made us a drink she called a Mimosa, invented at the Hôtel Ritz Paris in 1925, and told us that it was perfect for a beautiful Wine Country morning. Elsie knew we liked to try different cocktails and she kept up with such things. I turned and kissed Dan and said "It is sweet to do nothing." He smiled his agreement.

I decided to bring up something that was on my mind. "Do we really need this huge house? The rent doesn't cost us much but it feels too grand for my tastes" I said.

Dan knew there was more, saying "And you don't like living where one of our best friends was murdered."

"Yes, that's on my mind too. Maybe it isn't the best timing with the movie production beginning, but here's why I think we should consider it."

"I'm all ears" Dan said with his big grin turned on.

"It isn't your ears that I want but let's not get started on that, hear me out first, OK sweetie?"

"I'm still all ears" Dan said.

"Wise guy. I checked with our bank for winery properties on the market. I found four in Napa and two in Sonoma that fit our long-term plans. You and I talked about finding a winery property, even if we had to renovate the vineyards from neglect. When Prohibition is repealed, prices will shoot skyward and we will have missed a great opportunity. I would like us to look at them and choose the best ones for closer inspection. How does that sound?"

"It sounds to me like the cat's pajamas" he replied.

"You can take mine off later."

"I would if you wore pajamas" Dan grinned.

"Stop teasing. We have a mostly free day today with only one stop to get a contract signature. I picked out the properties to see if there's time." Dan wisely agreed. He knew that if I decided to do something, it was best to do it sooner than later. After we collected the contract signature in Sonoma we went to see the two properties there, with enough time left to visit one of the properties in Napa County.

Now that we started, our excitement built rapidly and the next day we looked at the others. At the end of the day, I was not surprised that we both liked the same property in Napa, a winery, three vineyards and an old house. The winery buildings and house were in need of repair or replacement but renovation of the winery buildings could wait. The vineyards contained more acreage than we wanted but they had not gone into serious neglect. We could decide later to keep or sell some acreage. The property was located outside of the town of St. Helena on Howell Mountain except for one vineyard on the valley floor. Vincenzo had told us that hillside vineyards produced exceptional wine grapes.

The hook was set and we went back every day to inspect various parts of the property. Then we asked Vincenzo Montanari to inspect the property with us and give us his opinion. When we drove up, Vincenzo looked pleased. "Dan, Laure, I know this property. Before Prohibition I tried to buy it but was out-bid. It will sell these days for less than I bid, but I'm not in a position to purchase it now. My vineyard is next to your valley floor vineyard. We could look into an agreement for combined vineyard maintenance and farming. I don't think it is too much land. It may seem so today, but when Prohibition ends you will be looking to buy land, not sell. I think it is perfect for you." Vincenzo's wise words moved us to make the decision to buy.

The next day Dan and I went to the bank and made a bid for the property. We were excited. It was our first home of our own and fit with our long term plans. When the deed was recorded, we created LaureDan Vineyards and Winery to add to our collection of businesses in The LaureDan Company. I was ecstatic with our property and its possibilities, but realistic to recognize that the house needed a lot of work. We asked Viktor look at it and he advised it would cost more to renovate than to construct a new house, but said we could make some repairs to live there temporarily and build after the movie production.

The days after we closed on the property were the last sunny warm days of the year. Dan and I enjoyed creating surprises for each other, so when he came home and found my note asking him to meet me at one of our vineyards he was not surprised. When he arrived, he found a small table set for two with a picnic basket along with two bottles of Montanari wine in a secluded place with a beautiful valley view. He did not see me yet but I knew he was alert for a surprise as he sat down and put together a plate of food and poured two glasses of wine. When he looked up, I was standing in front of him.

Shoe manufacturers were working with Goodyear to develop athletic shoes with rubber soles styled for men and women but I found them lacking in support and comfort. I had tried the hot new Keds shoes just before my order of the new Converse kicks arrived and this would be a good test for the promising new shoes. Dan was in good physical shape and I decided to find out if I could outrun him. To encourage him to catch me – not that he ever needed encouragement – I was wearing only my new Converse running shoes and sexy custom fitted camiknickers that I designed to provide support for my breasts for a short run. My Italian seamstress giggled with delight when I gave her my design and told her the plan.

The look on Dan's face told me he had taken the bait so I turned and ran. He was fast and almost caught me, but my running exercises gave me the ability to keep up the pace longer than he could.

I ran along a planned route through the vineyard that combined sprints, turns and a bit of hide-and-seek, but then I slowed because I wanted him to catch me. I knew he was close, but he was closer than I thought and I found myself scooped up and thrown over his shoulder, caveman style. Dan easily carried me back to the blankets that I had artfully arranged on a mat.

He set me on the blankets and I removed his clothes while he caught his breath and told me how sexy I looked running in my camiknickers as he removed them. I liked him to remove my clothing because he thrilled me with his sexy touches and soon we were enjoying our first hot romp in our own vineyard.

After a rest to feed each other, drink wine and laugh, Dan got that look in his eyes again. To my surprise, he took off running and I had to catch him, but that did not take long. Since I could not carry him, we walked back hand in hand, but sometimes his hand was on my butt until we were back on the blankets. I planned our first lovemaking on our winery property to be special so we would always remember it. My plan worked.

The sun was nearly down behind the Mayacamas, the western range of Napa Valley, and we were still naked on the blankets when the fall chill crept up the valley from the bay so we got dressed, packed up and went home. The next day we moved into the house. With help from Sven and Ole we did enough work on the old house to make it temporarily comfortable.

The winery house was much smaller than our previous rental, so until we built a new home we rented a cottage for Sunny and Elsie in St. Helena. Dan said when we built the new house, we would build cottages for Elsie and Sunny so they – and we – could have privacy. Both Sunny and Elsie were thrilled and said they would be happy to live in St. Helena until the new cottages were built. We also decided to build a third guest cottage for our families when they visited us. When I called my parents and excitedly told them our plans, Ma said I was getting the nesting urge like she had when she and Jake built their first home in Argo, Illinois, and I was born a year later.

November came with an interesting development. Sheriff Harris was running for re-election and we supported his rival, a deputy named Steckter. Harris was favored to win, but just before the election Harris dropped out and Steckter was elected. The fact that Giuseppe Giordano was in Napa at the time was not noticed by anyone but us.

Steckter was less strict about Prohibition, but in his campaign speeches he told the citizens that if anyone got out of hand he would quickly step in with the force of the law. It turned out that very little adjustment was required. The speakeasy operators knew it would be better to keep things low key than to get a sheriff's raid leading to fines and jail time.

GREEN LIGHT FOR ROAD TRIP BLUES

Dan and I took the Southern Pacific's *Daylight Limited* to Los Angeles for the public announcement of the Famous Players-Lasky green light for *Road Trip Blues*. Lasky gave us use of a studio to begin filming the indoor scenes a month before the outdoor scene filming, scheduled to begin in March or April 1927. We still had some open cast positions to fill but we had signed a director. Howard Hawks had expressed interest and we finally worked out a deal with Fox Films so he could direct for our new company, LaureDan Film Productions.

Dan's sister Claire was still missing and no one seemed very worried about it. I finally talked to Scott on the telephone and he said that Claire had just been there and left, but he became evasive when I tried to find out what she had been doing. It was not like her to disappear. Then I was not able to find my Uncle Viktor and his girlfriend Evelyn. What was going on?

Dan and I attended the final *Road Trip Blues* meeting with Jesse Lasky and other executives and more problems to solve before production began were put on Dan's shoulders. In front of Lasky, he acted calm, as if everything was jake, which reminded me to call my father and ask him what Uncle Viktor was doing.

Lasky gave us every break he could for our first movie production. We had budget approval for almost the full amount we had requested, including renting our locomotive to the studio for the movie, and we were able to get Bill's actor pay and associate producer compensation locked in. When we took our lunch break, Dan said "I'm glad you're here with me, you're an excellent negotiator. Then there's so much to be done, and soon you will be busy with costume designs and music and dance with Louise, not to mention our LaureDan business."

"I talked with Louise yesterday and she has already worked up some designs and choreography. She seems excited, unlike her usual attitude towards making movies. That's good because I don't really know much about either."

"Sweetie, you have a fine eye for fashion. I am anxiously waiting to see you in those camiknickers again. Just follow your vision, we're both going to be making it up as we go along. People will have no idea how much of the movie is based on real events. I am confident that you and Louise will come up with the best costume fashions and dance routines that Hollywood has ever seen."

"Mr. Smooth Producer, I know your type but you should remember that I know how to deal with fast-talking men like you who just want to get a girl on her back." I laughed as Dan wiggled his eyebrows and leered suggestively just like Groucho Marx did in his vaudeville routine. Rumor was that the Marx brothers were getting movie offers from the major studios. I thought they were outrageously funny and sure bets for success.

Lasky was full of confidence that an up and coming producer like Dan could handle everything. This was mostly because our friend and prankster extraordinaire Douglas Fairbanks was instrumental in making Louise's prank believable, but we were coming to the time when Dan was going to have to prove it. I gave him my commitment to do everything I could to help.

Dan booked us into The Beverly Hills Hotel's Bungalow #5, where we stayed after *The Great Gatsby* movie wrapped. When we arrived, there was a note from Scott to meet him in #8. We had not even known he was in town, but I looked at this as my chance to grill him on what Claire was doing.

We were dressed to the nines as Dan knocked on Scott's bungalow door, and it sounded like there was a party going on. Claire opened the door and had a huge sweet smile on her face, Scott right behind her. After they invited us in and gave us Champagne, Scott said "Dan, Laure, I hope you don't think I'm being presumptuous. This was all Claire's idea and she sealed my lips by threatening to cut me off if I didn't go along with her plan. Needless to say, I gave in." Claire's smile got even bigger.

Claire said "You know I've always been fascinated with the flickers, and Scott asked me to learn the business so he could turn over our movie investments for me to manage. I've been sneaking off to Hollywood to take lessons at an actor's school, and who should show up at one of my lessons but Douglas Fairbanks and Mary Pickford. That's when I found out they were the founders and owners of the school. They were impressed that I wanted to learn and along with your other friends began teaching me many things, even some of what a producer does. For the last two weeks I have been a guest at Dorothy Davenport's home. She comes from a family of New York stage actors and appeared in movies with Wallace Reid, and became a producer and director on her own after he died. She helped me learn as fast as I could absorb it."

"Well Sis, you're a sharp cookie so I expect you would do just that" Dan said with sincere admiration.

Dorothy Davenport was in the room and came over at the mention of her name. "That's right, she is a quick learner and Billie Dove introduced Claire to Lois Weber, a former actress and movie director. Lois was one of my mentors when I learned to produce and direct films. She is one of the most knowledgeable people in the business. Lois says Claire is a natural, and we recommend that you hire Claire to work in your production company."

Dan and I didn't even need to talk to each other, we both said "She's hired!" in unison.

"I'm glad you hired her, or I would have had a very disappointed wife to bring home to Long Grove" Scott said. "Jesse Lasky called me and asked if I wanted to invest in the movie, so I did, but I do not want you to think I did that so you would hire Claire. My investment was made before Claire decided to dive into the business, and my contract stipulates that I have no control over the movie production. Lasky assured me that with a hotshot producer like Dan, and with Laure and Louise Brooks and Buster Collier starring, all I had to do was sit back and cash the checks from my share of the profits."

Scott continued "Lasky thinks very highly of the both of you, and he's banking on your future by giving you every break he can. I'm happy to abide by the terms of the investment contract. By the way, Lasky says he has other investors if I wanted to back out once he heard about Claire so your movie was never dependent on my investment. Now that Claire knows more than I do about movie production she won't ask my advice, I'll be asking hers" Scott said. "Even if you don't show a profit, it will be worth it because Claire will have a business career she is developing on her own. She informed me that she would not be a stay at home housewife and I'd better get used to it. My mother isn't, she gets involved in the McLanahan businesses all the time. Besides that, my father has placed a huge workload on me so I won't have time to poke my nose into your movie."

Dan and I gave Claire big hugs. I was so relieved that there was no problem between Claire and Scott. Claire surprised us again, saying "I talked with Uncle Viktor and Evelyn at your wedding reception and they were happy to be invited to be cast in the movie but nervous because they had no experience, so I sent them a letter and told them to come out here. Douglas Fairbanks is the star, writer and producer of his next movie *The Gaucho* and offered us supporting parts for experience. We just began filming and don't worry, our parts will be done before *Road Trip Blues* filming begins. Viktor and Evelyn will not be here tonight because they are in rehearsal at Iverson Ranch. Viktor is learning to be a stuntman and Evelyn wants to be a cinematographer. At first, the camera crew gave her a hard time but she is feisty and showed she was willing to work hard and learn. James Wong Howe, one of the best cinematographers in the business is teaching Evelyn. With

Howe backing her, and the fact that she's so charming and Uncle Viktor appears so menacing, the male camera operators decided it would be better to make friends, and now they love their 'Little Evie' and fall all over each other to help teach her the craft. Douglas is going around bragging that his movie is Evelyn's first camera job and her practice takes have been the bee's knees. Mary Pickford is in Evelyn's camp too, and Mary's influence is legendary in Hollywood."

"We will have all our families in the movie business soon. Maybe someday we could start up our own studio" Dan quipped, but Douglas and Mary quickly appeared next to us.

Mary Pickford said "Shhh. Don't let Lasky hear you. There are a lot of new studio companies cropping up. Douglas and I, along with Charlie Chaplin and D. W. Griffith are the founding partners of United Artists so Jesse Lasky was worried that we might lure you over to UA. We did want to bring your production to UA, but you were already signed with Lasky."

Dan and I were learning about all the side deals, behind-the-scenes plots and sneaky plans that ran through Hollywood and hoped to stay out of them, but this made me see the impossibility of that. We decided to be as fair as possible in our dealings, and if we did not make it in the flickers, well, we had not sought to be in them in the first place. We had other business opportunities and we were not impressed with being celebrities. Fairbanks and W.C. Fields both told us that it was a necessary trait to want success in the movie business, but unwise to appear desperate. The top studio executives knew that if you were desperate they could bend you to their will and throw you away later.

The studio announcement of our movie's green light would be in tomorrow morning's trade papers and the studio arranged tonight's celebration dinner party. We went back to Bungalow #5 to change into our evening clothes, then walked to the banquet room. Dan disappeared, making me wonder why he left me so suddenly, but he came back with a tray of Champagne glasses. I wondered what that was all about until I saw behind Dan was my Ma and Pa and Dan's mother Dorothy. I dropped my Champagne glass as I went to hug them but W.C. Fields was nearby and caught the glass before it hit the floor. He was a juggler in his vaudeville days and still had quick hands. I thanked W.C. and gave him a nice kiss because I liked to see him smile, then introduced him to my parents, who were big fans of his. He talked with them for several minutes, even doing a short routine just for them and signed autographs on his studio photos. Before he wandered off for a fresh glass of gin, Louise and I put Fields in a Brooks sandwich and kissed him while photographers snapped cameras.

I hugged my Ma and Pa again with tears of happiness in my eyes. They looked great tonight, my mother's dress was almost flapper style and it looked great on her. Jake had flown the Fokker F.VIIa-3m out to help us celebrate, and had brought Dan's mother Dorothy. We introduced our parents to Douglas Fairbanks and Mary Pickford. Douglas grandly demanded that the photographer take pictures of him with Mary, Vera, Dorothy and Elaine, loudly proclaiming they were the most beautiful women at the party as he slyly winked at me and Claire and our mothers blushed. Then he went to talk to Jake about aeroplanes.

When Douglas came back he led Dan and me around the room to introduce us to everyone we did not already know. Douglas and Mary knew everything and everyone in Hollywood. I was glad they were in our corner. Alice White, Myrna Loy, John Gilbert, James Hall, Jack Mulhall, Dorothy Mackaill, Clara Bow, Marion Davies, Loretta Young, Buster Keaton and Buster Collier, it seemed like everyone was here to celebrate our movie production. Dan looked cool and calm as he worked the crowd, making his way confidently in this group. I literally backed into Herbert Brenon, my director on *The Great Gatsby* set. He asked me if I would like to look at a couple of roles and would send the scripts over to Bungalow #5. Louise and her husband Eddie Sutherland worked the crowd together looking elegant and chic. Louise and I posed for the movie news photographers, and those photographs showed up in the trade papers and gossip magazines for days afterward.

Dinner began and Dan was seated between Mary Pickford and Alice White, while I was seated between W.C. Fields and Eddie Sutherland, who had directed Louise and Fields in *It's the Old Army Game*. Sutherland was a good conversationalist but kept making suggestions about meeting me later, even though Louise was in the room. He told me that he would like to be considered as director for our next movie. *Fat chance of that*, I thought.

After dessert was served, Jesse Lasky took the podium to formally announce the green light for *Road Trip Blues*. The crowd stood and cheered. He praised Dan as a Hot New Producer in Hollywood and I wondered how many telephone numbers would find their way into his pockets tonight.

Lasky introduced Dan and he got a thunderous round of applause. Lasky recounted the legend of how Dan made sure good coffee was served on all Famous Players movie sets. No more of the swill that choked Captain Tracy. Lasky turned over the floor to Dan, who announced his cast and key production company people. Dan really looked great up there in his tuxedo and I anticipated taking it off him. I wore my sexy new lingerie that he would have to remove from me, but I had no worry, he was an expert at it.

Dan said he had three associate producers and introduced Bill and Claire. I almost fainted when he called my name to announce that I was an associate producer! He surprised me, having kept it secret. Then I realized that was why Jake and Vera had come to the party. I saw my father with the biggest smile ever on his face. I made sure to thank my parents when I went up to the podium to acknowledge my associate producer appointment.

After that was done, Dan invited Herbert Brenon to come up to announce that the theater release of *The Great Gatsby* movie would be November 21 in New York, and since I was in it he brought a nine minute reel of scenes for those who wanted to see it after dinner.

Later when I talked to Claire, she said "Laure, since I was a little girl I have wanted to be in the movies. Scott arranged with Lasky for me to work here, helping out and learning backstage work. I took to it like a duck to water and spent all my time soaking up knowledge." Then she lowered her voice and said "I'm so thrilled! I've met so many fascinating people and had to fight off a few of them, but I am faithful to Scott and untouched by the casting couch. Oh Laure I have so much to tell you."

We picked up fresh glasses of Champagne, went into a room set up as a theater, and took our seats just as the lights dimmed. Dan was next to me and it was a good thing it was dark. The film started and I was in the first scene, part of the trailer where I was running up a circular staircase with other party girls, and then the scene with several partygoers diving into a large swimming pool. Brenon had me in half of the nine minute feature reel. Most of the time I was dancing and Dan kept nibbling my ear and telling me what a great dancer I was and how sexy I looked. I thought about throwing him on the floor and having my way with him, but that might be too much even for Hollywood.

At the time of filming my scenes in *The Great Gatsby* I had not felt very sexy since most of the time I was exhausted with the long days on the set and Buster Collier keeping me awake late into the night. Brenon kept the scene in the movie where I wasn't a dancer. I was in front of the camera for about twenty seconds and Claire, whispered that I was a natural. When the feature clip ended Dan led the crowd's applause and it did not stop until the film was re-wound and shown again.

After that, Brenon called me to come up front, and told the audience that I had a big future in the movies and he was offering me a choice of good roles for my consideration, adding that he wanted Dan to produce those movies for him. I wondered how we were going to have time to build our new house and renovate our winery before the repeal of Prohibition.

We were exhausted by the time we got back to Bungalow #5 and unusual for us, we slept in late the next morning. The trade papers were on the doorstep of our bungalow, and we read about our movie production being green-lighted and all the gossip reporters wrote great things about us. Maybe we weren't interested in being celebrities, but it was heady stuff to receive all the attention and applause.

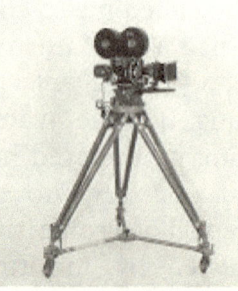

LIGHTS! READY! CAMERA! SPEED! MARKER! AND... ACTION!

The holidays flew by and it seemed like one party after another. The *Napa Register* featured write-ups about our movie, hinting that it was based on actual events. Little did they know! Uncle Viktor and Evelyn had come for the holidays and the Montanaris had offered the use of their guest cottage. It was small but luxurious and they began to learn about Wine Country, meeting our friends and neighbors. Bettina told them they could stay until they decided what they wanted to do, but Uncle Viktor would not accept it for free. Until the movie production began, he and Evelyn worked for a new speakeasy, and he paid rent for the cottage. Vincenzo didn't want to accept it, but not many people have successfully said no to Uncle Viktor. He bought a used car, a spiffy two year old Packard Single Six Runabout. He and Evelyn would go flying down the road until Uncle Viktor finally was stopped and issued a speeding ticket. He slowed down a little after that, but not by much.

We had Thanksgiving at our house, then celebrated Christmas and New Year 1927 with our friends. Dan and I agreed to exchange modest gifts for Christmas and our birthdays so we could save money for our new house.

The last role to cast was who would play me. Buster Collier wanted me to play the role and Dan agreed, but I refused. I liked Buster as a friend but did not want to open up the scars on our relationship from our affairs with Buster and Louise.

We considered Myrna Loy, Madge Bellamy, Josephine Dunn and others. Most of them were under contract to other studios and unavailable. Alice White's name came up and she was available. Despite knowing of Dan's long ago affair with Alice, all I said was that she was shorter than me, but I agreed to offer Alice the role and she accepted.

Studio filming for *Road Trip Blues* began on Monday, March 21 1927, the day I turned 24 years old. I'll never forget when the first film rolled.

"Lights" The assistant director (AD) called the command for the lighting crew to make a final check to ensure all the lights were set properly, even though they had already been triple-checked.

"Ready" the AD shouted. This was the command for all actors to be in position and the clapper slate checked that it was chalked with the correct scene and take number.

"Camera" was called next, the order for the camera crew to start rolling film.

"Speed" called by the Director of Photography (DP) when all the camera operators signaled that their cameras were functioning at the correct speed.

"Marker" the DP called and a young lad jumped in front of Evelyn's camera with the slate, clapped the sticks and jumped back.

"Action" After a quick look around, director Howard Hawks gave the order we eagerly awaited, the first command for action on the *Road Trip Blues* set.

We were impressed with his professionalism and style. He had gone over the scene with everyone to avoid glitches and misunderstandings. Some directors did take after take, but Hawks minimized that by spending more time in preparation before the cameras rolled to avoid wasting valuable film stock. We still had re-takes, but we agreed with his style and technique and stayed out of his way. The evening before Dan and I went over everything with Hawks to put in our observations because once the set was live, the director was the captain of the ship. Dan came up next to me and we held hands as the first scene unfolded. Our movie was alive! I admit to being thrilled at what we had accomplished. All the work we had done paid off and only one re-take was needed for the first scene.

Director Hawks was pleased but he was not one to waste studio time and soon had the next scene rolling. I had to go back to the dressing room because the scene after this was Louise and I doing the Charleston in a speakeasy. From acting in *The Great Gatsby* I learned that a movie was not filmed in the actual scene sequence, it was filmed to take advantage of the scenery in place and the actors and costumes currently on the set.

When I went to the dressing room Louise was having the finishing touches done to her makeup. She was so beautiful that I felt posilutely ugly next to her. When Louise was ready to go on the set she looked at me and told me I was beautiful and with the compliments we both received from those on the set I felt better. Dan told me I was sexier and prettier than Louise and offered to take me back to the studio bungalow to prove it, but I told him "sorry, Sweetie, the bank is closed, but it will be open later." We were ready and our dancing dresses Louise designed looked fabulous. A shout down the hall announced the AD calling us to the set. Hawks had a Victrola to play the music for our dancing. As Louise and I arrived on stage, Dan was placing the record on the turntable. Even though it was a silent move, it was easier to dance to music and I wanted to use the recording of The Charleston that Paul Whiteman had given us the night of our first date in Chicago.

Louise and I had worked out the timing with Hawks so that when the DP called "Speed" we were starting to dance and when the marker clapped it was timed for us to begin the choreography that Louise designed. For someone who had the reputation of being difficult to work with, Louise was enthusiastic, coming up with great ideas and teaching me more dance moves. She worked with the costume people on our sexy dresses that would show well on black and white film. Louise had been out with Buster Collier last night and I worried that she would be hung over, but she did not miss a step.

When Hawks called "Cut" everyone on the set broke into applause as Hawks declared "no re-take". We were confident that with Louise's creative choreography our dance scenes would stand out.

Dan walked by with the Paul Whiteman record safely in its envelope and said "Champagne and strawberries tonight Sweetie!"

"There damn well better be or I'm going on strike!" I replied, causing several people around us to laugh. Nobody on the set was allowed to talk like that, but we were considered unconventional, being from Chicago.

We finished with the sets three days later and had a day to relax while the carpenters and crews moved the old sets out and put new ones in place. We were assigned to a small studio but Lasky promised us a larger studio in two weeks when another production wrapped. Later, when the films of our first scenes were processed, we went with Lasky, Hawks, the AD and DP to the screening room to see the rushes. Lasky complimented our dancing and the entire production crew.

Dan was as happy as could be and I was proud of him for having learned from Fairbanks about the role of a producer and then without rehearsing, he pulled it off so no one suspected it was his first time.

The night after the scene changes, Dan and I had settled into sleep when the telephone rang. "That can't be good" mumbled Dan as I answered, being closer to the phone.

It was Bill. "Laure, you and Dan need to get down to the film locker right away. There's been a fire." I told him we were on our way. Before I hung up Dan knew that there something major had gone wrong and was pulling on his pants. When we arrived Lasky, Hawks, the AD and DP along with several firemen and the studio security chief were there.

"This fire was deliberate, set by someone who knew how volatile film is. Who is upset about this movie? Anyone got a grudge against any of you?" asked the security chief. None of us could think of anyone who would sabotage our film. We had told Lasky about my false murder charge, rather than have him find out on his own, and now he asked the obvious question.

"Could this be the same person or persons who set you up?" Lasky asked.

Dan replied "We don't even know who it was that set Laure up, or why, but it was someone who had political influence. I didn't think that the Chicago mob had that kind of pull out here, but Hymie Weiss is dead and we made our peace with Capone."

"The Chicago outfit does have influence out here. We get troubles with unions and things like that sometimes, but we are always able to sort it out with them. We have not had any problems with the mob for several weeks now" said studio Security Chief Higgins.

"We were lucky that the wind was blowing toward the gate because the guard smelled smoke and called out our fire department. He also called one of the Hollywood fire stations in to help us check the film lockers on all the sets. The film in this locker was unexposed; none of the film shot for our movie was here. With the studio's permission I'd like to put one or two of our watchmen in to augment the studio force. We will co-ordinate with studio security" Bill said. Lasky agreed although the studio security chief did not look too happy about others getting in his way, but he didn't have a choice once Lasky accepted.

"We've got more film stock and I'll have it brought in so we can keep filming. Meantime, everyone keep a sharp eye out for unknown people hanging around, and let's double check and search the studios when filming is done to make sure no one is hiding to come out and do mischief later" said Lasky.

We went back to our studio bungalow, but neither of us felt at ease. Trouble was starting up again and we had no idea who was causing it.

Dan and I ate breakfast at the studio café and just as we were finishing the AD came rushing in looking for us. "More trouble" was all he said before turning to run back to the studio.

"Now what?" Dan asked angrily as we ran to the studio. An angry DP was looking at the wreckage of two movie cameras, smashed to bits on the stage floor. "It looks like someone took a sledgehammer to the cameras" he wailed. "There are not even any salvageable parts."

We huddled with Hawks and Bill said it was unlikely that someone would try something on the set while the cast and crew were there. Several of our crew had experience as security guards, and two of them were armed. If these guys caught anyone messing with their livelihoods it would not go well for the perpetrators. Our 1911 pistols were in our studio bungalow and I went to get them. Hawks wanted to keep filming, but some of the studio crew were superstitious and threatened to balk at working on a set where there were unknown dangers.

When Louise and Buster Collier arrived, they took the news calmly and went to their dressing rooms. They both had seen danger with us last year, and neither of them were cowardly. Lasky sent over another camera but they did not have many more since all the studios on the lot were filming today. Evelyn arrived and Viktor stationed himself near her.

A minute later Louise came out and calmly informed Dan and me that there was a snake in her dressing room. She kept it quiet, knowing that the stagehands would be nervous to hear that. Bill and Viktor went in and Bill came over to whisper to us that it was a rattlesnake. He went to get a snake handler and a small revolver. Viktor stayed in the dressing room to keep an eye on it and promised Evelyn that he would not get snake bit.

But the saboteurs had another surprise for us. When the stagehands went to set the filming lights and turn them on, they found the arcs in several of them were smashed. Now everyone began to have the jitters. What next? Hawks told Dan he needed to scrap the day and have all the wiring and equipment checked. Dan agreed and Hawks gave everyone the rest of the day off. With everything inspected and the overnight security strengthened they would be able to concentrate on production. Dan went to tell the news to Lasky, who took it well, trusting Dan would get this resolved before long.

Bill called in an outside crew to inspect everything. We did not want the stagehands to discover more damage, but no other damage was found.

I called our office in Napa and Elsie answered, saying Josefina had gone upvalley to get a contract renewal signed. I gave her the short story of what happened and she offered to come down and help, but I told her I did not want Josefina left there alone, although Luigi had taught her how to shoot. Now that we knew there was something afoot we would not be caught with loose security. I told Elsie to keep Raider with Josefina for extra protection.

A few minutes later a studio messenger came and said there was a telephone call for Dan or me so I went to Dan's office. When the operator called back it was Giuseppe. He called right after I talked to Elsie and she told him what happened. Giuseppe asked me for details so he could make inquiries through his employer's organization.

We were not scared, we were angry. But who was our antagonist?

ROAD TRIP BLUES, THE MOVIE

Bill, Dan and I worked with the inspection crew until midnight and discovered no other sabotage. Viktor and Bill stayed overnight with the studio security people. In the morning Hawks and the cast and crew were ready to film. I went to see the studio security chief to make sure he was OK with us having private guards. He was an ex-deputy sheriff named Jack Higgins who had not been happy when Lasky approved our request for our own guards. As we talked he began to see that we were taking our movie production seriously and were not trying to undermine him with Lasky. In fact, Dan and I went to see Lasky and told him that Jack had added more security to the area and Bill, our associate producer and security manager was satisfied that everything that could be done was being done. Jack calmed down now that we understood each other, and after that he was always helpful.

During the rest of the filming in the studio we had no more trouble. We established 24 hour security. Dan, Jack and Bill inspected the set and talked with the guards when filming stopped and before the cast and crew arrived in the morning.

Dan left for Cherryvale in Kansas for a few days to meet Big Al and the Swedes for the final inspection of locomotive #3447 before the transfer of ownership to us. With Big Al supervising and double-checking they looked at everything from the cowcatcher to the coupler at the end of the tender and pronounced #3447 to be in first class condition. Bill obtained clearance and interchange routing from the railroads to move #3447 to Los Angeles where we would park it on a siding near our outdoor film location. We wanted to hire guards but the boys said they would take turns to patrol around the locomotive. With all the adventures we had with #3447, they were taking a protective attitude toward it now that it was ours.

In a week or two we would be moving to our outdoor location. Bill managed to teach Sven and Ole how to shoot, or at least to point their revolvers in the right direction so they would not shoot each other or the locomotive. We met Big Al Hudson's wife Joanne, who was short and very curvy with a larger than life personality, a perfect match for him and it was no wonder Big Al was happy to get back with her. We rented hotel rooms near the filming location for the cast and crew.

Howard Hawks, the crew and truckloads of equipment and supplies converged on the film location. The first outdoor filming would be in Southern California and it began without any problems the first two weeks.

The third week of outdoor filming began with Uncle Viktor's first stunt action scene. It was the scene when Dan and the crew took Pádraigh's train and rescued me near Albuquerque. We had an old boxcar and Viktor was playing the part of one of Pádraigh's men who would jump when the pyrotechnics started to simulate being blown out of the boxcar. Other stuntmen were jumping from the roof and inside. There were two camera operators filming outside the boxcar and Evelyn was filming inside the boxcar against Viktor's wishes, but Evelyn was not a wallflower and Viktor relented when she said "nothing could possibly go wrong since you're going to be right here with me." I cringed when she said it, but did not reveal my discomfort because I did not want to be seen as superstitious.

We watched as Hawks carefully went over the stunt with everyone. The stunt director personally designed the pyrotechnics explosion and verified the setup. Instead of letting the boxcar roll freely, Big Al was driving a small yard locomotive slowly on the other end of the boxcar where the cameras could not see it.

"Action" called Hawks and the boxcar moved. Big Al and the stuntmen practiced this stunt with everything except the explosives in place, but now it would be live. Hawks stressed the need for everyone to do their part on cue because we would not be able to re-take this scene.

The boxcar shuddered when Big Al jerked the boxcar back and forth with the yard engine to simulate the energy of the explosion. Evelyn, inside the boxcar would film Viktor as he opened the boxcar door and catapulted himself out to make it look like the explosion blew him out. In rehearsal, Viktor impressed the stunt director with his strength and ability to make it look real.

When the action started, Viktor tried to open the boxcar door and he was shocked to find it stuck. He knew he had to open it or the pressure wave from the pyrotechnics explosives would blow back to Evelyn, who was standing behind her camera just inside the open door on the other side. He yelled for the other stuntman to get out fast, turning and running across the boxcar toward Evelyn. He had no time to stop and explain, he just opened his arms and pulled her toward him as he jumped out the other door, in the process kicking the camera out. Viktor rolled as he landed so he would not crush Evelyn. They had barely cleared the door when the main pyrotechnics detonated. The flames were supposed to vent safely from both boxcar doors but with one door shut it was partially contained and the force of the blast vented toward the only opening, where Evelyn had been just a fraction of a second before.

The cast and crew were watching and when Viktor did not get his door open there were shouts from some of them. Dan saw Viktor with Evelyn in his arms flying from the opposite side of the boxcar with a tongue of flame on his back, and it looked like he landed hard. Dan was first to get to them, then Bill and then Hawks, me and the other stuntmen.

Dan was trying to talk to Viktor but I feared he was either dead or unconscious with blood running from wounds to his head and arms, his back singed from the flames. Evelyn was calling Viktor's name over and over, not realizing that from the loud explosion she couldn't hear and was screaming at the top of her voice. Dan gently moved Viktor's arms from Evelyn as he still held her tight and I thought he must be alive to do that. I helped Evelyn up and the doctor on the set was there with his black bag. Other crewmembers helped clear a place for the doctor to treat Evelyn's injuries. Ole came running up with water, Dan got Viktor sitting up, and I poured a small amount of water down his throat. He coughed and spit but his eyes opened, and I cleaned his eyes with his handkerchief. For a minute, his eyes were glazed and uncommunicative but then his head cleared enough for him to realize where he was.

"Get Lonnie! He was the last one in the boxcar! Quick, get him out of there!" Viktor tried to shout but it came out sounding as if he was choking. Bill and two stuntmen jumped into the boxcar, found Lonnie and carried him out, other stuntmen reaching to help him down carefully. He was still alive but had been trapped against the boxcar wall when the explosion went off and was badly burned.

The doctor said Evelyn only had cuts and bruises, and that Viktor saved her from being burned. Viktor roughly told him to stop talking and take care of Lonnie. Dan sat Viktor down next to Evelyn. One of the crew arrived with the doctor's second, larger bag with medications and dressings. I opened the bag and began to clean and dress Viktor's wounds. He smiled, but when Evelyn began to put her arms around Viktor, he screamed in pain. When she removed her arms they were bloody from the cuts on his back where he had landed on the broken movie camera, rocks and a blackberry bramble.

Someone brought blankets and I spread two out, one atop the other and helped Dan get Viktor on his stomach so we could treat ugly wounds on his back. As I cut off Viktor's shirt and exposed his wounds Evelyn saw them and became agitated. I told her that getting hysterical was not helping Viktor. She took hold of herself and helped clean the dirt and rock chips from his back. Later, she thanked me for getting her to focus.

The two stuntmen who had been on top of the boxcar had fallen off, both with scrapes and bruises and one with a broken arm but were otherwise in good condition. One of the crew who had been a medic in the Army gave him first aid until the doctor could come over.

The doctor went and spoke quietly to Director Hawks. Lonnie had died. The word got around fast. Hawks sent the doctor to talk to Viktor and asked Dan and me to meet him away from the crowd. He told us about Lonnie. Dan swore and I had a hard time breathing for a couple of minutes. Lonnie was dead because of our movie.

During the commotion, Bill and Big Al were investigating and found that the boxcar door had been deliberately jammed. Even with Viktor's strength, it would not have opened. It was an act of sabotage, and that meant Lonnie was murdered. Bill and Big Al came to us with their discovery of the door, and Hawks said we would have to suspend filming. Most of the crew would refuse to work until the saboteur was discovered, and Dan and I agreed that we did not want to go forward until whoever was doing this was apprehended. There was no sense in continuing to film, putting everyone at risk. This would cost the studio a lot of money but we didn't care. Hawks advised that Lasky might cancel the movie. We told Hawks the movie meant nothing to us now that one of our handpicked cast members, a well-liked stuntman with a wife and child, was dead.

Dan and I were beyond angry. We committed ourselves to use every resource we had to find out who was behind this. Nevertheless, where would we begin?

The doctor did what he could but Viktor needed more than field treatment. Hawks had three studio cars brought over. Evelyn and Viktor got in one car and the two injured stuntmen in the other to a hospital. Dan, Director Hawks and I went in the third car to call Jesse Lasky and give him the news.

I stayed with Evelyn by Viktor's bedside through the night. The surgeon said he would completely recover but should take it easy for a while to let the wounds heal. Just as the morning light appeared in the hospital window, Viktor woke up. Evelyn went to him and kissed him. He asked for something to eat so Evelyn went to get breakfast for herself and Viktor while I sat with him and talked. Viktor was sure there was a connection with last year's troubles but I could not see it. Pádraigh, Joey, Tony, Hymie Weiss – all were dead. We had made peace with Al Capone and had done to break our agreements. Despite his reputation for brutality, I believed that he respected us and had not ordered revenge.

But my frustration was growing. Who set me up for the murder of Col. Mosby, and now sabotaged our movie? Who would gain by doing this?

PHANTOM NEMESIS

Evelyn returned with their breakfasts and I left the hospital, first going to check our trailer but Dan was working with the crew to pack and load the movie equipment, so I left a note telling him I was going in search of food. I went to the only diner in the small town nearby and ordered ham and eggs and coffee. Lots of coffee. My order arrived just as the diner's door opened and I waved Dan to my table. After a quick kiss and a couple bites from my plate, Dan gave me the update about his conversation with Jesse Lasky yesterday.

"Lasky doesn't want to cancel the movie, he is putting the production on hiatus until the perpetrators are found and put away. He said the publicity would be good for the movie until I reminded him that one of our cast was murdered. Lasky wasn't very happy with me for reminding him of that but I don't give a damn what he thinks. I called Douglas this morning and he has not heard anything through the Hollywood grapevine about who could be sabotaging our movie. He said that Lasky was rude with the comment about publicity but added that Hollywood does not have much of a conscience so it did not surprise him. He added that putting the movie on hiatus was not necessarily the end of it, that would depend on the investigation and if the perpetrators were apprehended. He says if that happens the crew will come back to work because solving the crime would be seen in a positive light. Personally, I think that if the movie is canceled we have a lot of other things to do and we would be just fine."

Giuseppe and Dan were going to Napa, while I went to visit Lonnie's widow to see what we could do to help her. Lonnie had worked a few years as a stuntman and he had been a good provider. His wife Mabel was crying when I got there. I comforted her as best I could. I told her that we would cover the funeral costs and asked her if she needed anything. Mabel said Lonnie had an insurance policy but she had not had the courage to go through his documents. Mabel accepted my offer to send Josefina to help with the insurance claim and any other administrative matters.

Giving Mabel my address and telephone number, I told her to call me, reverse charges, if there was anything she wanted help with or just to talk. I added that when I returned to Hollywood I would call on her again to see what we could do for her and her daughter, who was just a toddler. I almost cried with Mabel when I realized the little girl would never really know her father. When I calmed down my resolve hardened and made me even more determined to find who had done this.

When I arrived home, Josefina was depressed about what happened on the movie set and readily offered to go to Los Angeles when I told her of our offer to help file Lonnie's insurance benefit claim and make sure everything else was in proper order. Josefina was a sweet young woman whose help would be a comfort to Mabel.

I invited Giuseppe to dinner with us, and asked Sunny to come up with a classic Italian dinner. He was getting to be a good friend to us and to the Montanaris.

We invited Luigi and Josefina to join us. Sunny served up an excellent dinner and Dan opened bottles of Montanari Barbera to go with dinner. Giuseppe brought a bottle of what he called Dolcino Rosso, or "little sweet red" wine, and a bottle of grappa.

We had the Dolcino Rosso with dessert and grappa later as we conversed in the parlor. Dan led off by asking if Giuseppe would tell us about himself, saying that he often seemed to be around when trouble came. The room became very quiet but we waited for him to speak. Giuseppe chose his words carefully.

"I am very surprised at the vengeance someone seems to have towards you. I have come to respect and like both of you and I believe my employer agrees, and that I should put your minds at ease about my role" he said, adding "My family came from Cuneo, a province in the Piedmont in the northwest of Italy, bordering on Switzerland and France, the same area where the Montanari family is from. It is mountainous there, the word Piedmont comes from a Latin word that means 'at the foot of the mountain'. The Piedmont is known for its excellent wines."

"My parents were shop owners. We were not wealthy but we had what we needed and my parents were able to send me to study business and economics at the University of Turin, which was founded in 1404 and one of the oldest universities in Europe. They wanted me to become a leader in business or government. I was determined to make them proud and I did so by finishing at the top of my class. As a present, my parents paid the ship fare for me to go with some friends to visit America. I then disappointed them by staying in America."

"I worked in New York to pay my way to Chicago, and there I started a small department store chain and became a partner in other businesses. I was a good businessman, a store owner like my parents and my stores were profitable. A few months later someone from the North Side Chicago gang came to my office and told me that I owed them protection money so nothing bad would happen to my business."

"One of my friends was associated with Al Capone and he took me to see Mr. Capone. I was fearful, I heard he was a dangerous man, but he received me graciously, put me at ease and asked me to tell him about the man who was threatening me. I described the man's visit but I did not ask him to do anything about it. I only asked his advice about what I should do. Mr. Capone seemed amused by my naivety. He said I did not live where the North Side should be collecting protection money and not to be concerned about it. He then abruptly dismissed me."

"A few weeks went by and I had not heard any more from the North Side protection collector and sent a note of thanks to Mr. Capone. The next day two men came, picked me up, and took me to Mr. Capone's office. He told me never to put anything in writing to him again, but he said I was still naïve and he would overlook it this time. We got to talking and he learned I was educated and good at business. He offered me a high-paying job to manage his legitimate businesses. My friend advised that it would be best for me if I took Mr. Capone's offer, so I sold my department stores and went to work for Mr. Capone."

"Mr. Capone has a vast amount of money to invest, and my job is to help Mr. Capone invest and run his legitimate businesses. By Mr. Capone's orders, I am kept strictly separate from his South Side Outfit business to avoid government agents harassing me to gain information. I began working with politicians and my influence in Chicago politics has grown, especially since I am perceived to be a neutral person, and a liaison for those who need to deal with Mr. Capone but cannot be seen to do so in public."

"I met Regina when she visited Mr. Capone. We had dinner and I asked her for a date, and that began an affair. Then Regina had to go into hiding after her uncle Don Coniglio was murdered by his stupid son Joey. You already know Mr. Capone sent Regina away for her safety and for special training since she was determined to pursue a vendetta against Joey. My affair with Regina ended. I have met other women but have not chosen one for my wife. Sadly, Laure and Josefina are taken" he said with a smile.

"Mr. Capone told me he asked you to work for him but you turned him down. He respected your decision because you had personal goals for your own businesses. Mr. Capone decided I should go to California to find new business investment opportunities and that I should get to know you to inform him if you entered the liquor business again, also to be of assistance to you or Regina if necessary. Mr. Capone did not think you would break the agreement, but understand that in his business you stay on top by knowing everything that your friends and enemies are doing. I am also instructed to learn the movie business for future investments" Giuseppe told us.

"When I heard Laure was charged with murder I went to Napa and began making inquiries, finding that the whole thing smelled like dead fish but no one was willing to talk about it. The influence was coming from somewhere, but it was not from Chicago. With Weiss, Pádraigh and Joey all dead, we were baffled."

"Even with my contacts no one would tell me anything, but I must have made Mr. Capone's dislike of how you were being treated known to someone who did know something about it, and I was informed through an unknown person that it was going to be corrected because the case against Laure was weak and the evidence insufficient to convict her. Bribery was holding the case together but our influence killed it. When I came to Mare Island I was merely the messenger and Mr. Capone's message was to assure you that things would change soon, but I was not to say more."

In the meantime, I renewed my friendship with Regina who holds both of you in high regard. I should tell you that when you safely brought Regina to San Francisco that day, I was in conference with the family there and had a long talk with Regina after you departed, after which I sent a coded letter to Mr. Capone. Because of how you helped Regina in spite of the danger, and that she likes and respects both of you, Mr. Capone decided to work on your side, but also because he hated Hymie Weiss, who wanted to make you dead. Weiss made a big mistake when he ordered an violent and public assassination attempt on Mr. Capone that nearly succeeded. As you are aware, a few days later Mr. Weiss was assassinated with extreme violence. Mr. Capone was nowhere in the area and does not profess any knowledge of it."

"The people in San Francisco where you brought Regina were specialists in training assassins. They took Regina in, but because she is not big enough to fight a physical battle with men, she learned to shoot, stab, slice throats, poison and other innovative ways to make someone die. She became very good at it and put her skill to work to kill Joey, upon whom she had sworn vendetta when he killed her uncle Don Coniglio, and because Joey raped her when she lived in the Don's house. I was there the day Regina allegedly died on your friend Bill's fishing boat. I knew Bill was not a fisherman but he is an experienced boat captain and the fishing boat was just a cover. He accepted the contract to fake Regina's death. There was a known agent of the North Side outfit on the boat, and Bill staged it to look like Regina was dumped overboard with bricks tied to her body so she would sink to the bottom and never return."

"What the North Side man did not know was that another man from the San Francisco family had slipped overboard from the other side of the boat. He cut the rope holding the sack of bricks and brought her to the surface to breathe until Captain Bill's boat was gone and another boat arrived to pull them from the water. Bill got the North Side man very drunk as he celebrated Regina's death. Then, after you left to recapture your missing train the man reported Gina's death, after which he died two weeks later of what was reported to be natural causes. Your friend Bill sometimes works for us on selected assignments. He is clever in making a crime look like an accident and deflecting unwanted attention."

"There's more to the story but that's enough for you to know. We have not yet discovered who has taken up vendetta against you. Whoever it is, they are very careful and they are unknown but have political influence. I am working on it, but you must let me do what I need to do without telling you what I do. Capisce? Otherwise I am compromised. Mr. Capone instructed me to help you but not be obvious about it, because he does not want anyone in government to know my work or who I work for. All the authorities know of me is that I am a very good businessman. I want to keep it that way."

Dan and I sat there, speechless. It was an amazing story but had the ring of truth to it, and Gina was in on it too. Regardless of Gina's trying to seduce Dan that day, she had not done so again. She killed Joey to fulfill her vendetta and that helped us. It was good that we did not know it then. Dan mentioned how Gina had put her index finger beside her nose, like the grifters do. Giuseppe just smiled and refilled our glasses of grappa. "Sometimes that is the only sign you will get from a friend."

But it was unsettling to learn that with all Capone's tentacles reaching into government, other mob organizations, unions, businesses and who knows what else, even he did not know who was attacking us.

"Giuseppe, what can we do to find out who is doing this? We don't know where to look" I said.

"I can only keep working on it, untying knots and pulling strings. Once we know, we can turn the tables but until then you must be very careful. When I find out, I must obey my order from Mr. Capone to tell him first. If he authorizes it, I can then tell you. He has assured me that he will deal rapidly with whoever it is that is causing you harm. I am sorry, but if I disobey him it is not that I get fired and have to find another job, I would have to find another life and that's hard to do if you are dead. Capisce?"

Later when we were alone Dan said "That's just great. We know some evil spirit is trying to kill us, and we have friends who will help but they do not know who it is either, and may not tell us if they find out. We have to be careful, but how would we know who or what to be careful of?" That night Dan and I did not feel like having a romp. Our 1911s were in special holsters by our bed where we could pull them fast if someone should enter the room. We also had shotguns under our bed and other weapons stashed all through our house. Elsie and Sunny were armed, as were Josefina and her parents. We had Raider, who seemed to hear almost everything and woke us up when he jumped up on alert to something.

Dan said "We are letting the enemy win by making us nervous and jumpy, which will lead us to making mistakes and that will be the end of us. Laure, I don't like to lose and I know you don't either. So let us be very careful like Giuseppe said, but we should live our lives as best we can. We can ask those of our crew who were with us last year if they are ready for another adventure. Add some new faces if we can to replace those out of the country. Let's keep on doing what we do but we cannot sit in the house like cowards and do nothing."

I kissed Dan and held him tight. "I'm not ready to lose. I won't ever be ready for that. I agree. We will be watchful and do everything possible to protect our families, our friends and ourselves."

LAURE ROLLS HER STOCKINGS

Louise Brooks was busy with an active schedule of movie productions and throwing parties with her husband Eddie Sutherland at their home in Laurel Canyon so I was a little surprised when she called. Her current role was in the Famous Players-Lasky movie production of *Evening Clothes* with Adolphe Menjou in the lead role. The story line was that his wife left him because he was too ordinary, so he tries to improve himself by becoming a Parisian gentleman. He steals Fox Trot, played by Louise Brooks, from Noah Beery who plays the role of Lazarre, a nightclub owner.

Louise told me that Jesse Lasky was going to offer me a role in *Evening Clothes* because a supporting actress had been dismissed from the set. Lasky needed a replacement who could dance, and Louise suggested me. It was a minor part, but Louise said it was made for me.

When Lasky called to offer me the role, I told him that I would call back within the hour. Locating Dan took almost that hour, but when I told him about it and asked if I could do it, he said "Laure, it's your decision and we have time now that *Road Trip Blues* is on hiatus. It would be good experience for you that could help us if our movie returns to production. If you want to do it, call Lasky and tell him you will be there."

Now that our relationship had become so close we shared our decisions. However, Dan was right and this was my choice. I called Lasky and told him I would be on the train the day after next. He said he would send a car and chauffeur to pick me up at the Los Angeles Central Station, and it would be at my disposal while I was in Hollywood. That was more than the studio did for supporting actresses and I knew it was because he wanted me to sign a studio contract with his studio.

In a flurry of activity I packed a trunk and sent Elsie to the train station to buy my ticket. Dan came home and gave me a big hug and kiss when I told him I had accepted the role. "You know, my dear, I hate to see you go, but I love to watch you walk away." He used that line on me before but this time he had such a wolfish grin on his face I had to do something about it. Later when we came downstairs we both had big wolfish grins on our faces.

Before I left for Hollywood Dan and I invited Josefina to come to our kitchen table and have a talk. Josefina looked worried, but that turned to surprise when I explained that we were making her a partner in LaureDan with ten percent ownership and a pay plan with a substantial raise and bonuses for bringing in new business and taking care of existing clients, along with other benefits. Josefina jumped up and hugged us both, saying we were the best employers a girl could hope for. She ran to the office to call her parents and give them the news. They said this called for an Italian celebration dinner, so we went to the Montanari's that evening.

The next day Dan drove me to the ferry and we spent the night in San Francisco so I could be on the Southern Pacific *Daylight Limited* tomorrow. In the morning he went with me to the Third and Townsend Depot and made sure

I was safely settled in the passenger car. Dan tipped the conductor and asked him to watch for any suspicious people and notify the police if necessary. I had my Colt .380 in my handbag and the 1911 packed with my dancing dresses and shoes. I promised to call as soon as my scenes were completed.

Louise asked me to stay at her house but with Eddie there I wasn't too keen on that. Dan said I should stay at the Beverly Hills Hotel but I told him it would feel lonely to be in Bungalow #5 without him, so he reserved a bedroom suite in the main building. He had a word with the hotel security manager who would have his people on special alert. Dan called Jack Higgins, the studio security chief, who said he would have an extra man patrolling in and around the studio while I was there.

On the train, I relaxed and studied the script. Arriving at Los Angeles, my car and driver were waiting as promised. Good thing I studied the script because Louise and Eddie would not take no for an answer when they invited me out to dinner. When her Rolls-Royce came to pick me up for dinner, I was surprised to see Louise, Eddie and another man in the car. It was Adolphe Menjou. He appeared as suave and debonair as he did on the screen and he introduced himself in the manner of a continental gentleman. He was an excellent conversationalist and I learned that he was from Pittsburgh and had grown up in Ohio. I was surprised because he seemed so European in his manners and clothing. I was glad to meet Mr. Menjou before arriving on the movie set tomorrow, but I told Louise I was not a date for him and hoped he knew that.

I think Louise wanted it to be a date, but she said "Oh, no, we just needed a fourth for the dinner table." I did not believe that feeble explanation for a second because Mr. Menjou had a reputation for being a ladies' man, although I did not know whether it was a deserved reputation. While we were waiting for our table, I had a moment with him in the restaurant foyer and told Mr. Menjou "I am a married woman. I don't know what Louise has said, but I will be going back to my hotel alone."

"I am sorry if you got the wrong impression, Laure. Yes, I know how Louise is, we have been in other films. But my dear Laure, this is not a date, we are simply actors enjoying dinner together."

Adolphe seemed sincere so after dinner when Louise and Eddie wanted to go dancing at a nightclub, I agreed to go along. Mr. Menjou was a gentleman except once when we danced a slow dance and his hand moved over my right breast on its way to my ass. "Nice try Mr. Menjou" I said as I moved his hand away "but please do not do that again." He apologized and it did not happen again.

Being new to Hollywood's ways, I did not expect gossip magazine photographers to be hanging around outside the restaurants and nightclubs where movie stars dined and danced. When we walked out of the nightclub I had my hand in Adolphe Menjou's arm to steady myself on the nightclub's stairs. Suddenly flashbulbs popped in my face and I knew the Hollywood gossip columnists would be writing about my failed marriage or some such nonsense.

The next day's gossip rags had the photographs at the top of their front pages. The photographs were cropped so Louise and Eddie were not in the picture and it looked like Adolphe Menjou and I were out on the town alone together and I was hanging onto his arm. The angle of one of the photographs made it look as if I was pulling Adolphe to me. A sleazy gossip columnist wrote:

"Now that his 'Road Trip Blues' movie has been put on indefinite hiatus, producer Daniel Lindner's sexy wife Laure Brooks may have left him. Last night Laure was seen at a lovers' nightclub canoodling with handsome leading man Adolphe Menjou, currently starring in the Jesse Lasky production of 'Evening Clothes'. Their hands were all over each other as they danced suggestively and Laure appeared to have tipped quite a few as she stumbled into Adolphe Menjou's limousine. Rumor has it that Laure Brooks is no

stranger to the casting couch and worked her way into a role in 'Evening Clothes' as a consolation prize after the suspension of Lindner's Road Trip Blues movie production. Like her cousin Louise Brooks, Laure is quite the vamp and moves fast when she is ready for a new man."

I was flabbergasted and outraged. Since I believe that taking the offense is a good defense, I bought the gossip rags to show Dan. Better that I tell him first.

When I arrived at the studio I showed the gossip rags to Louise and angrily complained "This sleazy write-up is all hokum! I did not have my hands all over Adolphe and I was not sozzled when we left the club. And I certainly did not leave Dan. He will be enraged when he sees this. What does this yellow journalist mean when she says I'm no stranger to the casting couch? The only casting couch I've ever been on is Dan's. And the limousine wasn't Adolphe's, it was the studio's car. I'm going to call the editors, tell them the truth and demand a retraction."

Louise laughed and told me "This is Hollywood and you'd better get used to it Laure. Ignore the gossip rags; they make up things to sell papers. If you complain, they will print it as proof that you are trying to cover something up, and they will assign reporters and photographers to follow you. Even if you don't do anything wrong, they will make up more banana oil because now they have fresh meat on the front page and their readers will gobble up every piece of gossip they can imagine. They will play you as long as they can. And Dan makes you get on the casting couch?" Louise smirked like a gossip columnist with a fresh scandal.

"My getting on Dan's casting couch is our little joke, a game that we play. I should not have said that."

Louise sent me to makeup right away so I would be ready when my first scene came up. My fury stayed with me all day, which must have been obvious in my acting. All of my scenes went perfectly except for one re-take and that was for a miscue by someone else. As for Menjou, Noah Beery and Louise, I was impressed with their professionalism on the set. Before each scene in which I appeared they helped me learn what I needed to know. Working with them was easy and fun. Near the end of the day while I was on the *Evening Clothes* set Jesse Lasky stopped by and came over to ask me to stay another two or three days.

"Laure, I hope you will accept another small role. One of our dancers has taken ill and had to leave the production. You are the perfect replacement for the role in *Rolled Stockings*. You would play a college girl who rolls her stockings and shows her knees. I know you can dance and you have lovely knees. At a roadhouse the girl has attracted the attentions of two brothers who both want her. It should only take a few days to film your scenes, and you and Louise work well together. This is a great opportunity for you. Are you in?" Lasky offered triple pay and I figured why not? But following Dan's example I demanded a higher number and Lasky gave it to me without bargaining. It would be more money for our new home construction so I said "I'm in."

Next morning I called Dan to let him know I was staying a few more days for *Rolled Stockings* and started to tell him about the gossip reporters and their made-up stories, but he stopped me when he asked "Is Mr. Menjou a good dancer? I heard he likes to grab cute little butts." I felt a chill down in the pit of my stomach but Dan was laughing. How did he know about that so soon?

I didn't think it was funny and said "Stop laughing for a minute, you're wasting long distance charges. I'll have you know that…"

"Oh Laure, Laure, Laure. You're so beautiful when you get angry. I know how you get that look in your eyes when you are determined to set the record straight. Well, that's already been done and I don't care what the gossip rags say. Lasky will call it good publicity. Do you remember that I met Menjou back when you were in the Napa jail and I was down there hobnobbing with Hollywood royalty? Don't worry Laure, he may have roaming hands and yes, if you had encouraged him he would have taken you to his bed, after all you are a beautiful woman. He called me yesterday to tell me what happened and that you threatened to kick his nutmegs up to his throat when he made a pass at you. Adolphe does not want you to be upset with him, he knows the story of the casting couch producer you threatened to neuter with your derringer. He is interested in working with us on future projects and he is a star that men and women like to see on the big screen. In Hollywood, any time anyone goes to lunch or dinner with a co-star, the rumors start flying. That's what sells the gossip rags. Ignore the rags and in a week they will be writing about someone else. Confront them and they will hound you for more."

"That's the same advice Louise gave me. But Dan, I don't recall threatening Menjou, I just nicely told him not to do that again, and he honored my request."

"Laure, as I well know, you are fierce when you are wronged, and I've no doubt you let Mr. Menjou know he should not have done that."

"You're not upset?"

Dan laughed. "No sweetie, if I didn't know you and found myself dancing with you, I would certainly try to feel your breasts and grab your ass."

"Hold on to that thought" I replied. "If you don't grab my ass when I get home, I will kick your nuts up to your throat."

"That's better than when you tried to shoot my nuts off."

"That makes you a lucky guy."

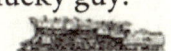

While I was in Hollywood I went to see Lonnie's widow. Mabel was wearing black and although she was very somber, we had a nice talk. I asked her what she would like to do next, but it was too soon for her to have thought much about that.

I found out that Mabel was from the town of Sonoma, where she had met Lonnie at a movie filmed on location there. She had family in Sonoma and I said if she wanted to come for a visit we would be happy to either bring her in our automobile if we were traveling back and forth or pay for round-trip train fare and she was more than welcome to stay at our house. Mabel liked that idea and said she would take me up on the offer when her daughter was a little older and better able to travel long distances. I asked if she needed money and she said no, but I noticed a very brief hesitation. I did not want it to appear that I was trying to buy her friendship, but I did not want her to fall into poverty.

I gave her some money and at first she refused it. As we talked she gradually came to be in better spirits. We had a good laugh over the time Lonnie had introduced her to Viktor, who had seemed very scary to her. Putting the money on her kitchen table, I said that if she did not accept it I would send Viktor over to convince her. I told her about the time Dan and I went to the Café Lulu speakeasy and I introduced him to Dan, whose hand was hurt from punching Joey got squeezed hard in one of Viktor's handshakes.

"OK Laure, I'll accept the money if that will keep Viktor from mashing my hand" Mabel laughed.

I asked her if it would be OK for me to visit her again and she said yes, she would like that.

When I arrived on the *Rolled Stockings* set the director seemed to be nervous and uninterested in the movie. He hardly gave any direction to me, but Louise took things into her own hands and arranged my scenes, which made it easy. I played the part of a girl at a roadhouse who dances with James Hall and Richard Arlen, the actors playing the roles of the brothers and I had a few lines. Even though the movies were silent, Louise said to always speak the lines because moviegoers liked to read lips. James Hall was a handsome gentleman, while Arlen was cool but not unpleasant to me. I later learned from Louise that she and Arlen did not get along.

I suspected that the reason Lasky agreed to my demand for higher pay was because he knew the production was going to take longer than he told me. The Hollywood scenes took two days and then the production moved to the University of California at Berkeley to add background realism by filming an actual college crew race. I was paid by the number of days worked, so I agreed to stay on, and as a bonus the studio paid my train fare to Napa when production wrapped up. I received extra compensation when they were short a driver for an automobile scene and I volunteered. The costume department dressed me like a college guy and hid my bob cut hair under a flat cap. I surprised the producer and director with my driving skill as I confidently raced the car around for extra camera shots. Louise laughed when she saw me dressed like a man, but then said she liked it and maybe she would like to do a movie dressed as a man.

Lasky had business in San Francisco around the time of my final scene, and I did not even know he was there until he came up to me. "Laure, that was another outstanding performance! Sign a contract today and I will put you in the Paramount Junior Stars program with Louise. You will get more visible roles and publicity. The Brooks girls appearing together will be magic on the movie screen, and you will both become major stars with Paramount."

While I liked acting, I did not have an ambition to become a major movie star. I reminded Jesse Lasky that Dan was my agent and I had to consult with him, which I would do the moment I arrived home. After he left, Louise said she wanted to celebrate my success in two movies by taking me out to dinner. Eddie was in Hollywood directing a movie so it was just us girls. When I am with Louise there is an abundance of drinking and whatever, so it was early in the morning when I finally arrived back in my hotel room.

Next morning I called Dan and told him I would be on the train home in the afternoon. I told him about my dinner with Louise and that made him laugh. Wanting some special attention from my man after not having any for so long, so I described what I planned to do to him tonight, knowing that would set his mind working overtime. When I arrived, Dan grabbed my ass as he had promised, and we both got what we wanted.

Over the next week Dan and I took long walks and tried to figure out who had such a grudge against us that it had become a vendetta. We made a list of everyone we knew but no one seemed to us to be that angry. Bill had been actively talking to people, and he was suspicious that some of them were not speaking freely.

Big Al moved our locomotive up to Napa where we could keep an eye on it. He found a small spur off the main track near Calistoga. Dan and I drove up to look at it and found a large vacant house nearby.

It took one telephone call to find that a family with financial problems because of Prohibition owned the house. They were barely hanging on to the house after moving in with the wife's parents in Napa, where her husband found employment. I offered to rent the house from them on a month-to-month basis and after a little negotiating, we made an agreement, and Dan had Big Al move the locomotive to the spur. Big Al, his wife Joanne along with Sven and Ole moved into the large house. The Swedes found odd jobs in the area, and they took turns guarding the locomotive and keeping it in tip-top condition.

MEET THE BOSS

The morning was chilly but Gilbert was sweating. The Boss wanted to see him and that usually meant bad news. The Boss rarely talked directly to anyone, and if he was singled out that meant trouble.

At 10 o'clock Gil arrived at the address in the message. It was a run-down house in a bad neighborhood where the houses were boarded up and the lawns taken over by weeds. The Boss continually moved about and meetings were always in run-down, out of the way locations. Gil went around to the back of the house and came upon a group of tough looking boys standing around, flipping switchblade knives open and closed while talking quietly among themselves. One of them called out "Hey mister. Yeah you, dumbfuck. What are you doing here?"

"I'm here to see The Stiletto" Gil said. The eight boys stopped playing with their knives and turned to him. They were young, around 15 or 16 years old, schooled on the mean streets. Gil was a tough street fighter himself and probably could have taken some of them out, but eight young thugs experienced with knives might be too many.

"Ain't no stiletto here dumbfuck, so go climb up your thumb." the leader said with a sneer. Gil had orders and The Boss did not accept excuses, so he waited. After a minute the punk turned back to him, popped his switchblade tip an inch from Erne's nose and said "Hey dumbfuck, what are you still doing here? Scram." The other boys started to circle around.

"My name is Gilbert and I was told to come here and ask for 'Stiletto', and I would be taken to see that person."

"Well why dincha say that the first time dumbfuck?" The leader turned to talk to his gang. "Rubes comin' 'round here are gettin' dumber and dumber, where are they from? Dumbfuck like this wouldn't last five minutes on our street."

Gilbert didn't want to tell him about the neighborhood he grew up in, where every day a guy went outside he would be just as likely to end up in the city morgue as return home, but these were feral teenage boys, and some of them were growling like stray animals who just found something to eat. "Stiletto" Gil said again. "Anyone know where I can find Stiletto?"

"First give me your gat." Gil reluctantly complied. The kid looked at it and laughed. "Stupid dumbfuck, bringing a five shot revolver to a knife fight with eight guys. Hey, maybe we should do Stiletto a favor and bring this moron over in pieces! Hahaha!" The boys laughed mirthlessly.

"Maybe I should tell Stiletto what a bunch of dumb asses you guys are. I gave you the proper password and you're making me wait. The Boss ain't gonna like this, and if you know what's good for you, you'll take me to The Boss pronto" Gil said as he flicked his hand and a knife slipped into it from his sleeve and at the same time a sharp blade popped from the handle. Gilbert smoothly pushed it to the ringleaders' face and cut his chin.

The boy showed just a moment's fear, then his courage came back as his toughs all flicked open their switchblades. It was still one against eight, but Gil had a bigger and meaner looking knife and looked like he knew how to use it. The punks knew he could not take them all down, but now they knew that Gil could cut some of them before they got him.

"Follow me dumbfuck" the leader snarled and turned, two of his young gangsters following behind. They went inside through a basement entrance where the leader pulled on a shelf and a hidden door opened. The leader motioned Gil through but as he stepped through the doorway, the boys tripped Gil and pushed him inside. As he fell, his knife skittered across the concrete floor and the door shut behind him. It was pitch black in the room but Gil sensed there were others in the room. He slowly got up. Just as his eyes adjusted to the darkness, a large bright spotlight came on, aimed directly at his eyes. Gil put his arm up to block it but a deep voice said "Keep your arm down asshole" and Gil did, having to almost shut his eyes to keep the bright arc light from burning his eyeballs out of their sockets.

Gilbert stood there for two minutes waiting for something to happen. A door opened and someone came in and sat in a chair behind the light. Gil had only met with The Boss twice before and both times The Boss was behind a curtain but now Gil was blinded by the bright light and could not see The Boss's face.

The deep voice said "State your name and number."

Gil gave his name and number 919, which was given to him when he came to work for The Boss.

"Where you from?" the deep voice barked.

"Wingo" Gil answered with the code word.

The dank basement room smelled awful and Gil could not identify what the smell was, but it wasn't healthy. He heard quiet whispers and something that sounded like radio static. The deep voice said "The Boss wants to know why you have failed to deal with the targets according to your instructions."

"The targets are resourceful" Gil whined. "The original plan to frame the female for murder failed because the payoffs and influence were not enough to overcome the weak evidence ginned up by the sheriff, and the targets have political, business, military and South Side Outfit connections. The next instruction was to stage a lynch mob attack on the female target at Mare Island. This attack would have succeeded but for her dog that alerted the Marine guards. We could not have foreseen that interference since our orders said the base commander was paid to send the military police away on a training mission but he failed to do so. Later that day when the men we hired were released from the stockade on the base commander's orders, they were severely beaten by a squad of military police. The men swore that despite the beatings, no one squealed but we killed two of them to give a lesson to the others to keep quiet. The Navy captain's actions came to the attention of his superiors and he was transferred. The new base commander is a Marine, one of her friends. We will not be able to bribe him."

"Next, we were instructed to harass and confuse the targets to soften them up and turn them on each other. This we have done. Since then we have kept hitting the targets, sabotaged their movie production and got it cancelled. Meanwhile my men are hanging around and waiting, doing a little damage, then running away and hiding. It's hard on them and they are getting antsy, but I told them they have to wait for orders to put the targets on a slab. We got other things to do too, you know."

Gil looked down to avoid the spotlight, but someone behind him and pulled his arms back while another thug delivered a hard punch to his gut, doubling him over. "Keep your face to the light. Do not turn away" the deep voice ordered.

Another voice, sounding thin, distorted and tinny as if coming from a telephone angrily said "You are not paid to think. You are paid to follow orders. When you were hired we discussed the penalties that would be inflicted if you failed to carry out your instructions. Do I need to remind you what those penalties are?"

"No Boss, no, I was just sayin' that the guys are eager to kill her and the guy. It just seemed like we are in a lull and the guys want action. We will do as we are told, Boss."

"Yes you will. Do your job but remember that if you run, we will find you. Your deaths will take days and be exceedingly painful. Do you understand?"

"Yeah. I mean, yes Boss. I understand. I'll keep my guys under control."

"You do that. Every step of our plan increases the pressure on the targets. They are being driven like game to the killing field. Your men will soon have their chance to satisfy their thirst for violence. We hired you because of your reputation for extreme violence and cruelty. Tell the men their time will come, but we want the targets to suffer and not know who or what is playing with them until the end. They will become desperate and strike out against everyone, even their friends, which plays right into the final scenario. If you and your men cannot precisely follow orders we have others who will."

"Yes Boss, I understand. I'll keep 'em in line. You also told me to let you know if anyone unexpected shows up. So far only a few of their old outfit are around but they haven't found out anything. Now there is a new guy poking around asking questions and we don't know who he is yet. His appearance is that of a businessman, but my nose tells me he has other connections. I was thinking to send him to sleep with the fishes before he wises up."

"You stupid sap!" the tinny voice screamed angrily. "Didn't I just tell you not to think? If we take this guy out, more will be sent to take his place and that will make the destruction of the targets more difficult. I will have this person dealt with when the time is right and not before. I have others waiting to take over should you fail. You are making me nervous and you don't want me to be nervous, I assure you."

"No Boss, I don't want you to be nervous. I will make sure my guys stop thinking and carry out your plans to a T" Gil said.

"Good, now go away you insect. You will receive new instructions by courier. Carry them out precisely. I do not want to have to meet with you to discuss your failures again. Do you understand?" the tinny voice howled.

"Yes Boss."

The voice became even more threatening, "Do not attempt to make my couriers talk. The goon you sent to try to make my last courier talk died a painful death. If you need to think, then think about that."

There were footsteps, a door opened and closed. The bright light in Gil's eyes went out as others in the room shuffled out unseen. Gil's eyes continued to burn from the arc light's glare as he tried to feel around the floor for his knife, but someone must have picked it up. Now fearful for his own life, Gil felt along the wall to the door. He couldn't get out of that basement fast enough.

When he found his way outside no one was there. The street urchins were nowhere to be found, nor was his gun. Gil felt like he was being watched as he ran away as fast as he could.

Gilbert returned to his gang, shaken and afraid. Not just because he had to tell his bloodthirsty misfits they had to stay on this job, but also had to tell them the news that his brother, who had not returned from his last assignment, was dead. Gil had sent him to interrogate and torture the courier to get information, thinking he would learn something to use to blackmail The Boss. Gil cursed the day he had accepted the ten grand to do this job. At the time it seemed like a lot of money for not much work. Now it was not nearly enough money for all the grief and aggravation, and they were no closer to finishing it than the day they started. Gil decided that in the future, they would stick to quick heist jobs and contract killings, where they went in, stole money or goods, then were often allowed to rape, torture and kill their victims.

TRUSSED UP LIKE A HOG

The investigation of Col. Mosby's murder was hitting brick walls. The Marine commandant sent two experienced investigators who got nowhere during a month of following clues and leads before being recalled to Washington D.C. Sheriff Steckter said that his detectives had also turned up nothing. Then the evidence files and physical evidence had gone missing. Dan called Captain Tracy of the California State Police. Capt. Tracy said he would send a detective to Napa as soon as he could, but the department was understaffed.

That the physical evidence was missing from the sheriff's department evidence locker was investigated by the Marine detectives, who found no information about what had happened and no one in the Sheriff's office remembered releasing it from the evidence locker, which was a secure room with no windows and only one door that was always locked. There was no evidence someone had broken into the room. It had to have been an inside job.

Giuseppe kept in contact with us but so far had nothing new. He talked to Capone, who questioned his capos, and sent messengers to the mob families who were allies or neutrals with no results. I asked about the North Side Outfit, and Giuseppe said Capone had inside informers who reported they could find no involvement.

Uncle Viktor learned through unnamed sources that the DA who had been so eager to bring charges against me had received a large sum of money just before the murder. He decided to have a meeting with the DA, who vehemently denied everything and threatened Viktor with unspecified charges if he continued to investigate. The fool did not know that he just made Viktor his worst enemy because Viktor would continue his pursuit of evidence to tie him to the phony murder charge.

I was just as determined to find Col. Mosby's murderer, but I had no clue where to look to find a clue.

Dan was out collecting contract signatures and supervising a property cleanup when I received a telephone call from a Sgt. Beauchamp at the Calistoga police department. He told me that Sven and Ole started a fight at a speakeasy up in the hills and were under arrest. Bail was set at $250 each, which seemed a little high, but I went to the LaureDan office and Josefina gave me $500 from our safe. I drove the Chrysler to Calistoga, following Sgt. Beauchamp's directions to the station.

I should have been more alert. When I arrived at the street I did not know it was a dead-end street until I got mid-way round a curve. There was a brick building with iron bars on the windows that looked like it could be a police station so I parked the Chrysler to look. I turned the doorknob and it was still in my hand when the door jerked open. I did not let go of it in time and was pulled inside where someone tripped me and I hit the floor.

Face down on the dirty floor I realized my failure to be careful. We had become less guarded as things had seemed to return to normal. I had not brought Raider, nor did I have a gun. *Foolish woman* was the thought running through my mind as I tried to get up, but someone put a knee on my back, another tied a dark piece of cloth around my head to blindfold me. I started to scream but a hand was clapped over my mouth. I bit hard but could not get my teeth into the hardened skin on the palm. I heard a yelp, so I must have caused some damage but it was not enough. As I was lifted to my feet I punched where I thought the hand was attached and heard a grunt, but still was not enough to get free. I felt the presence of another person very close in front of me and I kicked as hard as I could.

This time I got results as a male groaned and as he fell he said "Fuckin' bitch" in a pained voice.

Another voice said "Shut up Red."

A third voice said "You idiot, what did I tell you? No names."

More footsteps came toward me and hands grabbed my arms, pulling them together and snapping handcuffs on my wrists. I kicked again but only got air this time. Someone got a heavy band of cloth around my knees and tightened it so I could not kick. I was picked up and carried through the building, then thrown into the back seat of a car, face down. Unable to see, I felt someone remove the band from around my knees, replacing it quickly with a rope snugly wrapped around my ankles. My shoes were taken off and my legs were bent back at the knees while a leather collar was put around my neck, a rope was tied to the rope at my ankles, the other end fastened to a loop at the collar around my neck. I could not see, could not move my arms or legs. I let out a scream but someone stuffed some material in my mouth and tied a cloth around so I could not spit the gag out.

No one was in the back seat with me. The front doors opened and two people got in, the engine started and the car began to move. I tried to keep track of the turns but became disoriented as the car traveled up a curvy road. We must have been going over Mount St. Helena towards Lake County.

My black humor kicked in. *"Well, at least now I might be able to find a clue"* I thought, and would have giggled if I could but only a strange noise came from me.

The voice that had told Red to shut up yelled "Shut up you stupid bitch or I'll stop the car and have the guys beat on you." I thought about that. So far, other than being trussed up, no one had harmed me nor touched my body. They could have smacked me around or felt me up back at the fake police station. I speculated that I might not get a beating, at least not yet. I was glad that I was wearing trousers today. Not wanting to spend energy on trying to escape without eyes, hands and legs, I laid still and worked on my self-control with even breathing and kept my senses as alert as possible.

My prison car turned onto a steep and bumpy road, slowed, turned, backed up, and the engine shut down. Doors opened, hands pulled me from the back seat and carried me up six steps and a door opened. Inside, we went up another two flights of stairs, then the sound of a door unlocking. I was thrown face down on something that felt like an old couch. There were five or six people, I guessed men by their heavier footsteps. They left the room, locking the door. My eyes could not see anything through the solid black blindfold. My legs started to cramp from being trussed up like a hog, but I must have fallen asleep.

With no idea how long I had been there I awoke at the sound of the lock turning and footsteps entered the room. They picked me up, carried me to another room and set me on the floor face down. Now I began to be afraid, working hard to control my fear of being held helpless by my captors. I tried to make noise, my legs were cramping from being tied. "Shut the fuck up" a different male voice commanded, but the rope tying my ankles to my neck behind me was cut, and I let my legs down easy, letting the feeling return. I lay still, waiting. *"Not much else you can do, foolish woman"* I thought.

Everything was quiet and I sensed there were two other people in the room by the sounds of breathing and faint whisperings. I was amazed at how sensitive my hearing had become. "The boss is coming, sit her up." I was flipped over, the handcuffs and the rope around my ankles removed, then they sat me down on a hard chair. The gag was removed but not the blindfold. My mouth was stiff and sore. The deep voice asked if I wanted water and I nodded. A small amount of water in a tin cup was put to my lips and I took small sips, wetting my lips.

"So this is the great Laure, rumrunner, gangster, dancer, actress, adulteress, whore and murderer. That's quite a list of accomplishments for someone so young" the deep voice seemed to smirk as its owner talked. I waited.

Nothing I could say would help and very likely might hurt. "You and your troublemaker friend Dan probably think you will wipe us out as quickly as you did the others. But you won't. You can't. So think carefully about your answers." I remained silent. This seemed to aggravate my interrogator.

It was a very unpleasant voice that spoke next, shrill and tinny, a mechanical sound accompanied by a lot of static noise.

"Who is this person who got your murder charge lifted? You are a murderer, maybe not of the colonel, but of others. Who is this person? Who does this person work for?" The voice was getting sharper and sounded worried.

Realizing they did not know anything about Giuseppe I knew to not say nothing about him. "Many people helped me, some in the Marines, some in..." and I was cut off.

"You know who I am talking about. The person who came to you at Mare Island and then the next day you walked free. That murder charge was tight enough for a conviction, no shyster lawyer could have gotten you off and you would have been dancing at the end of a rope. Many people want to see that" said Tin Voice.

"I am not a murderer. I did not kill Col. Mosby. I only killed in self-defense those that were trying to kill me."

"LIAR!" shrieked Tin Voice. There was some whispering and Tin Voice seemed to calm down a notch or two. "You are not telling the truth. We want to know who this person is and where we can find him. Maybe we want to hire him for a job."

"I have no idea who he is or where to find him or if he wants a job. I did not ask him for help, in fact I don't know anything about him" which was close to the truth.

The deep voice took over. "Now see here, Laure. We only want some information and we will return you to your home. If you won't provide the information, we have a specialist on his way who guarantees that he can make you talk. You will babble like a baby everything that is in your silly head. If you are so un-cooperative that we have to pay him to make you sing, we will have no recourse but to kill you and your body will never be found. We will send information to Dan to make him think you ran away with another man."

The voice sounded chilling and worse, confident in the torturer's abilities. Bill, Dan and I had a long talk over drinks one night, and Bill told us some things that I really didn't want to hear about torture specialists. Some of the tortures Bill described sounded positutely medieval. But Deep Voice said that the torturer was on the way, so I had some unknown amount of time to devise a plan. "I do not know who this person is, but I might see him again and if you release me I could send you a signal when he appears again." Of course I was lying, what I would really do was have every gunman and Marine available to catch these trouble boys in a trap.

They were still for a minute then I heard whispering again. Tin Voice said "No, I think you will not do that. You are too devious and would instead have a trap set. No, you will be taken back to your cell to await The Doctor. He will cure you and then we will kill you. It's your choice. Dan will be next. Maybe both of you will meet at the gates of hell. In the meantime, think about this. Give us the information and we will return you unharmed, and pay you ten thousand dollars for your trouble. You will never see us again. Or you can die screaming when The Doctor performs operations on your body without anesthesia. Alternatively, he may put you in a barrel, fill it with shit and set the barrel in a pit of hot coals. You will scream for a few hours until you are cooked through. I would like to hear those screams. You will beg for mercy but it will be too late and none will be given. If you are lucky, we will capture Dan and have him in a barrel next to you. Wouldn't that be delightful? You can die screaming together. Good-bye Laure. I will see you one more time and you must have your final decision ready.

"Wait" I said, trying to buy time. "Could I have paper and pencil so I can write everything down that I know about this person you are asking about?"

More intense whispering. Deep voice said "Someone will bring paper and pencil. Don't even think about trying to get out, the stone walls are three feet thick. There are no windows low enough for you to reach and even if you could, they are too small for you to exit. Think instead how pleasant it will be at home with your make-believe husband and ten thousand dollars."

I was shuffled out of the interrogation room. The guards marched me back down corridors long and short, up more stairs, then I was pushed into a small room. "Just so you know, sweetcakes, they give us the women after The Doctor works on them. Red and me, we ain't had a good lookin' chippy like you in a long time and we will fuck you in every hole after The Doctor performs his surgery on you. Hahahaha!"

That did nothing but make me more determined to find a way out. When Red and his sidekick threw me into the room they did not put the gag in my mouth nor the handcuffs on my wrists. I took the blindfold off and looked around. It was a room that I estimated to be about twelve by twelve with rough stone walls and a very high ceiling. There were two small windows up higher than I could reach. A piss bucket. No table. No chair. Nothing but a metal bed shelf bolted to the wall with a thin straw mattress, no pillow or blanket. Hearing a key turn in the door made me put the blindfold back on. Whoever it was simply threw a couple sheets of paper and a pencil on the floor and locked the door again. I yelled "Guard! Hey, Red!" and the door opened again. "I need more paper, another pencil, and bring me my shoes. My feet hurt." That wasn't true but Red didn't know that. He laughed and made no other response, but a few minutes later the door opened enough to throw in a half-inch thick stack of paper, another pencil and my shoes.

The guard said "There's your paper, you better start writing. The Doctor will be here within the hour."

I did not need more paper or pencils, it was merely a request for something that had already been agreed to by their leader. By making a request for something that was approved, I added something that would seem innocuous. Weak thinkers would not notice that, they would just bring what was requested. After Red left, I opened secret compartments in each of the heels of my shoes and removed thin sharp pieces of hardened steel from each shoe. Uncle Viktor had told me he had made such a pair of shoes for himself when he was in a prisoner of war camp, but the war was over before he could put his escape plan into action. I would have a good story to impress my Uncle Viktor with if I pulled this off.

I thought about trying to open the lock on the door but my lock picking skills were not that good and I wouldn't know where to go to find a door to the outside. I began to pick indentations in the mortar between the metal shelf bed and the small window above. From the metal bed I only needed to climb about six feet to the window. The walls were old, the mortar and stone yielded easily to my hardened steel picks as I made a series of indentations up the wall. I worried that the window was barred outside, or would not open but there was only one way to find out.

It did not take long for me to get my laughable toe-holds picked in the wall and I was ready to take the chance on that rather than the nonexistent mercy of their doctor. I dumped the piss pot just inside the door. There wasn't much piss in it so I added what I could. Wickedly, I thought how nice it would be to have Dan with me for that, but then other thoughts came into my mind and I had to stop that line of thought.

I stood back to survey my work and almost cried. My makeshift ladder did not look as if I could get my fingers and toes in to hold my weight. I whispered *"Dan, I will always love you, no matter what"*. I took the thin worn out mattress and rolled it, set it on the metal bed next to the wall. Then I put the piss pot upside down on top of that so I could get as high up as possible before I had to commit to my finger and toe holds for the rest of the way up to the window. This reduced the climb until I would have to pull myself through the window if I got it open. I ripped the blindfold material and tied my shoes with it and made a loop to put my arm through to carry them. I was ready. Carefully, I stepped up to the top of the bucket, which wobbled precariously on the rolled-up mattress, I had no choice but to abandon my attempt or commit everything to it.

I committed everything to it. It was an easy decision – stay and meet The Doctor or take the slim chance to escape. As soon as I was on the wall there was no more nervous tension because fear and desperation took over.

In seconds I was halfway up the wall clawing desperately by fingers and toes to the meager holds I had carved out of the old mortar. My fingers were skinned and bloody before I got near the window. About a foot from the window my arms began to give out and I decided that if I got out of this, I was going to add some arm strengthening exercises to my exercise regimen. Not to get big muscles, I had seen women with big muscles and they looked very unfeminine, but enough to be physically fit when I was in trouble. My shoulders began to ache and my body was shaking from the exertion. I kept telling myself to climb – climb – climb – and ignore the pain. *Easier to say than to do it*, I thought when suddenly my face was at the window. It was dirty old glass in a metal frame with a latch that hinged at the top. I hoped it was not stuck shut.

It was, but I managed to get a steel pick in to cut around the window opening. I almost forgot the pain in my shoulders, arms, legs and feet. But it came back and I lost my grip. I dropped, catching myself about a foot below the window. My arms and fingers had no more to give but I had to ignore that. I had to make them work or The Doctor would be performing surgery on my delicate parts. I got back to the window but the steel picks had fallen to the floor.

With one fast solid yank I pulled the latch and the window began to slowly open. Pushing the window up I could see it would be real tight to get through. *Rhatz!* A metallic screech came from the rusty hinges but there was nothing to be done for it.

With another heave the window came open, in fact the entire window and frame came flying over my head and hit the floor with a smashing of glass and a smack of metal striking concrete. With that noise, someone would be at the door any second now.

The good news was that I now had a larger opening and there were no bars. I was able to get my arms through the opening and my legs and feet were scrabbling on the surface of the inside wall as I tried for as much traction as I could get. It was a three foot thick wall so I had a small platform. I pulled my shoes through and set them on the outside ledge. My boobs were crushed on the stone sill, but I kept wiggling and moving through an inch or two at a time. I had no idea how I did this, it happened out of desperation and adrenalin. I got my boobs over the lip of the sill, and that helped. *'They told Dan when I was caught I was hanging on by my boobs'* I thought. Whenever I am in serious trouble I get this weird giddiness that makes me think strange but funny thoughts, like that night in Cherryvale when I was running from Pádraigh's thugs. But I had to admit it helped. I recalled that Uncle Viktor had said something like that when he planned his escape from the prison camp. Weirdness must run in the family or else it is a mental release, a survival thing.

Almost through the window, but it was still so tight I could not get my knees up to crawl. *Was my cute little butt too big?* I looked down the outside wall. I should not have done that. It was a fifteen foot drop and the building was on the edge of a steep hill, so even if I made it to the bottom of the wall without killing myself I would be rolling down the hill, faster and faster until – what?

There was a tree nearby, but not close enough unless I could make a jump to it but suddenly I heard the door to my cell open and whoever ran in first slipped on the piss and fell because I heard the sound of a head striking concrete. Other voices were cursing and shouting at someone to get the hell out of the way. I had to get my legs out of the window, fast. No time left. I pulled them through. There was only one chance. If I could get my legs to give me one big push off the ledge I just might make it to the tree like a flying monkey. I could visualize the newspaper headline: *'Laure died when she tried to fly like a bird – the first real Flapper!'* Even under stress I had to laugh, but not for long. I could see the top of a ladder being set on the window ledge inside. *'Someone would be climbing up any second now and hands would grab me and painfully pull me back inside, scraping my boobs off on the stone ledge . . . poor Dan, he will miss them.'*

Getting into a position to leap, I skinned my knees on the stone sill. When I got my feet on the ledge I pushed hard and suddenly I was flying! No, not really, I couldn't flap my arms because they were hugging a tree. *'Hugging a tree? I made it! I am a Flapper!'*

But it was more like from the frying pan into the fire as I looked down. I lowered myself branch by branch until I was about ten feet to the ground but there was a steep bank with rocks studding the surface of the dirt below. No lower branches, no soft earth to land and roll. I saw an arm coming out of the window with a big revolver in its hand. Something dropped from the window – it was my shoes – I had forgotten to throw them down. The gunman must have accidently pushed them off the window ledge with his gun when he pushed his hand through the opening to shoot me.

I held on to the tree while wiggling my body down. I made it down two more feet when a bullet hit the tree trunk above me. I could not expect to be so lucky evading the next shot, so I let my arms and legs get looser and I went down fast, the bark tearing at my clothes. Trying to grip again near the bottom, my arms finally gave out. I landed on the ground, my head just an inch from a sharp rocky protrusion. I hurt all over but my body was in one piece. All I had to do was get on my feet and run. Run? My legs were like limp noodles. I couldn't feel my feet because they were numb.

No time to think about that. I pulled myself up and another bullet hit the tree trunk, this time closer. Someone was now hanging out the window from which I had recently defenestrated. I got up quickly, picked up a rock and threw it at the gunman. It struck him on the side of his head, causing him to lose his grip and fall back inside the room but good luck for me, his gun fell outside. It was a heavy .44 revolver so I took it.

But which way to go? I had not been able to track all the turns on the drive up to this place. A voice was shouting at others to tell them to get outside and grab me. Random shots were fired. A new gunman was poking out of the window and that gave me a fresh burst of adrenalin. I surprised the gunman by jumping toward the building, to the base of the wall, grabbing my shoes, then down the hill I went. I could not run very fast as I was slipping and sliding. A few hundred feet down there was a road. I stopped to put on my shoes and decided to cross the road and keep going through the woods. Not a good plan, because in a few minutes I almost went over a cliff. I managed to grab a branch to stop myself. I heard dogs barking. I could not outrun dogs. All this work and I would be taken back and turned over to The Doctor. I already hurt all over, I didn't think The Doctor could find a way to hurt me more, then realized that someone trained in medieval torture would come up with some novel ways to inflict pain.

'Rhatz! Oh Dan, I tried. I tried with everything I had. I'm so sorry.'

DOGFIGHT TO THE FINISH

I wanted to sit down but in my mind my father was telling me to get up and get going. My ancestors came from good Polish stock and I could not allow myself to give up. Knowing the road had to be close I moved along the cliff. Suddenly I popped out of the woods and there was the road curving away in front of me. On the other side of the road was a small rocky meadow surrounded by trees to the right, the road in the distance bordering the cliff to my left. There was nowhere to hide and my choices were to jump off the cliff or run across the meadow. It would be a close call if I could get across the meadow and into the forest before the guards and the dogs could catch me. Their shouts and barking indicated they were closing in fast. *'Rhatz!'*

Shots rang out as I made a stumbling uphill run over the rocky meadow. The heavy revolver was getting to be a burden so I crouched behind a large rock. Seeing a guard standing there looking for me, I aimed fast and shot, the guard fell backwards with a surprised look on his face. I aimed and fired off the remainder of the bullets but did not wait to see if I hit anyone. I threw the revolver over the cliff.

My legs that I thought had done their last when I climbed the wall somehow kept moving. Now I could see farther down the road where it curved ahead with trees on both sides, but here the terrain was going sharply uphill. Men were emerging from the trees behind me and two big dogs barked and growled, signaling that they saw me. I had to get into the trees on the other side of the meadow. My father's voice commanded *'Laure, do not give up'* so I kept going. Around the curve of the road ahead came the sound of a motorcar grinding its way uphill. *The Doctor was arriving.* I made my decision. As long as I could move, if I died today it would be from overexertion and not from some quack doctor of pain.

I made it into the trees beyond the meadow. Bullets were now whistling through the branches around me, and I began to zigzag to throw off the gunmen's aim, but that resulted in twisting my ankle when my shoe caught between two rocks. *'Rhatz!'* I rolled behind a log, wishing I had not shot off the revolver and could have taken some of the goons out before they got to me.

They could not see me so they quit shooting but I could hear they were in the trees. My hands felt some small rocks I could throw. *'I'll throw rocks at gunmen but I'm not giving up.'* When the footsteps got close enough I would have to get up to throw the rocks. I closed my eyes, concentrating on judging the distance of footsteps to time my rock throwing to be close enough to surprise them and give me a good chance to hit them.

A dog licked my face. Thinking my mind was slipping away I managed to open an eye. It was Raider. *'Raider? How did he get here?*

Raider jumped as one of the guard dogs came within a few feet from the log. Their dogs were huge beasts, bigger than Raider, and as he jumped the guard tried to shoot Raider but missed and shot his own dog, and it went down with a horrible scream. Raider turned to the second dog a few feet away from him, moving in fast with a huge mouthful of sharp teeth. Too close. Raider moved sideways but the teeth bit his tail and he yelped. But he got free, still on his feet.

Raider leapt onto the back of the other dog and sunk his teeth into its neck. The noise was horrendous as the dog let out angry painful howls and snarls and I could hear its teeth snapping. The big dog shook and Raider was flying through the air again. Raider and the other dog snarled and bit and screamed, blood flying everywhere. The big dog reared up to jump but Raider came up under the bigger dog and sunk his teeth into its throat. While the dog was trying to throw him off, Raider was flapping like a flag in the wind. The bigger dog lurched back and forth to dislodge him, but Raider's teeth remained firmly clamped to the dog's throat. The guard dog began to stagger and slowly fell to the ground. The sound of running footsteps and shots were getting closer and I discovered the shots were coming from in front of and behind me.

Dan was next to me. *'Dan? I must be hallucinating.'* Suddenly Bill, Luigi, Josefina, Vincenzo and Viktor came past me, shooting my pursuers as they advanced. Josefina stayed with me if a guard doubled back. She moved me behind a rock and took a covering position. The pursuers, now without their two big dogs and facing opposition from accurate rifle firepower, turned and ran. All I could say was "Thank you, Josefina" before I passed out.

I awakened as Dan began to lift me, but I told him to stop. He did so, afraid that he had hurt me. "No Sweetie, you did not hurt me. But I posilutely need a kiss to make sure that it is you and not a dream."

When he kissed me I found strength in my arms to pull his head close to mine and we kept kissing until Uncle Viktor came up and offered to stand watch while we barney-mugged. Making sure I was OK except for my twisted ankle and noodle strength legs, I told Dan I wanted to get out of here, the faster the better. He picked me up and carried me, saying that Bettina and Evelyn were a short way down the road with the automobiles. Raider followed us, limping badly.

At first Dan and the others wanted to go after the gang but I could not tell them how many gangsters there were, and since I was blindfolded except for the time I was in my cell I could not give them a description of the building's interior. Dan said Raider and I needed medical treatment, so everyone got into my Dodge and Vincenzo's Star automobiles.

I told Vincenzo the street address in Calistoga where I was kidnapped and he and Luigi went to check it out. No one was in the building but the Chrysler was still where I left it. Vincenzo knew where the real Calistoga cop shop was located and he went there but there was no Sgt. Beauchamp in the department. It had been a setup that I did not see coming.

On the way home Dan said what I was thinking. "I want all this to be over. Laure, I just want to have a normal life, write books, drink whiskey, make wine and make love to you. Not necessarily in that order."

After we were home I began to write down everything I could think of, hoping to find a clue to the identity of our nemesis. When I finished, I was so exhausted that I asked Dan if he would hold me tonight, saying "Sweetie, you could give me the best screwing ever but my body wouldn't feel it."

"I'm just relieved to have you back and we have a lifetime to do the horizontal Charleston."

"Oh you are so sweet. I love you" I told him tenderly. "Where's Raider?" I asked as Josefina came into the room with a basin of warm water and supplies to clean my cuts and scrapes.

"You fell asleep in the car and we took Raider to the veterinarian on the way home. He had several wounds. As soon as you are safely resting I am going back to the vet to check on him. The vet said he will recover, but he is probably not going to feel very good for a while. Josefina volunteered to clean and dress your wounds. You can rest easy, I'll sleep in the guest bedroom tonight so I won't wake you."

"No, you will not do any such thing."

"Why not?"

"If I wake up without you next to me I might panic. Then I'll have to find you and get in bed with you. So save us the trouble and get in bed with me and hold me gently tonight."

"Yes dear." I had taught him to say that as the correct way to acknowledge agreement.

I awakened with pain in every fiber of my being. I had over-stretched, over-exerted, over-used, over-every-thinged every part of my body. Even my breasts hurt. Dan was asleep with his arm loosely over me. I took his hand and put it on my breast. He was not awake yet but his natural reaction was to gently massage the breast and I gasped with discomfort. Dan woke up with a start and his arm retreated.

"I'm sorry Sweetie, my arm must have slipped around you."

"No, I woke up and moved your hand there, forgetting how I was hanging on the window ledge by my boobs and now they are sore. It's not your fault."

"They must really be sore. Maybe I should carefully inspect them."

"Even that would hurt right now. They took a lot of abuse on a stone ledge when I crawled out the window. Don't be worried, I'm sure in a day or two the girls will be wanting your attention."

"I know" Dan said with a smile.

"You're an animal. Speaking of animals, how's Raider?"

"He's doing very well, resting here at home. He asked me to give you this" and leaned over to lick my face, making me laugh. I needed that.

"I want to get him a big meaty bone. He risked himself again to protect me" I said.

"That's already taken care of. When Sunny returned from shopping I told her what happened and she went back to get a bone for him, saying she knew you would want to do that. The vet ordered Raider to have no strenuous activities for a few days, so don't go getting yourself in danger right away."

"Oh so you're a wise guy now?"

"I was wise enough to ask you to marry me" Dan replied.

I tried to move to kiss him but every nerve ending sent pain messages to my brain. "Don't worry, it will be awhile before I'm rested and recovered enough to get kidnapped again."

"I'll go make some breakfast and bring it to you" he said.

"Bring the coffee first please, and while you're putting together the breakfast I'll go sit at the table by the window. That lovely view of the Mayacamas is so peaceful and it will help me feel better."

Sunny offered to make my breakfast but Dan wanted to do it personally. He fixed me a great omelet of ham and eggs with cheese and vegetables chopped in, served with Sunny's fresh biscuits and jam. We ate and enjoyed the view, then Dan read the newspaper to me.

When he was done I said "Dan, I'm starting to remember things. Would you bring that list I started on and write down what I add to it? I'm just going to throw it all out there. It might be a nothing jumble, but we can go over it together and something will come up. Oh, I sorry, I shouldn't have said that."

"That's OK but you'll pay for it."

"And I promise you will enjoy it" I replied.

A BIG MEATY BONE

The door to the bedroom opened and my hero dog came in with a slight limp. Despite the bandages on his sides and tail his eyes were bright and clear. He came and put his head on my lap. I gently scratched his ears, thankful he was alive.

Dan walked in holding something behind his back. He gave me the package and I knew what it was. Raider knew too, since he could smell it. I took the butcher paper off the bone, still with a good amount of meat on it. Raider was a gentleman dog and did not grab it from me, he waited until I had it unwrapped and held it out to him. He sat there with the bone in his mouth and we looked into each other's eyes. I said "Thank you Raider. You are the best dog ever." He wagged his tail and Dan called him from the room to eat it in the kitchen, but I asked Dan to bring in a couple of towels and set them down. The dog knew immediately it was for him and moved to the towels, setting himself down with the bone between his front paws. Before he went to work on the bone, he looked up at me and licked his lips. I thought it was his way of saying thank you.

"Sometimes I think Raider has a human brain. He seems to know what we think" I remarked.

"Yes, I've often thought the same thing" Dan said.

Dan was excited at what I remembered. Once I started, all the recollections of yesterday came roaring back and he asked good questions that helped me think of other things. "How did you know to come up that road to look for me, and bring your private army?" I asked him.

"Josefina said you took $500 from the safe and said something about going to see a Sgt. Beauchamp at the Calistoga police department to bail out Sven and Ole. You were already heading down the road when she remembered that Big Al had sent them down to Napa for lubrication oils and other things they needed to perform maintenance on our locomotive. She knew something was wrong and called her father. Viktor was working for Vincenzo repairing winery buildings. He called Viktor in and had Bettina call me to report you were kidnapped. We gathered our crew and drove to the real Calistoga police station. Officers had noticed two unfamiliar automobiles driving fast out of town and up the road to Mt. St. Helena. The police have no jurisdiction outside of town but they gave descriptions of the automobiles and a list of seldom used buildings up the road."

"Since we had two automobiles, we leap-frogged each other as we inspected the buildings. We were getting worried that maybe you were taken up to Lake County. Our police notes for the next property said there was a big house with a stone tower that seemed to be occasionally used, but whoever lived there was unknown to the police. We stepped on the gas and were rounding a curve when we heard gunshots. We pulled off the road and there you were, running across an open meadow toward the trees. By the way you are extremely sexy when you run" Dan said, making me laugh. "I was hurting everywhere and about to collapse and you thought I was sexy?"

"Yes. You just made it into the trees with those goons shooting at you with the two big dogs closing in. They were moving fast and we couldn't get a shot because you were between them and us, so we advanced as fast as we could. When we had clear lines of fire we opened fire on the goons and Raider disappeared. He reappeared next to you and I saw him take on the dogs just as you fell down. Josefina and I were nearest to you and we came as fast as we could. Our people put up fast and accurate covering fire to drive the gangsters off. We did not want to run straight into an ambush, and there was the possibility that if we ran ahead some of them might double back to harm you. We did not know how many of them there were and I wanted to get you and Raider some medical attention." As he spoke, Dan was holding my hands in his, and I saw the worry in his eyes.

I told Dan "I managed to escape but was out of ideas and out of strength. In my mind I heard my father's voice telling me not to give up. My body was on the edge of complete exhaustion but my father's words kept me going. When I fell and twisted my ankle I still wasn't going to give up, but I was out of options. Then Raider was there and took on the dogs and you and Josefina were next to me. My mind thought it was a dream but you kissed me so I knew it was real."

"Laure, if you had not made your escape, we would have been there too late and they might have moved you, or if they were holed up in the stone tower they could have held us off a long time before we could get reinforcements to winkle them out. You're amazing, doing what you did. And your father's advice was on the money – you didn't give up" Dan said.

"I paid the price for it though."

"Laure sweetie, it was a price you could pay. Your regular run along the river keeps you in shape, and I happen to love your shape and your mind and your lively spirit very much."

We sat together at the table by the window and talked through the list a second time to see if one or the other of us noticed something we had not seen before. He brought us two small glasses of something very tasty called Southern Comfort. I asked him how he acquired it and he said Giuseppe had left it at our house after his recent visit. It has a nice flavor, sweet and pleasant. My insides began to warm up, and with that came an inspiration. "The voice I call Tin Voice. I've heard it before, but it wasn't tinny. I don't remember when or where, but I will remember when I think more about it."

"That's progress. If you've heard the voice before, then it is someone that you or maybe both of us know. Maybe the voice was disguised because he knew you would recognize him."

"It could be, but I don't know how a voice could be disguised like that. It sounded like a bad telephone. Is there a machine that can do that?"

"There are Victor Talking Machines and radios, and the dictation device Scott uses. With all the new science these days, things are developing fast. In Hollywood they already have prototype machines to show movies with color and sound. It will revolutionize the movie business. We have teletype machines able to send messages direct to anyone who has a similar machine. We are putting one of them in the LaureDan office. I wanted to do it last year but the telephone wires in Napa weren't good enough at the time. So yes, it is possible there could be such a machine that could disguise a voice. Did the voice move or was it in a fixed location?"

"No, as far as I could tell, it came from the same place. Why do you ask?"

"If it was an electrically operated device, it could only move as far as the power cord. It could have a battery cell, but that would add weight to be carried about."

"So how does that help us?" I asked.

"I called Giuseppe and Bill went to meet the ferry boat from San Francisco to bring him here. I thought your experience is something he should be made aware of, and this doctor of torture might be someone Giuseppe's contacts can identify. Let's keep going on the list, maybe more will come up. Oh there, now I've done it this time. I'm sorry Sweetie."

"I am feeling better and unlike you, I don't take teasing very well. If you take it slow, we might do a slow horizontal waltz but I'm not ready for the horizontal Charleston yet."

"I want you to be recovered. I will not do anything that could hurt you. I will wait."

"Hm. Most guys would just jump on me and have their way. You're a good man to consider my feelings first. I'm impressed" I said with a laugh.

"You have always had a positive effect on me, polishing my rough edges. I'm becoming quite cultured and refined, you know" Dan said, mimicking the voice of an English butler.

"Maybe I'd better re-think this. I like your rough edges. I like that when the time is right and we both want it, you take charge and have your way, but you will let me run the show when I want. In everything we do we are like that. It is one of the things that I love about you" I said.

"Was it on your list of 100 attributes your husband should have?" Dan asked.

"It certainly is, at number 8."

"What are numbers one through seven?"

"Not going to tell you. A girl has to have some secrets and things to brag about to her friends."

"You brag about me?"

"Absotively posilutely" I responded. "I've bragged about you to your sister Claire, to Josefina, Elsie, Dawn, Billie, Evelyn, Carole Griffin and Louise. Don't worry Sweetie, when I brag about something, it is a good thing." We looked into each other's eyes. We both had that familiar look.

"If we take it slow, is there enough time before Bill and Giuseppe get here?" I asked.

"Yes, but..."

"I made the decision. The correct answer is 'yes dear'."

"Yes dear" Dan said with a smile.

I don't know if it was the Southern Comfort or Dan, probably both but I felt a nice warm glow during and afterward. We cleaned up and were ready when Josefina opened the door for Bill and Giuseppe. Viktor and Evelyn arrived in their Packard.

"You are looking mighty pleased with yourself Laure," said Viktor with his slightly lop-sided grin. "Good to see you're feeling better."

"Dan has the same look on his face" said Evelyn.

We just kept grinning. "If must be that Southern Comfort liqueur that Giuseppe gave us" I said.

"Yep, that's what it is" Dan said agreeably.

No one believed us.

Giuseppe wanted to hear the entire story from the start so I began with the call from the fake Sgt. Beauchamp all the way to my suspicion that I'd heard Tin Voice before but had not been able to come up with who or when. Giuseppe said that could be a big clue if I did remember it. He also said he would find out about a torture specialist called The Doctor.

An hour later, after examining the information, nothing further was discovered. Delightful aromas came from our kitchen where Sunny had been preparing a roast beef dinner with vegetables and a salad. Giuseppe brought several bottles of an imported Italian wine, perfect with our dinner.

After dinner Bill told us that he had a job to do and expected it would take a week, maybe two. I didn't say anything, but it sounded suspiciously to me like he was going to visit a new woman in his life.

THREAT ESCALATION

The next morning I had to inspect our former rental house now that The LaureDan Company was managing the property for the bank. The bank had potential buyers coming in to look at it in a few days. Dan did not want me to go alone, so we packed a lunch and our shotguns and M1911 pistols. Raider volunteered to ride with us.

No one lived in the house since we had moved out. I had an inspection checklist. Dan carried his shotgun as we walked the outside of the property, Raider roaming about smelling everything and marking his old territory again.

Unlocking the front door, we cautiously went inside. Everything seemed OK on the first floor. Raider became interested in going upstairs when we were startled by the sound of footsteps and a door being slammed. We went up slowly, Dan leading with his shotgun.

Dan stopped and raised his hand. I listened, and thought I heard faint steps. "Back stairs" I whispered. We turned back down the main stairway and moved quickly. The sound of glass shattering came from a storeroom behind the kitchen. We went out the back door and a man was running towards the road. Dan called for the man to stop and fired the shotgun over his head. The intruder didn't stop so I took aim and fired two quick shots with my M1911 at the running figure and he flinched. It was a hit but not enough to stop him. We ran to our Chrysler and Dan asked me to drive while he watched from the passenger seat. It was a long driveway and when we got to the road, a dark roadster was leaving fast, heading north. I accelerated the Chrysler to give chase but even though it could make over 80 miles per hour, the roadster was faster and we lost sight of it. As we passed our winery house Dan said "We're not going to catch this guy, so let's finish our inspection and go back to our house."

Later, when we pulled up our driveway Sunny and Elsie were outside, Elsie holding her rifle. They came running up to us fast. "I heard something outside in back of the house" Sunny said. "I got Elsie and we were going to take a look."

"OK, you two don't have to get involved in this, we will go check it out" Dan said.

"We are already involved in it, and we can help flush the bum out" Elsie said. Our intrepid Irish maid did not lack courage.

"Then you two go around that way while Laure and I go the other. Don't shoot unless you're sure who it is, then shoot to immobilize. Maybe we can interrogate him" Dan said.

We went our separate ways and sure enough, as Elsie and Sunny were coming along the side of the house a man jumped out of the bushes and ran to the vineyards. Neither of us had a clear shot so we pursued on foot, being vigilant to make sure we weren't running into a trap.

We almost had a clear shot when the man turned, raising his hands. But something was not right. I yelled "Gun! Left hand!" as his hand came around with a hidden gun and he fired at us but missed, then ran fast, changing his direction and ran toward the Silverado Trail.

"Sunny, please call the sheriff. Tell him we had an armed intruder. Don't offer any more information, just ask them to get here on the double" Dan ordered.

Sunny came back outside. "I reported an armed intruder and gave the address, but I hung up before they could ask for more information. We should expect a sheriff's car eventually."

A few minutes later, Vincenzo drove up, having heard the gunfire from his nearby winery. Dan filled him in on what happened. After that, I added "I'm sure I nicked an intruder in the leg at our old house, we saw blood on the driveway, but this intruder moved too fast to have a leg wound and left no blood. There might be multiple troublemakers."

We started looking around the property for anything amiss, when suddenly there came an explosion from inside the house and a fire erupted immediately. Vincenzo jumped in his automobile, calling out that he was going to call the St. Helena fire department from his home.

About fifteen minutes later, a Chevrolet police sedan arrived. A large man got out along with the driver, a patrolman. The large man introduced himself as St. Helena Police Chief Dave Quinlan. We told him what happened. He said the firemen were on the way, and since we had no firefighting equipment at the house we could only stand there and watch it burn. A minute later a St. Helena Fire Department truck pulled up and firemen jumped off to get their pump started.

The fire chief and his crew did what they could, but the fire had enveloped the house quickly, and we sadly watched the old house die a fiery death.

We were fortunate. Our winery house was much smaller than our previous rented house so we had moved the LaureDan offices to a storefront in St. Helena, and most of our personal belongings were still at the Montanari guest cottage.

Chief Quinlan gave us his private telephone number and said he was going back to St. Helena and would check to make sure our office was secure. He also requested that we stop by tomorrow and give him a report. He seemed a very straightforward kind of guy and we agreed to meet him in the morning, since we wanted to stay to retrieve whatever we could from the house for now.

The sheriff's car came up our driveway and Sheriff Steckter got out and walked over to us. While his deputies searched outside our burning house, I began by telling Sheriff Steckter about our visit to our previous house. He was a man of fewer words so he mostly listened, asking just a couple of questions. Finally the sheriff said "I'm running out of investigators, there was also an attempted robbery at a jewelry store in Napa. Shot and injured a clerk but didn't take much loot. I hope you two aren't going to give me any more crimes to investigate today."

"That's everything we know at this time" I said. Sheriff Steckter smiled. His lead investigator called the sheriff over and they talked for a couple of minutes. After his discussion with the investigator, the sheriff came back over to us.

"My deputy and the fire chief are convinced the fire was started by an incendiary device. I sent a deputy to the other house to look around."

A few minutes later the deputy returned, jumped out of his patrol car and went straight to his boss. We watched as he showed Sheriff Steckter a box containing a disarmed bomb he had found at our old rental house. He called the fire chief over and they agreed that it could be the same type of device that started the fire here. The man must have been here long enough to set the bomb's timer, but we interrupted the other man at our previous rental property, and he ran rather than be captured with the bomb. I told the sheriff that I had wounded the man in the right thigh, and he said he would contact the hospital to see if anyone showed up with such a wound.

"You two seem to be at the center of a lot of suspicious activity lately. I heard about the problem north of Calistoga the other day. Mind telling me what's going on?"

"Sheriff Stecker, we really don't know. Last October someone tried to frame Laure for Col. Mosby's murder and almost got away with it. Then more things began happening to us, our movie set sabotaged and a stuntman killed, now all this. We just want to live a quiet life here in Napa and be prepared to make wine when Prohibition is repealed." I hoped the sheriff would not take exception to what Dan told him, and he did not.

"Just so you know, I have notified the Prohis that I will turn over any crimes related to the Volstead Act to them. I don't have the manpower nor the inclination to go after every poor winemaker in the county. I know there are wineries and distilleries in the hills and they are making wine or distilling liquor. As for me personally, I like to have a shot of whiskey now and then, but it is getting to be almost impossible to find any these days." He looked us in the eyes as he said that and we looked back with as blank an expression as we could manage.

The sheriff gave us his card and asked us to call him directly if we had any more trouble or could provide information sufficient for him to make an arrest. Dan and I agreed we would inform him right away. The sheriff went to his car, his driver pulling away smoothly.

I noticed Elsie had made herself scarce when Steckter was here and now she reappeared. "Sorry, but the sheriff knows a thing or two about me and its better if he don't see me. Nothing too serious, but I like to be careful."

"It would be best if we know what it is so we don't inadvertently say something to the wrong person" Dan said.

Elsie agreed and told us more of her background from her days in Ireland along with some minor infractions here. "We don't have any trouble over those days Elsie. We appreciate your telling us and you can be assured your secrets are safe with us. I would like to have you talk with our attorney at our expense, who may be able to clear up those minor scrapes here in California" I added.

The next morning we went to St. Helena for our meeting with Chief Quinlan in St. Helena. He received us in his office and had coffee brought in. "Sorry, I can't offer any wine" he laughed. "And I know that most of the people who live around here would not be upset if I did."

"I always like to know the people who live in or near St. Helena. Your property is outside the city limits but close enough that the sheriff sometimes calls my department if they cannot get a deputy to the scene quick enough. He can give us temporary jurisdiction until his people arrive. From what I've heard, you are both fine young people who try to avoid trouble, but it seems to find you. I can't stop that from happening unless someone commits a crime in

St. Helena, but I'll work with you if you'll work with me. All I ask is that you not break the law in town, and if something out of the ordinary happens, let me know. In return, I'll be fair to you."

"We agree, Chief Quinlan. Laure and I will work with you in any way we can" Dan said.

"If you would, please give me some background on what has happened and who causes trouble for you" the chief asked.

Dan and I took turns telling our story, leaving out the parts that might still incriminate us to the point where the chief would have to take action. We liked Chief Quinlan and were glad we talked with him, feeling better having developed a good relationship with local law enforcement.

We found a house to rent in St. Helena until we could build on our property. It was small but we would be close to the winery and walking distance to our office in town. Elsie and Sunny were already living in St. Helena and only lost a few personal items in our house fire, and I gave them an allowance to replace those items. Dan and I lost some clothing and furniture and I felt fortunate that our treasured photographs and personal mementos were safe at the Montanari guest house. Vincenzo told his workers to keep a close eye on all their buildings and report any suspicious activity immediately.

We received a letter from the Duesenberg brothers. After several delays, the work on our Model X was finished. Dan and I had talked about buying a sedan, which would be more comfortable in the winter rainy season. I thought we would buy another Chrysler, but Dan wrote to the Duesenbergs about acquiring a sedan. Most Duesenbergs were sold as running chassis, and buyers would contract with a body company like McFarlan or Murphy to install a body to their specifications.

The brothers asked us to wait to purchase another automobile until we arrived there, because they believed a customer was going to cancel a sedan order because of unforeseen financial difficulties. I surprised Dan when I agreed.

On the same day, Laure got a call from her father Jake. Scott had purchased a new Ford 4-AT-B Trimotor and sold the Fokker F.VIIa-3m. After Jake made safety and performance modifications, Scott asked Jake and Claire to test fly it out to see us, and they arrived three days later. I was happy to see my father and we went out for dinner. Later, when I gave my father an update, he was not amused.

LAURE AND THE DUESENBERG RACECAR

Jake offered to fly us to Long Grove for a visit with our families, after which we would take a train to Indianapolis to pick up our Duesenberg. The new Trimotor was a stronger aeroplane than the Fokker with its all-aluminum construction, but was not significantly faster. The Ford 4-AT-B carried upgraded engines and Jake, as usual, worked his own magic on them for power and reliability. The flights were smooth and we enjoyed seeing the country from above. With a good tailwind we made it to Gauthier's Field in Wheeling in two days with Jake and Claire taking turns flying. Dan and I were drafted to be student co-pilots and began to learn about aviation.

We enjoyed a whirlwind round of visits with family and friends, noticing the new houses being built near Long Grove. Scott and Claire's S Bar C ranch was beautiful, and Claire enjoyed showing us everything. She still had her first horse and he looked to be in splendid condition. When it was time to leave there were tearful good-byes. Scott and Claire drove us to Chicago's Dearborn Station for the train to Indianapolis.

The Duesenbergs sent a driver to pick us up at the Indianapolis Union Station and at the Duesenberg factory the brothers received us with warmth and welcome, as always. We were numbered among their favorite customers.

Our Model X was completely rebuilt and looked posilutely gorgeous. Fresh red paint, new chrome, tires and wheels, dashboard – it was a new automobile. The Duesenberg technicians painted the area around the bullet holes but kept their promise not to repair them. Even the brothers had come to accept them as proof that a Duesenberg could take almost anything.

The brothers asked Dan if he would like to drive a Duesenberg Special they were testing for the Indianapolis 500. I answered "Yes, I would love to drive it first" and the brothers laughed but Dan knew I was serious. Next morning they took us to the Indianapolis Motor Speedway, also known as "The Brickyard" when it was first paved with bricks in 1909.

1927 was the first year that the rules did not require a mechanician or co-driver. The new single seat chassis appeared narrow compared to the previous Duesenberg Indy racecars. The Duesenberg brothers seemed worried as I put on a driving suit, gloves and goggles and settled into the seat. I overheard Dan telling the brothers not to worry, that I was an excellent driver and experienced with high speeds. The brothers advised me to go slow because it was a very powerful racing automobile. Dan grinned. He knew I would not go slow as he kissed me and whispered in my ear "Have fun but please, Sweetie, don't do anything rash. I couldn't bear to live without you." I knew he didn't want me to get hurt, but all the same he supported my ambition to drive the racecar, even though the Duesenbergs were skeptical.

Driving the first lap around the two and a half mile racetrack with a lap time that showed the Duesenbergs I was not careless with their car, I almost unmanned their confidence when I downshifted and stepped on the power crossing the start/finish line at the start of the second lap. The racecar squirmed as the supercharged straight eight responded beyond my expectations. I was thrilled with the acceleration but felt in complete control.

Drivers and crews from the other teams lined the inside rail of the track upon hearing there was a woman driver pulling laps in a Duesenberg. On the third lap I found the line through the corners that the Duesenberg factory test driver told me about. My fifth full lap felt smooth and fast and as I went by August and Frederick had big smiles on their faces and Dan told me I had an even bigger grin. I put in eleven laps, claiming that I had not seen the sign to come in at the end of the tenth lap. Nobody believed that feeble story but all was forgiven when I brought the car into the pit and August showed me the chart of my lap times. News of my achievement quickly made the rounds and the men watching along the inside wall roared their approval. Each lap was faster than the previous lap and by the end I was within a few seconds of the factory drivers' times. Dan just smiled, knowing that the feeling of power and speed created in me another kind of lust with him being the beneficiary.

Dan got into the driver's seat while the mechanicians refueled and completed their final checks around the racecar. I whispered some tips in his ear about the line through the corners because each one was different, then I told him I was excited from driving fast and what I was going to do to him tonight. The crew started the engine and Dan was so charged up that he let the clutch out too fast and stalled the motor. While the crew restarted the racecar I told him to stay calm until we were back at the hotel and then I would attack him.

Dan went out inspired. By his fourth lap he was as fast as my fastest lap and improving. He completed ten laps and came in. The crew checked the racecar over and August came up to show Dan the lap times – he had been as fast as all but their top factory driver. I was not surprised he did so well. What the Duesenbergs did not know was that Dan and our friends had cobbled together a racecar from various wrecks and parts they scrounged and ran the car at local racetracks in Northern California. These were rough graded dirt ovals of half mile to mile in length. Dan was one of the best of the local drivers. He had only crashed once but was not injured other than bumps and bruises, however I almost had a panic attack when I saw it happen.

That night we had to postpone our planned romp because the Duesenbergs invited us to dinner, during which August floated the idea that they needed a driver for one of their five cars in the Indy race since one of their drivers had broken his leg, and would Dan like to drive in the Indianapolis 500? Dan was excited but I was scared all the way down to my rolled stockings. I did not want him to do it. Crashes, injuries and death were frequent and unpredictable even among the experienced drivers. But how could I deny him this opportunity, when he never denied me what I wanted to do?

That night Dan wanted to call Jake, who was not surprised and did not have the same reservations that I had. By the end of the conversation, we agreed that Dan should drive the Duesenberg, on the condition that Jake was the crew chief so he could oversee the preparation of the racecar, which was what Dan's secret agenda had been when he called my father. The next day we presented our condition to the Duesenbergs and they accepted. They knew Jake from his Elgin days and had tried to hire him, but were too late when we made our business agreement with Scott McLanahan.

The catch was that Dan had to stay in Indianapolis for testing, practice and qualifying. I was uneasy about going back to California without him, so we decided that I would stay in Long Grove and go to Indianapolis on the weekends. In Long Grove I stayed at the S Bar C Ranch where Scott asked his cowboys watch over me should our phantom vendetta seeker come looking. But that did not happen and the weeks before May 30, 1927 passed without difficulty. Our teletype machine was installed in the LaureDan office and Scott had one in his office at the ranch, which he offered for my use. It was quick and easy to communicate with Josefina, who had already proved that her promotion to partner status was a smart move.

Dan became fast in the new racecar. It was the #21, and he considered that a lucky omen since my birthdate was March 21. Jake reshaped the driver's seat to fit Dan, and made many other adjustments to increase reliability. He told Dan speed was important, but finishing the race was more important. "Can't win if you can't finish" he said.

In the last two weeks before the race I stayed in Indianapolis, where we had a short-term rental house. Every one of our family and friends wanted to be there for the race. Since the word had gone out that Dan was driving a Duesenberg racer at Indy, Viktor, Evelyn, Josefina and her parents said they were coming. Luigi arranged for special leave and when Major Griffin heard the reason, he arranged for leave so he and his wife Carole could be there. Sgt. Reilly proposed the idea to Major Griffin to assign his squad to field exercises, using our vineyard property. His real motive was to guard our property so we would not worry about it. That way we could rest easy that our phantom nemesis would have a difficult time sabotaging our property or the St. Helena office, and Reilly's squad would have new turf to practice on. Bill and Giuseppe were coming for the race and our mothers and distant relatives would be there. Dan joked that they would have to build another grandstand section just for our families and friends.

At the last minute Louise Brooks showed up with Buster Collier. We were even more surprised when Douglas Fairbanks arrived. He said Mary Pickford wanted to come too, but she was on a location shoot and could not get away. W.C. Fields sent his regrets, but Keith Aldridge, our deputy sheriff friend from Cherryvale came for the race with his new wife Amy.

Dan really got excited when Erwin "Cannon Ball" Baker and his wife Elnora arrived. Baker had raced at Indianapolis, winning the first motorcycle race at Indy in 1909, and had driven a Frontenac in the 1911 Indianapolis

500, finishing 11th, and his advice proved as good as it was on our first trip west. The Duesenbergs were pleased to add Cannon Ball Baker as a crewmember so he could help Dan with training and strategy.

Jake was in his element and having a great time doing everything possible to make the Duesenberg fast and reliable, and the Duesenberg factory engineers were enthusiastic as they learned a thing or two from Jake. Some of Jake's aeroplane customers were flying in for the race. It was bragging rights for them that their aeroplane technician was also an Indianapolis 500 crew chief. I was busy arranging hotels or rentals for everyone. Dan and I were often so tired at the end of the day we would collapse on the bed and fall asleep.

When Bill and Giuseppe arrived they took charge of security. Bill brought in a couple of Pinkerton agents that he knew and trusted. Bill and Giuseppe helped Jake inspect the race car at random times every day for signs of tampering, but our phantom nemesis either didn't come to Indianapolis or was plotting our demise elsewhere. There were no incidents, but we felt better being prepared.

This year the field consisted of 39 entrants who had to qualify for 33 starting grid spots and the qualifying was brutal. Dan got a case of nerves during qualifying and his best time put him 28th on the grid. He was disappointed but the Duesenberg crew along with Jake and Cannon Ball were not in the least worried. I was the one doing all the worrying.

At first it was just me with Claire, Louise and Jodie, a girlfriend of one of our mechanicians having fun finding the local speakeasies for drinking and dancing. Then Evelyn and Josefina arrived and we began to get noticed by the press. As race day came closer I felt less like drinking and dancing. I wanted to spend every minute with Dan, hoping these would not be our last days together. My attitude toned down our party activities. We continued to go out two or three nights a week to dance, but tried not to create any scenes. The last days before the race Dan and the crew were busy with practice and fine-tuning so our nights out were girls only. But that was OK because I had no desire to play around, although Buster made his usual offer.

On May 20, Charles Lindbergh took off from Roosevelt Field in Long Island, New York. Thirty-three and a half hours later he landed at Le Bourguet Field near Paris, the first person to fly solo across the Atlantic. Jake had met Lindbergh and said he had seen the passion for flying in him and expected Lindbergh to take the challenge. Lindbergh's accomplishment took some of the publicity away from Indianapolis but we did not mind. We were photographed just going to and from the racetrack and the publicity frenzy increased during the last week before the race.

With Cannon Ball's experience guiding him, Dan calmed down as he gained confidence and let go some of the pressure he had placed on himself. Dan's qualification speed was 107.360 miles per hour, while the 1926 Indy winner Frank Lockhart took the pole position at 120.100. The Duesenbergs said for a rookie to qualify was impressive. Dan received his competition license and prepared for the race with physical strengthening and endurance exercises. He even lost a couple of pounds. "Got to be faster than the others" he laughed "and every lost ounce helps."

Monday, May 30, 1927 came and I was awake before Dan. I was never so afraid. Now I wished that we had not come to Indianapolis. Dan said he was respectful of the peril of the racecar, the track and the other drivers. I thought about begging him not to drive, but I knew that would be futile and hypocritical of me. I had been able to put the fear out of my mind up till now but this morning it was like an elephant in the room and it would not leave. I was holding Dan close, my head on his chest taking in his masculine scent possibly for the last time. A tear escaped from my eye and fell on him, waking him up. "Laure, you're awake. Is something wrong?"

"No Dan, I'm fine. It's just sweat, it is warm in here."

He looked at my face and found another tear. Gently he wiped the tear away from my cheek with his finger and put it in his mouth. "Mmm. I will think about how good you taste all day and I will come back to you tonight. I promise" he said softly.

I got out of the bed and ran to the bathroom, where I cried as quietly as possible. I rarely cry, but the emotion just overcame me. All the build-up of the recent weeks, all the challenges we had overcome since we met, everything ran through my mind. I had not locked the bathroom door and Dan came in, pulled me to him and kissed me. We silently held each other for several minutes.

"Just think that tonight you might make love to the winner of the 1927 Indianapolis 500" he said, trying to be cheerful.

"I don't care if you finish in 33rd place. You are a winner, my winner in life. Come back to me tonight. That's all I ask."

"Do you have faith in me? Do I have your complete support today? Because that is important to me. That's what will keep me going, keep me safe, along with you sending positive thoughts to me for each one of those five hundred miles."

I had to be strong for him. He should not have to think of me as a weeping wife. I took control of myself. "Sweetie, in spirit I will be riding with you in the race car, every mile. I will be cheering for you so loud I probably won't have a voice later to tell you how much I love you. But I will make sure you know it tonight, whether I can talk or not."

"Now that's something that will give me confidence." We kissed, got dressed and went out for breakfast. Dan's photo had been in the newspapers, along with the 32 other drivers so many people recognized him and stopped to wish him well. He always responded positively and left them with a smile, always glad to sign photographs. Many of them recognized me and remembered me as the cousin of Louise Brooks. It was amazing what a little publicity and ties to a famous movie star could do.

My mind was in a daze as we arrived at the speedway. There was a parade followed by the driver introduction. My father took me to the #21 garage and all the crew cheered me. "The boys stayed up late and went over the racecar again and again until it was as perfect as we could make it. Bill, Giuseppe and the Pinkerton boys stayed in the garage and took guard shifts overnight to make sure no one came to sabotage the car. Cannon Ball and I will check it again before we roll it out to the track. Laure, this is a great automobile and Dan is an excellent driver. I predict he will finish in the top 10 today."

"Thank you, all of you. I want you to know much I appreciate your work and Dan does too, although I am sure he has already told you, and..." I was cut off by a commotion at the door. Louise was trying to get in but the door guard, who was probably one of the few people in the United States who did not recognize Louise Brooks, would not let her in. Jake told him she could come in, and when she did the crew all wanted to get their picture taken with her and get her autograph.

"After the race, men, after the race I'll be back to kiss every one of you!" Louise said as they cheered, seeing this as a good omen. They noticed that we looked enough alike to be cousins.

"Wow, I heard you were cousins but seeing you together, now I believe it!" said one of the crew.

"OK guys, we've still got work to be done" Jake said. I kissed Dan for maybe the last time. I took a yellow scarf from my pocket and gave it to him. It was the scarf that Claire had dropped from her aeroplane with the message for him to pick me up in at the Union Station in St. Louis, the first day that we made love. I had put some drops of my perfume on it. Dan put it up to his nose and smiled.

"It's you. I'm going to carry this in the pocket over my heart. I love you, Laure." After we hugged and kissed I had to turn away to keep him from seeing me cry again. Jake sent one of the crew members escort Louise and I to our seats in the grandstand, where the others in our party were already situated. Louise and Claire sat on either side of me, my mother behind my seat, choosing those seats to be near and help keep my confidence up. Louise banished Buster down to the opposite end of the row. She knew it would not be good for Dan to drive by and see me sitting next to Buster. Louise had a good heart.

The festivities before the race seemed to go on and on. There were marching bands, parades, speeches. Finally the race cars were brought out to the track and lined up on the grid. I saw Dan in his Duesenberg driving suit talking to Jake and Cannon Ball Baker, going over their race strategy again. Dan had a peek of my yellow scarf showing in his breast pocket. It helped me feel better.

The grid cleared and the command "Gentlemen, start your engines" came over the loudspeakers and almost 33 engines roared. We were seated where we could see the start/finish line, but the cars were stretched out so when the starting flag waved the last car crossed the line several seconds later. The stragglers, those whose engines did not start, got started or pushed off the grid to their garages. There was so much dust and exhaust smoke I did not see Dan go by, at first thinking his car didn't start, but as the field crossed the line at the end of the first lap I spotted him.

Dan started in 28th position and stayed there for several laps. He seemed to be stuck in traffic and did not try to put too much speed on. I began to wonder if something was wrong with the racecar. Frank Lockhart, starting at pole position commanded the lead for 91 straight laps, eventually leading for a total of 109 laps until his engine broke a connecting rod and he was out. I thought of Jake saying "if you do not finish you cannot win". Jake had gone through the #21 engine and told me it was a strong motor.

Dan began to improve his lap times, moving up in the standings to 20th place, then 15th, where he stayed for several laps. By this time the race was more than half over but Dan still looked strong and alert, not tired like many of his competitors whose shoulders sagged as exhaustion set in. There were five Duesenberg racecars, and by lap 152 of 200 laps, two Duesenbergs were out of the race, one with a mechanical failure and the other crashed. Dan was now in 10th place. There were other crashes and every time one happened my heart stopped until I saw Dan go by on the next lap. With 190 laps run, two Duesenbergs were in first and second. Dan was still in 10th position and began to make his move up the leader board.

On lap 198 and two to go, the second place Duesenberg dropped out with mechanical failure. Then they were on the last lap and Dan moved past another car to seventh place. Everyone in our section of seats was standing and cheering, even Buster. It seemed so long before the field came around and the cars were starting to close up to each other as every driver struggled to improve his position during the final seconds.

The winning Duesenberg, driven by George Souders crossed the finish line where a race official waved a checkered flag. Three other racecars crossed, and I looked at the next car approaching the finish line. I could not see the car's number or color because the car was so dirty it did not look like Dan's car, but as the car crossed the finish line, a yellow scarf waved from the driver's hand! I jumped up and down, shouting with my family and friends, only partially for his excellent finish, but mostly because I was relieved that he finished without harm.

Once past the checkered flag, their positions were recorded and the cars took a triumphant parade lap. When they came across the line for the last time they had slowed down into a rough single file in their finishing position, all the drivers waving to the stands. Dan was still waving my yellow scarf. I was so relieved that I sat down, unable to move now that the adrenalin was wearing off. The cars stopped and crews came out running, surrounding the automobiles. Dan's crew lifted him out of the seat. They set him down standing on the seat and he looked across the track. Louise and Claire got me to stand and I began waving and cheering like a crazy woman. I think we saw each other at the same moment. I laughed, cried, and laughed again. Dan put my scarf to his mouth and kissed it, then waved it at me as I blew kisses to him. I wanted to do a whole lot more to him, but that would have to wait. Suddenly Bill and Giuseppe were next to me. Bill took me by the arm, and along with Claire and Dan's mother Dorothy they led us through a tunnel under the grandstands, up some steps and through a door. We were on the bricks. I was running to Dan and passed his mother and sister. No one else was going to win this race. His crew chanted "Laure – Laure – Laure" as I ran into him so hard I would have knocked him down but my father was there and held us upright. Poor Dan, he was so filthy dirty, oily and smelly. I did not care. I held him close as long as I could. The dress I wore was utterly ruined with oil and grease stains, but that was the least of my cares.

The race had taken 5 hours 7 minutes and 33 seconds, and Dan was exhausted, as were all the drivers. He was in better condition than most, but even so he was worn out. All we did for those first few minutes was hold each other. I had to let go of him for a few seconds when the race officials came by to congratulate him, then his crew crowded around. I heard them say "blazing fast finishing lap" and "top 10 finish by a rookie driver" and "one helluva race". Cannon Ball was there and I hugged him too, and thanked him for his advice and strategy that had worked so well for Dan. He had advocated for hanging back at first, then work up through the pack in the middle of the race, and finally put on his best speed near the end, taking every opportunity to move up. Dan recognized good advice and used that strategy. Cannon Ball said if Dan finished in the top twenty it would be a fantastic drive, and here he was, a rookie finishing in fifth place.

Someone gave the winner a bottle of milk and soon more bottles came out. Dan got one and almost drank the entire bottle. Claire and Dorothy were on each side of Dan now, but he motioned me to come and held me in front of his body, turning me around and putting his arms around my waist. I noticed that he may have been exhausted, but a part of him was feeling quite lively as he pressed his body to mine. I wiggled to let him know that I noticed.

The news photographers were making their way down the line. Dan lifted me up and put me in the seat of the racecar, placing his helmet on my head, and my picture was taken at least a dozen times. Then Louise was on the track and a photographer shouted "Both Brooks girls are here" and that caused more uproar. The crew lifted Louise to join me in the driver's seat, which was tight with the two of us, but the photographers loved it. Then we got out and Dan got in, and I managed to sit on his lap with my legs hanging off the side. A bit too much leg, although no worse than I had done at speakeasies. Just then, along came August and Frederick Duesenberg, big smiles as they stopped to admire my legs. Claire and Dorothy had their photos taken with the Duesenberg brothers and with Dan. The crowd was thinning out and Jake had the crew take their tools and pit equipment to the garage, and a technician drove the car to the garage. Bill, Giuseppe and Viktor came to shepherd us back across the track, where cars awaited to take us to our rented house. As soon as the crew finished Jake would bring Dan and Cannon Ball to join us.

Josefina was at the house with helpers putting out sandwiches and fruit, pastries and other goodies. Buster brought me a glass of punch and I didn't have to taste it to know it had been generously spiked. He said he was trying to get me drunk so Dan could take advantage of me. I said "Thank you, Buster, but Dan's only problem will be fighting me off."

At the Duesenberg victory dinner that night, the brothers asked Dan to come to the stage to thank him for his great drive. Jake, Cannon Ball and others congratulated Dan on his drive. Dan gave a short speech thanking the team for building a fast and safe racecar that ran flawlessly throughout the race. One of the technicians came up to say that "the Brooks cousins brought us good luck." Dan's share of the prize money was $3,000, almost all of which would go to our house construction fund.

Later in bed, after Dan was asleep I laid my head on his chest, just like when the day began. I felt a tear slide down my cheek again but this time it was a tear of joy. "Dan, you're my winner" I whispered, holding him close as I fell asleep.

A DUESENBERG SURPRISE

On Wednesday, June 1st there was a celebration for the victorious Duesenberg racing team at the factory for all the employees. E. L. Cord, who now owned the Duesenberg marque was there and gave a speech but no one seemed to pay much attention to him. It was easy to tell that the employees were still loyal to the Duesenberg brothers.

Afterward there was a lavish buffet lunch set out on long tables on the factory floor for factory, office employees and management. We stood among them, eating and chatting when a spry old machinist came up and introduced himself. "I am Oscar, I help build special cars, the racing cars and prototypes. That car you drove in the race was one of the best I ever worked on and I am proud of your taking it to a top 5 finish. It made all the extra work worthwhile. The word is that the car will be kept to run in next year's Indy 500." Dan thanked him, and Oscar turned to me and took my hand and said "I've seen you in the newspapers, I like going to the movies and I saw you in *The Great Gatsby*. You are a lovely woman. I had a lovely wife who also liked to dance, but she passed away three years ago. She was always by my side, and I pray that you two have a close relationship. It is important, yes?" I gave him a hug in response.

As we talked to Oscar we learned that he also worked on the prototype automobiles, and remembered our Model X when it was first built. He also worked on the fresh restoration. "That is a fine automobile. Frederick and August let us read the journals of your drive to California and back. It was as exciting as those dime novels. I liked that you asked us not to repair the bullet holes. We inspected them and after reading your journal it felt like we were there with you. The paint man put some metal protector around the holes to prevent rust, but the holes need to be cleaned and the metal protective finish renewed every year. He went to get some for you to take home. Don't leave until he gets back. The interior designer was impressed with the shade for your dog, it was made of high quality leather like we use here. He only had to put some leather conditioner on it and replace the fasteners to make it look like new."

We enjoyed talking to Oscar, he was a delightful man and so very happy when I held his hand as we walked around the shop floor. Later, he told us "These employees are the reason that Duesenberg automobiles are of the highest quality. The brothers perfected the design and engineering and hired the best craftsmen to build the automobiles. I wish we had been able to put together the financing to keep the Duesenbergs with their company. They admitted to not being the best businessmen and we could have helped them. I'm not sure this man Cord who bought the Duesenbergs out is the right guy for what needs to be done." Those were frank words for an employee, but this man really cared. From all I had seen here, I fully agreed.

We both liked Oscar so much that Dan didn't mind that I was still holding Oscar's hand when August and Frederick came to take us the prototype shop. When the brothers waved, men rolled covers off two automobiles. One was a four-door sedan, all black, even the radiator shell. Not sporty, it was like a royal limousine with a luxurious black leather interior. The other was a two-seat boattail roadster, dark blue in color with a red leather interior. August said the body was custom made by McFarlan.

"Wallace Reid was a fan of McFarlan automobiles and they are made here in Indiana. McFarlan also makes custom bodies and this is a beautiful example" Dan said in admiration.

"The automobiles are yours" said the Duesenberg brothers, "The sedan you are purchasing at our dealer discount if you approve of the automobile, and the roadster we give to you in appreciation for Dan's outstanding drive in the race."

"But I didn't win" Dan said in amazement.

"You gave us more than a win. The publicity from your rookie drive from twenty-eighth to fifth place, along with the glamorous photographs of you and your lovely wife Laure and her cousin Louise Brooks appeared in the morning newspapers all across the country. We already have over twenty confirmed new orders from Hollywood celebrities and business leaders for new automobiles and our distributors telegraphed us that many more orders are in process. The McFarlan roadster is your new sports car. Jake tells us you two like to drive around your beautiful California wine country, enjoying the beautiful scenery. Why not travel in Duesenberg safety and comfort and great McFarlan design?" August said.

As for the reference to Louise, I remembered that the Duesenberg brothers had become very fond of her when she visited us in Napa, telling her she should go to Europe and make movies since she did not seem to like Hollywood.

For once, Dan and I were speechless. Both automobiles were gorgeous. The sedan, regal and proud, the roadster "with smooth curves that remind me of your beautiful body" Dan said in front of everyone, making me blush, which rarely happened.

"We are doing this because our power here is waning in favor of Mr. Cord. We are making the best arrangements we can for our employees and although you are not on our payroll, the work you have done for us more than pays for the roadster" said Frederick. "But there is one catch. We would like you to keep journals for each automobile and send them to us, even after we are no longer at the factory."

We did not know what to say. Thank you did not sound like enough although we said it over and over. We were happy to keep journals. "Now how do we get three automobiles home?" I asked.

"Your friends Scott and Bill have taken care of that. As you know, they have connections at the highest level with the railroads and they are preparing special boxcars, one for each car, to ship them to you. The only problem the railroads had was a shortage of locomotives, and your friend Bill told us you have one. We took the liberty of asking him if he could send it here, pick up the boxcars and Scott said he would pay the expense and arrange for your train to run as a special. He contacted your train crew and they are on the way."

"Sounds like everything is planned, there's nothing for us to do but accept these fine automobiles and enjoy them" Dan said.

"I think we will have to build a garage now that we have five automobiles" I said. "I'll call Uncle Viktor and see if he would build it for us. He's been talking about starting a construction company."

"What about Viktor and Evelyn's careers in the movies?"

"After the sabotage of the stunt and Lonnie's death, Evelyn still wants to work behind the camera and do some bit parts. Claire told her that color movies are sure to happen, there are different processes under evaluation. She wants to be the first female color film cinematographer. However, Viktor took Lonnie's death hard. He is re-thinking about his plan to be a stuntman. He blames himself for not checking everything out, but it was the stunt assistant director who was supposed to do that" I said.

Suddenly, we looked at each other with the same reaction. '*Why hadn't we thought of this before? Why didn't the assistant stunt director check everything that day? Or if he did, why didn't he find the sabotage?*'

"The stunt AD should have personally opened the boxcar door to make sure it would work. Dan, we have to go to Hollywood and find that stunt AD. I want to talk to him" I said in a rush.

"Viktor will want to be there for that talk too" Dan added. "OK, let's get things wrapped up here, make a quick visit to Long Grove to say goodbye to our families, and head west. We can take the *San Francisco Overland Limited* and make further plans on the way. Let us not tell anyone about this. We don't know who to trust and I don't want that assistant director to have a story prepared and we will have made a trip for biscuits."

I thought that finally we might have a way to find out who was behind this vendetta against us. It set my mind working again on all the details of recent events. So far, the only thing had been the impression that I had heard Tin Voice before, but I could not pin down who, when or where.

After spending two days in Long Grove, Jake drove us to North Western Station in Chicago to begin our trip home on the *San Francisco Overland Limited*, taking about two and a half days. This time we were going to get off the train at Port Costa in California. I had sent Viktor a telegram to meet us there with our Chrysler B70 sedan.

We were excited to take our first ride on the new bridge from Crockett, just up the road from Port Costa, to Vallejo. The Carquinez Bridge opened on May 27, 1927. Crossing the country was becoming faster every year. Cannon Ball said that many of his cross-country driving records were set to be broken as the roads improved.

I sent a letter to Viktor, who showed it to Giuseppe. Through his contacts Giuseppe found the stunt AD, a fellow named Foster Pell, was expected to return to the studio from a remote location shoot in ten days so we had time. Another thing – the name Foster Pell sounded familiar, and I remembered that Foster was the AD from *The Great Gatsby* movie, the one who did the backwards scheduling and laughed at me when I pointed that out. I did not recall seeing him on the *Road Trip Blues* set, but he could have easily blended into the crew. I had been busy with other things and Dan did not know him. I was looking forward to making that worm squirm. Viktor had let it be known that if Pell was proven guilty, he would have a very short life expectancy.

We arrived at home amazingly fast compared to previous trips home when we had to go to San Francisco or Oakland to get a ferry. First thing we did was to take a shower together. We loved the incredible sensuality of washing each other. I commented to Dan that he looked even sexier, having lost four pounds preparing for and driving in the race. That was all it took and two minutes later I was being nailed to the mattress, still wet from the shower. That was my sneaky plan and Dan fell for it. I knew he would.

THE MISSING ASSISTANT DIRECTOR

Viktor wanted to bring Evelyn along to Hollywood because she had knowledge of how the stunt was designed and he thought it would look normal for them to be traveling together. I agreed, Evelyn was a kick in the pants to hang around with, and she and Viktor were a team.

After resting for two days and catching up on LaureDan business we started out early the next morning in our trusted Chrysler on the road to Hollywood. Taking shifts behind the wheel we arrived at The Beverly Hills Hotel in the late evening.

We decided that I would go to the studio office on my own to inquire about where to find Foster Pell, using the cover that as the associate producer I had to tie up some loose ends for the *Road Trip Blues* production, now on hiatus. In fact, we were in the process of combining our Hollywood activities under our new company called LaureDan Film Productions to manage our Hollywood interests. Even though we might not do much if *Road Trip Blues* was never finished, but we could take on other work. I officially made Dan my agent. It was a fiction, since I managed my own career, but it would make it easier to brush off casting couch invitations.

The Famous Players-Lasky Studio personnel office was my first stop. But what I found there was not good news. "Rhatz" I said as I found that our man Foster Pell had left the movie production he was working on and disappeared. The director was furious because Pell left suddenly and found that Pell had not kept up the paperwork properly.

I was able to get Pell's address from the studio and I read the directions to Dan as he drove. Viktor was concerned that Pell had somehow gotten wise to us looking for him and had gone into hiding. We arrived at the address, an apartment block in a seedy neighborhood.

There was no Foster Pell or similar name on any of the mailboxes. I knocked on the apartment manager's door and she told us Pell had moved out without notice a week ago and without paying the rent. Now we were certain Pell knew we were looking for him, but how?

Dan came up with the idea of finding out who Pell's friends were. We went back to the studio and luckily found Herbert Brenon, my director on *The Great Gatsby*. He was glad to see me and said the only friend of Pell he could recall was Lester, Brenon's assistant clerk. I remembered Lester from the night that Shorty and Slick tried to kidnap me from the tent colony on the shoot.

After I got Lester's address at the studio office, just as we pulled up to another Los Angeles apartment block, I spotted Lester walking out the door carrying a suitcase. He did not see me so I ducked below the window as Dan drove to cut Lester off at the street corner. When I opened the door Lester panicked and ran, but Viktor jumped out of the back seat and ran faster, tackling Lester on the lawn.

A passing Los Angeles patrol car stopped to see what was happening. Dan went over and told the officers that he was a movie producer and we were filming a scene. The officers wanted to talk to the victim to see if he agreed with that story, but just then quick-thinking Evelyn, who always traveled with a small movie camera, stepped from between two parked automobiles, pretending she was filming the action. When one of the officers recognized me from the Gatsby movie they accepted our story and drove off. We were lucky. Evelyn told us that there was no film in the camera.

I was worried that Lester would yell, but Viktor had whispered that if he made a sound, Viktor would break his scrawny neck, and with Viktor's menacing looks Lester was terrified that he would do just that.

"Lester, I am surprised that you are running. You were such a good guy on the Gatsby set and you helped me, especially when those men tried to kidnap me. What made you change?" I asked, trying to sound neutral.

"I'm not running, I'm going to the store" Lester replied.

"With a suitcase full of clothes?" I asked. Viktor was standing behind Lester and pulled his coat partly down behind him, trapping his arms. Evelyn reached into Lester's coat pocket and pulled out a train ticket to New York. Lester looked down, defeated. There was not much he could say. I felt sorry I had to put pressure on him. "You and Foster Pell were friends, was he the one who told you to get out of Los Angeles?"

"Yes" Lester said with a sigh. "He sent me money to buy the ticket and said I needed to disappear and he would tell me when I could come back. He said if I did not go to New York, someone would come to question me and torture me to get answers. Are you going to torture me?"

I laughed. "No Lester, I like you and will not torture you. But this is important and if you don't level with us, Viktor might. Lester, I need your help. Do you trust me?"

"Yes, yes I think I do. You were always nice to me and everyone else. That Buster guy was too when he said you were his girlfriend. He gave me a big tip to be quiet about you going to his trailer at night when I checked the tents on the Gatsby shoot." As soon as he said the words he realized it was the wrong thing to say. I glanced at Dan and he remained calm. I should have known that my affair with Buster was not going to go away quietly.

"Let's leave that subject for now. I made a mistake and learned from it. I am not now nor ever was Buster's girlfriend, OK?"

"Yes, Mrs. Lindner. I'm nervous and scared. Listen, Mr. Lindner, I don't know what the hell I'm talking about, and I'll never say anything like that again. I'm sorry."

"That's OK Lester. Laure told me everything and we trust each other. And Lester, Laure would very much appreciate your help by telling her about Foster Pell" Dan said, sounding calm and sincere, while Viktor stood nearby with a menacing look.

"Yes sir, I'm worried because Foster said whoever asked me about leaving L.A. would hurt me to get me to talk. Then he said he would hurt me if I did talk, so now I just want to leave town and never think about any of this again. Foster seemed nice on the Gatsby set but now I'm afraid of him. He threatened to beat me up real bad if I didn't leave town. I don't even know what I could say that would be so damn important to get beat up over. I had to quit my job with Famous Players. I liked my job, so I'm upset about that too. Foster said I was not to tell Mr. Brenon why I was leaving. Mr. Brenon said he didn't want me to quit and he wanted to know why but I couldn't tell him. I did a good job for Mr. Brenon. Now what am I gonna do?"

"Lester, we promise not to beat you up or hurt you, but we will protect you if you agree to go where my friends can protect you until this trouble is resolved. It will not be jail, it will be pleasant surroundings with good people, but you have to stay there to be safe. Laure will fix it with Mr. Brenon so you can get your job back when this is over, and we will pay for your return to Los Angeles. Will you do that for us?" Dan asked.

"That big mean looking guy is really your Uncle Viktor?" Lester asked Laure.

"Yes, he is my father's brother. He is here to help me because evil people want to harm me. As long as you don't try to hurt me, Viktor will not hurt you, in fact he will protect you." Viktor nodded and tried to smile, which just made him look more menacing. Evelyn went to Viktor and put her arm in his, which softened his appearance.

"OK, I'll help. What do you want to know?" said Lester, still nervous.

"Lester, I'm hungry and it's lunchtime. Let's get sandwiches and we can sit in the park and talk where there are lots of people around. How's that sound?" Dan asked, seeking to loosen Lester up to speak freely.

"Sounds great Mr. Lindner. Say, can Laure really fix me up with Mr. Brenon? I liked working for him and learning the movie business. I want to be a director someday."

"If you like we can go over there right after lunch and you can sit in the meeting. Laure will talk to Mr. Brenon and I believe he will be glad to have you back on the job when this is over" Dan said.

"OK, let's get lunch" Lester said, and we went to a diner and ordered hamburgers and fries, salad for Evelyn and Laure and a hamburger for them to split, and iced tea to drink. We went to a park with picnic tables, ate our food and Lester told us everything he knew. He said that Foster told him he was in with some people who were working on a con job to make a lot of money, and Foster said he would give some to Lester if he followed orders. Then Foster threatened him, which confused and scared him.

When Lester asked what was happening, Foster told him that Laure and Dan were trying to kill him, but why we would do that he never said. Foster said that his boss was going to fix the problem by driving Dan and me out of Hollywood, and if that didn't stop us, we were going to have some sort of accident.

"Did Foster say what that accident might be, or when it would happen?" I asked.

"No, he didn't say what the accident would be, but he said that by the end of summer it would all be over. He said his boss was doing stuff to scare you, to make you nervous so you would make mistakes. That way when you died people would think it was an accident. Then Foster's new friends were going to put you both in Chicago overcoats. I know it gets cold in Chicago so I thought that an overcoat would be a good thing there. But the way he said it sounded dangerous, and when he realized he told me too much, he ordered me to keep my trap shut."

"Foster liked to be the big man in charge and he let it get to his head when he could step on other people. Foster met his new friends not too long after the Gatsby movie wrapped. He was sore that Mr. Brenon would not give him a recommendation to become a first assistant director, telling him he had not done a professional job on the set. So when the bad people came to Foster he jumped in with both feet. He made it sound like these powerful and dangerous people came to him to solve their problems. I thought he was full of horsefeathers, but I did not tell him that. He was getting mean and slapped me around, so I kept my mouth shut around him." Now that Lester had relaxed with us, he let it all out.

"Lester, a Chicago overcoat is a coffin. Did Foster describe his new friends that he was working for, or with?" Dan asked.

"Yeah, I even saw some of them. There was a bunch of guys who looked like really mean gangsters. Just like the gangsters in the movies, except these guys were scary even without makeup. But they wasn't the brains, they was just the muscle. Foster said he was the brains and could control the gang because he was smarter than them. I didn't figure it that way but I kept my mouth shut, you see? There was a big boss but I never seen him or her. This big boss was like a ghost, rarely appearing to Foster and a few other gangster types" Lester said.

"Him or her? What makes you say that?" I asked.

"Like I said, I never seen the big boss, who had some kind of voice problem and didn't talk like normal people. It was evil sounding. I heard it once, when I went with Foster to a meeting and I was inside the abandoned house where they met. Only Foster knew I was inside. It was cold and there were bad guys in the neighborhood who might beat or kill me just for fun. Foster said I could come inside, but I had to be quiet as a churchmouse. It seemed like whenever I was with Foster, he was telling me people wanted to kill me when I done nuthin' to them. I was hiding in another room and Foster didn't think I could hear them talk, but there were holes in the walls and I could. The voice sounded like a machine, real creepy and shrill. I was learning from the voice coaches about voices, y'know, I learn everything I can from the smart people.

Funny, I never learnt anything from Foster except that I was gonna get beat up" Lester said.

"You were saying about the voice" I prompted.

"Oh yeah, the voice was like screeching metal or something unnatural. But like I said, I learnt a lot about voice coaching and how to listen to someone with a bad voice to coach them to get better. Y'know, they say that not too long from now we will have talking movies. Wouldn't that be something, eh?"

"Lester, please tell me why you said him or her when you were referring to the big boss" I asked again. Lester liked to ramble.

"Yeah, I was learning voice coaching and underneath the metal screeching I thought it could be a woman's voice. But who ever heard of a woman running a gang? Women couldn't do that."

It got real quiet as Lester realized he had put his foot in his mouth again. "No, I didn't mean you Mrs. Lindner, or you, Miss Evelyn. You sure could run a gang. Heck, I'd follow you. I just meant women are too weak to boss a bunch of gangsters." Lester finally figured out that he should stop talking.

"Enough of that" I said. "Tell me more about why you think the voice was that of a woman."

"Like I said, I learned to listen to the person's voice, to identify each part of it to find out what needed to be trained to make the voice better, clearer or sexier. When talking movies come, a lot of actors and actresses are going to be out on their keisters. At least that's what most of the voice coaches are saying. But I could be wrong, maybe it was a male voice. I just remember the first time I heard it, my first impression what that it was a woman's voice. Sorry I can't describe it better, but it was a terrible sounding voice no matter whose voice it was. It gave me the heebie-jeebies and I hope I never hear it ever again."

"Thank you Lester. You have been very helpful. I called from the restaurant and we can go see Mr. Brenon this afternoon, but after that we must ask you to go with

Viktor and Evelyn up to Northern California, where we can arrange for you to live temporarily with a nice family until we get this problem resolved. Until then it would be dangerous for you to stay in Hollywood or anywhere in the Los Angeles area" I said.

"Do I have to go with Uncle Viktor? Why can't I go with you?"

"Lester, in this family, the big man listens to me" Evelyn said. "I won't let him hurt you unless you do something stupid."

"But you're so little, and he is so big. How could you stop him?"

"Lester, you should listen to Evelyn, because I listen to her" laughed Viktor.

We then went to see Brenon, who I knew to be a reasonable man and I had asked him in advance to re-hire Lester, and that I would explain it to him when we got there. Brenon knew the sabotage problems that we had on the *Road Trip Blues* movie locations. I described the situation to him and he agreed to re-hire Lester as soon as everything cleared up. Lester's mood brightened considerably and he even started to joke with Viktor.

Dan and I talked it over later. Lester had not told us very much we did not already know, but since we had next to nothing to go on it seemed like a lot. We contacted Giuseppe, only saying on a public telephone that we were inviting him to dinner when we returned. It was a little more crowded in the Chrysler than on the way down, but we made it. I arranged with the Montanari family for Lester to live with them for a few weeks, and if it didn't work out we could move him to other friends over in Sonoma County. I offered to pay Vincenzo but he refused, saying that's what friends did for each other. He was very happy and proud that his daughter Josefina was now a partner in The LaureDan Company and glad to do us a favor. Vincenzo was even more pleased when Lester offered to work while he stayed with the family.

I sent a telegram for Bill not to go to Los Angeles, but he had already left. When I got to talk to him I asked him to look in on Mabel and Marigold and let me know if they needed anything. What I did not know was that he was already there.

We arrived in St. Helena late in the day and Giuseppe was there early the next morning. Sunny and Elsie set out fruit, brioche, pastries and Italian coffee. Lester told Giuseppe his story, which he did a lot easier than before now that he felt better about his future. When Lester finished, I asked Elsie to take him to the Montanari ranch.

We sat outside in the light morning breeze, enjoying our coffee. "Lester's speculation that the Tin Voice might be a woman is interesting" Giuseppe said. That certainly had our attention. But a woman? We could not think of a woman we had so completely angered that she swore a vendetta on us. It was definitely not Gina, Giuseppe assured us of that.

I asked Giuseppe a question that had been bothering me for several weeks. It seemed unlikely, but so many things that had happened were unlikely. "Is it possible that Pádraigh is still alive? He came back from the dead once before, you know."

Giuseppe had thought of that too, and had asked Gina. She said that he was most assuredly dead; she checked his body before she left the hotel. He had been shot twice at close range by me, poisoned by Bill and Meghan, and his throat cut by Gina. Any one of those would have caused his death. I thought he was near death before I escaped from the room. Bill told Giuseppe the type and amount of poison he and Meghan administered, and he agreed it was more than enough to do the job. Gina told Giuseppe that before she left the hotel room after cutting him, she checked his pulse and there was none, nor was there any blood coming from his neck wound which would have been the case if his heart was still pumping. Before Dan and I departed from Cherryvale, the Montgomery County sheriff's office and the county medical examiner had taken the body to a local funeral home where it was put in cold storage for three days before they released it. All the evidence was clear. Pádraigh died in Cherryvale that day. But if Pádraigh was dead, who was trying to destroy us?

A call came from the Famous Players-Lasky studio office asking for Dan. He went to our office to take the call, coming out a few minutes later to say that Lasky's secretary called because he wanted to meet with Dan about a movie project. Dan told the secretary that they had just returned home and he would be down next week. She pressed him to return earlier because the project needed help now, but Dan held out. He was glad he did that because the next call was from Big Al, telling him that they would be coming up the Napa rails in two days with our Duesenbergs, barring any unexpected delays.

The next day Luigi came in, wearing his Marine uniform. Maj. Griffin had sent him to check on me and to stop at any other places in the county that might concern the Marine MPs, such as speakeasies. Griffin had told Luigi to return in two days with his findings. This was Griffin's way of giving Luigi a visit with his fiancé. Josefina was in our office and they had a grand reunion. Their relationship was lustful, a lot like how Dan and I were, and I wouldn't stand in the way of that.

Two days later Big Al and the Swedes sent a telegram that they were an hour from Rutherford Station where there was a siding with a ramp where they could unload the cars. The cars arrived in perfect condition. Luigi was still in the area and he drove us to the station. The boattail speedster was the first off. Dan was being the perfect gentleman offered it to me, knowing I liked fast automobiles as much as he did. But it was his reward, and I pushed him behind the wheel and took our new sedan. The Duesenbergs told us that the automobiles were regular production with the improved Model X Straight Eight but when Dan started it, we could hear the whine of a supercharger. We opened the hoods to find that the Duesenberg brothers had installed superchargers on both of our new automobiles. Dan said I had a radiant smile on my face when I saw the superchargers. He knew me well.

We had a romantic dinner the evening before Dan left for Hollywood. He set everything up, candles and all. He grilled the steaks while Sunny prepared the side dishes. During dinner, he kept looking at me, so I said "You really didn't have to put on a full seduction for me tonight, you know I'm a sure thing."

"I like to keep in practice at seducing you, and even after nine months I still can't believe how lucky I am to be married to the love of my life. You're posilutely the caterpillar's spats."

"Posilutely? Caterpillar's spats? Since when do you speak Flapper?"

"Since the night we danced at Café Lulu and made love for the first time at The Mayfair Hotel in St. Louis. Every now and then I even say Rhatz."

MEETING AT STUDIO 9

Dan was up early the morning after our romantic dinner with a ravishing for dessert. When I woke up, he was shaving and I went downstairs. A small vase of fresh wildflowers sat on the kitchen table. Dan must have picked them earlier that morning. The note said:

"You are smart, beautiful, and sexy and at least a thousand other wonderful things. I will always love you. Dan."

I made breakfast for us and set it out on our patio in the sunshine of the cool morning. "Laure, where are you?" he called.

"Just follow the smell of the fresh coffee to the patio Sweetie" I called back. He was there in a lickety-split second, grabbed me up from the chair and planted a sensuous kiss on my lips. "I can hardly walk this morning and you want more?" I teased.

"Yes, because I am such a guy, as you well know."

"You're an animal, but I'll miss you because your beautiful wildflowers melted my cold hard heart." He looked pleased that I liked the flowers. At breakfast our house chef Sunny joined us and a few minutes later Elsie arrived with her boyfriend Darcy. In our house, our employees ate with us.

We laughed and chatted and passed around the *Napa Register*. I had never talked to Darcy outside of his job as a waiter at one of our favorite restaurants in Napa. He seemed a nice enough fellow, and was asking Dan and me questions about Hollywood and the movie business, saying he wanted to go down there some day and see about a studio job.

Dan loaded his suitcase and briefcase in the Duesenberg sedan, having prepared it for the trip the day before. The large black sedan looked menacing yet stately and rich. The Duesenberg Straight 8 supercharged motor purred as it warmed up.

We had been inseparable since the day I came back to him at the Union Station in St. Louis. I was uncomfortable when he was not next to me in our bed. Dan kissed me goodbye and I had such a horrible premonition I could not let go of him. "Sweetie, are you alright?" Dan asked.

"Oh I was just having a moment of anxiety. Do you really have to go?"

"I agreed to meet with Jesse Lasky at the studio, the secretary said there was an important movie project he wanted to talk to me about. Say, why don't you come with? I can wait while you pack and don't worry if you forget anything, we can get whatever you need in Los Angeles. I would love to have you with me, the trip promises to be boring but I'm never bored when we are together." He made it sound like it would be fun, and I was sure it would be, but then I thought I was being silly and worrying about nothing.

"I should stay here, there's lots of work to do with our LaureDan companies and Viktor is coming over to talk about what we want for our new house and garage if we start construction this year. Don't worry about me, I'm just missing you already" I said. We kissed again, Dan got into the sedan. Before he closed the door I leaned in and kissed him, and I wanted to jump into the car with him.

"I'll be back as soon as possible. I love you" Dan smiled.

"I love you too. Stay safe, don't take any risks."

"I won't, and when I come back we will celebrate something, I don't know what, any excuse will do" he grinned as I shut the door. Putting the Duesenberg in gear he accelerated slowly down our driveway. At the end he stopped, got out of the car and waved to me and I waved back. Then he was gone.

My feeling of doom and despair failed to clear up even though I threw myself into my work. I wanted to talk to someone in Hollywood, so I called Billie Dove. Her maid said she was on a movie shoot and would be back next week. Douglas Fairbanks was also on a movie location. I called Louise Brooks.

Eddie Sutherland answered and I told him who I was and asked for Louise. He said she was at the studio today and would be staying there overnight. Then he told me he wanted to come up and see me while our spouses were in Hollywood. I wanted to bang the telephone down but I politely told him I was not interested. Then I banged the telephone down. I thought about Louise spending the night in Hollywood, but remembered that Dan would not be there until sometime tomorrow.

I did not hear from Dan that evening, which did not worry me since he said he would call from the Famous Players-Lasky offices after the meeting. I decided to stop worrying and sat on the couch to read a novel.

Dan was staying at the Beverly Hills Hotel in a suite, saying if he was in our favorite Bungalow #5 he would miss me a lot more. Now I was wishing I had jumped in the Duesenberg and gone with him. Bungalow #5 was one of our special ravishing places.

Dan had an uneventful drive to Los Angeles but he knew something serious was bothering me because I was usually self-confident and did not allow things to get to me. He tried to think of what it might be, but we had been in good spirits the night before and he could not find a reason.

After checking into the Beverly Hills Hotel the next day, Dan called our LaureDan office to see if I was there. Josefina answered the telephone and told him I had gone to Napa to drop off our property reports at the banks and collect payments. Dan asked Josefina if there was something I was upset about. At first she didn't want to talk about it, but then told him. "Her intuition told her that something was not right and that you might be going into danger. She doesn't get like that very often. You know, sometimes women get these feelings and all too often we are proven right. I'll tell her you arrived OK."

"Thank you Josefina, tell her that and that I love her and will be back as soon as possible, and I will be careful. There was a note for me at the front desk to go to the studio and meet with Lasky as soon as I arrived, so I will do just that. I told Laure I would call after the meeting or first thing in the morning if it runs late. Everything going well with you and Luigi?"

"Oh Mr. Lindner, it could not be any better. He's thoughtful and kind, a gentleman in public but his hot Italian lover comes out when we are together. And to think I would not have met him if Laure and I had not been kidnapped and you had not gone to the Marine MPs at Mare Island for help. You and Laure are our role models. We are waiting until Luigi gets his discharge from the Marines so we can get married and we want both of you to be at our wedding."

"Thank you Josefina, we want to be there too. I'm sure it will be a great wedding with lots of fun, food, wine and dancing."

"You can be sure of that. My parents love Luigi almost as much as I do and they are putting on a big traditional Italian wedding. Good-bye, sir. Hope you're home soon."

"Count on it. Good-bye" Dan replied.

In a decrepit old house in one of the worst parts of Los Angeles, several gangsters were gathered. Some of them were nervous, not liking or trusting their new boss, but all of them were afraid to back out, having been paid in advance and threatened with dire consequences if they failed. The money had been good, more than good in fact, and these types of people always took the well-paying jobs as soon as they heard about them. They were uneasy because they felt more danger from the boss than the victims.

A man came into the room followed by a shadowy figure covered in what appeared to be a hooded monk's robe. This was their boss, and from the appearance there didn't seem to be much to worry about, but they knew what happened to those who failed this boss. The lights at the front of the room were turned off so they could not see his face, and bright lights shined on the assembled group, making it difficult to get a good look at their boss.

The cloaked figure started talking in a shrill metallic voice. It was worse than listening to fingernails on a chalkboard, and the words were hardly anything to make them feel easier. Details of the job were assigned, threats issued, and the usual offer for anyone who wanted to leave, to leave now. They all knew that anyone who got up to leave would be dead before they made it through the door.

As the plan unfolded, they regained some of their confidence because it was a simple snatch, grab and deliver the victim to the boss. What could possibly go wrong?

CAUGHT IN THE NET

Dan narrates

After lunch and a change from traveling clothes to a business suit, I was on my way to the new Famous Players-Lasky Studio location on Marathon Street. It was an impressive location, much larger than the previous studio on Vine Street near Sunset Boulevard. The guard at the gate must have been new because I had not seen him before, but the studio was growing as it geared up to make more movies. I thought it unusual that the gate guard did not have me sign in, but since Lasky's secretary called me to the meeting maybe I was on a special list. The gate guard gave me a pass to put in the windshield of the Duesenberg and directions to Studio 9.

I drove around the new studio to get familiar with it, and who should I see but Louise Brooks in a publicity photo shoot at the historic old barn, where *The Squaw Man*, the first Jesse L. Lasky film and the first feature length film made in Hollywood was filmed in 1914. The historic barn had been carefully disassembled and reconstructed on the new studio property. Louise was on a ladder in a fur-trimmed coat pretending to dab paint on the building while photographers snapped their cameras. I decided not to stop because I did not want to get in the way, and I thought that in the black Duesenberg sedan Louise would not recognize me.

At Studio 9 I parked the Duesenberg and entered through the main door. There was no activity in the studio, which seemed rather strange. Why would Lasky want to meet in a vacant studio? I briefly thought about going back to the Duesenberg to get my M1911, which I had left locked in a small safe under the seat but I went ahead to take a quick look around just in case Lasky was in the back of the studio. I did not get more than thirty feet inside when a large net dropped from above and trapped me. I knew not to get into a frenzy but calmly tried to find an edge to crawl under to get out. Suddenly six men rolled me up in the net and carried me through a door. "OK, tell Fairbanks to call off the prank" I said loudly, thinking this was something that he would think up. Douglas was a notorious prankster and had helped turn Louise's prank into my becoming a movie producer. Fairbanks told me it was the best prank he had ever successfully carried out. So here I was being carried out but I didn't fight it, figuring that Fairbanks, Mary Pickford and Billie Dove would soon be laughing uproariously when I was dumped on the floor in front of them.

But to my surprise, instead of being dumped on the floor in front of a laughing Fairbanks, I was carried out another door and directly into the back of a panel truck. The rear door was open and I was made to sit on a bench on the right side. Men reached through the net to put handcuffs and leg chains on me. This was not a Fairbanks prank. These men did not look like a studio crew and acted like gangsters. Two men stayed in the back of the van, sitting across from me. The engine started and the truck began to move. One of them cut a link of the net, reached in and shoved a piece of cloth in my mouth so I could not call for help.

'This wasn't a prank nor a meeting with Jesse Lasky. I should have taken Laure's intuition more seriously and carried my 1911' I thought to myself, but managed to stay calm.

I heard the sounds of cars and trucks and the shouts of newsboys hawking their papers on the street corners as well as screeching tires now that the truck seemed to be speeding quite rapidly. Suddenly there were horns honking, the truck slewing around as it braked hard. The truck hit something with a loud crumpling of metal and breaking glass. It tilted and then tipped over on the side I was on, so I was laying on my back on the wall. Both of the goons sitting across from me landed to my right when their bodies flew through the air before they came to a stop. *That was close, if they had landed on me I would have been severely injured.* One of them was motionless after hitting his head on a metal rail. The other thug hit the wall next to me with a thump and was moaning, his leg twisted at an unnatural angle.

My hopes were raised because a bad accident like this would bring the police. Sounds of angry shouting came from outside the truck but there were so many voices I could not make out much of what was said. Two police sirens approached and started to wind down when the cars stopped nearby. An authoritative voice called out "Stop. You're under arrest!" The next sounds were those of fighting, police batons and brass knuckles striking flesh along with a moan that sounded like someone being stabbed. This was answered with gunfire, more screaming and moaning, the sounds of breaking glass, bodies hitting automobile fenders or the pavement. More gunfire, then it became quiet. Even the normal street noise was silenced.

Someone began to pry the van's rear door open. The truck body must have buckled when the truck fell on its side. The door lowest to the ground dropped down and two men crawled in but they were gangsters, not cops. The bodies next to me were pushed aside so they could carry me out of the van and two other gangsters went in. It sounded like they were checking the injuries of the men that had been in the back of the truck. I heard a gunshot from inside the truck, then a man's voice begging for his life, silenced by the sound of a second shot. They must have killed their own gang members because they could not leave them to be arrested and interrogated, and they were too badly injured to be moved.

There were spectators but they were moving away after the sounds of the shots and gangsters were pouring gasoline around the truck. One of them threw a lit cigar into the pool of gasoline and the truck burst into flames. I would have called for help but the gag was still in my mouth. I tried to look around, but did not recognize any familiar buildings. I saw the bodies of four policemen being thrown into their patrol cars and they were doused with gasoline and torched. Burn the evidence to throw off the investigators, who might initially think there was a multiple collision and the vehicles caught fire. It could take hours for them to arrive at the true cause of the deaths. By that time the gang would have taken me a long way away from here.

They carried me about two city blocks, down another street for a block when a large Buick sedan came down the street. Three gangsters forced the driver to stop at gunpoint and an elderly lady was pulled from the automobile and pushed rudely to the curb. The car's back door opened and I was thrown in the back seat face down. Two gangsters sat in the rear jump seats, two more got into the front and drove off fast. About twenty minutes later the driver began cursing as the engine quit. It sounded to me like the automobile had run out of gas. The gangsters pulled over and in a few minutes had stolen another automobile and I was stuffed into another rear seat. I was beginning to get the idea that these thugs had not worked together before and were nervous and scared. In fact, one of the thugs took off running down an alley. The gangsters took a couple shots at him but did not chase him. Maybe they didn't have a leader, but someone had to be in charge to set this elaborate trap to catch me.

By making small movements I managed to turn my body and head so I could see up out of the car's windows. So far I had not been able to identify any buildings or landmarks when one of the mugs caught me looking. "Foster – pull over and get some newspapers, quick-like."

"No names you idiot" and I wondered if that was Foster Pell's voice. The driver pulled up at the next corner where there was a newsboy shouting his newspapers. One of the thugs from the rear seat got out, ran up to the boy, grabbed the kid's newspapers and hustled back to the automobile. The kid started shouting "Help, thief!" when someone in the front seat shot at the newsboy, who was killed, wounded, or scared quiet. I hoped it was the latter.

The back seat thugs spread the newspapers over me so I could not easily be seen. A gang of thugs with sub-standard intelligence had kidnapped me. That meant they were more dangerous.

They drove for three hours, stopping at a gas station to buy gas and gas cans to extend the range of the car. Later the car turned onto a rough road, probably a farm track from the barnyard smells. The two goons in front, one of whom I thought was Foster Pell, got out and went to the ramshackle farmhouse.

When they came back, orders were whispered and they were careful not to use names. I was pulled from the back seat, the net cut away and I stood there in handcuffs and leg chains. Someone put a black cloth blindfold over my eyes and tied it behind my head. We went inside and I told them I needed to take a piss. They had to go ask someone in the back of the house. He came back and said "The boss says I got to go in there with you and hold your dick."

"You want to hold my dick? What kind of banana oil is that?"

"The boss don't want you seein' out the window."

"Is there a window in the bathroom?" I asked. The dumb dope went to look.

"No, there's no window in the bathroom."

"Then just get me through the door and take off the blindfold, close the door, and wait outside the door. I'll use the toilet and knock on the door when I'm done. I'll stand with my face to the wall so you can put the blindfold back on, even though I have already seen your faces." I felt ashamed for having been captured by what had to be the dumbest criminal enterprise in the United States.

This was confirmed when he said "I'll have to go ask the boss first" and went down the hall. The idiot evidently did not realize that I was in the room alone. I tried to slide a wrist from the handcuffs but they were too tight. A door slammed and the thug was back.

"Nah, the boss says I gotta hold your dick while you piss." He led me to the bathroom, pushed me in but before he could get in behind me I turned my body and elbowed him as hard as I could in the stomach. "Ooof" he said as he went down. I listened and he wasn't moving. Bending my head down as far as possible to my hands, I managed to pull the blindfold off. I got on my knees and checked his coat pockets, found a handcuff key and got them off, but it did not work on the leg chains. I stood at the toilet and took a much needed piss. I thought of pissing on the guy, but decided against it. I might need a stupid guard once I figured out an escape plan. I put the handcuffs back on and the key in my pocket. I put the blindfold on the guard, then threw water on his face from the sink. He woke up. "Who turned the lights off?" he moaned.

I kicked his leg and said "Take the blindfold off asshole, and give me your gun so you don't shoot yourself."

He pulled the blindfold off and said "Hey, you're the captive and you're calling me an asshole?"

"Well, you've got a point there. What's your name?"

"Sylvester" he said, then he thought about it. "But maybe that's not my real name."

"OK Sylvester" I said. "What should I call you?"

He looked was as stupid as he looked. "Well, I guess you can call me Sylvester but not when we go in to see the boss. You're not supposed to know anything about us."

"I don't know anything about you. Who is the boss?"

He started to move his mouth but clamped it shut. "I can't tell you."

"OK, then I'll just call him Asshole" I said.

"No! No, don't call the boss that. You'll be tortured and killed, and me too." Just call the boss, 'The Boss', OK?"

"OK. I'm tired and hungry. Where's the kitchen?"

"The boss is having food brought in. You'll have to wait like the rest of us. Go sit in that chair." Then he realized he had not put the blindfold on me. He put it back on, but he didn't do a very good job. Sylvester had not checked his pocket for the handcuff key.

There was a dull roar of voices arguing somewhere in the house. I managed to push the blindfold up when Sylvester wasn't looking. A car drove up and I could see out the bottom of the blindfold as a drunken gangster came staggering in with a bag of sandwiches and two pie boxes. I was led to a table and the drunk sat me down. "There's a sandwich on a plate in front of you. Better eat before the boss asks for you. That sandwich might be your last supper, so enjoy it." He left the room and I felt around and picked up the cheese sandwich. Neither the bread nor the cheese smelled fresh. I smelled the pies nearby so I dropped the sandwich and felt around the table. I had to stand up and lean to reach, but no one said anything, so Sylvester must have left the room. I found a pie, already sliced. I pulled a piece out with my hand and tasted it. Apple pie, and smelled fresh so I ate it. I was still hungry.

I felt around the table again and found the other pie. I took a slice in my hand and sniffed. Blueberry pie. I ate a slice. I was thinking about going for another slice when I heard footsteps and a new voice said "What are you doing? Who said you could have pie? You're supposed to have one cheese sandwich."

"Pie? Someone else had pie. A guy came into the room and I smelled pie and then heard someone eating."

"Don't try to con me, I'm not as stupid as these idiots. The trail of crumbs goes right to you." This sounded like the Foster Pell character.

"Someone must have sat here before I was pushed into this chair. Can I have some pie now? I'm hungry." I wanted more pie, even though I might be shot and killed in the next five minutes. I thought about Laure. '*How would she react when she was told of my death, face down in a blueberry pie?*' Just then there were more steps, sounded like four or five people sitting down at the table.

"Take the prisoner over to the couch while we eat" ordered Foster. Hands pulled me from the chair and dropped me on a couch. The others were eating pie. No one ate the sandwiches. I thought about recommending the blueberry pie over the apple pie, but decided against it. No need to hasten my death by being a smartass.

They left the room and I was told to lie on the couch by a guard who was watching me. I was tired and almost fell asleep but the sound of someone snoring kept me awake. By rubbing my head on the couch I was able to slide the blindfold up enough to peek. I couldn't see very much but it was better than being completely blind. The pies were gone, leaving only the stale cheese sandwiches.

Someone told me to wake up if I wanted breakfast. It was the Foster Pell voice. "Hey Foster, I have to use the bathroom for more than a piss."

He didn't deny the name, so it must be Pell. He moved me to the bathroom but this time instead of trying to come in with me he just pushed me in. "Hey Foster, how about freeing up a hand so I can wipe my ass?" Foster came in and opened the cuff on my right hand.

I was waiting for that and swing around to coldcock him, when another voice said "You try it and I'll cut your hand off." I heard the sound of a switchblade flicking open. It was last night's drunken gangster, looking hung over but able to see what I had planned. I sat down, did what I needed to do and cleaned up. "How about getting me a toothbrush?"

"Fuck you."

"That's not very nice. You mean to tell me that I can't brush my teeth?" I asked.

"If you can find a toothbrush in there, go ahead and use it. That's what we do." I decided to have dirty teeth today.

Pell, despite his denial, was as dumb as the other gangsters because he had not locked the handcuff, so I pulled it around my wrist under my suit coat but didn't lock it. No one bothered to check as I was led to the table and two pieces of bread were put in my hand. "No coffee?" I asked. Pell poured something into a mug and put it in front of me. "How about cream and sugar?" I asked.

"Drink the fuckin' coffee black or don't drink it. This ain't no fuckin' diner."

I drank some, and learned the truth in the old saying "Never think things can't get worse, because they will." This was worse than the swill they served in the commissary on *The Great Gatsby* location, but I drank it because there wasn't anything else.

I had all my senses on alert looking for more stupidity from the guards that I could use to make my escape. But after the coffee I was taken out to the car by the guards, blindfolded and pushed into the back seat with one of them on each jump seat and a third next to me. I kept my hands down between my legs so it appeared I was handcuffed. We drove most of the day and arrived at a railyard, evidenced by the sounds of locomotives.

They took me out of the automobile and to a railcar, pushing me awkwardly up the stairs and inside. Someone opened another door and shoved me through, closing the door too quick for me to see anything. I was alone in the room so I took off the blindfold. It was pitch black in the room even though we had just come in from bright daylight. My right hand was still free so I felt around the door, but it was a metal clad door. I went around the room feeling along the walls. I found a small metal sink attached to the wall and a crapper next to it. Continuing to work my way around the room I there was a metal bunk attached to the opposite wall. Its major features were a thin mattress and a scratchy blanket. No pillow.

Then I found a window. It was covered with wood and smelled like fresh paint. They must have painted the window black and covered it with boards to keep me from breaking a window and jumping out. I managed to get a couple of fingers into a corner of a board, but it was fastened with screws, not nails so I could not easily pull it out. I decided to keep trying and got another finger behind the board and felt metal. There were wide flat metal straps under the boards, so even if I pulled the boards I couldn't get to the window. *"Rhatz!"*

An hour later, the railcar lurched as it was coupled to a train and soon it was moving steadily if not very fast. I had no idea where I was or what direction we were heading. I didn't know the time of day. Getting one end of a window board loosened I pushed my fingers to the glass. By scratching enough black paint off to see outside, I was able to determine that it was near sunset.

A key rattled in the lock and I barely got turned around in time to see a guard come in with a food tray. I did not recognize him but he appeared to be upset because I had taken my blindfold off. He set the tray down and put it back on me, tight. I couldn't see, but I sensed that he was moving before I felt his fist hit my gut. He was a hard hitter and I went down on my ass. The guard was angry and kicked me in the ribs and stomach a couple of times. He had set the food tray on the floor and I heard him kick the tray and the contents went flying around the room. Throughout his visit, he made no verbal sound except for some grunts before he left the room and locked the door.

I got up on my knees, my rib cage and stomach hurting. It hurt to stand so I felt around the floor to see where the food and tray had gone. The guard must have taken the tray, all that was on the floor was food. No dishes, no spoon. Whatever it was smelled horrible, I guessed it was soup and bread. Not wanting to lick soup off the floor, I ate the bread. There was nothing to drink since the soup would have washed down the stale bread. Taking off the blindfold, I crawled over to the bed, pulled myself up and laid down to let the pain in my ribs subside. It did not feel like anything was broken, but it sure was sore. I fell asleep, dreaming about Laure seducing me to stop me from going on the trip to Hollywood.

The train halted and I woke up. It sounded like a fuel and water stop. I looked through my little window scratch to see it was night. Later the train backed up and stopped, probably to throw the switch, then the train moved forward. Who were these people? Were they the ones who had sabotaged *Road Trip Blues*? Where were they taking me, and why? My only conclusion is that they wanted me alive, at least for now. If they wanted to kill me they would have done so already. I dozed fitfully but got no sleep.

By my reckoning two days had gone by. I had been locked in the small dark room for most of that time. The train, however, had only been in motion for about half the time. The rest of the time it sat on sidings waiting for the next connection. This told me that my captors did not have much clout with the railroads, like Pádraigh's gang had through his connection with Hymie Weiss and the North Side Chicago gang. I knew that having connections was essential for getting dispatch clearance for private railcars. Not knowing where they were taking me I had no idea how much longer I would be locked in this room, or what would happen when we arrived at wherever I was being taken.

The conditions were miserable. The next day my fat, sadistic guard noticed my right hand was free and secured the cuff back on. He didn't even ask why it was loose and I decided he must be used to gross negligence on the part of the other goons. The room stank of spoiled food, and the room was hot as the railcar sat in the sun. Twice during the day I pounded on the door demanding water and relief. It took a long time until someone came. They had stopped forcing me to wear a blindfold when inside the room because I always took it off. When they took me outside, they made me wear a blindfold, and whoever put it on made sure I could not see anything as I was led off the train. By counting the voices, they always had four or more men guarding me. I could not see nor could I run because of the leg chains, and couldn't fight because of the handcuffs.

So far the only guard to come into the room was the same fat guy who knocked me down and kicked me. He blindfolded and knocked me down every time he came in, and he always threw my food on the floor. It did not make much difference because it smelled terrible. The bread was stale but I would crawl around to find it. I was able to drink some water by cupping my hand under the weak stream coming from the faucet at the sink and lapping it up. I knew the water was in the railcar's tank too long because it smelled bad and tasted worse. I refused to lick the floor to eat what the guard threw down even though my hunger was taking a toll on me, but my sadistic guard knew I eventually would have to lick the floor to survive.

There was no shaving, cleaning or bathing. I still had Sylvester's handcuff key, and checked it to make sure it worked. Since the day I had taken the key from Sylvester, no one searched me, so either Sylvester was embarrassed and did not want to tell anyone he had lost the key, or he was just so dumb he forgot about it.

I had to keep my mind disciplined for whatever was coming. Laure must know that I am missing since I should have called her. But how would she know where to look for me? She would call the studio. That's when I recalled that I had not recognized the gate guard, and he did not ask me to sign in. I thought of the gang as a band of dumb misfits, but someone had created a brilliant plan to make me disappear. My heart sank as I realized Laure might never find me, so I had to make an escape plan.

The next day the railcar was coupled to a train and it was moving somewhat faster than before. This morning the fat guard began a new routine. He would call for me to put the blindfold on. If he came in and the blindfold was not on he would quickly back out and lock the door. I couldn't see much because with my eyes accustomed mostly to darkness, it hurt when there was a bright light, and he had a flashlight that he would shine in my eyes so I had very little idea what he looked like except that he was shorter than me and much heavier. This day the train traveled until mid-afternoon and was making a stop for coal and water. It began to get hot inside my cell.

The guards brought me outside to a picnic table, grumbling but careful not to say anything that would give me a clue. Someone gave me a sandwich and I ate it. It tasted like something found while grubbing around in the garbage behind a grocery store. It was not fresh, but at least it had not been on my filthy cell room floor.

The locomotive whistle sounded and I was hustled back inside the railcar and into my cell. Now I had an escape plan. I unlocked the handcuffs but left them sitting on my wrists to look like the handcuffs were on if the guard didn't look too close. When the fat guard came in with food, I pulled the blindfold off just as he was throwing the food tray on the floor.

I pulled the cuffs off and rushed him hard and fast, hitting him when he was turned and slightly bent over. As we dropped to the floor I took hold of the tray firmly in both hands, rolled away and jumped to my feet. He got up and pulled his fist to give me a roundhouse punch, which gave me time to hit him on the nose with the metal tray as hard as I could. He reacted by putting his hands in front of his face so I flicked my foot and tripped him onto his back. His heavy body hit hard enough to knock the breath out of him. I jumped on his chest with my knees and heard ribs crack. I smashed the heavy metal tray hard on his face. He swore in surprise and I knew he would give me a beating if I did not win this fight.

With that desperate thought I continued to smash the tray again and again on his face and head as he tried to squirm. He raised his fists to punch me but he was weakening. He began to swing a big punch, but as his fist came up I slammed the heavy tray down to strike his fist as hard and fast as I could. Something cracked, and his wrist was useless after that.

I took a chance to lift my knees from his chest and drop back down, landing one knee on his stomach and by chance the other knee landed on his groin. Now he was really hurt and angry, but I was fired up with adrenalin and the possibility of escape. I banged the heavy metal tray on his head and face and until his nose was broken and his face a bloody mess. His breath was coming in short shallow gasps with one fist flailing around but it was doing no harm. The fat guard finally managed to knock the tray out of my hands but I kept hitting him with my fists until his groaning stopped. I watched for signs of movement. His eyes were still and glassy, blood was coming out of his nose and mouth, but he was breathing.

I had nearly beaten him to death but did not feel the least bit guilty. Searching the guard's pockets I found a key but it didn't work on the leg cuffs, so I searched in the guard's other pockets and found a small jackknife. I got up slowly, listening for the sounds of other guards, but it was quiet outside the room.

Looking around the corner of the doorway, I saw there was no one in the outer room. There was food on another tray, probably his dinner. His food was not much better than what I had, but not having had much to eat for the last few days I felt energized by it.

Searching the desk for a key to the leg chains, I found a small tin in a desk drawer, and I was rewarded with the discovery of several keys inside. One of them fit the leg chain locks. Freedom! I checked the guard again and found he was still breathing. His weight was mostly from fat so he ran out of energy soon after my surprise attack commenced. The heavy metal tray that he dumped my food from was the instrument of my retribution.

I found no weapons in the outer room. All I had was the cheap little knife. My wrists and ankles were raw but there were no cuts, just bruises and soreness. 'So now, what to do?' I thought to myself. Jumping from the train seemed to be the best idea even though I did not know where I was and the train was moving fast enough to concern me if I could not roll fast enough. Looking around the room, I tried to find anything that would tell me who these people were. The guard had a wallet with two dollars in it and a union membership card in a railway clerk union based in San Francisco. I put it back in his pocket. There was nothing else in the room I could use.

"Rhatz!" I said as the train began to slow down. A mixed blessing, the slower speed would allow me a safer jump, but it also meant the train was stopping and the gang would be getting off, leaving me less time to get away from the train. The door of the larger room opened to a corridor with no windows but there were five doors on one side and one at the end. I walked the corridor and tried each door only to find they were locked. The railcar was a design I had not yet seen, it was not a post office/package express car and not an executive car, nor a boxcar. I thought it might be a construction crew car, with small rooms for two or three men to each room and a larger room at the end for a foreman's room and office. My cell was one of the crew rooms.

I grabbed food to stash in my pockets, took the knife and went to the end door of the railcar. I reached for the doorknob just as someone was opening it from the other side. That someone was the most hideous apparition I could ever imagine. It smelled terrible and it was wearing a monk's heavy brown hooded robe tied with a rough rope. Instead of a face it had an ugly metal mask. Behind the apparition there were two thugs carrying Thompsons with large drum magazines. I slammed the door and engaged the lock. This was silly, with Thompsons the door would be sawdust in seconds, except the apparition was temporarily in their line of fire. I looked around and two more thugs were coming down the corridor from the opposite direction. I went to side window. It was stuck shut. Ripping a curtain from the window, I wrapped it around my hand and punched out the glass. The other guards were almost done breaking the doors down, but I had worked too hard for this moment. Luckily, I was thin from my forced diet so it was easy for me to defenestrate.

LAURE FOLLOWS THE TRAIL

* Laure narrates *

Dan had not called so I called the studio. Lasky was out of the office but expected back in the afternoon, so I talked to his secretary and left a message for him to call. I was getting sick with worry when a telephone call came from Jack Higgins, security chief for Famous Players-Lasky Studio. I feared the worst when Josefina summoned me to the telephone.

"Good morning Mrs. Lindner. I heard you called Mr. Lasky about a meeting with Dan, but Lasky did not have a meeting with Dan on his calendar so I smelled a rat and Lasky told me to investigate. Also, a new black Duesenberg sedan was parked overnight in the Studio 9 lot and no one was assigned to use Studio 9. My security office could not determine who owned the automobile because the registration plates were new and not yet in the files in Sacramento. I tried the driver's door and it was unlocked. Inside, I found the bill of sale to you and Dan. I asked around and no one knew if Dan was on the studio property, there was nothing at any of the studio gates to show he had entered. Someone told me to ask Louise Brooks and she told me she had seen Dan the day before as he was driving by the old historic barn where she was in a publicity photo shoot with Adolphe Menjou and some other Famous Player stars. She said Dan did not stop but kept going as if he had not seen her. So he was here, but no one has reported seeing him since."

Before he could go on I said "Dan thought he was going to meet Lasky for a movie project based on a telephone call from someone who represented herself as Lasky's secretary. Dan did not call yesterday as expected and I have been trying to find out what happened to him, but he has disappeared. I called Lasky's office and his secretary says she did not call Dan, nor has Lasky. I called the

Beverly Hills Hotel where he was staying. They told me he checked in but did not return to his room. I called the Los Angeles and Hollywood police but they told me it was too soon to file a missing person report. That's stupid, if someone is missing, the best time to find the person is right away and waiting a week or ten days lets the trail go cold. I expect there are policemen in both departments that are very annoyed with me for being cross with them. When you called I was packing to come down there."

"Laure, it would be a good idea for you to stay where you are, because there is evidence of foul play. Here's what I've learned. Someone rigged a net inside Studio 9. When I inspected the site, it appeared that the net was dropped, but it was gone except for some cut pieces still in the rigging. Normally the movie crews clean up things like that. I checked with the gate guard, but he was not on duty that day. He had gotten food poisoning the day before and called in sick, and a temporary guard from the agency was posted there for the day. As it turns out, the replacement guard only worked that one day and the agency can't locate him. It looks to me like someone arranged a guard change to put their own man inside. He let Dan in without signing the gate register, and Dan was captured at Studio 9" Higgins told me.

The chief continued "That same day, the Los Angeles police reported a truck crashed into another truck and tipped over. Men from the rolled truck pulled the driver of the other truck out and began to beat him. Two patrol cars arrived on the scene and according to witnesses the four patrolmen tried to make arrests but were beaten with their own nightsticks, shot and their bodies thrown into their patrol cars. The bad guys drained gas from the tanks, poured it on the vehicles and burned all of them with the bodies inside. Two bodies were in the back of the rolled truck, shot and burned. The police have not identified them yet, but their initial description does not fit Dan."

"That's not all. A few blocks away from the crash, a woman was pulled out of her Buick sedan and thrown to the curb and the assailants stole her car. She said the men put a net with something in it into the back seat of the Buick before they drove off. When questioned, she could not say for sure if there was a person in the net or not. About an hour later her Buick was found in the middle of a street, key in the ignition and no gas in the tank. Nearby, a man had his car stolen the same way the woman's Buick was taken. To make it worse, about two miles down the street from there, a newsboy was wounded by gunfire. He told the police that a man jumped out of a car, grabbed his newspapers and ran back to the car. It was a busy corner and the newsboy shouted for help. The man who got in the car produced a revolver and shot the newsboy, who is listed in serious condition at the hospital, but the surgery was successful and he is expected to recover. These random events strung together tell me that your husband has been kidnapped. Have you received any calls, ransom notes or any news from Dan?"

"No, nothing at all. Do you have any idea who could have done this?"

"No I do not" said Chief Higgins.

"Are you investigating this?" I asked.

"No, I am limited to actions taken on studio property, which would be the kidnapping, but the DA says we haven't even proved it was a kidnapping without witnesses or a ransom note. The Los Angeles police department is investigating the murder of four policemen, a truck driver, two men in the back of a burned truck, attempted murder of the newsboy, car and truck arson, the theft of two automobiles and the stolen truck."

"I'm coming down there" I said.

"Please don't do that just yet. If your husband is kidnapped, they could have done that to lure you here to kidnap you. I can't order you not to come here, but I hope you will take my advice and get some bodyguards and stay there. Let the police do their investigation. If you come here and the perpetrators grab you too, it makes their job harder, and you and Dan could both be killed" he said.

"Dan could be dead already, but I have a strong feeling that he is alive. I'm coming down there and I intend to conduct my own investigation. I am not going to sit on my ass while my husband is in danger, and I don't care if I'm in danger doing it. Staying here is not the answer. I am bringing my people, Bill, my Uncle Viktor and others. At least one of them will be with me at all times. I will be armed and I know how to take care of myself. I would like to meet with you when I get there to be updated on the situation, but I am not going to sit at home waiting."

"Well, I can't keep you from coming here, and Viktor and Bill certainly seem capable of protecting you. Come to my office when you get to the studio. I'll have your name on the gate guard's list and when you arrive I'll give you all the information I have and a contact name at the LAPD" Chief Higgins said.

"Thank you chief, I'll be there tomorrow."

"Tomorrow? Are you flying here?" he asked.

"No, we will be coming by automobile and taking turns driving. I'll see you tomorrow morning."

"OK, but please be careful. I like you and Mr. Lindner and don't want to see you have any more trouble. You've certainly had more than your share. Travel safe."

"Thank you chief, I will" I replied.

I called Uncle Viktor and told him what I had learned. He didn't say much, and I knew that meant he wasn't pleased with what I told him. He did not want me to go, but there was nothing he could do to stop me short of locking me up. Evelyn understood how I felt and told Viktor she was going too, whether he liked it or not. Viktor told me to bring my guns and he was going to pack for the trip. "My guns are cleaned and ready, Uncle Viktor. Luigi just finished checking over the red Duesenberg and it is ready to go. He arranged for emergency leave and wants to come with."

"That's good, he's a Marine so he knows how to commit violence when necessary and we may need some of that. I'll pick Bill up on the way over. Has anyone heard from Giuseppe yet?"

"No, Bill is our only contact to Giuseppe and he hasn't heard from him. See you in an hour Uncle Viktor. And thank you for all you've done for me. I don't know what I would do without you" I told him.

"You would do just fine. You certainly are just like my brother's daughter, smart, stubborn and passionate. Keep it under control and we will find out what's going on" Viktor said. I loved my Uncle Viktor as much as I loved my father. Well, they are brothers, smart, stubborn and passionate, and Viktor was right, I'm just like my father; at least the stubborn and passionate parts. There was no need to waste time sitting around when Dan needed me. He came for me when I was in trouble, now I'm coming for him and I'll send to Hell anyone who gets in my way.

Viktor, Bill and Evelyn arrived. I was glad for her to be with us because I might need a shoulder to cry on. *'Rhatz!'* I said to myself. *'No more thinking like that. Dan and I will be together again.'* My intuition told me that he was alive but in great danger. Dan told me that he sensed that I was near when he and the Marines boarded the ship to rescue me and the other kidnapped women in San Francisco, and now I sensed that Dan was alive.

Viktor told me that he called Jake, and he is going to leave tomorrow morning to fly out. "Should make it by the next day, because Claire is flying co-pilot and I've heard those two are getting the reputation of being the best aeroplane jockeys in Chicago". I was happy to have my Pa join us, but I knew he was building up his aeroplane business and had just begun selling as well as servicing them. Viktor said that he had trained technicians and a shop manager working for him now, so he could take a few days off. I also knew that just as Viktor could not stop me from going to Los Angeles, I would not be able to keep my father from coming to help.

Luigi went to Mare Island to get his leave pass, clothes and guns. We had to stop at Mare Island to pick up Luigi and that would make five of us in the Duesenberg. Since we had no lack of drivers and shooters I asked "Why don't we drive both the Duesenberg and the Chrysler, so we have two automobiles if we have to split up in Los Angeles? The Chrysler's in good condition and reasonably fast." So we did. Viktor and Evelyn offered to drive the Chrysler while Bill, Luigi and I roared down the road in the Duesenberg. It was faster than the Chrysler, but we couldn't use top speed on all the roads, and I calculated they would get there not much later than we would.

When my father had modified our red Duesenberg Model X Dual-Cowl Phaeton, he installed the most advanced main headlights available and a pair of the best driving lights linked to the steering gear so those lights turned with the wheel. This gave us a look at what we turned towards before we got there, and that is what saved us. I had just finished my shift at the wheel and turned it over to Luigi. As we came around a sharp curve the driving lights revealed a car in the middle of the road. Luigi was able to slide by the car without slowing down much, but it made me wonder who would park in the middle of the road?

Shots rang out after we passed the car and I heard a bullet hit the Duesenberg's body. That explained the bad parking job. I was already in a bad mood and I ducked down to get out of their line of sight and get my rifle. Luigi put the power on and the big Duesenberg Straight Eight was wailing its familiar and much-loved supercharger song. I set up to shoot but the Duesenberg accelerated so fast we were already out of range.

Bill said "Those trouble boys must have thought we would stop when they were in the middle of the road and they could shoot us as we sat in our automobile. Now the mugs are trying to chase us" and I looked back to see two guys jump in their car and the lights come on. Luigi said with the Duesenberg's power he could easily lose them, but Bill said "Let's slow down and let them get a little closer." I remembered Dan telling me how Bill liked to shoot the radiators and gas tanks in the cars and trucks when they ambushed the Capone 5 near Cherryvale. Sure enough, that's what he did. Bill got out his long barrel sniper rifle and before they got in their range of us, they were in his range. Three shots from Bill's rifle and their car stopped and both headlights were gone, coolant pooling under the radiator.

"Do you think they were highway robbers?" I asked.

"No, they were waiting in ambush for us" Luigi said.

"But how would they know when and where to wait for us? And they would have to know when we left" I said.

"I'm worried that we may have a snitch in our midst who is telling the other side what we are doing. Too many things have been too coincidental. Let's sneak back and take a look at them" Bill said.

Luigi, being a Marine and feeling the need to commit violence on those who tried to kill us agreed. Luigi switched off the Duesenberg's lights and pulled off the road around a curve where the other guys couldn't see us. We did not want to get too close because a red automobile, even at night, could be noticed. We took our rifles and Bill went down the east side of the road while Luigi and I took the west side, working our way among the trees and bushes by the side of the road. In a few minutes we were close enough to hear the guys talking but couldn't make out their words. Getting closer we could hear. "Boss ain't gonna like this. Boss wanted us to take them out. Now what are we gonna do? Can't go back and tell the boss we fucked up. We will get zotzed for that."

That confirmed it. These guys were part of the gang that was trying to sabotage our lives and kill us. I whispered to Luigi "They are worried about their boss killing them. We can solve their problem." Luigi smiled and made hand signs to Bill across the road, who nodded agreement. We moved up another ten feet. Then I had another idea, and whispered "Maybe we should catch and interrogate them, try to get some information."

"Do you really think they will voluntarily tell us anything? I've been in the Marine MPs long enough to know these kind of people won't talk. They kill or get killed, or go to prison if the cops catch them, but they won't talk. If they do, their own people kill them. The other thing is, if we waste time trying to get them to talk, we don't get to Los Angeles until late. You're the boss Laure, but if they find out we are close they will shoot to kill. We may be better shooters but even a bad shooter can get lucky."

I thought about it. We would have to sneak up to grab them, and even if we got them without getting ourselves injured, how long would it take to make them talk? "You're right Luigi, let's finish the job here and leave. We could be here all night and get nothing. I'm sick and tired of killing, but we know they were sent here to kill us, so they are not innocent tourists. Let's get this over with."

Coordinating by hand sign, Bill indicated he understood and was ready. Luigi opened fire when he had a clear shot, then Bill and I added our firepower. Luigi squeezed off a round and one of the men dropped. The other pulled his handgun but never had a chance to shoot before Bill finished the thug with one bullet. Bill and I crept slowly ahead while Luigi went back to bring up the Duesenberg in case we had to make a fast getaway. Bill and I watched the men for movement because they could be playing dead. We came up slowly and still seeing no sign of movement, I covered for Bill as he went closer to inspect the bodies. Both men were dead. Bill waved for Luigi to bring the Duesenberg. When the headlights flooded the scene we looked for identification but found nothing. In the distance we heard the sound of an automobile coming up fast so we got in our Duesenberg and Luigi was turning it around when I saw the approaching car was our Chrysler with Viktor and Evelyn.

Luigi backed up to be between the gunmen's car and the Chrysler, tapping the brake lights to get their attention. The Chrysler slowed and sharp-eyed Evelyn had her rifle ready before she saw it was us. Seconds later we were telling them what had happened. Viktor was angry about the attack and the suspicion that we had an informant that set us up. I watched how Evelyn calmed Viktor and he agreed there was nothing to gain by wasting time here.

Viktor said we should travel together, close enough to support each other if there was another ambush but far enough apart so we could not both be ambushed together. I went back to the Chrysler to ride with Viktor and Evelyn and we arrived in Los Angeles by mid-morning. We went straight to Chief Higgins's office at the Famous Players-Lasky Studio. He sent for coffee and doughnuts while we changed our clothes and washed up in his office bathroom. The first thing Higgins said was that it had been confirmed that neither of the men burned in the truck was Dan and the newsboy was recovering nicely. I felt relieved and it reinforced my belief that Dan was alive. Chief Higgins told us there was nothing else new, but the Los Angeles detectives suspected that the gang had left the area by train and not by car. However, the gang had a four day head start and we did not know in which direction.

With the report that the gang might have taken to the rails, Bill again worked his magic with the railroad dispatchers and district managers to see if there were any unusual train or private railcar movements. Turned out there were four reports of unusual movement in the area.

The next morning Jake and Claire arrived and I was surprised to see that Scott was with them. "I managed to talk my father into giving me some time off. You and Dan helped me last year when the gangsters turned me into a morphine addict. Claire is just as bad as you are, telling me she was not going to sit around and wait. I don't know what I can do to help but I know how to shoot and after last year, I'm not afraid to pull the trigger on a bad guy. I called in more resources, the crew from last year but they will not join us for three or four days, depending on where they are coming from. Laure, I took it upon myself to contact Big Al to tell him to get steam up and come down here with your train when I heard the gang might be on the rails. He sounded happy to have something to do, he and the Swedes have been restless waiting around and they are itching for a fight. If that wasn't the right thing to do, I'll pay the expense for the locomotive's return trip."

"Thank you Scott. I'm glad you sent for our train. This is getting to be déjà vu all over again when we had planes, trains and automobiles. All we're missing now is Frank, Meghan, Dawn, Buster and Louise."

"Frank and Meghan are in Europe on a top secret assignment from the President. No word on when they will be returning. Last I heard they were in Paris, but that was a cover story, their mission was not in France. Dawn is finishing up an assignment in the New York area. As for Buster and Louise, you'll have to call them, but I heard they are on movie locations."

DAN MEETS TIN VOICE

* Dan narrates *

At first I was glad that the train was slowing down as I jumped and rolled like Lonnie the stuntman had showed me a few months ago, when everything was peaches and cream. But several thugs also jumped off the train, at least one of them broke an arm or leg from the sound of his cursing and cries of pain. That didn't lower the odds enough, there were still a half dozen or more of them looking for me. I tried to roll down into a creek next to the track but it was too shallow to cover me. When I stepped back onto the bank, some sticks cracked and the sound brought everyone running toward me. I took off, but I was weak from the fight and lack of nutrition. I did not see a fallen log and tripped over it, going down face first. Rolling myself up I was ready to keep on because they must have orders not to shoot me. But two of them were on me, holding me down until the others got there. *'Rhatz! I almost made it.'* If the train had been going faster I might have gotten away.

The gang controlled the engineer and made him stop when I jumped off. The thugs pulled me roughly back to the railcar at the end of the short train. They were about to throw me in the cell, but Foster Pell's voice told them to bring me to the boss. Pushed down the narrow hall with a Thompson jamming me in the back, I hoped the thug did not have his hand on the trigger or he could shoot me accidently, not that he would care.

When we got to the other end of the railcar I decided to take another chance and jumped as soon as I cleared the door at the end of the car. That didn't work. There was a gangster waiting, Thompson aimed at my chest. I was lifted back up and frog-marched through the door of the next railcar. The décor in this executive railcar was of a sumptuous, decadent bordello style. "Bring him here. Hold him." I didn't even have to see to know this was the voice of what Laure called Tin Voice. A chair turned around and there was the apparition I had seen before. The sound of its voice sent chills through my body. I was unable to try another escape since the Thompson barrel poked at my spine and three thugs held me.

The apparition stood up with difficulty. I got a good look at the metal mask and wished I hadn't. It was filthy and crudely made. I saw the apparition had a box on a leather strap hung around its neck, and the metallic voice was coming from it. Was this horrible wretched person responsible for trying to frame Laure for murder, sabotage our movie, and send people to harm us?

"Why are you bruised?" the Tin Voice asked without any introduction.

"Your jail guard threw my food on the floor of my cell, then hit and kicked me every day."

"You are lying. I told him that you were to be treated carefully. My client expects you to be in prime condition."

"Well, this guard must not have received the message. He hit and kicked me every day and all I was able to retrieve was the stale bread. The rest of it was on the floor, but I refused to lick the floor" I replied. "You can see these bruises on my arms and chest" and I pulled off my shirt. The apparition seemed to stare for a minute, so I kept talking. "And what client is this? What does a client of yours have to do with me?"

"That is none of your business." Tin Voice turned to one of the guards. "Reese, go look in the cell and tell me what you find." Reese was back in a couple of minutes.

"The cell floor is covered with rotting food" Reese said, with no mention of the guard.

"Take that guard out and shoot him. I personally gave him explicit instructions." It occurred to me that the thugs had not told Tin Voice that I had beaten the guard, and I wondered why. But I waited, and no further words were spoken until the sound of two gunshots were heard. It appeared that the thugs were covering for the guard's mistreatment of me, and were now covering themselves for not telling Tin Voice that I had beaten the guard. This gang was inept at best, yet they managed to keep me captive. I guessed that did not say much in my favor.

Tin Voice spoke to Foster Pell "I now must spend time and money to bring him back to health or the client won't pay. Tie Mr. Lindner to a chair and get that cell cleaned. Give him better food. Foster, I want two guards who will follow my instructions exactly. I will hold you responsible if they fail. We have a short time to get this deal done because we have other things to turn our attention to. I will personally inspect the cell before Mr. Lindner is put back in it. Now go, hop to it."

Tin Voice turned to me. "I have information for you. Laure has been informed that you are dead so forget about her coming for you. She seems to be glad you are gone, because she has been enjoying the company of male visitors who come to your house every night."

"That doesn't sound like Laure" I said.

"Forget about Laure. She was never interested in you. She only needed your help so she pretended to be your girlfriend and now that you are gone she lost no time to take other lovers to your bed. Many of your former acquaintances have made the trip from Hollywood to sleep with her. Buster Keaton, or was it Buster Collier? Maybe both. They have bedded Laure in your house, in your bed. They drink, dance, laugh and have sex. Sometimes she takes more than one man at a time. That's how easily she has forgotten you. She has also taken to smoking opium. There is nothing for you to go back to, so do not concern yourself with that whore any longer." Tin Voice turned and abruptly left the room.

I could not believe Laure would act that way. It just did not ring true. Opium? Laure would never do that. Yet, being disoriented from lack of nutrition and the stress of being in captivity, plus being so near to escape and freedom but caught so fast, there was a small part of my thoughts that said it might be possible. But Laure? No, I could not believe it of her. But what purpose did it serve for Tin Voice to tell me this?

I also was getting the impression that I'd heard the voice before, but it was so distorted there was no way to be sure. Two hours later I was back in the cell. This time, the paint was scraped from the window and the wood slats removed, however the iron straps were there and it seemed that there were more screws holding them than before. The floor was cleaner but still smelled bad. The mattress was the same but the blanket was clean and there was a thin pillow. A small viewing port had been cut in the hallway door, with the lock to open the viewport on the outside. When the next meal arrived, it was marginally better than before. The new guards told me my meal would come with one plate or bowl, one spoon and one cup. All these items would be retrieved in twenty minutes of the food being served, so I had to eat it or lose it.

I lay on the bunk to think. Why would a client of Tin Voice want me to be healthy? Was I being sold as a slave? And telling me Laure was acting like a cheap whore and smoking opium? Why?

I did not have another visit with Tin Voice and the train stayed on the siding for another day. At least it did not get as hot as before, and there was now a vent in the roof. The hole was too small for me to get through if I got any ideas for escape.

The next afternoon the railcar was attached to another train and we began to move again. I tried to see out of the window, but the glass was so bad that it was a mess of distortion, and I could see only vague shapes. I watched when we slowed down for towns to try to find anything that could tell me where I was or where I was going. I thought we were traveling northeast and guessed Philadelphia, New Jersey or New York was the destination.

The guards were careful to place my food tray on the table and returned to pick up the tray and dishes twenty minutes later. One good thing was that my hand and leg chains were removed when I was in the cell. If the train stopped long enough the guards put leg chains on me and take me outside, and they walked with me for exercise. When I was in the cell there were always two guards in the room outside the door who looked in the viewport every five or ten minutes. When the food came, one guard brought it inside while the other stood in the doorway with a big wooden club in the event I tried to escape again. I vowed to try to escape again just so they would try to hit me with the club, because then I would not be in good condition for their client. None of this was making any sense to me.

My mind remained filled with thoughts of Laure. Did she only want me to help her against Pádraigh? Was Laure so happy to be rid of me that she took other men? I was in a turmoil. Part of me said that it was possible what Tin Voice said could be true. The other part of me said no, remember Laure's kisses? And the look on her face of pure happiness when we made love? Could she fake that for such a long time? And why, after Pádraigh was finally dead, did she stay with me if all she wanted was my help to kill him? Every time I thought about it I decided that Tin Voice was lying because Laure was not that kind of woman, so I kept my faith and hope in her.

STUDIO HAIRDRESSER GOSSIP

* Laure narrates*

We were still in Los Angeles, following up clues in hope of finding where the kidnappers had taken Dan. There were so many reports of strange railcar movements that Bill began to suspect there was a deliberate attempt to spread false information to create confusion.

A telegram arrived from Giuseppe saying he would be arriving soon and I hoped he had good news. Waiting was difficult. I wanted to go somewhere. Viktor pointed out that would be fine if we knew where to go. Meanwhile, the word must have gone out that I was in Hollywood without my husband and the calls started rolling in. Men I had never heard of before, various casting couch producer types who must not have heard about my history. Men who wanted me to help them get a movie role – many of them generously offering to take me to their bed to comfort me while my husband was missing. Then there were men I knew from Adolphe Menjou to Buster Collier. Buster asked me out to lunch, which made me think he was up to his old tricks. He was a handsome man, and my mind briefly wandered to remember how much fun he had been, but that was before Dan and I got married. I told Buster that if Viktor could come with, I would meet him. He was not happy about that, but he said it was important. As it happened, Viktor was following up leads in the stunt actor community, so Evelyn went along as my chaperone. She thought it was funny that I needed one.

Buster took us to the Famous Players-Lasky studio lunchroom. I was wrong thinking he wanted something else from me. Well no, he did want that, but this time he said there was some information I needed to hear straight from the source. After lunch Buster took Evelyn and me to one of the studio hairdresser shops, this one with twenty stations, filled with men and women getting their hair ready for a role or audition. When one of the hairdressers saw us, she finished with the actor in her chair and told her supervisor she was going on break. We went outside and Buster introduced us to Betty, who lit a cigarette and offered one but I declined. I tried cigarettes when I was with Pádraigh because he smoked, but I disliked them and never got the habit. When we first started dating it was a plus to Dan's status that he did not smoke.

Betty was of average height and had a good figure under her hairdresser's smock. She might have been attractive but she wore too much makeup and her voice was scratchy, probably from the cigarettes.

Betty began her story. "So this chippy named Janice is at my station a few weeks ago, getting fixed up for a casting couch audition with an assistant director – although he told her he was a director. Buster said you know him, guy by the name of Foster Pell who was the assistant director on *The Great Gatsby*." Betty definitely had my attention now.

"Janice is young and good lookin' but a bit chubby for the flickers 'cause, you know, the camera makes people look heavier than what they are. I seen you in that Gatsby movie and the camera loves you, just like your cousin Louise. Janice had been in the shop several times, she's had small walk-on parts and was doing auditions for bigger roles. The word is around that she is now ready to do it on the couch 'cause she's getting desperate to get her big break in the flickers, and when word like that gets out it attracts cake-eaters like Foster Pell. So I'm fixing her hair and Janice is talking about your movie *Road Trip Blues* and said that this Foster Pell guy told her that he could get her a part in it. Too bad it was shut down because the word around the studio was that it looked good, real good. I remembered Foster because he made proposals to me to go out with him and get sozzled and screwed, but me, I don't find him attractive, not at all. If it had been a real good lookin' guy like your husband Danny I would have taken him to the back room and done him right there, but Foster don't have what I want. Sorry, didn't mean to say anything about your husband, I don't know him, just seen him around. Some of the other gals talk about him when they bump gums about the good lookin' actors and directors and such. Nothin' bad, y'know just that they all want to get on Danny's couch and some wouldn't care if there was a movie part offered or not. Now I don't know of anyone who has, I'm just repeating what others have said" Betty told us.

"Tell Mrs. Lindner what you told me, Betty" Buster prompted.

"OK, I'm getting to it. Anyway, she says that Pell was quitting the movies to work for a gang that had a big deal going down. They needed a front man, since the mark knew the grifters. But the deal was outside the law, if you know what I mean, and Pell was gonna do a reverse sting and keep the money for himself. I got curious and tried to ask Janice more but she suddenly realized what she was saying and clammed up. A couple days ago I was doin' Buster's hair – and I'd heard you'd been doin' Buster" and she stopped talking to giggle. "So I mentioned it to him, and he said I had to tell you what I told him. But hey, I don't want no trouble over this. Lots of people talk big in a hairdresser's chair and we don't pay no nevermind to it."

"Did Janice say any names, or where the deal was going down?" I asked.

"No, I don't remember a name. No wait, she did say Babette. Yeah, Babette, that was the name, but I don't know who Janice meant by that."

"Betty, you didn't tell Laure where the deal was supposed to go down" Buster prompted.

"Yeah, Janice said something about New Jersey" she said.

"Where in New Jersey?" I asked, hoping this could be the break we needed and we could get going to find Dan.

"She didn't say, but the mark was someone who worked for someone named Johnson. Oh, I talk too much.

I hope this don't get me in trouble, that Pell guy seems like a dangerous sort."

"No, I won't get you in trouble" I promised Betty.

"Thank you Mrs. Lindner. Well, I gotta be gettin' back to my station, I overstayed my break. Hope what I said helps."

"Thank you Betty, what you told us is very helpful" I replied. I thanked Buster for getting Betty to talk to us.

When Evelyn and I got back to the Duesenberg we had a good laugh. She said she understood why I enjoyed fooling around with Buster. I told Evelyn that Buster was still a difficult subject for us, because Dan thought I had been too willing to make what should have been a short experiment into a serious affair, and I agreed that was what I had done. She said she was not being judgmental, but could see why I allowed myself to be seduced. Evelyn said that while I was listening to Betty, Buster had been giving her the eye. Evelyn admitted she was beginning to fantasize about being with Buster.

When Giuseppe arrived with Bill, I told them the studio hairdresser's story. Giuseppe was interested and asked questions. "This may be the key to your puzzle. I have to talk to my contacts about this. I'll let you know if it stirs up anything" Giuseppe said. But Giuseppe's eyes told me he knew more than he was telling me. After Giuseppe left I was upset. Bill told me to be calm, that if Giuseppe was holding back it would be for good reasons because Giuseppe was definitely on our side.

After Giuseppe left, he called Al Capone and told him the story. When Al heard what I learned from Betty, he gave Giuseppe his thoughts on who was involved. Capone told Giuseppe not to reveal anything to me for now, because of the extreme danger I would be in if I went there. After the call from Giuseppe, Al Capone sent word for Gina to come to his office as soon as possible.

Next, Giuseppe made a call to a hotel in New York City. He spoke to a covert operative he knew and gave instructions to go to New Jersey. He also gave vague orders to "use your discretion" and to "do what you determine is necessary" to achieve the objective and to "be very careful because you will be on your own and I won't know what actions to take until you are able to contact me again." It was very fortunate that the operative was highly experienced in this line of work.

THE STING

Dan narrates

I kept a vigilant watch for another opportunity to escape and now I knew the train was in New Jersey. I did not know why, but Tin Voice sent messages every day through my guards offering to procure a woman for me. I wondered *'Why would Tin Voice care if I had sex or not? Blackmail? To make me forget about Laure? There was no woman in the world who could make me forget about Laure'.*

The next morning I had a bath in the parlor car and Sylvester brought in a new suit and shoes that fit reasonably well. A gunman ordered me into the back seat of a limousine with Foster Pell. A few minutes later, the car stopped at the front door of a major luxury hotel fronting on the ocean. I was in Atlantic City.

Tin Voice did not accompany us. Foster Pell had wormed his way into Tin Voice's confidence and convinced Tin Voice that he could handle the deal. Pell told me we were going to a meeting and that I was to shut up and let him do the talking.

Pell and three of Tin Voice's gangsters walked me through the hotel lobby to an elevator, Pell gave his name to the operator and as he called for authorization, Foster told Tin Voice's guards to go back to the train and that he would take a cab back when the business was completed.

The guards went out there was Dawn. Before Pell turned to her, she quickly tapped a finger on the side of her nose to tell me to play along. She walked up to Foster and took his hand. "Are you ready, my dear?" Foster asked and she gave him a kiss on his cheek and a smile in response. I felt better with Dawn there, knowing she was an experienced and capable field operative.

The elevator arrived at the ninth floor and we were shown into a large room filled with mobster-types. We were directed to sit in leather armchairs about ten feet in front of an enormous desk. No introductions were made nor any names offered. The man sitting behind the desk did not look like a mobster, more like a banker in his conservative business suit and horn-rimmed glasses, but everyone was deferential to him. I recalled from news photographs that he was Nucky Johnson, boss of the Atlantic City outfit. He motioned to a hard looking older man seated in a large leather chair next to the desk who did look like a mobster, saying "Vinny will handle this."

Vinny started by asking who spoke for us. Foster Pell stood up. "I am here on behalf of my employer, who discovered where this man, Pádraigh Herlihy, has been in hiding and as a service to you I have brought him here." I began to get a bad feeling about this.

Vinny asked "Mr. and Mrs. Herlihy, can you identify this man?" An older couple at the side of the room came over to look at me. I saw the resemblance between Pádraigh and the man. I naïvely thought the man would say I was not Pádraigh, but instead got my second major surprise of the day.

"Yes, this is our son Pádraigh." The woman who might be Pádraigh's mother burst into tears and began sobbing.

"Mr. Herlihy, are you positive? We had word that Pádraigh died in a train wreck, but he faked his death and later was assassinated in Kansas by his wife."

"My wife and I are positive this is our son Pádraigh. He brought shame on our family and we are pleased that he will now be held responsible for his actions."

"Thank you, Mr. and Mrs. Herlihy. You may leave."

The pieces were falling into place. The mobster named Vinny sitting next to the desk must be the father of the New Jersey mobster that Laure told me about, whose son Pádraigh tortured and killed even when he knew the contract was canceled.

Tin Voice's plan to capture me and put me in front of Vinny as Pádraigh was as twisted as it was brilliant – and thus it clicked over in my mind that Tin Voice was our former employee Enid Hanlon, aka Rose Herlihy, Pádraigh's sister who had set Laure up for capture by the Cranston gang. Now I knew why both Laure and I thought we heard the voice before it was destroyed by Meghan's sniper bullet in Kansas.

Rose hired Foster Pell to be her front man so the New Jersey mobsters would not know she was Pádraigh's sister, in which case the mobster might kill her too. With her brother dead she had no difficulty in framing me as Pádraigh to collect a big payoff. It was a cruel joke that they wanted me healthy so I could withstand more hours of torture before I died.

The plan allowed Rose to kill several birds with one stone. She collects money, gets revenge for her brother's death and the New Jersey mob gets their revenge on someone who they think is Pádraigh. I get dead. Rose would then find and kill Laure, completing her vendetta. Rose must have paid off Pádraigh's parents, or maybe she hired actors to take their place, otherwise why would his parents make a false identification? Then it hit me – they were his parents and had lied for him before when they identified the body from the train wreck as his. They were in on it because they would also get freedom from the New Jersey mob, who probably kept them under watch in the event Pádraigh showed up. It tied up a lot of loose ends, and now Laure and I were the last loose ends.

Dawn casually walked to the back of the room to talk with one of the New Jersey mobster's gunmen. Foster Pell stood up and said "If you are satisfied, our contract calls for a payment of $100,000 plus our expenses which are $82,780 for a total of $182,780, cash on delivery for the man known as Pádraigh Herlihy in good health. We have conclusively proven that this is Pádraigh Herlihy. He will claim that he is not Pádraigh, but his parents confirm it.

I thought Vinny must really want Pádraigh bad to pay that kind of dough. Vinny said "I am satisfied that this is Pádraigh Herlihy. Pay the messenger the full contract amount." A large thug brought in two suitcases and set them on a table in front of Foster Pell. He opened a suitcase and looked at the cash, pulling the banded bills out to riff through them to make sure they were real, but when Pell started to count the money, Vinny became angry. "I don't cheat those who fulfill contracts for me. There is $200,000 in the cases and that covers the contract and expenses and a bonus for your employer. Do not insult me by accusing me of not paying on my promises."

The gunman talking to Dawn approached Vinny and whispered in his ear. He looked surprised but nodded in agreement. "My men will take you to a room where you can count your money out of my sight. Don't ever come around here trying to do business again."

Foster Pell noticed Dawn standing at the back of the room and assumed she was ready to go with him so he shoved the money in the suitcases and the gunman picked them up, motioning for Foster to walk ahead. Foster seemed surprised when Dawn did not go with him.

Less than a minute later I heard Foster Pell begging "Nooo, don't" followed by two gunshots. The gunman who had gone out the door with Pell came back with the suitcases. "Mr. Pell decided to donate the money back to you" the gunman said with a grin. So that was the end of Foster Pell, caught in his own sting when he tried to take Rose's money.

Nucky had not yet said a word. He had only watched the proceedings. Now he laughed, drank from a wine glass and laughed some more, saying "Wait'll I tell Luciano, he's gonna get a big laugh outta this."

Dawn was smartly dressed in a businesslike ensemble. She confidently walked up and stood in front of the big desk to address the big boss. "Mr. Johnson..." but he stopped her.

"Please call me Nucky" he politely requested.

"Nucky, my name is Dawn and I'm sorry we did not meet earlier but I am appreciative that you trusted me when I sent word that there was a sting being played on

Vinny. The perpetrator is Rose Herlihy, who you know as Pádraigh Herlihy's sister, who had been shot but survived with serious disabilities. I can verify to your satisfaction that this man is not Pádraigh Herlihy" and she put two photographs in front of Nucky and Vinny. "The photos are marked Pádraigh and Dan. You can see they are two completely different men. Daniel Lindner is a Hollywood movie producer and husband of Laure Winiarzski Lindner who had been Pádraigh's girlfriend, but she was never Pádraigh's wife. As you know, Laure Lindner is alleged to have assassinated Pádraigh last year in Cherryvale Kansas, but the case remains unsolved. At the time Pádraigh was trying to kill Laure and persons unknown intervened to hasten Pádraigh's death. I saw the body personally and I can vouch for his death. Rose decided to get her revenge by framing Mr. Lindner as Pádraigh to collect a large reward from you. Mr. Pell got involved and was working his own sting to get hold of the money and disappear."

Dawn calmly continued "Further proof that this is not Pádraigh can be obtained from Mr. Al Capone of Chicago, whom I believe you are acquainted with. Mr. Capone knows Dan and Laure, as they were caught between the North Side and South Side Outfits when they ran contraband wine and spirits from California to Chicago. Mr. Herlihy associated with Mr. Weiss and the North Side Outfit, and there has been bad blood between the rival organizations for several years."

Nucky held up his hand for Dawn to stop talking. "My people discovered this with help from a man named Giuseppe Giordano, who is vouched for by my associate Lucky Luciano. Giuseppe said you would make your presence known but he did not tell me you are a most beautiful woman. I believe Luciano and Giordano, and I believe you, but I do not give a fuck what that *stronzo pazzo* Capone says. He thinks he's got a tiger by its ass in Chicago, but I can crush him like a bug whenever I want." Nucky shook his fist. "He can't tell me nuthin'. But since you came here to bring us knowledge of this fraud, and I don't like to kill beautiful women who have not done me harm, I'll grant you and Daniel Lindner safe exit. Give Mr. Capone my regards and tell him I will see him in hell, but if he shows up here before then I'll personally send him on his way. Please give my thanks to Giuseppe, who has proved to be an honorable man. You and Giuseppe have saved my capo Vinny a lot of money so I grant you freedom as your reward."

"Dawn, if you are ever looking for a job, please come see me. I don't mean to work in my clubs and houses of pleasure, I mean in your current field of work. I have heard of you by reputation. Vinny and I thank you for exposing Mr. Pell's game, and he" Nucky stopped to laugh "will not ever be doing that again."

"Thank you, Nucky. Giuseppe and I will be glad to work with you on projects beneficial to both of us."

I kept my trap shut as Dawn and I got on the elevator, even though she did not like using elevators. But we were under Nucky's protection and he sent his man Digger to escort us to the lobby so it seemed OK, but two floors down the elevator door opened and two gunmen stood in the opening. Dawn and I were standing behind Digger and the elevator operator, so the gunmen had to shoot them to get to us. Dawn reacted with a quickness that astounded me. Even as the bodies in front of us were falling to the floor, she pulled a gun from her leg holster while I pushed the elevator operator's body aside and took the controls to close the door and send the elevator down. One of the thugs tried to put his foot in the door, but Dawn shot him in the foot and he fell back, screaming in pain. The other got off a shot that went through the door a couple inches above her head. Had I not been able to get the elevator moving, she would have been dead. Digger was dead so I took his guns. He had two, a .22 pistol in an ankle holster and a Colt Police Positive chambered for .38 S&W rounds under his suit coat. They were both loaded and I took them, but there was no extra ammunition in his pockets.

Dawn stopped the elevator, saying they might be able to control it from the lobby and we had to get off. We were on the fourth floor and after checking the corridor, we ran towards the rear staircase. Before we got there we heard footsteps running toward us. I saw a door ajar and went in, pulling Dawn in with me.

The running steps kept going past our door. We waited and listened until Dawn decided to turn on the light. We were in a linen supply closet. We found maids' and janitors' uniforms. Without a word we changed, and Dawn put our street clothes in a laundry bag. Cautiously checking that the corridor was clear, we got to the staircase and went down quietly. In the lobby there was no panic or screaming. The sound of shots on the upper floors must have gone unnoticed. We walked like hotel employees in a luxury hotel, casually but with a purpose. Ten feet into the lobby I spotted Red and Sylvester from Rose's gang, scanning the lobby looking for us.

Dawn and I moved quickly through another door, this time it was a housekeeping supply room. Dawn locked the door while I took stock of what we might use. Dawn found a feather duster and some cleaning cloths and I pulled a large garbage container on wheels with a broom and shovel in holders on the side. Sneaking out of the closet we headed to a rear door. Looking back to the lobby, Red and Sylvester were pushing people down to get to us. "We have to get out of here, now" Dawn ordered. We saw an exit door and ran to it. Red and Sylvester were approaching and I shoved the garbage container on wheels at them to slow them down.

Bursting through the door, we discovered it was a back door entrance for VIPs and those who did not wish to be recognized. There was a valet station for automobiles, the valet gone. A big black Locomobile sedan pulled up and a man and much younger woman got out, furtively looking around. The man spotted me and threw the key to me, thinking I was a valet because I had the hotel name sewed on the front of my shirt. He shouted "Keep it nearby, we will be leaving in about an hour" and they went inside.

I replied "Yes sir" with a shout and jumped behind the wheel. A boy in a valet uniform appeared and began shouting. Dawn waved her gun at him and he ran while she got in the back seat of the Locomobile to watch for followers.

"I didn't think Nucky would do that to us" Dawn said. "He doesn't like mob violence like Capone does. He and Luciano say fighting only gets you more fighting."

"It wasn't Nucky, those two gunmen who shot Digger were from Rose's gang" I said.

"That may be, but with Digger was killed, unless we can get word to Nucky, he may think we did it. Until then we have to watch out for everyone, including the police since we stole this car." Neither of us knew the streets of Atlantic City but we were starting to get to the edge of it and traffic thinned out.

"Turn right" Dawn said as an Oldsmobile came up behind and someone began shooting at us. I had the Locomobile going fast enough to scare Dawn. She said to slow down and I jammed on the brakes. The Oldsmobile following us didn't have a chance as Dawn put slugs from Digger's .38 into its radiator and windshield.

Following Dawn's instructions I turned down a side road but immediately ahead was a police blockade and no place to turn around. There were police officers in covered positions behind their cars. "Get low" I yelled and aimed the Locomobile directly between two of the police cars. The heavy Locomobile pushed the lighter Fords aside, but one of our fenders was bashed in so that if I turned left the tire would rub on the fender. I went at top speed for a mile, turning right on a side road, then another right to a dirt road where I could stop the Locomobile out of sight of the main road. I told Dawn I had to bend the fender back or we would not be able to turn left.

I tried to pull the fender away but the Locomobile had thick, heavy fenders that resisted my efforts. I got the car's toolkit and tried to pry it away and it began to give slowly. Not soon enough, because two cars came around the corner and men popped out of the side windows with Tommyguns. Dawn shouted for me to go to into the trees and as soon as I went one way, she went the other way. I started back toward her when the gunmen started shooting at her. I shot two of them with and they turned their attention to me. A few seconds later Dawn fired at them and we briefly had them in crossfire, so they retreated but kept watch at the end of the street. They sent one of the thugs away, probably to get reinforcements. Slowly circling to sneak across the road out of their view to look for Dawn, I found where she had been but she was gone. There were empty revolvers and blood. 'Rhatz!' She left no other trail that I could find.

There were only two shots left in the .22. I managed to elude the gunmen, but Dawn was nowhere to be found. I went back to the Locomobile and got the fender pried away from the wheel. Searching the car, I found a 1922 Beretta with a full magazine under the front seat, but no extra ammunition.

It was getting dark and I drove until I found a place to park in a wooded area and slept in the Locomobile. In the morning I went to a gas station to get a map but the reality was that I had no money and the Locomobile contained less than a quarter tank of gas.

I began to get hungry and the houses were fewer and farther apart but they all appeared to be inhabited. I drank water from a garden hose near a house and decided to walk towards a group of houses to scrounge through their garbage cans for food. I did not want to go to anyone's door, because there might be a police report with my description and the resident would call the police, who might turn me over to the mobsters if they were on the pad. I was watching from behind a garage and saw a man came from a house to put a bag in a garbage barrel. When the man was out of sight I went and looked in the barrel, finding enough vegetable cuttings, stale bread, thrown out leftovers and various other semi-edible things to stave off my hunger pangs but my hunger returned a couple hours later.

I thought *'Dan Lindner, hot shot Hollywood producer and whiskey runner, Indy 500 top ten finisher, owner of three Duesenbergs, successful businessman, Napa vineyard and winery co-owner, married to the most beautiful woman in the world, was reduced to stealing gas and feeding himself from garbage cans. How the mighty have fallen!'*

Late in the afternoon, I returned to the Locomobile after scrounging for food only to find a police car parked next to it. When the officer went to get a doughnut I slipped around the houses, sneaked up to the Locomobile and grabbed the laundry bag of clothes. When I heard the sound of a locomotive's steam whistle I moved in that direction.

A few minutes later I came upon a single railroad track in a warehouse zone. During the day I watched the sun to make sure I was heading west. I decided if I went west far enough I would get to the Pacific Ocean. When that thought registered its utter foolishness I realized that I was getting scatterbrained from lack of food. Staying in the brush near the track, in the dark of night a slow moving freight train of about ten cars was coming. When I saw a boxcar with open doors, I began to run, angling to get to the open door when I would be at top speed to jump and pull myself inside. I could not see much since there was only a sliver of moon. I went to sit down at one end of the boxcar and did not see that someone was already there as I sat on top of him. He did not take very kindly to that and tried to hit me. I moved away but he kept following and swinging his fists at me. He was a small man, determined that I should leave the boxcar, but I needed to get to a town or city where I could get help. I was not going to be thrown off by a bum defending his corner of a boxcar.

Going to the other end of the boxcar and hoping to find a place there to sit, there was another guy who joined with the first guy to throw me out of the boxcar. After a couple minutes of pushing and shoving it seemed to be getting rather comical. The two guys were thin and weak. I was in marginally better condition than they were, but there were two of them. I did not want to hurt them, figuring they were just poor bums trying to go somewhere just like me. I got hold of one of the men by the neck and slammed him up against the boxcar wall.

"Stop!" I yelled. The three of us stood there, out of breath. "Guys, I just want a place to rest, I won't bother you and when we get to a town I will jump off to send a message for someone to come for me."

The two men shuffled a few feet away and whispered, then came back. I raised my fists to protect myself but one of them said "If you're just wanting to ride tonight, you can have this side of the boxcar. Moe and I will go to the other side, but if you come over there you'll have both of us to deal with." I laughed, because I was too weak to beat them and they could not beat me.

"It's a deal" I said, and turned to go sit in the corner. I wanted to establish that I held no animosity toward them and hoped that in the morning they could tell me where I was. I called "Thanks guys. My name is Dan, what's yours?"

"We ain't got names so shut up and get some sleep. We don't got money neither, so don't come looking for any."

With no more sounds from the other end of the boxcar except for loud snoring, I drifted off to sleep. I dreamed that Laure was outside, calling my name. I tried to call to her, but she could not hear me.

ON THE WRONG SIDE OF THE COUNTRY

Laure narrates

Vera had not heard from her husband Jake for three days and she was getting worried. She knew all the stories of Jake and her daughter Laure and son-in-law Dan's adventures last year and had thought all that was behind them. Laure and Dan were married and Vera was silently hoping for word that a grandchild was on the way. She wanted so much to be a good Polish grandmother and spoil her grandchildren, and they would love their Nana.

She was cleaning her kitchen when someone knocked on her front door. In the peaceful Village of Long Grove hardly anyone knocked. Her friends and neighbors would just call out and Vera would answer for them to come in. It made her uneasy that someone was knocking on her door. Suddenly she got a chill – what if Jake was hurt? Or her daughter Laure? What if someone wanted to rob her?

Vera went to the front door. Her rifle was upstairs in their bedroom, unloaded and in the back of her closet. She decided to open the door, more worried it would be bad news of Jake or Laure than fear of an intruder in Long Grove. Pulling the door open, there was a large man filling the doorway. He was not as tall as Jake but he had wide shoulders, a strong physique and a scar just below his chin. He appeared to be someone who was used to dealing in violence. He smiled when he saw her but the scar and his crisply trimmed thick black moustache made his smile look menacing. Vera sensed movement behind the man but she could not see who it was before the man reached out with his powerful arms to grab her. She let out a loud scream, hoping a neighbor would hear.

"Giuseppe, I know Bill trusts you, but I think you are holding back information from me. Let me make a guess. You don't want to tell me something because you think I will go off like a crazy woman with guns blazing to rescue my husband. Well, my mind is becoming more frazzled every day I sit around doing nothing while Dan is being held captive. So tell me what it is you are keeping from me. I need your help."

Giuseppe considered the situation. He had been holding back information on Capone's urging, but now it just didn't seem right. "Laure, I'll tell you everything I know, but I warn that you will be uneasy afterward. I will be blunt. Your nemesis is Rose Herlihy, who worked for you as Enid Hanlon and set you up for kidnapping by the Cranston Gang. One of the reasons my contacts never thought of her was because she was reported dead in a gun battle near Cherryvale, Kansas. Rose survived but suffered severe injuries to her face and throat. She has difficulty eating, her face and neck are so frightening that people turn away and vomit so she wears a metal mask that is almost as ugly. My source tells me Rose's vocal chords are badly damaged so that it is nearly impossible for her to speak, her natural voice is merely a squeak. A device that allows her to be heard was made for her, but the device is primitive and the sound is scratchy and tinny."

"One of my contacts was able to talk to a small-time gangster by the name of Gilbert, who confirmed that Rose is fixated on ruining your reputation and destroying you and Dan personally. She is obsessed with putting you to the most horrible death she can conjure up. And I expect that with her internal rage and mentally unstable condition, she can imagine more horror than most."

"Can I talk to this Gilbert fellow?" I asked.

"No. Rose hired Gilbert and his gang, and I suspect they were the ones who murdered Col. Mosby and framed you, and then hired some disgruntled Mare Island base employees to beat and hang you. At the time, Rose was hooked on the idea of hanging you from a tree. They even had a camera to photograph it and send the photos to Rose. Your dog alerted your Marine friends and saved you. Rose is so twisted she wants to kill your dog too."

"Gil made the mistake of trying to get Rose's courier to talk. He knew if he and his gang failed they would be killed, but was suspicious that if they succeeded she would have them killed anyway. Gil was not very smart and thought the courier would tell them, but the courier had no idea, he was just a messenger. Rose found out that Gil's brother had captured and tortured the courier, and Rose had Gil's brother tortured and murdered. There is no compassion inside Rose. She orders the death of her own gang members for the slightest transgressions. Gil and his gang went into hiding, but Rose found them and there was a massacre. Shortly after my contact talked to Gil, he and his gang were brutally murdered, each one tortured and then shotgunned in the face. Other criminals, even the most hardened types fear Rose."

"So both Rose and Pádraigh have come back to life after being thought dead. I must find Dan. Where have they taken him?" I asked nervously.

"Hold on, Laure. You're not going to like this. Someone who knew I was looking for unusual information told me that Rose was holding someone as a hostage and expected a big payoff. I think the hostage is Dan but some of my conclusion is based on guesswork. One of our operatives, you know her as Dawn, was in the area where they were reported to be and I got word to her to go in undercover and check it out. Dawn is an expert in that kind of work. In addition, I have contacts with other mobs as well as the work I do for Mr. Capone. When the information came to me, Rose's gang was on an eastbound train near Nashville Tennessee. I have had no news from Dawn since. She is very capable of taking care of herself, but for now all we can assume is that she is either on the job and incommunicado or they found her out and killed her."

"If she is on the job, she is with Dan" I said more to myself than the others. *'That also makes me worry.'* I knew the attraction between Dan and Dawn that went way back before me. I never told Dan but that brief affair worried me like my affair with Buster worried him. She was gorgeous and sexy and had been Wallace Reid's lover when he was on the road making movies. Tears welled up in my eyes but I held them back. Nothing I could do about it, either they would fuck or they wouldn't. But now Dan and I were married and that made it different. Affairs before engagement or marriage were forgivable, after was something else.

Giuseppe must have seen the despair on my face and continued. "The information I received this morning said Rose was taking her gang to the New York/New Jersey area. So far there's no word of contact with Rose from any of the mob families in the area, but I don't have good relations with all of them, while others, such as Lucky Luciano, I do have an understanding with and we communicate. The others see Mr. Capone as a threat, especially as he has continued to weaken the North Side Chicago Gang and if he does knock them out, he would control the entire Chicago area. Mr. Capone's outfit would then rival the power of all but the biggest gangs in the eastern United States."

"Why would they take Dan to New Jersey?" I asked, but as I asked the question the answers fell into place. I remembered Pádraigh killed a New Jersey mobster's son when a hit was put out on him, and had tortured the man before he died. There were two things wrong with that – first, torture was not part of the contract, and second the contract was revoked and Pádraigh knew it, but bloodthirsty as he was, he made the hit anyway and demanded to be paid, lying that he was not told of the cancellation. That did not go over very well in New Jersey, but at the time Pádraigh had the backing of Dion O'Banion and Hymie Weiss of the North Side Gang, which at the time was as powerful as Capone's South Side Outfit. I had broken up with Pádraigh after learning of his work for the mobs and wanted nothing to do with him.

Pádraigh became angry and was on his way to Chicago to talk or force me into staying with him. Then he was declared dead in a horrific train wreck so the New Jersey mob stopped looking for him when his parents identified a body as his. But the parents were going along with the fake identification to keep their son alive, because he had in fact survived and killed the man whose body was identified as his. Pádraigh went to work for Hymie Weiss and found out where I was, hunted me down to get revenge just after Dan and I began our relationship. Scott came in while I was telling this to Giuseppe and Bill.

Giuseppe made the connection. "That's the answer Laure! She is going to convince the New Jersey mobster that Dan killed his son, or possibly try to convince the Mafioso that Dan is really Pádraigh. She will demand a reward for bringing Pádraigh to them. Dan won't last long once Rose gives him to the New Jersey boys. Rose needs money, so she will turn him over to the mob for the reward. We have a serious problem now, because Mr. Capone's poor relationship with Nucky Johnson and his mob means we have very little influence with them. The police departments are on the pad, often all the way to the top, so the police will not help us and may help Rose by telling the Jersey outfit where we are and what we are doing."

I was in a rage of anger and despair. We were still in Southern California and had to get to New Jersey right now to have the ghost of a chance to help Dan. "I'm leaving for New Jersey today. When do we expect Big Al and our locomotive?"

"They'll be here tomorrow depending on how they get through the connections to Los Angeles" Bill said.

"Then we will fly" Scott said. You've got Jake, Claire and me for pilots. My new Ford Trimotor can carry eleven passengers besides the two pilots, but we will need guns and ammunition too, so we should figure nine passengers for safety."

"If we rotate the flying duties, we can stay in the air more hours each day. How many of us are going?" Claire asked. "I know you only want volunteers Laure, but let's be honest, everyone will want to go. I think the passenger list is Laure, Viktor, Luigi, Bill, Scott, Giuseppe if he wants to go, and me as the third pilot. That's seven passengers, who else?"

"If they can get to New Jersey with our locomotive, we would have Big Al and the Swedes. Big Al can shoot, the Swedes are not so good at that but their size and physical fighting capability might be needed" I said, remembering how they had saved me when I was on the run from Pádraigh's gang and they found me in a blind pig in Cherryvale.

"Big Al will check in with my security office when they get to Coalinga. If Bill and I get on this, we can divert the locomotive east at Bakersfield. I'll use every bit of influence I've got and I'll call my father too, he's got a lot of pull with the railroads, he's on a couple of their boards of directors. Let Bill and I work on that" Scott said, and I could hear a bit of excitement in his voice. He missed out on the adventure last year and I think he wanted to be in on this, especially since Claire was going.

"What about Evelyn? Viktor asked. "She's here, she's quick, smart and a damn good fighter, and Laure, we come as a pair. You want one of us, you get both of us."

"Well, that answers that question. What do we need? Let's make a list and buy whatever we need today including some nonperishable food. Medical supplies since we don't know what shape Dan will be in when we find him."

Giuseppe smiled and said "See what I mean Laure? As soon as you knew the whole story, you are ready to go, guns blazing regardless of the danger to yourself. You don't have to go, Rose is clearly insane and she is far more dangerous than Pádraigh."

"Giuseppe, I like you but I always seem to want to shoot you. My sister-in-law is going, my Uncle Viktor's girlfriend is going. It's my husband who is in trouble, and I don't want a life without him. Why the fuck should I sit and wait by the telephone? Do not even think about telling me not to go or I *will* shoot you" I told him.

Giuseppe held his hands up in the air and laughed "OK, OK! I surrender! Don't shoot! Do what you think best and I will help in any way I can."

An hour later everyone was either shopping for what we needed or making calls or sending telegrams. There was no way to plan what we would do when we got there. Giuseppe was right, I was ready to go in with guns blazing but it was better than sitting in Los Angeles. Dan and I had developed a sixth sense. We somehow knew if the other one was near, so I thought he would know if I was near, and this time I would be bringing help.

After the passenger list was set, Jake, Scott and Claire had gone to the airport to check out the Trimotor and make sure the fuel tanks were full. We would take off just before sunrise. Bill told us that he had been in contact with Big Al and the AT&SF and our locomotive was now east of Bakersfield with priority clearances all the way to St. Louis where they would interchange to the eastern railroads.

I hoped that we would not get to New Jersey too late. I also hoped that Dawn had not had her way with Dan, but I would have to face that when the time came. I certainly did not want to find Dan and get him away from Rose and her gang, only to find he was with Dawn. We had not even been married a year, so I put those thoughts away. They would not do me any good during the job that we had to do. I reaffirmed my decision to keep my trust in Dan.

TRAIN MAN DAN

Dan narrates

My eyes popped open in the morning and I tried to remember where I was. Then I focused on the two men sitting up watching me from the other end of the boxcar. The train was moving slowly and it looked like we were still out in the country.

"Good morning gentlemen" I said, trying to be pleasant. No response. "I suppose there is no room service at this hotel." This time I got a chuckle from one of them.

"How is it you're wearing a dirty and torn hotel janitor's uniform?" one of them asked. "And why do you have a man's suit and women's clothing in your bindle?"

"I don't remember" I said, immediately realizing how lame that sounded. I didn't want to tell them that there were nasty people looking for me. They might turn me in, and at the moment I wanted someone to tell me where the hell I was and where we were going. "What's a bindle?"

"See, I told you he ain't gonna tell us nothing." The other one nodded.

"You're running from someone, probably the law. You're going to have to leave, we don't want trouble from the cinderdicks."

"I am hoping some people don't find me, but they are much worse than the cops. If you're going to be unfriendly I'll take my leave as soon as this train stops" I said.

"Not only did he not tell us anything but he expects us to be friendly. Probably wants food or money and we ain't got neither."

"I don't want what you don't have. If I had some food I'd share with you, but I'm traveling light" I replied crossly.

"We know. We checked while you were sleeping." They must have been light-fingered because I didn't wake up. "And you don't want to wait to get off when the train stops. You gotta get off while it is still moving, otherwise the cinderdicks will catch you. You haven't been doing this for very long, have you?"

"No, this is the first train I've hopped on since I became a bum" I said.

"You're a bum?"

"Guess so, I don't have any money or anything but the clothes on my back and I'm trying to get home. I'd be glad to do something to make money so I could call my wife and friends to come get me."

"Then you're not a bum if you're willing to work."

"I don't understand. I thought a bum had nothing and traveled around looking for work or handouts."

"If you'll work, you're not a bum."

"Maybe we need to educate him. He's new to this and I think he is telling us the truth."

"I guess we haven't taken a chance on anyone in a long time. But remember the last time we took a chance on a new guy? We almost got skinned alive. But if you think so. OK Dan or whoever you are, I'm Moe and he's Joe."

"Hello Moe. Hello Joe. Pleased to meet you. I still don't understand what you mean about being a bum" I said.

"What you are is a hobo. A hobo is someone who moves around, looks for and accepts honest work. A tramp is someone who moves around but won't work, and a bum is someone who doesn't move and doesn't work, who lives off handouts. If you're going to travel like this, there's a whole community out there and you should learn the basics, real quick like if you know what I mean" Moe said.

I did not realize that people who rode the trains had a social hierarchy, but there it was. I was a hobo by that definition. "So what's your story? Why do you travel?"

Joe said "We're hobos, we will work. A couple years ago we traveled on the trains as paying customers. We are vaudeville artists, singing, dancing, telling jokes, whatever we could do to make people laugh and pay to see our act. Now vaudeville is in decline because many of the vaudeville palaces are showing flickers and we don't get hired like we did in the old days."

"I'd like to see some vaudeville" I replied.

"You buy a ticket? Joe asked.

"No, I don't have any money, remember?" I replied.

"Well, then when you find a job and get paid, you can hire us. We gotta eat too, y'know" Joe said.

"You're right, and I promise that I will hire you some day. But look guys – I've only been doing this since I hopped into your boxcar yesterday. I sure would be obliged if you could smarten me up on how to ride the boxcars and find work."

"You were right Joe. He really doesn't know what he's doing. First of all son, you don't ride the boxcars, you ride the rails. You gotta learn the lingo and rules" Moe told me.

"I'm your eager student, and when I make some money I'll be glad to share with you" I said.

"You seem OK, so learn this first, because in about a half hour this train is going to come into a railroad yard and we want to get off just outside of town. The Hobo Code was created by Tourist Union #63 during the 1889 National Hobo Convention in St. Louis Missouri. The code was voted and passed as laws for the Nationwide Hobo Body. I was selected as a representative to teach it to others, and you need teaching so listen up. This is what it says:"

"Number 1 – Decide your own life, don't let others run yours."

"Number 2 – When you're in a town, respect the law and act like a gentleman."

"Number 3 – Don't take advantage of someone who is in a vulnerable situation, like local residents or other hobos."

"Number 4 – Always try to find work, even if it's temporary, and take the job nobody else wants. That way you'll be hired again should you ever come back."

"Number 5 – When there isn't any work, make your own work by using your talents. Make something and sell it."

"Number 6 – Do not let yourself become a stupid drunk. It'll set a bad example and the locals treat drunken hobos poorly."

"Number 7 – When jungling near a town, respect clothing handouts, pass them along, another hobo might need them."

"Number 8 – Always respect the land, do not leave garbage where you are jungling."

"Number 9 – If you're in a community jungle, pitch in and help."

"Number 10 – Try to stay clean and boil up when you can."

"Number 11 – When traveling, ride your train respectfully, take no personal chances, and cause no problems with the operating crew. If you can, earn your way by helping out. Act like an extra crew member."

"Number 12 – Do not cause problems in a train yard, other hobos will be passing through that yard."

"Number 13 – Do not allow anyone to molest children. Turn them in to the authorities. Molesters are the worst garbage to infest society."

"Number 14 – Help runaway children, we see lots of them. Try to get them to return home."

"Number 15 – Help other hobos whenever you can because you'll need their help someday."

"You're not kidding me, are you? There really is a code of laws for being a hobo? I never knew that. Do most hobos follow the laws?"

"Most of them do, most of the time. There's always those who can't or won't. The tramps and bums don't respect the code because they don't do anything or respect anything."

"What's a jungle?" I asked.

"Usually just outside of towns and cities there are places called jungles where hobos gather together for protection and camp when they find work. If we don't cause trouble, most local police let us alone. Some of them won't, they hate anyone who rides the rails. You always have be careful."

"Is there such a place by the next town? I want to find work so I can call my family and friends. They have no idea where I am. In fact, where am I?" I asked.

"We're on the West Jersey and Seashore Railroad. You hopped on just outside of Atlantic City. We were there looking for work and found some, but didn't make much money and we spent it on food. The next town is Newfield, New Jersey and there is a small jungle there. You can hop off and go in there. Introduce yourself, tell the truth, and ask if anyone knows where there is work. They probably won't tell you since you're new, but it don't hurt to ask. Someone like us might take a likin' to you" Moe said.

"Where are you guys going? I want to go to Chicago where I have family and friends."

"We are going to the end of the line at Delaware Bay to avoid Philadelphia, take a boat across the bay and pick up the Philadelphia, Wilmington and Baltimore going to Baltimore. We have sometimes been able to get work in Baltimore doing our vaudeville act. Don't pay much but we like to keep our show sharp. Never know when we might find a town that still likes vaudeville" said Moe.

"Do you know a fellow by the name of W.C. Fields?" I asked.

"Who? Oh you mean William Claude Dukenfield? I heard he calls himself Fields now. Yeah, we know him, he showed us some stuff back in the day and we opened shows for him. Good juggler, oddball jokes, heard he was in the flickers now" said Joe. "You talk like you know."

"I have met him I have not worked with him on stage. I've seen some of his routines and his movies. Makes me laugh. He's quite a character" I said.

"That he is, son. He was lucky to make the transition into flickers." Joe said.

"Would you tell me when I should hop off before Newfield? I'd travel with you guys but I want to be heading more to the west, you know, for Chicago."

Joe and Moe whispered to each other. "Well, seeing as you're a nice fellow, we might be willing to travel as far west as Chicago, if you're willing to share out your money. We'll share with you, kind of like having an agreement to travel together. We decided that if you traveled alone, naïve as you are, some cutthroat will have you for lunch."

"I'd be much obliged gentlemen" I said.

"Look, he calls us gentlemen, Moe. Son, if we travel together you have to follow the code and if we tell you to do something, do it, because we won't tell you unless it is important. Sometimes there are people we have to be careful of, so don't be volunteering information to people you don't know."

That's how I became pals with Moe and Joe. I later found out that they were big time vaudeville stars before people turned to the movies. I was glad to have their experience to help me ride the rails. I did not mind sharing out my money I earned while hoboing. Once I was able to send a telegram to Laure I'd give it all to them, except what I needed for food until my friends arrived.

In Chicago I could call Jake or Scott or my old friends Otto and Fritz, who now owned my former auto repair shop in Long Grove. They could pass the word to Laure and someone would send me money for a ticket home.

Home. That made me think about Laure and how much I wanted to hold her to me, taste her sweet kisses. I loved how she smelled, her hair, her skin, her beautiful face and that brilliant smile. I wanted to kiss her neck and lick Champagne from between her breasts, then trail on down where I liked to drive her wild. I made myself stop thinking that as my cock began to get hard. And I was worried about Dawn. I couldn't find her trail. She might have been caught or be injured or dead somewhere. I hoped she had not died creating a diversion for my escape.

Moe, Joe and I hopped off at Newfield to find work. We were starving and needed food. Moe and Joe found work washing dishes at restaurants while I worked as a farm hand. It was hard work but they fed me well and my strength returned, although I had become seriously thin. I remembered ruefully when I had lost four pounds at Indianapolis, and Laure had complimented me on looking great. The suggestive way she said that earned her a barney-mugging, which she later told me was her plan, saying it was more fun to turn me on to get seduced. Oh how I missed her sense of humor, not to mention getting a good romp in bed almost every day.

The jungle at Newfield was not a big one and I met other hobos, mostly guys down on their luck trying to get it back. There were a few bad guys that we had to watch out for. Two days after we arrived I returned from work to find a big guy trying to force Moe and Joe into giving him their money. I walked up to him and told him to leave them alone.

He got real angry. There are guys that are just that way and I figured him to be one of them, always mad at the world and willing to take it out on those that weren't. The big guy telegraphed his intentions as he took a step back to swing at me. As he did, I stepped inside and gave him a quick flurry of gut punches which slowed him down, then I gave him two to the chin as hard as I could. He went down, his back in the fire. We pulled him out and rolled him to get the flames put out. He wasn't burned, but he was angry.

The next day he waited in ambush for me, but he hadn't figured on Joe standing about twenty feet behind the guy and pointing into the brush where the big guy was trying to hide. I made like I was going to walk right into his trap but I was ready and sprung back when he jumped. He landed on his stomach because he put everything into his jump, wanting to smash me into the hard packed ground.

He was stunned long enough for me to get his arm behind his back and pulled up tight. He screamed in pain and other hobos came to look, but they knew the guy was bad news and most of them liked Moe and Joe and me, so they ignored our fight.

He kept screaming and I kept pulling his arm up higher. Finally he begged me to stop, saying he would not bother us again. I knew I should not trust him, but did not want to dislocate his shoulder either, so I let him loose and jumped up. He got up slowly and turned away from me, but then quickly whirled around to sucker punch me. He wasn't fast and I ducked and parried his punches, getting in close for more gut punching, which was his weak spot. He went down, moaning and holding his stomach. Moe and Joe came over and kicked him. I stopped them, but I told the guy if he ever bothered us again, I would put him down and let everyone kick him until he couldn't get up again. He got the message and left us alone after that.

Next day we were on the rails, then got on a ferry across the Delaware Bay then back on the rails of the PW&B to Baltimore. After that we rode the Northern Central to Harrisburg, stopping there for a couple of days to make money for food. I found farm work again since I didn't like washing dishes. I would rather do the harder physical work that Moe and Joe, being older guys, could not do as easily, and it helped keep me in shape. I lived by the Hobo Code and I found that I enjoyed these relatively carefree days. Moe and Joe told me stories of vaudeville I admitted to having written a screenplay for a Hollywood studio, but did not tell them I owned a winery.

I missed Laure so bad that I decided to take the chance to send a telegram. I had been afraid to do that because Rose's gang would be looking for me, and they might have friends in Pennsylvania. They might have telegraph operators on the pad to let them know if I showed up. The cops might be looking for me about the stolen Locomobile. It could even be Nucky looking for us if he thought I had killed poor old Digger. I wanted to get word to him about what really happened.

I sent a telegram to the LaureDan Company because I knew Laure might be on the road looking for me. Josefina would get the telegram and get the news to Laure. I sent a cryptic telegram signed with my initials DJL.

Unfortunately I was right to worry that someone was looking for me. We heard through the jungle grapevines that some guys were asking around about me. They didn't know I was traveling with two other men and hobos don't give out information about their own. I guessed correctly that the telegram was not sent and I had wasted my money. I decided to get closer to Chicago before I tried that again.

From Harrisburg we hopped a long Pennsy freight to Pittsburgh. We earned money for food and camped at jungles outside of Pittsburgh for a few days to get more money saved up, since Moe said some of the conductors on the railroads in Ohio and Indiana would let you ride but expected a bribe to overlook your presence. Another couple of hard guys tried to grab Moe and take his money but Joe let out a warning and I came running to drive away the poachers with a few well-placed punches. From all the farm work I was doing, I was getting stronger and becoming a tough fighter. The word had gotten out not to mess with us because we stuck together, along with a couple of other guys who asked to join us, glad to share money and food and because Moe and Joe insisted we be fair and share ours. I was able to afford used clothes from a church thrift shop, and I bought for myself and my friends. I washed my old clothing, worn but in serviceable condition, then gave it to hobos who needed it.

In Pittsburgh I worked at an auto repair shop and my friends found jobs here and there. Moe and Joe and I had become close friends. We shared our food and although it was not cooked like my mother or Sunny our home chef, we had enough and it kept us going. Laure was a great cook, but she did not like to cook except for making pies at holidays, when I would help her in the kitchen until we couldn't stand it and I would grab her and have my way, although she said she was having her way with me.

Fond memories of Laure kept me in good spirits. Always enchanted by watching her shoulders and back and her cute little butt as she leaned over the table to roll pie crusts, one day I was overcome with desire and lifted her up, putting her on the sturdy butcher block kitchen work table where she had been rolling pie crusts and proceeded to have my way with her. There was pie crust and flour all over the kitchen and all over us, and we danced and laughed when we were done. After we cleaned up and made more pie crusts, we made love on the table again. I pointed out that she was violating her rule that if we were near a bed, that's where we should make love. But Laure told me it was so much fun she was making an exception. The pies, by the way, turned out to be excellent. After I had teased myself with the memory, that evening I bought a couple of pies on the way back to camp and shared them out with my hobo pals although I did not tell them why I felt the urge to have pie. Moe, Joe and I each had a piece of pie and Moe cut the rest of the pies into equal slices and served them around. It wasn't much, but they were pleased that we shared the treat with them.

The hobo life was good common sense and it agreed with me, especially as our circle of friends grew. Moe and Joe knew most of them, and let only those hobos who followed the code into our group of friends. However, as a group of men that were doing relatively well we attracted the bums who preferred to steal or cheat and my fists were becoming harder as I got better at knocking them down. I showed some of the other hobos how to fight and it did not take long until no one except the foolish or the newcomers tried anything.

Our group was a hard working bunch and we made some money. I was getting anxious to get home and Moe said we could ride the Pittsburgh, Ft. Wayne & Chicago all the way to Chicago. We would have to hop five different trains but there they knew the hobo jungles across Ohio and Indiana to spend the nights. On our last night in Pittsburgh I treated our fellow travelers to pies again. The next morning Moe, Joe and I said goodbye the jungle and settled into an empty boxcar for the first leg of our trip to Chicago. But it was not to be ours for long. The train made an unexpected stop in the middle of nowhere and a large and ornery conductor with three big cinderdicks were going from boxcar to boxcar, rousting out the hobos and giving each one a beating. Some of our guys tried the trick of hiding out of sight up under the boxcar or on the roof but the cinderdicks were experienced in the tricks of the hobo community and found them, pulling them out of their hidey-holes. We heard the sounds of hobos being beaten up getting closer, and the conductor and his goons would soon be on us. These thugs were big, mean and fast and could bring in the local law on their side. Our little ragtag group would not have a chance to stand up to them.

"I'm sorry Dan, we knew of this guy but he was said to be down near Cincinnati, but they must have transferred him up here. If we knew we would have taken a different railroad" Moe said, not looking forward to a beating.

"It's not your fault Moe. I just took a quick look and they pulled five men out from a boxcar, so they're going to be busy for a minute or two. I can't fight all the railroad guys, and if I'm knocked out you guys will be next so let's hoof it out of here. It's a couple hundred feet to the tree line of that section of woods, you two head for it as fast as you can. I'll be right behind you. If they get close I'll keep them busy long enough for you to get away" I told them.

"Thanks Dan, if we get split up the next jungle is on this side of Massillon Ohio. Don't let the dicks get their hands on you. They are vicious and hurt men just for the sake of hurting them, and those who fight get beaten worse for it. Because it is our word against theirs they never get in trouble. They just say we fell out of a moving boxcar and the town cops and sheriffs won't do nothin'" Joe said.

"You two get going while the thugs are busy. Go!" and they took off. I counted to ten then jumped and ran. The guys were only ten feet from the trees when the cinderdicks spotted us and came running. Moe and Joe made it into the trees and I was right at the tree line when the first cinderdick tried to grab me. They had told me not to fight the dicks, but my natural response was to defend myself. I spun when the dick grabbed my shirt and it ripped as I came around with my spin momentum and landed a hard fist to the dick's face, breaking his nose. He went down howling but I made it into the woods. Moe and Joe were nimble old guys and made their way deep in the woods by following along a creek. I caught up with them a few minutes later. They said the cinderdicks rarely went deep into wooded areas because they might get ambushed, and anyway there were several more hobos to beat up on the stopped freight train.

The hobos that were beaten had been left lying on the ground, some with broken limbs. I went back to the edge of the woods, becoming angrier by the minute. The locomotive whistle blew, the thugs got on as the train began to move. Moe and Joe tried to stop me but I was madder than hell and told them to go help the others. Then I ran to get ahold of the caboose that the cinderdicks and the conductor climbed on. My time learning how to get on and off a moving train paid off. I got up on the rear platform of the caboose and peeked through a window. The thugs were sitting at a table passing around a bottle of white dog and laughing. They had blood on their clothing from the men they had brutalized, and were counting out a small pile of cash taken from the hobos. It was bad odds at four thugs to one of me, and I wished I had Viktor with me but my companion was the element of surprise. After a minute I saw how to fight one or two at a time.

I opened the door silently and went in. The dicks had not seen me yet. There were bunks and lockers on either side of a narrow corridor so if they came at me they had to attack one at a time. I grabbed a short-handled square-ended spade hanging on a wall bracket.

After they counted out the cash they laughed and drank as they played cards, so I was able to move quietly behind them as they sat at their table. I got their attention when I swung the spade and smashed their bottle of moonshine. I raised the spade to hit the closest thug, swung fast and clocked him upside the head with the back of the spade and he slumped over and fell from his chair, blood pouring from his scalp. The other dicks stood up and tried to lunge at me but the table was between us. I held the spade horizontal and jabbed it at one, striking him in the chest and cracked a couple of his ribs. He went down.

The conductor reached inside his coat and pulled out a .38 short-barreled revolver, but I had seen him reach in and my shovel was already in motion. I smashed it down with all my strength on his hand and he dropped the gun. It skittered across the floor, I positioned the spade to slap his head with the flat side, and the bully began to blubber and beg for mercy. He was much bigger than I was, but seeing two of his goons go down so easily he didn't want to mess with me. I was so angry at what they had done to those poor hobos that I kept swinging and chopping the shovel until all four were groaning lumps on the floor. I shouted "Get off this train. Jump now, off the back platform. Do it!"

The others jumped but the conductor kept begging for mercy so I had to poke him with the spade a couple times to get him to move to the door. He went out on the platform but did not want to jump because the train was moving too fast. I poked him again and he got to the side of the platform holding on to the railing. I smashed the back of the spade down on his fingers until they were bloody but he kept holding on. I raised the spade to his face. "Jump now or the next strike will be to your neck".

His face went from being a cowardly bully to a look of fright and fear. I didn't want to kill the guy, I wanted him to jump and break a leg or arm and feel what it was like to be helplessly beaten. I gave his fingers one more smash and his grip loosened. Down he went off the platform. I watched his body bounce as he rolled down the side of the railroad embankment.

My anger subsided with the sight of the conductor hitting the ground hard. I found his gun and put it in my pocket, took some food and pulled the emergency brake handle. The train began to slow down and I made a safe jump off and disappeared into the woods.

Circling back I found Moe and Joe looking real scared. "Dan, you did a brave thing and the boys will always remember what you did for them, but now you are in a heap of trouble. These cinderdicks stick together and they will pass the word up and down the rails to take revenge on you."

"The dicks didn't get a good look at you, I'm the guy they can identify. Let's get all the hobos moved to safety so when the dicks return they will not find them."

Some of the injured men who could walk had left the area and we did what we could to help the others, which wasn't much until one of the hobos who ran away saw us and came back. He was a medic during the war and soon we were helping him fashion splints from pieces of wood and binding wounds with whatever clothing we could rip into bandages. I gave the medic my ripped shirt because I had another shirt in my bindle. The men were grateful and some reached into their pockets to give us coins, but they came up empty because the dicks had robbed them. I got pissing angry again but there was nothing for it.

We rested in the tree line until another slow freight came by and we hopped on. Getting off outside of Massillon, we found the jungle and began to settle in when a group of men came over and told us we had to leave. "Word is up and down the line about you beatin' up a conductor and three dicks, and the railroad gumshoes are hoppin' mad. You gotta leave because they will be looking for you, and if they find you here they will drive us all out and we'll get beat up too. Now git!" So we did. We were moving deeper into the woods when sounds of fighting came from the jungle. The dicks arrived in force and beat them up even though we were not there. I told Moe and Joe to keep going while I went back. The dicks beat up the hobos and set fire to the jungle camp.

Next morning we walked to Massillon. I found a telegraph office at the train station. Taking a chance I pulled my hat down over my face and went into the office. I was filling out a message form when Moe tugged my sleeve and pointed at a handbill tacked up on the wall. It was a good pencil drawn likeness of me with a reward posted of $500 for information leading to my arrest for assault on a railroad employee and three railroad policemen. The clerk deliberately ignored us so Joe took the handbill off the wall, folded it up and put it in his pocket. I called the clerk over to send the telegram, hoping this one would go through but now I was worried that he would tear it up and call the railroad dicks.

The telegraph operator did not look at me as he said in a low voice "My cousin was on a freight east of town. He was ridin' the rails to get here for his mother's funeral. Some dicks pulled him out of a boxcar and beat him up real bad, breakin' his arm and leaving him bloody. Some men who had been on the freight helped clean him up and splint his arm good enough to get to Massillon where he was able to send word to me. I got him to a doctor and he will be OK. I don't wanna look at you, but I know who you are. There's a handbill on the wall…" and he looked over and saw that it was gone.

He gave me a small smile, now he could look at me. "Whoever you are, thank you for helping my cousin. Not many folks will stop to help a hobo. And if you're the guy who stomped the dicks, good on ya, but don't tell anyone I said that. Take my advice and get yourself out of Massillon as fast as you can, and don't get on the tracks in or out of here. The railroad sent a small army to clean out the jungles up and down the Pittsburgh, Ft. Wayne and Chicago tracks. If you stay in the area they will find you. I'll send this telegram but let's change a few words OK?" It took us a minute to adjust the words and we left before a pair of cinderdicks came to the office to ask about me.

My actions had stirred up a hornet's nest. I had no idea how riled up these dicks would get when they got a dose of their own medicine. I told Moe and Joe, "like I always say, fuck 'em if they can't take a joke."

"Hey, maybe we should work that line into our act" Moe said.

FRIENDS FROM FRANCE

Laure narrates

Vera turned away but the man was strong and pulled her to him. He was saying something but Vera was so scared she did not recognize his words. Suddenly the man tried to kiss her on the cheek, and at the same moment she saw that the person behind the big man was her childhood friend Marie-Laure. Things quickly calmed down as she introduced Vera to her husband Jean-Philippe and their son Charles. Despite his ferocious visage, Jean-Philippe was a fun-loving man and apologized for his mistake in assuming Vera had been expecting their arrival. The telegraph line had been down the day before because of a thunderstorm and tornado, and the messenger didn't deliver the telegram until after Philippe and Marie-Laure arrived. *"Je suis désolé de vous surprendre. Je voulais vous saluer avec un gros câlin et baiser français!"* Jean-Philippe said, ashamed that he had been the cause of shocking his wife's best childhood friend.

The confusion was not over. A neighbor heard Vera's scream and called the constable's office. Constable Sherman was not there so the neighbor came running over with his shotgun after sending his son to find the constable. The neighbor held Jean-Philippe at shotgun point until Constable Sherman got there and Vera told him who her guests were and that it had been an unfortunate misunderstanding.

Vera and Marie were thrilled to see each other again and to celebrate their reunion they made a dinner to exceed any gourmet's expectations. The next day she took her guests over to the McLanahan Ranch and introduced them to the McLanahans and Dorothy Lindner who was there visiting. Another big dinner was put on, and it was a full and weary trio who arrived back at Vera's later that evening. Vera did not see the new telegram envelope on the tray in the hallway where her maid had placed it several hours before.

The next day Vera jumped when she finally read it, blinking with disbelief. It was from Dan and sounded like he was in trouble somewhere in Ohio. She tried to call Laure but Sunny answered and said Laure was somewhere back east searching for Dan. Josefina did not know for certain where Laure and her crew were, telling Vera that Laure's last report was from New Jersey.

"Vera, what is wrong? You look so worried" said Marie-Laure.

"Oh I don't know what to do. My daughter is searching for Dan in New Jersey but he's in Ohio and needs help" Vera said to Marie-Laure and Jean-Philippe.

"Why was Laure-Marie searching for her husband? Was he running away from her?"

"No, no, nothing like that." Vera told them the short version of their recent adventures.

Jean-Philippe whistled. "Mon Dieu! C'est terrible!"

"Father, you should speak English since we are in America" Charles told his father.

"Of course, I am just so shocked. What can I do to help?" Jean-Philippe asked earnestly.

"I don't know how you could help. Laure has several good people with her and they are looking for a person known as Rose Herlihy. Until I find out where she is, I can't get a message to my daughter and she will not know that Dan is in Ohio."

Marie-Laure said "Jean-Philippe can be of assistance. He is a Colonel in the Gendarmerie Nationale, a national police force in France. He is experienced at investigating, solving crimes and finding people. He has been working hard without a vacation and I finally talked him into taking some of his leave, and here I am telling you to use his experience to help you. I do this willingly. You can send Jean-Philippe and we will spend our time laughing and talking and catching up on what's happened in our lives, *nous aurons du plaisir ensemble à nouveau.*"

"But my dear Marie-Laure, he will have no jurisdiction here. He can only help as a civilian."

"That is so Vera, but he is a most experienced civilian, and you need his expertise" Marie-Laure responded.

"I don't want to spoil your vacation, please do not worry. I will keep trying to contact Laure" said Vera.

Charles spoke up. "Aunt Vera, we do not see this as spoiling our vacation, it will be part of our American adventure. Since I was a little boy I remember my mother talking of you as part of our family. You need help and my father can provide that help. Besides, if I can talk Papa into taking me along, I would get to see more of America. I am enchanted by your country and all its opportunities."

Jean-Philippe added "I ask you not to be concerned, I am pleased to do this. Tell me more about this difficulty. Do you have photos of Dan so I can see what he looks like? And yes, I would take Charles along with me, he has a brilliant analytical mind, a university trained architectural engineer who would have made a good police officer if he wasn't designing buildings. Charles came with us to see as much of America as he can, and this would be a way for him to do that."

Vera didn't want them to be in danger, but if all they were doing was helping find Dan, she would be glad for any help they could give. "Thank you for your offer of help. I'll go to the bank and get some money for your expenses" Vera said.

"No that is not necessary. Marie-Laure now controls her family's trading business and shipping interests she inherited from her father and I earn a good salary as a Colonel, which is a military title because the Gendarmerie Nationale is a branch of the French military. Our responsibility is to police the areas of France outside of the cities and large towns of France, which are served by the Sûreté, also known as the Police Nationale. The Gendarmerie Nationale police the coast, the airports, the roads and we are often called to assist city police agencies. Finding people and dealing with gangsters and kidnappers is something I have much experience. I place myself at your service, Madame Winiarzski, and ask you to accept my humble and sincere offer of assistance. Besides, I am happy when I am in action. Marie-Laure thinks I need a vacation, and I am enjoying our time here, but some action would be just the right tonic for me."

"How can I refuse when you say it that way?" Vera laughed and told Jean-Philippe everything she knew about the situation and gave him photographs of Dan and Laure. Jean-Philippe asked about maps as he was unfamiliar with our cities and roads. Vera called Elaine McLanahan and she said Thomas was at home and put him on the line. Thomas immediately offered to send a ranch hand on his way over with maps and timetables of Ohio, Michigan, Indiana and Illinois roads and railroads.

After consulting the timetables, they decided that Vera and Marie-Laure would drive Jean-Philippe and Charles to Chicago that afternoon so they could get on a morning train to Massillon, where Dan's telegram originated. "Jean-Philippe, Charles, I am so thankful for your assistance. Here's a list of telephone numbers for me, for the LaureDan Company where their partner Josefina will help in any way she can, and the telephone number for the McLanahan security office in Chicago. The office will relay messages and provide information, and Thomas has put you on his list of friends. Thomas is a stockholder in several railroads and is well connected. Here are letters I have written for you and Charles to present to the authorities to explain your presence and ask for support in your investigation."

"Merci" Jean-Philippe said. "I am prepared better than sometimes in France with all the information you have given me. I will send telegrams when I have news to report." Vera and Marie-Laure drove the men to a hotel near Chicago's Union Station. Jean-Philippe and Charles kissed Marie-Laure and Vera, and the ladies returned to

Long Grove. Jean-Philippe's professionalism helped Vera feel better and she called Josefina to tell her who they were. There was nothing to do now but wait. In the excitement Vera began to understand why Laure refused to sit by the telephone and wait. Vera now wished she could help her daughter in person but she had put the experience of her friends on the case and had nothing to add to their expertise.

"Well Laure, what do we do now? Giuseppe asked. "We have been chasing our tails trying to find Rose. All we know is that she is in the area, we have seen some of her gang, but she herself remains invisible to us. We are sure that Dan and Dawn have long since left New Jersey but we can't get any word of where they are. They have not turned up in Chicago. We have run up blind alleys at every turn."

"I'm sure Dan was here, and if we keep Rose pinned down in New Jersey she can't run him down and kill him, which I'm sure she will do if she finds him before we do." An hour later a telegram delivery boy came with an envelope for me. I signed for it, gave the boy a tip, and ripped open the envelope. It was from Josefina, telling me to call Vera who had received a telegram from Dan. Why didn't he send it to me? *'Well, that was a silly thought, he had no idea where I was'.*

Had I received the telegram earlier I would have flown to Chicago with my Pa. He told me that my mother's childhood best friend Marie-Laure was due any day now on their tour of the United States. I wished I could be there, sure that she would not understand why a woman would be traveling all over the country with other men to find her husband. That was not done a few years ago, but I embraced the Modern Woman, the Flapper social revolution, except for smoking cigarettes and having sex with any man who looked interesting. The call I placed to my mother came through in less than ten minutes. Telephone service was improving rapidly.

"Hello Ma, this is your missing daughter Laure. I heard you had news of Dan."

"Yes and you would know this if you were home so we could find you to tell you the news." The line went silent. My mother and I had talked this subject over thoroughly and I had no desire to do it again, but she surprised me by saying next "I'm sorry my dear, that was wrong of me. I am filled with anxiety" my mother said. I was amazed – my own mother was now implying that it was OK for me to be all over the country to help rescue my husband? "Now that I am waiting for someone to call with news, I understand better why you do not wait. I'm not nearly as competitive and adventurous as you are. You must have gotten that from your father."

"Thank you Ma, but what is the news you have from Dan?" I tried to be patient but my mother was not telling me anything and we had been on the telephone for over a minute. My mother apologized and read Dan's telegram to me, then told me about her dear friend Marie-Laure and her husband and son arriving and how Jean-Philippe and Charles volunteered to go to Ohio to see if they could find Dan. I was impressed. Here were two men from France who I had never met and they volunteered to help. I felt even better when Ma told me about Jean-Philippe's background as an experienced investigator with the rank of colonel in the Gendarmerie Nationale of France. He was someone who could look at things dispassionately and not miss any clues. Now that I knew Dan was traveling west there was no reason for us to search for Rose in New Jersey, although we would have to be careful or Rose could be a problem if she came up behind us.

Calling my crew together I told them the latest news and that we were going to Ohio as fast as possible. Big Al and our private locomotive – which I once considered an extravagance but now I was happy to spend the money on it – would roll as soon as Bill arranged clearances with the railroads. I had purchased an old executive railcar with a worn out interior. Bill and Big Al declared it to be a good railcar, just needing some cosmetic refurbishment. And the Swedes did a great job fixing it up.

I continued to worry about Rose, but we had no clues to follow, and I so desperately wanted to hold Dan close to me and make him swear that we would never be separated again. Then I would fuck his brains out to make up for time lost. I had to stop thinking like that. What if he and Dawn had run off together? Then I would never feel his loving and would only be left with forlorn desires. I wondered if Buster might still care but threw that idea away just as fast as it arrived. Yes, Buster was a good man, a great lover and fun to be with, but he would never have the place in my heart that Dan held. Never.

In just a couple of hours we were all aboard and the train began to move toward home. Home. I wondered if we would ever have a safe, secure home.

SS GRAND RAPIDS

Dan narrates

With the cinderdicks on a rampage looking for me, I reluctantly parted ways with Moe and Joe because I did not want them to be found with me. I disguised myself with a different name and grew a beard but despite that the cinderdicks came close to capturing me twice. I feared to send a telegram when I found the handbill with drawings of my likeness on every telegraph office bulletin board. A friendly telegraphist told me that the cinderdicks threatened the telegraph operators if they failed to report my appearance. I had not been able to get a mile west of Massillon because they were watching the highways as well as the tracks. I created a distraction by paying a boy from another town to use my name to send a telegram for me to Josefina, telling her that I was going to ride the rails in a southerly direction. That opened up a brief chance to ride the rails north and I arrived in Monroe, Michigan where the town's claim to fame was being the birthplace of General George Armstrong Custer. Now I was able to ride the rails under the slightly less angry eyes of the gumshoes of the Grand Rapids & Indiana Railroad.

I ran out of money just east of Grand Rapids Michigan near the town of Ada and I found employment in a remote hilly area working for a persnickety old geezer who made beer and moonshine. He trained me on the moonshine still and I learned fast. Bootleg whiskey often deserved the name coffin varnish and the old geezer was careless of the quality of his product. Not wanting to make something that could blind people, I befriended a local farmer who hauled the moonshine for the old coot. He was impressed that I wanted to make good whiskey and taught me the right way to do it. This got me in trouble with my ornery boss who complained it took me too long to make whiskey, but he did not fire me because no one else was willing to work for him. One night I had enough of the old fool's whining so I punched his lights out when he pulled a gun on me. I picked up his revolver and kept it. He became more reasonable after that.

Buying used clothing from church thrift shops helped me to have enough money to eat better, but I was still thin from hard work and worry. My plan was to earn money to buy a car. Even with the cinderdicks watching the roads I thought I could sneak away at night and get to Chicago.

By now I had no idea if Laure was still my wife. She might have assumed I was dead. Although in my heart I hoped she waited for me, I had once told her if something happened to me she should move on and build a new life. These were unpleasant thoughts so I tried not to think on them.

Working at the still on a hot afternoon I noticed two men coming up the hill. I grabbed the old rifle that my boss had left. Not to protect me, he said, just to protect the still, damn the old coot. The men were getting closer and were coming up the path to the still. One of the men was middle aged with broad shoulders, a very sturdy fellow who looked like a policeman. The other was young and tall and looked like a professor.

I thought they were railroad dicks who discovered my location. When they got close I stepped out of the shed with the rifle pointed directly at them and called "Stop right there. Who are you and what do you want? Speak plainly and quickly. I have no patience for cinderdicks who beat defenseless hobos." I knew that might enrage them, but I was getting tired of not being with my Laure.

"I agree, I do not like policemen who beat up people for sport" said the wide-shouldered man with a distinct French accent. "What did he call them? Cinder-dicks? Charles, what does that mean?" he asked the other man.

The younger man smiled, saying "it translates literally as 'cendre flic', or 'mâchefer flic', but in France we call them 'la police des chemins de fer.'"

"Interesting" said the older man. "Allow me to introduce my son Charles, who is making a study of the English language because he plans to live in the United States for a year or two to further his education. I am Jean-Philippe Lamoreaux. At home in France I am a Colonel of the Gendarmerie Nationale. As such I have no police authority in the United States, but I have been searching for you at the request of Lady Vera Winiarzski. I have a letter from her attesting to that fact." He held out the letter.

"No, I'm not going to fall for that trick. Put the letter on that tree stump and take ten steps back." He obeyed my request and I went to the stump. It looked to be Vera's handwriting but I could not be sure. "How did she come to ask you to look for me, especially since you have no police authority? That does not make sense" I said.

Jean-Philippe laughed. "Yes, she told me you would be wary. Perhaps I should tell you that my wife is Marie-Laure Lamoreaux, her father was Baron Peel. Vera and my wife are best childhood friends. Her daughter Laure-Marie was named after my wife, who asked that the names be reversed because a ship named after her was lost with all hands in a typhoon. Marie-Laure is superstitious and thought that would turn away any bad luck."

I remembered the story that Laure had told me and wanted to believe the man. But what if he came from Louisiana where French was a common language and was working for Rose who had found this information and told him what to say so he could grab me?

"What do you know about Laure?" I asked hopefully.

"That I cannot say as I have not met her. Vera said Laure-Marie was with your friends on a train searching to rescue you from someone she called Rose who has a bad voice from a gunshot wound. May I reach into my pocket to produce my police shield? It is from France but it is real, and perhaps it will ease your doubts about us."

"Yes, but do it slow and easy." Jean-Philippe carefully took out a leather wallet, opened it and turned the badge toward me. He walked to the stump, set it down and moved back. I went to look at it. It was in French and could be fake, but if it was fake someone had done an impressive job of making it look real. Still, it proved nothing to me. "You have all the right answers but I don't know if Rose coached you to say these things."

"Monsieur Lindner, I do not know what I can tell you to convince you. I understand what you have been through. I talked to the conductor on the train that you and your hobo friends were on, when this conductor and his men beat up several, what do you call them Charles? Oh yes, unpaid travelers. He and his cendre-flics didn't want to talk to me and gave evasive answers to my questions after I – um – persuaded them to talk. I know the signs of deceit from my years of dealing with criminals. I thought them to be reprehensible men who should not have police authority, but sadly, that is not for me to decide. I also talked to two men who say they are friends of yours. They are old-fashioned gentlemen who introduced themselves as Moe and Joe. I am sorry if you cannot believe me, and I knew it might be difficult for you. Charles and I will go, but I advise you that I will telegraph Lady Vera to report I have seen you."

"Yes, I understand, but I cannot take any chances to go with you, even if you are who you say you are. I'm sorry, but if I am wrong please tell Laure that you saw me, and tell her I love her and miss her very much."

"I will tell her. Vera told us Laure-Marie is terribly worried for you, and she misses you as well. Your family and friends desire your safe return." The man went slowly to the stump, picked up his badge and the letter, took an envelope from his coat pocket, set it down and walked back down the trail with his son. I watched them go down the hill until they were out of sight. I went to the stump and looked in the envelope. It contained $50, which I was glad to add to my meager wallet. Now I was conflicted. I wanted to trust them but Rose was clever and vicious, and it was possible that she could have found out this information and coached this Jean-Philippe guy on what to say to trick me. Then I would find myself standing in front of the New Jersey mob again, and without Dawn to rescue me. No, I could not take that risk. But I was heartened at the thought that Laure and my friends were looking for me and had also found out who was conducting the vendetta against us. It also meant that Laure was not at home taking male callers to our marital bed after I disappeared. If that were the case, Rose was lying to cause trouble between Laure and me. It meant that as long as Laure and I were together in spirit, we must be a considerable threat to Rose.

Now that I was discovered, leaving the area was my only option if Rose had sent them. I was sorry about that because a couple more weeks of making whiskey would have provided enough cash to buy an old jalopy to drive the back roads south around Lake Michigan to Chicago.

That night I slept at the still with the rifle next to me. I planned to hitchhike to Grand Rapids in the morning, where I could look for work. Now I was willing to wash dishes to get the last dollars to purchase a car. The more I thought about it, I found myself thinking I should have trusted the Frenchmen. In my regret, I drank most of a bottle of good whiskey from one of my own batches before I fell into a drunken sleep.

During the early hours of the morning, three people quietly slipped into my camp. Seeing me sound asleep on the ground, they approached carefully. As the eastern sky began to lighten I must have rolled over and they saw and removed my rifle and pistol. Someone sat next to me and I awakened, dreaming that Laure was sleeping next to me. I was putting my arm around her as we snuggled up close and I mumbled an invitation for morning sex, one of our favorite things.

Instead I woke to the laughter of the Frenchman who looked like a policeman. My eyes blearily recorded the presence of another man and a woman, also laughing. My senses began to wake up and I tried to strike at the Frenchman as I scrambled to get up. He easily blocked my punch but did not punch back. I tried to move fast but when I stood up, I was so hung over that everything spun around and I fell back down. The three were still laughing when a familiar female voice said "Here Dan, drink a little hair-of-the-dog and you'll feel better" as she pushed a bottle to my mouth. Taking a slug of the whiskey, my head was still pounding but I recognized Dawn with the two Frenchmen from yesterday.

"I am pleased to find you alive but alas, I must turn away your request for a morning fuck" said the man who introduced himself again as Jean-Philippe.

"Well this is a surprise" I said as calmly as I could manage. My head was still spinning and I was now suspicious that Dawn was the leak in our crew that was telling Rose and her gang every move we made. Unlikely, because Bill checked out everyone who worked for him, and she had worked at Pinkerton's with Bill. But it was still a possibility.

"So whose side are you on?" I lamely asked Dawn.

"Yours. With all we've had between us, you think I'd turn on you? No, I was, and still am, in love with you but Laure got to you first. I'm not angry, she won you fair and square. For me, it was a sad lesson learned" Dawn replied.

"I'm sorry Dawn. You know I like you a lot, maybe too much, but I love Laure."

"OK, but unless you want to stay here and make moonshine for the rest of your short life until Rose finds you as I suspect she will, I have an automobile nearby. It's a worn out old flivver but it should get us to Grand Haven where we can get on the Grand Trunk Western ferry boat across Lake Michigan to Milwaukee. Laure and your train could meet us there, or if they are too far away maybe Jake could fly up to bring us home. By the way, two nice old vaudeville gents named Moe and Joe send you greetings. I talked to them two days ago."

"I am sorry Mr. Lamoreaux, for thinking you were my wife."

"I should think Laure-Marie would find it as amusing as we do" laughed Jean-Philippe.

"Did I say anything else stupid?" I asked as Jean-Philippe and Charles moved away to watch the trail, giving Dawn and me a chance to talk privately.

Dawn said "Your honor is safe. I found your bottle of whiskey and finished it as I listened to you talking in your sleep. You were drunk and dreaming you were talking to Laure. You said you loved her and your description of what you wanted to do to me – her, I mean, was very sensual and I pretended you were saying it to me. You two must have a hell of a good time in bed. You never licked Champagne from my tits. But do not worry, I will not say anything to cause problems for you. How's that for stupid? I love you enough to help you get back to Laure."

"Thank you for that Dawn. You are a true friend and I am grateful. I'm tired of being on the run and was so disappointed at being discovered that I drank too much moonshine. Dawn, why didn't you wake me up last night?"

"Until it got light enough to check, we didn't know if you were sleeping with a pistol under your pillow. In your drunken fog I might have surprised you and gotten shot for it. Besides, I was enjoying your talk with Laure" Dawn said with a wry smile.

"How did you and the Frenchmen get together?"

"I was tracking you and learned someone who fit your description was working at a moonshine distillery near Grand Rapids. I thought you might be working to get money to travel. Moe and Joe said you liked to work outside of the cities. I was following leads and early yesterday I noticed these two were behind me so I hid and waited for them. As they passed I was close enough to hear them talking, and I heard your name, so I began to follow them. I was hiding down the trail and watched them when you came out of the shack. I'm glad you were careful because I had no idea who they were. My gun was out and ready if they made a false move. I saw you talk to them and was glad to see you appeared to check them out, but then you did not seem to trust them. They came back down the trail and I followed unnoticed, like I was trained to do. When we got near the town they stopped to get a sandwich" Dawn told me.

We traded the bottle and took small sips of whiskey, and Dawn continued. "Wanting to get a closer look I casually walked past them and was surprised to find out they knew I was following them when J-P said 'Madame, would you like to join us for lunch? It was a hard trail and you must be as hungry and thirsty as we are. Please join us. But first, there is a public telephone in the grocery over there. Call Vera and describe us to her, and see what she says.' And so I did. They made no move to confront me. I got Vera on the phone and she agreed with the description so I waved them to come over and gave J-P the phone so he could talk to Vera to confirm who he is. Vera called J-P's wife inside to put him on the line and he passed the test. J-P, Charles and I joined forces and came up with the plan to be here when you woke up. I was concerned that Rose may also have found your whereabouts and we wanted to be here before her goons showed up. Just so you know, since you are not available I'm becoming attracted to Charles. I cannot remember how long it's been since I've had my ashes hauled and unless you would like to volunteer your services I'm going to try him out when there is an opportunity. But I'm here for you if you want it. I know you're married to Laure, but it would be only between us and no one else would ever know."

My dick began to respond to Dawn's invitation but Laure and I had developed a synchronicity between us that made it difficult for us to lie to each other. Our minds often seemed to become one. When one of us tried to hide something from the other it quickly became obvious, so we didn't try to lie or cover anything up, and by now I didn't want any woman but Laure.

I did not even have to say no to Dawn, she understood when I changed the subject. "But Dawn, what happened in New Jersey? I was worried for you, thinking you were hurt. I circled around to your hiding place in the woods and there was blood where you were, but I couldn't find a trail to follow."

"That's kind of an embarrassing story I'd rather not tell, but I might as well spill the beans. Don't laugh, but I got shot in the ass. It was a flesh wound and I found a small town doctor to treat it to make sure it did not get infected. The doctor fixed me up, no questions asked, although he did enjoy squeezing my ass cheeks. I am so angry about being shot there because I'm going to have a scar on my ass for the rest of my life. Imagine some guy I liked who was ready to jump my bones and noticed the scar. How would I explain it? 'Oh, my old boyfriend and I were running from the mob and the police and I got shot in the ass.' A wise guy might try to make a joke about my big butt and then I would have to shoot him. You don't think my butt is too big, do you?"

I knew that question should be answered carefully, but in fact Dawn had a sweet ass, nice and round, just a bit bigger than Laure's cute little butt. "No, your sexy ass is not too big, it is just right for a man to grab and hold while he's – oh never mind. I'm sorry Dawn. You are a great friend and that night in Illinois you taught me a lot and helped me become a movie star lover for Laure. I owe you a lot. I love you too, as a sister or good friend."

"I do too, although I have never been able to decide if you or Wally was the better lover. Please take that as a compliment because Wallace Reid was as great a lover as most women fantasize, even better before his morphine addiction got bad."

"I will take it as a compliment. Maybe you should tell Laure, she still fantasizes about him. Sometimes when we role play, she asks me to pretend that I'm Wallace Reid."

"Laure never had the experience of Wally making love to her. I have. All I can say is that you and Wallace Reid are the best lovers I've ever known. You should let Laure keep that dream; it is not a bad thing. Women love to live their dreams in real life and if it is her choice that you play the role, then you are her dream lover, the man she knows will send her into ecstasy. It will keep your lovemaking exciting and special. Doncha know Laure and I had a long 'girl talk' about you. I am a little jealous of how much she is in love and in lust with you. So my advice is to make love to Laure like you made love to me whenever she asks you to be Wallace Reid."

Dawn gave me her sexy dangerous smile and the conversation was driving me wild with desire but I wanted Laure to be my wife and lover forever. I hoped we would be able to handle our pent up sexual emotions when we were reunited.

My bindle was ready to go and I went to tell the old coot I was quitting and to pick up the pay he owed me. He did not want to pay me because he had pushed me to take shortcuts in making the whiskey that I knew could be dangerous and I had refused. The old coot told me I did not follow his instructions so I did not earn my pay. I jumped at him to beat the money out of him, but Dawn came between us and pushed me away. He smiled when he saw Dawn smile and get close to him. The old bastard raised his hands to fondle her breasts, but his smile and hands dropped as he felt the sharp point of a knife at his chin. Dawn said "Pay him. In full, and add a bonus for putting up with your horsefeathers. And no more shortcuts making whiskey. You could blind or kill someone. If you ever make coffin varnish instead of whiskey again, I'll come back and believe me, you won't like what I will do to you." The old coot nervously reached in his desk, got his money box and paid me. Dawn saw a gun and a box of ammunition in the drawer and took them, removed the bullets from the gun and threw everything out the window. By the time he went out, picked them up and reloaded we would be long gone.

In Grand Haven we bought sandwiches and soda pop from a small grocery and went across the street to a park to eat. Jean-Philippe told me more about his wife Marie-Laure and her friendship with Vera while Charles and Dawn took a walk around the park, talking and laughing comfortably together. Dawn looked over at me and winked.

Jean-Philippe was able to get a call through to Vera and she gave me the best news I ever heard except for the day Laure agreed to marry me – the news that Laure and our crew were on the way to Long Grove with Big Al and the Swedes driving #3447 as fast as the railroad clearances allowed. Next time Laure called, Vera would tell her to keep going up to the ferry boat dock in Milwaukee. Not even drinking good wine or whiskey made me as high as the thought that I would soon be with Laure again. It had been over three months since we last held each other.

Dawn sold the old worn-out flivver to a used car dealer and cadged a ride to the ferry terminal where the Grand Trunk Railroad's *SS Grand Rapids* was docked and ready to load railcars and passengers. Although it was a beautiful day we paid the fare for a private stateroom since Dawn said it could get cold out on Lake Michigan, even in the summer. The departure time came and went and the ship did not leave the dock, so I went to find out why. The purser said the departure was delayed for three important passengers who were expected to arrive soon. I walked the upper deck to watch the pier for the arriving VIPs and was surprised to see a fast speedboat approach, slow down as it came to the pier and three men disembarked. The men each carried suitcases and appeared to be businessmen. As they were escorted to the ferry the lines were cast off and the big boat began to move. I wondered who the passengers were that were so important that the railroad would hold the boat for them.

Dawn and Charles seemed to be getting on very well. I figured that Dawn was in need of a man's attention while Charles was enjoying giving her his attention. I was glad Dawn found someone to scratch her itch. I had been sorely tempted to do it myself.

The sea breezes were chilly on Lake Michigan, and we went to the lounge for a hot drink and something to eat. Afterward Dawn and Charles stayed on deck while J-P and I went to the sitting room to sample some of my good rye whiskey. I was looking forward to hearing stories of Vera and Marie-Laure, but my mood was dampened when J-P told me he felt like we were being watched. I had not noticed, but J-P was an experienced detective and would notice such things well before I did. When I asked J-P to describe the men he saw, it was a good description of the three special passengers. I dismissed the obvious thought. How could anyone know I was on the *SS Grand Rapids* and how could they get there that fast? It had to be a coincidence. But then I remembered Viktor and Bill having a conversation about there not being very many true coincidences in life. J-P and I went looking for Charles and Dawn to warn them.

J-P and I walked the upper decks and a lower deck without seeing Charles or Dawn. J-P took another stroll on the upper deck in case we had missed them while I went to check our stateroom. Dawn and Charles were not there, but as I came out, the three passengers were waiting outside the door. All I had was the pistol I took from the old geezer, which looked like it would fall apart if I pulled the trigger. I didn't have time to pull it before they grabbed me, one at each arm and the third behind us. I was frog-marched down a corridor when J-P came around a corner and took in the situation. His gun appeared in his hand so fast I didn't see how it got there. The three men were momentarily surprised so I twisted away from my handlers and pulled my pistol. The tables were turned as we had them from two sides.

J-P told them to go back into our stateroom, but one of them spotted a fire alarm box and pulled the lever. Immediately the corridor filled with the loud clanging of emergency bells along with passengers and ship's crewmen. We couldn't shoot as the bad guys vanished into the crush of people. Charles and Dawn heard the bells and came running to our stateroom. Knowing that there was not a fire, we went inside and locked the door. Each of us had revolvers.

Our two outer stateroom windows opened to the promenade deck, and just as the bells were silenced those windows were smashed open followed by Tommyguns pushed through the openings to spray the room with Chicago Lightning. There was no place for us to take cover so we hit the floor, but the shooters saw us and began to lower their aim. J-P rolled on the floor next to a window, grabbed the shooter's Thompson from the side and pulled. J-P was strong and agile and he pulled the shooter inside, clean through the window. The shooter was still trying to turn his gun to shoot when J-P hit the goon in the face, wrestled the Thompson from him and threw him back out the window. The goon pulled a pistol and started shooting wildly. Dawn, deciding that enough was enough, gave him one shot between the eyes and he was dead before he hit the deck. The other two ran away.

J-P stripped the Thompson down and hid the various parts and we put our revolvers under the couch cushions just before the stateroom door was kicked open by the ship's crew. Dawn sat there with a section of the newspaper and casually pretended to read. The ship's officer demanded to know what happened, and we told him someone broke the windows and shot their guns while we dived to the floor, and we had no idea who the shooters were.

This was true but not the full story. The crewmen were assigned to check all the rooms for injured persons but they were unarmed and panicky. They left for the next room without searching for guns and left the dead gunman on the deck.

A few minutes later, two sailors with a stretcher and a man who appeared to be a doctor came, pronounced the man dead and removed him without saying a word to us.

A half-hour later, the boat's captain came in with four of his crew and asked where the body was. We told him and described the men who had taken the body. The captain made no reply but eyed us as if we were the gangsters.

We decided to wait up on deck until we arrived at the Port of Milwaukee terminal. It would be less cover but easier for us to watch for the thugs and melt into the crowds on deck. J-P put the Thompson parts in our travel bags and we carried our revolvers in our pockets, Dawn in her handbag.

Charles went to get coffee for us but came back immediately, saying he spotted the two men who ran away from outside our stateroom earlier. J-P wanted to go to the captain but Dawn said the captain might have been bribed. I found a porter and he said there was no exit check for passengers at the departure gate, so I told my friends to follow me. Walking down two decks we found a way into the railcar hold. I nosed around and found a boxcar that would suit our needs, first in line and partially filled with freight that would make good hiding and defensive positions if need be. Only one sailor was patrolling the railcar deck. When he was on the other side we hopped into the boxcar.

The SS Grand Rapids slowed and maneuvered to line up at the Milwaukee dock. J-P reassembled the Thompson but warned that the magazine was only half-full. He told us "We must remain unseen. No shooting unless there is no alternative. We not only have to watch out for Rose's gang, we have to consider that the sailors don't know we are the good guys and will detain us and turn us over to the railroad police if we are caught."

The ship vibrated as the large doors at the end of the ship swung open and hardworking yard locomotives came steaming in to couple up and pull the strings of railroad cars to the nearby sorting tracks. I had chosen this railcar because the freight contained machinery and fermentation tanks consigned to a Milwaukee brewery. At least we wouldn't be stuck on a train going to Texas.

I expected the boxcar would be moved to the local brewery so there was nothing to do but hide and wait and this time Lady Luck rode with us. The yard locomotive took the train to the sorting tracks, the crew uncoupled the other cars and re-coupled the locomotive to our boxcar and delivered it to a siding next to a brewery. Our boxcar sat next to a large industrial building dock for the equipment to be unloaded and, at the moment, no one was there. I thought we should get out now and the others agreed. We would be in serious trouble if brewery workers found us when they came to unload the freight. J-P disassembled the Thompson again. A few city blocks away we found an abandoned warehouse, windows broken, weeds growing around it. There was an unlocked door and we went inside to wait until dark when we could find our way to a telephone, then go to where Laure's train awaited us.

A SPEAKEASY BRAWL AND A CAT FIGHT

Laure narrates

Our old executive railcar rode well and the Swedes had applied their magic to fix it up and make it comfortable. Before leaving New Jersey we stocked it with food and supplies. We used the kitchen of the railcar so we did not have to stop for anything but what the railroad required and for fuel. I wanted to call my parents but every time I tried there was no answer. I worried, but if Marie-Laure was there, they probably were out and about somewhere. I had never met my namesake Marie-Laure, the woman who befriended my mother when they were little girls. I looked forward to hearing the stories, but I was most excited with the hope that Dan and I would be together again if Jean-Philippe was successful.

We went through some thunder and lightning storms, which did not bother the train, but did cause slowdowns to remove debris blown onto the tracks. Normally only one of the Swedes at a time had to be with Big Al because it was an oil-burning locomotive so there was no coal to shovel, but today both men were up front to watch for hazards and remove them from the tracks. Ole told us that Sven was getting to be an old lard-ass from not working very hard now that they did not have to shovel coal, and the way he said it made us all laugh.

Arriving in South Bend Indiana, I had Big Al stop the train on a siding near a general store so I could call my mother to get the latest news. Vera and Marie-Laure took turns by the telephone and were happy to have an important part in bringing us together. Pa was at home and gave me the news that Dan, J-P, Charles and Dawn last reported that they were at the pier to board the GTW Railroad's ferry from Grand Haven to Milwaukee and would be checking in when they arrived in Wisconsin.

Jake would have flown to Milwaukee to pick up Dan and company, but the current weather forecast showed marginal conditions for flying because of large thunderstorms with lightning and high winds. He would be at airfield where the Ford Trimotor was in its hangar to prepare it for flight as soon as the weather cleared. I put Bill on the line to discuss the best locations to meet. We were being careful because there was no report of Rose Herlihy except that she was moving west. It was another bit of evidence that there was a rat in our midst.

Bill and Jake made a short list of places in Milwaukee where we could meet, and when Dan's group called in later, Vera could tell them the list. Bill and Scott obtained priority clearances and routing for our train through Chicago, but the direct north line to Milwaukee was busy and we would have to wait, so Bill got us priority clearance on the C&NW's northwest line that would pass through Arlington Heights close to Long Grove. We decided that we would not have time to stop so we would keep going to Janesville Wisconsin where we would get on the track toward Jefferson Junction and then east direct to Milwaukee. Bill and Big Al looked over the routing and decided that we could be there around midnight if there were no delays. Thomas McClanahan got us priority over all other railroad traffic except the premier passenger trains and express freights.

Bill called our crew together to put security measures in place. We had been watchful but if Rose learned where Dan and I were together, that's where she would strike. Besides Big Al and the Swedes, Bill and Giuseppe would take shifts riding in the locomotive. All of us were armed with a variety of Thompsons, shotguns, rifles and handguns. Viktor would be in command of security in the railcar and Luigi volunteered to ride on top of the railcar or the tender when we were not in thunderstorms. Evelyn and I would be in the railcar, ready to go wherever our firepower was needed. In Chicago we topped up fuel and water while Sven and Ole checked everything on the locomotive and tender, the lines, couplings, undercarriage and roof to make sure there were no signs of sabotage.

My joy at thoughts of Dan and I being locked together in intimate embrace tonight were shattered when the train abruptly came to a halt about halfway on the last leg to Milwaukee. Our train was on double tracked rails in a run-down industrial area, with sidings and spurs going to warehouse and manufacturing facilities and there were no residences anywhere in sight. We were stopped because a dispatcher reported a derailment had closed the track, and since it was already after 9 PM it would not be cleared until morning. The dispatcher shunted us off to a siding since a work train was on its way to clear the derailment.

Sven and Ole could smell a speakeasy a mile away, and they saw people coming and going from a small building a few hundred feet from the tracks. Sven went over to check. "Ya sure" he said when he came back "Ve got us a speak-easy over dere. C'mon Miss Laure, Ole and me, we take you out for drink, ya? You look like you need a drink tonight since Dan won't be here" I did not want to go but their enthusiasm was infectious and I could use a drink. Big Al said he would come get us if there was any news. Part of my decision to go with the Swedes was to get my mind off thinking about Dawn and Dan being so close for so long. I wasn't dressed for a night out, just a leather jacket over a shirt, form fitting riding pants and knee-length leather boots because Dan always told me that combination showed my long legs and cute little butt and looked sexy. I knew looking sexy would not make much difference when we saw each other – the only question was who would begin stripping the other's clothes off first. But then, we had done it with our clothes on before, so it was a moot point.

Uncle Viktor and Bill accompanied Sven, Ole and me to the speakeasy. It was in a rough part of a small manufacturing zone that could be referred to as the wrong side of the tracks except the right side did not appear to be any better. We had a little trouble getting into the speakeasy since we were not locals but Bill negotiated with the doorman, who looked nervously at the big Swedes and Viktor and kept repeating that he didn't want any trouble. I smiled at him and he let us in.

We got a table and decided to get beer because Bill took a whiff of the whiskey and said it was rotgut and he would not drink it. It would be accurate to call the joint a blind pig, a low class speakeasy that often served bad booze. I didn't usually drink beer but since the whiskey was bad and there was no wine we had no other choice. The room was in a high-ceilinged industrial warehouse, dirty and poorly lit with music coming from a player piano across from the bar. I could see two other women in the room. They were not happy to see me, no doubt they thought I was competition but I wasn't there to sell my body like they were.

I began to get nervous when some of the locals staggered close to our table and deliberately bumped into us. Viktor casually remarked that things were looking like trouble. I should have expected this. Sven and Ole were grinning like Cheshire cats, while Bill looked more eager for a fight than I would have expected.

Some men at a nearby table started to make loud remarks about how our table should be more willing to share the dancing girl after I turned down several requests to dance. Viktor got up and disappeared to the other side of the room. I wondered why. One of the denizens of the roadhouse grabbed my arm and began to pull me out of the chair, saying "I'm buying this dance, chippy". I stomped his foot as hard as I could and his friends got up and came over to get me. They were a bit fazed when Sven, Ole and Bill stood up. All three were big and tall with the look of experienced bar fighters, but the locals pulled knives and demanded "give us the chippy or we're gonna have ta cut ya."

My crew waited until the others made the first move. A knife went slashing toward Bill but he stepped back, got hold of the man's wrist, and twisted it hard. The man howled with pain when his wrist cracked as it was turned to an unnatural angle, but he tried to swing at Bill with his other arm. Too bad he didn't know that he was already beat. Bill twisted harder and with the sound of another bone cracking the man dropped his knife. Bill spun him back around, put his boot on the man's backside and propelled him back to crash into his table. '*Rhatz!*' I thought, '*Going to a speakeasy with these guys, why didn't I expect to end up in a bar brawl?*' A group of men from the other side of the room came toward my crew and soon half the room was in the fight using bottles, knives and fists. A man came running at us swinging a rickety chair. Bill grabbed the chair and pushed the man down, smashing the chair on his backside, breaking it to pieces. I only had to reach down to get hold of a chair leg and déjà vu of the saloon fight in Cherryvale washed through my mind. None of the local men expected me to use the chair leg so that's what I did, and was able to clock two of them on the head. '*Rhatz. I am starting to enjoy this!*'

Nevertheless, I was not an experienced bar fighter and made the mistake of getting a step too far away from my guys. Two men grabbed me and dragged me away while several of the others jumped on Bill, Sven and Ole to keep them busy. The two men who pulled me away began making comments about getting my boots and pants off as they took me into a corner. The big talker pulled a knife, grabbed my shirt to cut it open, and began telling me what else they planned for me. I did not like their plans and was relieved when I spotted Viktor on his way over and looked the other way so they would not look in his direction.

The big talker cut the front of my shirt open just as Viktor took hold of both men by their hair and knocked their heads together. They let go of me as they tried to squirm around to hit Viktor. They made a big mistake because Viktor was waiting for that. "Knife!" I called to

Viktor. As they turned toward him, the men screamed when they lost handfuls of hair as Viktor smashed their heads together again. After the sounds of skulls cracking together and knives clattering to the floor, Viktor threw them into the corner where they were planning to take me. I used the opportunity to stomp one guy's foot, and the one who cut my shirt had not learned it was time to quit. He tried to get up. His lesson came with my delivery of a solid kick to his balls. His howl was so chilling that the room seemed to stop for a few seconds. That man would not be using me or any other woman tonight.

Viktor shepherded me back to where my crew were fighting. They were doing some real damage but there were a lot of tough customers in this blind pig and my guys were slowly being pushed back and now were only a few feet from the wall. I saw my chair leg and picked it up just in time to jam it into some guy's gut who was moving toward me, then whipped it around to hit a kidney when he bent over from the gut hit. He went down with a sharp gasp followed by dull moans. With Viktor in the fight, we started to push the locals back.

My crew kept me close but that limited my ability to swing my club, so I moved between Bill and Uncle Viktor. I had to stay in their shadow but I made a few good hits when the local gang tried to form a scrimmage line to rush my men. Sven and Ole stood there and absorbed a few punches to let the other guys in close where the big Swedes would simply bear hug them to crush their rib cages, then get them in a headlock and pummel their faces. Any who still wanted to fight after that were picked up and thrown at the others, or simply body slammed to the floor. The Swedes were very effective bar fighters and dished out a lot more than they took and the local gang began to shy away from them. I found my place to fight when a couple guys tried to force their way behind Viktor. The two tough guys must have thought I would be easy to knock down but I remembered some of the moves Dawn had taught me. I sidestepped one of them, tripped him to swing the chair leg underhand and hit the other one in the knees. He tried to slide sideways so I swung around with my club and backhanded him hard on his shins. Viktor was taking out two guys in front of him but had time to give my opponent an elbow to a kidney. When the first guy was getting up I almost got caught again when his hand grabbed my left arm. My club was in my right hand. There wasn't room to swing it so I made like I was trying to free my left arm from his grip and he grabbed my arm with both hands. When my right arm got free I brought the club around for a solid hit to his head. It sounded like a bat hitting a Chicago softball and he went down.

The second guy flicked his wrist and showed his switchblade knife, weaving it back and forth like he was charming a snake, but it didn't charm me. My chair leg club was blocked so that there was no room to swing it. The guy jumped at me and slashed a couple of times as he leered at my ripped shirt. I needed to buy a few seconds so I stopped him by smiling at him and pulling my shirt open. His eyes got real big as he stared at my bra. "Do you like that?" I smiled and winked. He could only nod and I swear he was drooling. "Well then, move over here and take a closer look. The dummy did as he was told and now my chair leg was free so I used it to smash his wrist and the switchblade dropped to the floor. He face showed enough pain to indicate I had probably broken his wrist. But he wasn't very smart and as he dived down to get the knife with his other hand, I put my foot on his hand as it grasped the knife and brought the club down on the back of his shoulders. He collapsed with a long eerie wailing sound. I pulled my shirt back together and found one button that hadn't been ripped off and buttoned it. It looked ridiculous but it did cover my bra. Mostly.

Big Al burst in, pushing the door open so hard and fast that it swung around and hit the wall, breaking the hinges. In New Jersey Al bought a police whistle and now he blew it, yelling "Police! This is a raid! You are all under arrest! Do not leave this room!" Big Al had a big voice and most of the men in the blind pig started running for the windows and exits, not even looking to see if the cops were really there. Many of them who went for the windows were thrown through by my crew.

One last tough guy made his way toward me. He had a wild look in his eyes because he was roaring drunk so it was easy for me to clunk him on the shoulder with my chair leg. Sven was looking at me in case I needed help, but my attacker was on the floor so I put my finger next to my nose, grifter style. Sven did it too, just when a guy swung at him. Bill was there, punched the guy hard and away from Sven towards Ole, his muscles flexing as he picked the big man up and body slammed him to the floor. With that sickening sound, much like a bag of overripe vegetables hitting the floor, the fight was over.

Two bartenders armed with axe handles were still behind the bar to protect the booze but when we walked over to the bar they threw down their axe handles and raised their hands. "No fight" they said. Ole looked disappointed.

Big Al and Bill demanded the bartenders break out the good whiskey. The barmen did not move fast enough so Bill and Big Al each grabbed a bartender and threw them over the bar while I picked up the axe handles and passed them back to Big Al and Bill. Seeing that there were no cops at the main door and my guys were ready to use the axe handles, the barmen decided to make a run for it. We let them go. Bill searched the back bar and found the good whiskey and some cigarettes he called jujus. We each had a shot or three of the whiskey and Bill lit up one of the juju cigarettes. He took a drag on it and passed it to me. Although I don't smoke I tried it anyway. It smelled funny and I started to feel strange.

"You're getting stoned" Bill laughed. With a shout Luigi ran into the room and told us that Dan had arrived at the train. They had heard the derailment story and had got hold of a motorcar and drove the roads alongside the railroad tracks to find us. It wasn't hard for them to spot the #3447 lighted number panels on the front of our locomotive. My heart leaped with joy and despite being behind Bill and Big Al and feeling woozy from the juju, I got around them and was the first out the door. My men were unable to keep up as I sprinted to our train. Tonight my running exercises paid off and I wasn't winded when I got to the train.

Instantly my joy turned to shock when I came near the railcar, and through a window recognized Dawn inside one of the rooms. Then I saw Dan come up behind her, his back to me so he could not see me outside. He pulled her back to his chest and circling his arms around her waist, kissed her neck, unbuttoned her shirt and played with her breasts before turning her around to face him. They pulled each other close and began to kiss and it was not the kiss of casual friends. It was an open mouth seduction kiss, and I saw his hands move to pull her to his. At first I was frozen in disbelief at what I was seeing, but when Dan pulled her shirt and bra off and began to gently twist her nipples my mind snapped.

I ran the last few feet to the end of the railcar, leapt up on the platform, through the door and down the corridor, arriving in the bedroom just as Dan began to suck on Dawn's breasts. Not stopping, I launched myself at them, knocking both of them to the floor. I screamed to Dan "Get the hell out of here" and jumped on Dawn. She was so shocked that I was able to sit on her, hold her down and straddled her body. I punched her, pulled her hair, slapped her face, ripped her clothing and punched her some more. Then I began to punch her in the stomach and rolled her over to punch a kidney. She tried to cry out but it turned into a low moan after my second punch. Dawn rolled herself back enough to take advantage of my hesitation. She grabbed my wrists and flung me over and onto my back. She now was on top of me, held my hands down over my head and slapped my face. She finished ripping

my shirt off when Dan tried to intervene. Dawn and I
were both fired up with the anger of the fight and said "Go
away" in unison. He backed off and left the room.

Dawn looked up at him and watched him leave, but I
did not, so I was able to surprise her when I got my leg in a
position to use it as a lever to disengage Dawn and spring
to get up. I stood over her and as she tried to get up I
grabbed her by the hair and boxed her ears. In return she
got hold of my leg and pulled it out from under me,
twisting me around on my face as I went down and
jumped on top of me. Now she was giving me kidney
punches. She straddled my ass as I tried to push up to
unseat her and rode me as if I was a bronco. She did not
fall off but she had to hold on and that kept her from
hitting me again. Dawn leaned forward to take a hunk of
my hair in her hand and pull my head up. It strained me so
that I lost my breath and she whispered in my ear "Stop
Laure, or I'm going to have to hurt you" which I knew she
could do. She was the one who had taught me how to fight
but I never had the opportunity to finish the lessons. She
was trained and experienced in hand-to-hand fighting and
now that the surprise of my attack was gone she held the
advantage and pummeled my back. Dawn flipped my body
over for more punching. Now I was taking a beating and
running out of energy and again Dawn leaned over me,
our boobs rubbing on each other and told me again to give
it up.

I said "I'm not giving up to you, husband poacher."
Dawn looked surprised and I was able to roll and push her
off. I pretended to move away but when I got my feet
under me I jumped down on her to land on her ribs, just as
she was raising her fist to punch my stomach again. The
combined force of my body coming down while she was
pushing her fist up at me caused me to collapse, limp and
out of breath, with a long gasp. I was hurting all over as
Dawn took control. She got me on my back and slapped
my face, this time really hard and I tasted blood on my

lips. My body was so limp I could barely lift my arms to defend myself, but I refused to give up.

Worn down from sadness and worry, the speakeasy fight, the whiskey, the juju cigarette and being thrashed by Dawn, I couldn't stop her from rolling me over, grabbing my hair from behind and putting her hand on my right breast to pick me up to throw me. "Give up Laure, you're not going to win" Dawn warned. "Save yourself from a beating."

This enraged me and with my last reserves of strength I kicked her arm as she reached to pick me up to throw me again. It must have hurt because she was down on her knees as I came around, ready to grab her hair and pull her face up for a punch to her nose. Arms wrapped around my waist and pulled me away as I threw the punch and all I hit was air. Another man grabbed Dawn and held her arms behind her before she could give me a couple of fast jabs to the ribs. The fight was over, and for me it was a good thing. Dawn was escalating the fight and I knew I would lose. It was only my anger and shame at losing my husband to Dawn that kept me going.

Charles was surprised as he held Dawn in his arms and kissed her when I kicked open the door and rammed into them. He was shocked to see me hitting Dawn. He got in between to separate us and stop the fight, instead he was hit and roughly pushed aside and told by both of us to get out. Charles went down the corridor to find Dan and was told that he was in the bathtub. Charles knocked on the bathroom door and when Dan asked who it was, he said "This is Charles. Two women are fighting. One is Dawn, the other I think is Laure who is trying to give Dawn a beating. I can get between them but they are both partially naked and I thought it better that you put hands on your wife."

"Are they hurting each other?" Dan asked as he pulled a towel around his body.

"No, not yet. I think they like each other and are holding back or they would do more damage. There must be a terrible misunderstanding to cause such a fight."

Dan followed Charles down the corridor to the second compartment from the end of the railcar. They opened the door to see Dawn and me rolling, pushing, shouting, hitting, pulling at clothes and hair, punching and slapping each other. The room was dimly lit so we did not see them until the men got their arms around us to pull us apart.

Instinctively I knew Dan's hands were on me, and he held me firmly while the other man held Dawn. I couldn't see Dan but I knew his hands, I knew it was him by the way he touched me. It felt like he was holding me lovingly, not like someone who had recently been cheating on me. When the other man took Dawn and carried her from the room Dan pulled my back close to his body and kissed my neck, just like I saw him do to Dawn a few minutes ago. I felt his stiff cock as he rubbed it on me and I began feel the core of my body heat up. But I reached back and scratched his arm and tried to kick backwards as he lifted my feet off the floor so I kicked air, having lost the push for leverage.

Dan began to kiss me and my brain wanted to make him stop but my body, denied the physical act of love for so long wanted him to continue. My anger at his arrogance to touch me after he touched Dawn won as I spun away from him and slapped his face as hard as I could, leaving a red mark on his cheek.

I don't know what I said, but my fury vented as I told him that he was not going to touch me again, and that I was leaving him right now and he should never try to contact me again.

"But, Laure, I..."

"No. No more talk. You have humiliated me. Go to Dawn if you want her. Don't ever come near me again or I will shoot you, and I won't miss. Get out of here now! Viktor! Help!" I shouted as loud as I could.

"Laure, please listen. I don't know what this is all about but..." Before he could finish I picked up a bottle of whiskey and threw it at him, but being enraged I missed breaking it on his skull. Instead, it hit him on the shoulder and fell to the floor and broke, filling the small bedroom compartment with broken glass and whiskey fumes. Everything seemed to stop for a moment as Dan had a surprised expression on his face. I weakened, pulled him to me and kissed him, then pushed him away so hard he fell to the floor backwards and was cut by a shard of the whiskey bottle. His arm began bleeding from the gash.

"I loved you with all my heart, believing you were the love of my life, but you have scorned my love. You are shallow and contemptible. Go to your new lover, you will never know my love again!" He started to say something but I yelled for him to shut up and get out and called again for Viktor. Dan looked into my eyes with confused innocence, and I had a fleeting feeling that I might be wrong. But I had seen it with my very own eyes. How could I misbelieve that?

He got up from the floor slowly, as if hoping I would start laughing as if it was a prank, but it was no prank. My mind sank to the depths of despair as I ordered the only man I ever truly loved out of my life.

I started to cry and softly said "Leave now. Please leave. I never wish to see you again."

Now I saw hurt in his eyes, and innocence. Without a word, he turned and left the compartment. I sat down on the bed and cried. I stopped suddenly with the realization that he only had a bath towel tied around his waist. *'How can that be?'* I wondered *'When I saw them in the window he was fully clothed.'*

I hated him. I loved him. And that's when my mind cleared up for a few seconds and I realized I should not have smoked that juju cigarette.

I did not hear Viktor come into the compartment until he gently said "Why did you attack Dawn?"

"I saw Dan passionately embrace and kiss her, remove her clothing and intimately touch her body. After all I have gone through since he was kidnapped, this was the first I've seen of him in three months and he's seducing someone else. He is a beast and I am divorcing him."

"You might want to reconsider. Dan was taking a bath to be clean for you upon your return from the speakeasy. He was in the bath the entire time until Charles came to get him to help stop the fight. Dan could not have been with Dawn" Viktor told me.

"Then who was..." and my heart plummeted, realizing I wrongly accused Dan and attacked Dawn.

"Dawn hasn't said anything yet. She's bruised but she will be OK" Viktor said. "You're my niece and I am protective of you. I need to know if Dan has done anything wrong to you" Viktor asked, with a little more growl than I wanted to hear.

I was stunned. I had attacked a friend and worse yet, I told the man I loved that I was leaving him and to stay away from me. My mind, which had been swirling with despair, was clearing. "No Uncle Viktor. Dan has done nothing wrong to me. From the very beginning, he has been a gentleman and treated me with love and respect. That's why I fell in love with him, and I still am. This mess is entirely my fault. I must immediately apologize to Dawn. Then I must convince Dan not to leave me even though I have made a complete fool of myself. Oh Uncle Viktor how could I have been so stupid?"

"Laure, you are an intelligent woman. Maybe you should not smoke those marijuana cigarettes. They are very strong and combined with whiskey they paralyzed your thinking."

Viktor left the room while I changed my clothes. Dawn had given me some hard hits and the bruises were adding physical pain to my emotional agony.

I went to look for Dan, but was told he left the train. I went back inside the room, condemning my foolishness. All I could think of was the look in his eyes when he wanted me, the tender and sensual times we enjoyed and his desire for me to equally enjoy it, how happy I was when we danced, how we faced danger side by side, how he respected me and gave me room to be myself. Now all of that was gone because of my foolish behavior. I felt devastated and ashamed.

A little bit later I found Charles and Dawn sharing a hug and a kiss. That's when I noticed that from the back, Dan and Charles were of similar height. His hair was lighter in color but in the dim light I had not noticed. I had seen Charles, not Dan, with Dawn.

Charles prudently exited the room to leave us alone. I told Dawn about my foolish assumption and apologized sincerely to her. She accepted without hesitation. Dawn surprised me when she offered to finish my fight training if I promised never to attack her again, because she had been surprised at my ferocity and under different circumstances may not have been able to take control of the fight away from me.

I wanted to go to Dan, but what would I say? I had to make my case and not just beg and cry for forgiveness. I had to convince Dan that I was still the woman of his dreams, who would stand by his side when facing danger and passionately make love to him after the danger passed. I decided that was exactly what I would tell him before I dragged him back to our room.

For some reason, I thought of the day Dan caught me making pies and took me on the butcher block table as flour and pie crust flew all over the kitchen. Why did that pop into my mind?

THE WRONG SIDE OF THE TRACKS

Our lookouts sounded the alarm. Seconds later, two men pumping a handcar approached our train. Sven covered them until Dan got there and introduced his friends Moe and Joe, who were speechless from being out of breath.

"You've been set up – there is no derailment" Joe shouted. "If a dispatcher ordered you to this siding, it is a trap because Rose is on her way with at least twenty gunmen. Get out of here, fast!" Bill had set up a grasshopper telegraph, a device patented by Edison in the 1880s. Using electromagnetic induction it allowed a passing train to communicate with nearby telegraph wires running parallel to the tracks. It worked well enough when the wire was a few feet from the train, but there was little demand from passengers so it never gained widespread use. Bill decided this would be a good test of the grasshopper telegraph so he communicated with a dispatcher he trusted who confirmed there was no derailment on the C&NW system in Wisconsin.

Bill sent Giuseppe and Luigi forward to ride in the locomotive and report back if they saw anything unusual, telling them to get #3447 moving. Big Al was already in his engineer's seat with Sven as fireman and he sent Ole ahead to open the switch at the end of the siding. Steam was up as Bill arranged with the dispatcher for us to reverse our direction at an interchange about a mile ahead.

Moe and Joe departed, telling Dan they would scout around and find us when they had something to report. As Big Al began to move our train he could see that Ole was frantically trying to break the lock so he could open the switch. Sven grabbed a crowbar and ran to help.

"Rose's gang must be close to be able to lock the switch. We checked it when we stopped here, and it was open" Big Al reported. Viktor came in with a grim look on his face. He had gone back to the other end of the siding and found that switch had been sabotaged as well. Had Moe and Joe not warned us, Rose's attack plan would have succeeded and we could have been dead on that siding in the next few minutes. On everyone's mind was *'How did Rose know where we were and the rail route we had taken?'*

It took almost ten minutes but thanks to the strength and ingenuity of our Swedish railroad men, the sabotaged switch was opened and we rolled.

I found Dan and we agreed to discuss my fight with Dawn and my angry words with him after we were out of danger. "I'm worried about our security leak" I said unhappily. "Rose knows when and where we are going, so this is what I want to try. Who do we tell when we change our plans? We call Josefina or send a telegram or teletype if we can get to one. We also have been checking in with Jake and Vera in Long Grove. Giuseppe keeps in touch with his boss. Scott was probably advising his father Thomas where he was going. Who else is telling someone of our plans? Big Al? Bill? I could add Jean-Philippe to our list but the leak has been going on long before he arrived. I think we should send false information and despite the problems with confusing our own people, we should not tell anyone until we expose the spy. To know where the leak is coming from, we can make up different false information for each contact. Evelyn has offered to help keep track of what we tell to who." Evelyn nodded her agreement.

All of the people we kept in our confidence were people who we knew well and had earned our trust. Most of them had been with us for two years. It would be an enormous disappointment to find one of them had betrayed us.

"Let's make up some places in different directions where we are going to next, and I'll start feeding the information out" I said. In ten minutes we had several false bits of information to send out. Dan said he would call Josefina when we stopped at a telephone. Bill was sending information on the grasshopper telegraph to McLanahan, and Giuseppe said he might be in a lot of trouble for lying to Al Capone, but he would do it for us. I told him Dan and I would get an audience with Capone and explain it to him, hoping Al Capone still liked us. Giuseppe said that Capone did like us because we provided timely assistance to Gina last year without asking for any favors in return, and we had kept to our agreement about not going into the liquor business.

"Gina, I thought. *I wonder where she is and what she is doing. Could Gina be the leak?"*

As I cleaned our guns I looked out the rear window and noticed something wrong. "I think we are in another kind of trouble" I said, my voice quavering. "We're going fast on the wrong side of the double tracks."

Bill had just returned from the locomotive and replied "Don't worry Laure, the Chicago & North Western is what's called a left handed railroad. Instead of traveling on the right side track when there are multiple tracks, the North Western travels on the left because one of the ancestors of the North Western, the Little Galena and Chicago Union Railroad Company started with one track. When they added a second track, they placed their stations for their trains to Chicago so customers did not have to cross a track to get to their train. For whatever reasons, the C&NW kept that arrangement as it expanded. Today it would cost a fortune to change all the switches and signals and everything necessary to be right handed like most American railroads." It sounded strange to me but Bill knew more about transportation systems than anyone else. Even Scott McLanahan kept trying to hire Bill to work for McLanahan Enterprises, but Bill liked to be independent so he could work for whoever had the best deal, and he liked working for us because we played it straight.

Our train was heading east toward Milwaukee when Big Al found the interchange to get the train's direction reversed and soon we were heading west to go back on the same route we used to get to Milwaukee. We spread our misinformation that we were going south from Milwaukee to Chicago using the C&NW north route. Everyone was watching for any sign of Rose's gang.

A few minutes later, as we rounded a gentle curve with as much speed as Big Al could maintain and still keep #3447 on the rails, a train approached, moving fast on the opposite track. It was a Pacific 4-6-2, one of the big North Western units. They had some of the largest 4-6-2 locomotives ever built. This one was roaring along the curve when Bill saw the train's consist was only three cars and called a warning that this could be Rose's gang. That was confirmed when the train went by. Two goons on the rear platform picked up something and a loud rattling noise was heard. J-P shouted "Get down! Chauchat mitraillette!"

J-P sometimes mixed English and French when he was excited. "What the hell is a sho-sha me-try-yet?" I asked. When the sound stopped and we picked ourselves up off the floor, Viktor told us that it was an early design French machine gun that was rushed into production too early. It was disliked by the soldiers who had to use it during the war because of its slow rate of fire, and because it jammed easily in the muddy trenches. Viktor added that there could not be many Chauchats in the United States so Rose's gang must have stolen or imported them. Fortunately for us their aim wasn't very good as they sprayed rounds randomly about and only a few bullets struck our railcar. Viktor said the design of the gun made it jump around as it fired.

"Rose's train now has three cars behind the locomotive. Moe and Joe said she picked up twenty more gunmen" Viktor said. "They must have thought we would be waiting on that siding track like sitting ducks and all they would have to do was park their train next to us and rake us with their Chauchats until we were destroyed. I'll bet we surprised them."

"We can't keep running from Rose forever. They almost trapped us and she will not give up" I said. "There must be something we can do."

"Damn! Damn! Damn!" Rose screeched angrily. "Now they know we have machine guns bigger than their Thompsons. That crazy bitch Laure must have discovered that she has an informer telling us what they are doing. The last report said that they were trapped on the siding. Do we have any other pigeons that can get us information?" Rose demanded. "Next time we stop, someone get Desmond on the telephone. Why were our machine gunners on the rear platform asleep? Break their arms and throw them off the train when we cross the next bridge over a river. And where's that boy, my driver? Send him to me, at once – I'm almost out of whiskey!"

"I arranged for a clearance for a fast run to Madison, where we have to interchange south to Chicago or north to Eau Claire, because going west on that branch of the C&NW takes us to dead ends" Bill said. "I've asked Big Al to stop if he sees a pile of railroad ties near the tracks because I want to build a shooting bulkhead at the back of the railcar. Machine gun bullets, even from inaccurate guns, can kill us and they will go through thin railcar walls, so right now we have no cover."

Dan, Viktor and I discussed our route plan with Bill as we looked over his C&NW route map. "Let's go south toward Chicago. That's what Rose would expect us to do but we can put out more disinformation to confuse her."

"That's true, and there are alternate routes south of Madison on the North Western to get us to Chicago" Dan replied.

"And a long list of interchanges to other railroads in the Chicago area" said Bill. "Going north to Eau Claire, the main routes are to Green Bay in the east and Minneapolis in the west, although we could drop south toward Omaha at several junctions"

"Take us south at Madison then, and monitor as best you can for Chicago routes where we can move fast" Dan agreed.

"We need to come up with a plan to deal with Rose" I said.

"You're right Sweetie, but for the moment we need distance between us and Rose's train" said Dan. "Then we will get the crew together and work up some ideas."

A few minutes later, Big Al brought #3447 to a stop and we loaded some railroad ties to set in the rear of our railcar for a bulkhead that even a Chauchat couldn't shoot through.

As we walked down the corridor, Dan stopped me at our compartment door, opened it and guided me through, and I went willingly, closing it behind us. After my misguided outburst I wanted to seal our relationship with tenderness and loving. It was dark in the room and he pulled me close and planted an invitational kiss on my lips. I knew what kind of party he was inviting me to and asked "Do you ever think of anything else?"

"Not when I'm next to you."

"Does this mean I'm forgiven for attacking Dawn?"

"Since you were in a jealous rage over me, it would be wrong to say that it didn't excite me. And we have not had sex together in over three months."

"What do you mean 'together'? I have not had sex with anyone but you."

"I've been true to our marriage too, although I admit to having erotic thoughts about Dawn. But don't get angry, I was not going to let anything happen. I love you, my beautiful, smart sexy woman."

"I briefly had an erotic thought about Buster Collier, but I was feeling lonely and it is normal to have an erotic thought sometimes. But nothing is ever again going to happen between Buster and me. Nothing."

"So Buster was that good you keep having thoughts about him?"

"Dan, don't take this the wrong way. Buster is a nice man and an exciting lover. If I had never known you I would have been happy to be with him. But I don't want Buster, I want you. I know you have been upset about my affair with Buster, but my decision is made. I'm yours, all of me, now and forever" I said.

"All this time apart and we stayed true to each other and our relationship is strong. I'm not upset about you and Buster any more, and as for Dawn, Charles is planning to make sure she will be fully occupied with him, and Dawn has the same plan for him."

"Tell me, Dan. Is Dawn a better lover than me?" I asked teasingly, even though the question could backfire on me.

"I had my first affair with Dawn when I was eighteen and I was far less experienced than Dawn, so I learned a lot from her. But today, Dawn is to me like Buster is to you, a friend and former lover. You can think of him as a great lover, that's what Louise thinks and she's had more experience than all of us on this train put together. What I hear us telling each other is that it's OK, we've had that experience and we both decided that our future is us. I'm not letting anything in the past get in the way of our future, even though Dawn told me that she can't decide if Wally Reid or I was her favorite lover."

"Well, she should know. But I can't decide either, between you and Wallace Reid. He's pretty damn good, you know."

"You had sex with Wallace Reid? I didn't know that."

"Sure, many times. Every time I asked you to role play Wallace Reid, since you were educated by Wallace Reid's lover Dawn, it might as well have been Wally who made love to me. You do act different when you're Wally. I don't know what it is, but you seem different. So yes, I've made love with Wallace Reid several times."

"You really think that when we role play you're with Wally?"

"Let's leave that question unanswered. That way it will remain mysterious, as if we were wantonly taking other lovers. I want to keep us excited for each other. I know one of the difficult things is making love to the same person for a long time and not get bored. When you play Wally, we are exploring having sex with different lovers. We can do that without cheating on our marriage or our love for each other."

"Dawn said women love to live their dreams."

"I am living my dream, with you."

"Hmm. You should ask me to role play Buster some time."

"Maybe I should. I don't know how it might be different, but you are different when you're Wally."

"Let's find out. But first, would you like to role play Dawn?"

"Take me now and you will find out" I replied.

This late at night we seemed to be the only train on the Chicago & North Western tracks. Big Al had #3447 running fast and smooth. Big Al, Sven and Ole loved the locomotive and maintained it to perfection. Now when we needed it most it paid off and Big Al had a big shit-eating grin on his face as he drove as fast as safety allowed. We were closing in on Madison, Wisconsin where we would interchange to head south.

"There's no headlight but something is gaining on us" Charles and Dawn called out. They had the 2 AM to 4 AM watch on the rear platform. Luigi was up in the engine cab. No one was in bed, all of us slept as best we could on the floor and chairs and couches in the railcar's parlor. In two shakes of a lamb's tail everyone was up and ready. "Less than a minute ago it was just a shadow but now it looks like the end of a boxcar coming at us at a high rate of speed. It could be Rose's train pushing a boxcar in front of the locomotive. That gives them a platform to shoot from and protects their locomotive from us shooting at it."

Bill looked at it and said "It is a boxcar being pushed ahead of a locomotive. My guess is they have their Chauchat gunners set up and ready this time. Get your guns and ammunition and take your positions, I'm going up front to talk with Big Al." Since there were too many of us to shoot from the rear of the railcar all at once, Viktor organized us into teams. One team fired until empty, then dropped back to reload and the next team moved up to shoot.

When Bill returned the boxcar was very close. "Big Al says if they are gaining that fast, they are going too fast for this section of track. We are five minutes from Madison but we will have to slow down for other rail traffic soon. This is gonna be too close for my comfort."

The boxcar was now within range and two Chauchats began to chatter. Viktor was eyeballing the stack of railroad ties we had picked up and made into a shooter's barricade. "I have an idea. Where's J-P?"

"Over here Viktor. I'm on the next fire team."

"Laure – Dan – Bill – here's what I'd like to do" and we circled around to listen. We agreed to try Viktor's idea.

J-P and Viktor were the two biggest men on the train except for Sven and Ole but they were up front in the locomotive. Charles and Dawn on the first fire team began shooting their rifles from behind the barrier while everyone else was flat on the floor.

"OK, we gotta do this fast. Ready J-P?"

"Je suis prêt."

They crawled out onto the rear platform. Viktor counted out a fast "One – Two – Three!" Viktor and J-P jumped up and each picked up a railroad tie and dropped it down on the track behind our railcar. The ties bounced and we could not see where they landed. Bullets immediately sought the men out but they had surprise on their side. The ties were overboard and the men were back safe behind the barricade before the Chauchats were able to zero in on them.

It was only a second or two, but it seemed as if it were a long time as nothing happened. Then we heard a thud from Rose's boxcar. We watched it lurch over as it jumped the rails with one side of the boxcar's wheels between the tracks, bouncing on the ties and the wheels on the other side outside the track. Leaning sharply to the left as if a large hand was pushing it, sounds of screeching metal, men shouting, wood smashing and splintering were heard and sparks were flying. The boxcar leaned over further and toppled over on its side. The headlight on the locomotive was now visible and Dawn knocked it out with one shot. Rose's locomotive smashed into the wreckage of the boxcar, now sideways across the tracks, pushing it several hundred feet along the track until it slid off the rails and down the low embankment. Wreckage from the coupler of the boxcar and a chunk of the frame had been caught in the front coupler of Rose's locomotive and that created the sounds of metal being torn apart, screeching and sending sparks flying.

The Chauchats and the boxcar were gone, but there must have been two or three of Rose's gang who were able to leap back to the locomotive to shoot at us. Evelyn crawled to the rear platform with reloaded rifles for Charles and Dawn and brought one for herself. "Shoot where you see the flash of a rifle shot" Dawn said. It only took a few shots to quiet the shooters on the locomotive and soon we were safely out of range.

Big Al reduced speed as we entered the Madison traffic zone. Everyone congratulated Viktor on his plan, and J-P for his help throwing the ties off to land in front of the boxcar's trucks. It appeared that the boxcar had hit at least one tie which derailed the boxcar. "Great throws, well done Viktor, J-P! Without that, those Chauchats would be picking us apart" Dan said. Evelyn was already getting a bear hug from her guy. One might think Viktor could have easily crushed her but if you looked carefully you could tell Viktor was very gentle with her. Dawn was hugging J-P and calling him 'Papa'. Her relationship with Charles was becoming comfortable if she was already thinking of herself as a family member.

Bill said "We've won that round but I don't think there was any significant damage to their locomotive except for the headlight and front coupler, and once that is repaired Rose will be pursuing us again. But we needed a break and this will give us time to get through the interchange at Madison without being shot at. Good work!" Claire found a couple bottles of wine and we toasted our small victory.

Railroad traffic was heavy around Madison. Bill and Scott worked all the angles. Both men went to influence the dispatcher to give us priority and slow down Rose's train as much as possible. They were also able to get priority for our locomotive to take on fuel and water.

"Where do you want to go?" Bill asked us. Good question, I thought. *"Where could we go with Rose chasing us, and what would we do when we got there?"*

"Dan, we can't stop anywhere near Long Grove. Rose knows our families are there, and she could send her gangsters out to harm them, or worse yet take them hostage to force us to surrender. We can't let that happen" I said.

"You're right. Bill, we need to have some options on interchanges to get south of Chicago as fast as we can to draw Rose away so she doesn't have time to send out a hostage taking party."

"If we get to a place where I can contact Café Lulu in St. Louis, I might be able to get a few shooters to join us" Viktor offered.

"I don't know if my boss would loan us any men, but I can ask. I might have success it I ask for men to set up an ambush that we could lure Rose into" Giuseppe said.

Dan made the decision. "OK, let's do this – as we get near Long Grove – the C&NW line we use is the one we came north on and that takes us through Arlington Heights – let's get Scott, Claire, J-P, Charles and Dawn off to go to Long Grove and prepare our families and provide protection if Rose sends her thugs there. We should send Giuseppe to see if his boss will help us. For the time being, Big Al told me that if we can get to the Monon or the Central & Eastern Illinois he knows those rails and has dispatcher friends there. He can run Rose on a wild goose-train chase to give us time to put a plan in place to shut her down. That leaves you and me, my dear, to act as bait for Rose all over the countryside. We will have Bill, Viktor, Evelyn, Big Al, Sven, Ole and Luigi with us."

I told everyone to get some sleep if they could, and Viktor set a watch schedule before he went forward to the locomotive to relieve Luigi. At first none of us could get to sleep, but then the locomotive began to move and that lulled us to sleep for about two hours till daybreak.

DÉJÀ VU TRAIN/AUTOMOBILE CHASE

Dan and I awoke when the train stopped briefly at Arlington Heights for J-P, Charles, Dawn, Scott, Claire and Giuseppe to disembark.

Later that morning, Bill updated us with the news that we were well ahead of Rose's train. His grasshopper telegraph was working well and found that Rose left Madison about a half hour ago after making repairs to their locomotive, and they did not get to refuel. But we were running out of food. Since there was a refueling stop ahead Bill suggested that Viktor and Evelyn find a store and get some groceries while Sven and Ole filled the tender's oil and water tanks. Big Al came back to the railcar to catch some shuteye. Sven could drive the locomotive well enough for now. At least we were off to a good start. We began moving down the track and we got our crew together to see what ideas we could come up with while we had something to eat.

"Would Rose be able to read telegrams you send and receive on the grasshopper?" I asked.

"Yes, if they had a grasshopper, but I took the precaution to give our people going to Long Grove a code to use to scramble and unscramble messages. It is not a difficult code to break if someone knows how, but it would take time and from what Dan told us about the brainpower of Rose's typical gangster, they probably don't even know how to read. I think the risk is minimal" Bill advised. "Just so you know, when we get Rose buttoned up and things get back to normal, I've got business to take care of in Los Angeles that will take three or four weeks."

"Someone to visit?" Bill, do you have a girlfriend hidden in Los Angeles?" I asked with a laugh. I received no answer, which I took for a yes. I knew Bill easily found women whenever we stopped long enough for him to scout around, but since his last trip to Los Angeles he had not been out wolfing like usual. I suspected there was a girlfriend coming into Bill's life. "If you're not going to answer that, maybe you'll tell us where we are going?"

"Big Al wants to get on the Monon because he knows that railroad and all the connections. Says he can run circles around Rose's train down there. Viktor will call Café Lulu in St. Louis at our next stop. If he gets a good answer, we can interchange to another railroad and run to St. Louis. If Viktor gets a half dozen or more gunmen, our odds against Rose are better and we can take the offense."

We asked our Long Grove contingent to send us a code word by telegram when they arrived so we knew they were safe. Scott and Claire were going to their S Bar C Ranch and would instruct the ranch hands at their and his parent's ranch about Rose. Many of the ranch hands were good with guns but not experienced with city slickers and their tricks. J-P, Charles and Dawn were going to Long Grove to protect Dorothy, Vera and Jake. Not that Jake needed help, but it would free him up to concentrate on his aeroplane business. We received the safe word from both parties.

Big Al drove #3447 to Indianapolis on the Monon. From there, we could turn around and go back to Chicago on our choice of return routes or interchange for St. Louis. Dan and I were working on our next disinformation distribution. Dan was sitting next to me on a couch in the parlor, writing our messages to send to Long Grove and Napa. Suddenly I began to feel depressed that we were running away. I leaned into Dan and put my head on his shoulder. It all seemed so hopeless.

Dan put down the papers and put his arm around me. He didn't say a word, he just held me, understanding why I was upset. Suddenly our reverie was broken when all hell broke loose. Dan threw me to the floor as glass flew through the air. So were bullets. Lots of bullets. Wood splinters and bits of the window curtains were flying around. Viktor and Bill shouted for everyone to get down. When my mind focused, I realized that the hailstorm of bullets sounded like Chauchats. *'Chauchats? It had to be. Didn't sound like Thompsons and no one could shoot rifles that fast. But here? How did Rose catch up with us when we were at least an hour ahead of her train?'*

From the floor, I was looking at the settee were Dan and I had been mere seconds ago. It was stitched with bullets, exactly where I was sitting. Had Dan not thrown me to the floor I would have been stitched as well. Where was Dan?

"Dan! Where are you? Bill! Viktor!" I shouted but it seemed I was alone on the floor.

"Right here Laure. Here's yours." Dan was crawling toward me with my rifle and 1911. Now that the bullets had stopped, Dan cautiously peered out for a look.

"Laure, that road paralleling the track is the same road my father, Jake and I were on in 1919 racing our Elgin against the Monon express train. Only now I'm on the train and there's a car racing down the road. Big Al was driving the Monon locomotive that day, and he is driving ours. Big Al poured on the power and we are pulling away. There are three people in an open car, a driver and two Chauchat machine gunners." I peeked and saw the car, now just out of range of the Chauchats.

Dan pushed me down again. "Get down Laure! There's another automobile coming from the opposite direction, another open car with machine guns. Rhatz!" Dan laid down on top of me to cover me. Dozens of bullets went through the walls of the railcar, traveling through and exiting the other side, shredding the interior on the way, and they were aiming lower this time. They knew we would be hugging the floor. Dan was on top of me but high enough that he could be hit.

"Dan get off me, those bullets are coming in low" I shouted. "Please, I don't want to watch you die" I said and pushed Dan off. We crawled down the middle of the railcar to the private rooms until the Chauchats were out of range.

Now the sound of battle was coming from the front of the train. Our locomotive picked up speed as we went around a slight curve and the railcar lurched, rocking side to side as the sounds up front started with a bang and then a crashing, crumpling sound followed by a metal-rending screech.

The bullet barrage from the front stopped and I took a fast looksee. Our railcar was passing through a grade crossing and there was the mangled wreckage of a truck. I got a glimpse of a bloody arm holding what I guessed was a Chauchat. Rose's gangsters tried to block the tracks with a truck but instead of slowing, Big Al pushed the throttle and smashed through the truck. We were moving forward so I knew we had not derailed, but the gangsters' cars caught up with #3447 when it slowed, and bullets from the gunmen on the road were coming in again.

Dan and I crawled for our rifles and I looked for a place to pop up for a look. Bill and Viktor were shooting, ducking and rolling, moving and shooting again. I popped up and took a shot but the car was not where I thought it should be. Just as I ducked and dived I saw a muzzle flash and a bullet came through our railcar, once again right where I had just been.

Now I was angry. Some asshole was shooting at me, and now I had a good picture of where the cars were in relation to where we were. I moved a few feet, popped up again, got a fast bead on a head in the open car, pulled the trigger and dropped down, rolling from where I had been. There was another crunching crashing and rolling sound of metal crumpling and glass shattering.

"Great shot Laure! You shot the driver and the car rolled into a ditch!" Viktor shouted. Bill and Viktor were up, both firing like crazy people and I heard another thump and crash from the road. The shooting stopped and the train slowed.

The wreckage of the cars and the truck were about four hundred feet back. "Luigi, Ole and Bill went back to see if there are any survivors, but I don't think there will be any" and just as Viktor said that, we heard another gunshot. "Well, maybe there was one but he's not a survivor now."

"Grim work" I replied, feeling sorry for our people having to kill like that.

"This is one of those times where it is us or them" Dan said.

We walked back to the scene to join our crew looking over the wreckage while our locomotive crew made repairs. The truck had been blocking the tracks, the driver expecting the engineer would stop rather than risk derailment but Big Al applied more power and the truck was now a pile of smoking, twisted metal, wood and rubber. Big Al admitted that the truck could have derailed the locomotive, but stopping would have meant the sure destruction of the locomotive. Our locomotive was tough, but there was some damage. Sven replaced a section of pipe and the other damage was minor. There were still bits of the truck stuck in the cowcatcher. Sven and Ole were cleaning the debris out while Big Al kept up steam.

Dan was looking at the truck's wreckage and said "This is what the 1919 Elgin my father and Jake were driving in the race would have looked like if we had not made it across the track."

Walking back to the wrecked automobiles, the car with the driver that I shot had dropped into the ditch and rolled at least twice, Dan estimated. I could not look at the bodies. Although I had killed Pádraigh up close, that was different. I had seen and felt his violence against myself and others. Dan, sensing what I was thinking said "They were sent to kill you. Don't be angry at yourself, direct your anger at Rose, who sent them to attack us."

The other car had gone off the road, stopping when it hit a tree. The bodies of the driver and gunmen were ejected from the open car and had flown several feet before landing in grotesque, unnatural positions.

Big Al called out that the train was ready to roll so we went to the railcar and got on. Big Al was right that he could lead Rose on a wild goose chase in Indiana. But without a clear plan, it was an expensive and time consuming cat and mouse game with no end in sight.

We arrived in Indianapolis. While Big Al was supervising the refueling and watering of the locomotive we contacted our people and passed out more disinformation. We received bad news from Viktor. He called Maybelle Manx at Café Lulu and she told him that Café Lulu was at war with the big speakeasy again and regretfully, no one could be spared. A car approached our locomotive and two men emerged. Instead of the worn out clothes that Moe and Joe usually wore, they were now sharp dressed men in spiffy new suits. I wondered how they suddenly came into money. *'Could these two be the spies in our midst?'* I wondered.

Moe and Joe saw us and smiled. "Knowing you were on the way here, we got a two night gig at a resort on the river at the edge of town. Most of the guests there were old-timers, people who like vaudeville and detest the flickers." They used the old expression "flickers" to describe movies because the old movie projectors were not as smooth as the modern ones. "We had them roaring with laughter. See, it's a good thing that we keep practicing our act."

Dan came over and greeted his friends. "You're not dressed for the kind of train travel that you know best, so what have you two been doing?"

"Spying."

"Says you" I replied as my breath caught in my throat and I turned to look around, expecting gunmen to appear behind every automobile. They were admitting they were spies! A dozen of Rose's goons could be closing in while Moe and Joe grinned and laughed. My 1911 was in the railcar but my Colt M1908 .380 pistol was tucked under my shirt in my belt behind my back since I usually wore jeans or pants when traveling. When I turned to face Moe and Joe the Colt was in my hand, pointed at them.

"No, wait! Dan, tell her we're on your side!" Moe screeched. He was visibly frightened.

"Laure, I trust them. We have been through stuff together. Don't shoot them yet" Dan said to me, then turned to Moe and Joe. "You'd better explain truthfully to Laure who you've been spying on. I will not be able to stop her if she doesn't believe you."

"We were nosing around and found Rose's train, hidden on an abandoned siding near Carmel, about 27 miles north of here. The train was in a wooded area near the White River and we were able to sneak around and get under the railcars. We could hear this strange, awful voice so we knew it was Rose by your description. She was giving orders to attack your train north of Carmel with three vehicles" Moe said. "This was the group that attacked you. She was ordering a second group to attack you south of Carmel. She threatened her own people, said she would kill them if they did not kill you. I don't know why her people don't run from her" Moe said.

"They would have guards watching their train, how did you get past them?" I asked.

"Yeah, there were guards but they were not watching very carefully. It was easy to get around them while they were drinking the local moonshine" said Joe.

"We only had one attack, why didn't the second group attack us?" Viktor wondered.

Joe grinned. "We put sugar in the gas tanks of their vehicles. Take away their transportation, and they're campers, not travelers."

Moe added "We went to a store and bought sugar, but the first group left before we got back. We sugared the second group's cars and a truck."

"How did you know where we were going, and where Rose was going?" I asked, still not convinced that Moe and Joe were not spies.

"You're not the only ones with connections to railroads" Moe said. We know most of the dispatchers all over Indiana and Ohio. And we hear about you in the jungles all the time. Dan is a hero in the hobo community, standing up to that corrupt conductor and his henchmen. Beat them up all by hisself" Joe told Laure.

"I was lucky and had surprise on my side" Dan said modestly.

"It was still four large, cruel railroad goons, merciless men who took pleasure in beating up hobos. That reminds me of the bad news; those four goons are now working for Rose. They are her personal bodyguards and enforcers, that's why the other gang members do what they are told. They killed two of their own guys up in Wisconsin because they failed to shoot you. Broke their arms and threw them in a river. Those guys are the devil's own thugs" said Moe.

I put my gun back in my belt, not sure if I believed what they had told us. However, Dan vouched for them, so I decided to trust for now, but I would be watching them carefully.

Moe and Joe gave Dan his wanted handbill from a telegraph office wall. "Something for your family scrapbook" said Joe.

"I'm going to get this framed to hang on my office wall" Dan said. "Too bad the reward was only $500. Next time I piss off a railroad I'll do a better job of it."

Moe and Joe took to the road in their automobile and planned to meet us in Long Grove. They were not shooters and would be safer where Rose least expected them, on the highway.

Joe's comment about taking away Rose's transportation gave Dan an idea, and he wanted to see what I thought. We took a walk, staying close by our train if Rose showed up. I liked the plan and we hashed it out enough to present it to our crew. Dan called everyone together and made a diagram to illustrate the plan. It was a risky plan with many details to work out and we needed everyone's expertise, along with a great deal of outside assistance. Many favors would be called in to make it happen. An interesting discussion began and ended with Bill calling Giuseppe and then his railroad, Pinkerton and government contacts. As it turned out, Dan's idea came at just the right time. It was just what some people were looking for.

While we were holding for our railroad clearance to leave Indianapolis, Bill sent a telegram to our McLanahan security office contact and received an immediate reply for me to call Josefina in the LaureDan office no matter what time it was.

Josefina related that our chef Sunny had inadvertently listened to a telephone call and it sounded suspicious so she told her and Elsie about it.

Elsie and Sunny began surreptitiously watching their suspect and caught Elsie's boyfriend Darcy Moynihan red-handed, intercepting telegrams and listening to telephone calls to The LaureDan Company. If the contents were important, he would leave, saying he was going on an errand but instead went to a small one room rented office in St. Helena where someone had installed a teletype machine and sent the information to Sacramento.

Josefina called St. Helena Police Chief Dave Quinlan who came out personally to arrest Darcy, who would be charged with accessory to kidnapping and attempted murder. Quinlan's interrogation techniques caused Darcy Moynihan to confess his true identity. He was Dabney Herlihy, Rose Herlihy's cousin, and he was being paid by someone in Sacramento to send information about our movements. It had been easy for Dabney, since we had a party line for our house telephones in several rooms so Dabney would hang out where no one else was, or pick up a telegram and read it. Dabney had moved in with Elsie and came and went as he pleased, saying he ran errands and deliveries for the restaurant where he worked. Chief Quinlan's investigation cleared Josefina, Sunny and Elsie from any suspicion of assisting Dabney.

When Chief Quinlan began to investigate the Sacramento address he was contacted by Captain Tracy of the California State Police, who claimed jurisdiction and took over the investigation, although he named Chief Quinlan in his report as the arresting officer. We knew Captain Tracy from last year's events surrounding my attempted kidnapping from *The Great Gatsby* movie set.

I passed the news to Luigi, who was proud that Josefina and her friends had discovered one of the spies Rose planted in our midst, and told me "I miss Josefina so much and as soon as Rose's gang is fini I want to go to her as fast as I can." I told Luigi we would buy him a first-class ticket home on the next fast train from Chicago. He was so happy that he hugged and kissed me, then ran down the corridor of the railcar singing an Italian love song.

Later, while we waited in the Monon Indianapolis railyard we received four telegrams, one from Jake in Long Grove, another from Josefina in Napa. The third was for Bill from one of his associates, and a fourth came from Giuseppe. The pieces of Dan's plan were coming together, and I was excited to think that we might finally get Rose out of our lives.

DRAGON'S FIRE

Locomotive #3447 glided smoothly on Monon rails north by northwest toward Chicago. Bill received a coded grasshopper telegram from Scott instructing us to arrange new clearances to interchange at Frankfort to the Nickel Plate Railroad to Crawfordsville, then pick up the New York Central direct to Danville, Illinois where we would interchange to The Milwaukee Road and then the Chicago & North Western to Long Grove. Bill told us that the clearances went through so quickly that it seemed as if the railroads knew our requests in advance. Dan saw it as a sign that our plan was being implemented.

I sat with Dan in the rear parlor to watch for any train closing up on us. There was the possibility that Rose would not chase our train, but instead get in front to block it. Bill was in the locomotive and had given us a whistle signal he would use to warn us if Rose was in front. But so far, there was no sign of Rose or her train. At Danville we interchanged to the Milwaukee Road for our northbound leg to Chicago. Almost as soon as we moved onto the Milwaukee Road double track Dan spotted a black plume of locomotive breath gaining on us. Rose's gangsters must have been waiting and watching for us to pass through the interchange, which meant there was a second leak.

The chasing locomotive came into view on the parallel track, which could result in a head-on collision with a train moving the opposite direction. Dan had expected that possibility. We watched the distance diminish between us. Dan said this one was a 2-8-0, not the locomotive Rose had on the C&NW. Luigi, looking through his binoculars, said he could see a Chauchat gun barrel on the front of the locomotive so he crawled above to crawl up front to tell Bill and Big Al that Rose was behind us and closing fast. Rose's locomotive was sending thick black smoke up its chimney, which indicated poor fuel management leading to incomplete combustion. Big Al, as always, had our locomotive running efficiently. The smoke from our stack was pale or white, showing very little unburned oil.

Dan estimated that Rose's train would be pulling next to us about a quarter mile from the bridge span over the Vermillion River. As soon as they got close they would use their Chauchats, Tommyguns and grenades to disable our train so they could close in to finish us off. The gang's locomotive was less than a half-mile behind, close enough to see the barrels of at least two more Chauchats protruding from the sides of their railcars that would be facing us when they closed up. Clearly seen were metal plates bolted to their locomotive to protect the front Chauchat, which soon began chattering and bullets ripped into our railcar, but we were down behind our reinforced railroad tie bulkhead.

The grade was smooth as we approached the bridge because the road bed was elevated above the alluvial plain with embankments and trestles. The area along the river was mostly flat with couple of a hills covered with trees about a quarter mile away.

"Shit" Bill hollered when we heard a flat "whump" followed by an explosion about 200 feet behind us and 100 feet from the left side of our train. "How in the hell did they get a mortar?"

"Sounds like a Stokes 3" mortar, the Tommies used them in the war. They are deadly within about 750 yards" Viktor told us. "If one of those falls direct on our railcar or the locomotive…" Viktor stopped when the second "Whump" sounded, closer than the first. It exploded about 100 feet behind us but still 100 feet to our left. "It will be difficult to aim on a fast moving platform like a train."

"You don't have to have a good aim if you get lucky" I said, although my comment wasn't appreciated much. No one seemed visibly scared, and it wouldn't help anyway.

Bullets were striking our railcar like a hard, fast hailstorm, coming through above our railroad tie barricade, blowing holes and sending splinters through the car. I pulled Dan down tight to me and waited.

At last we heard the sound that Dan and I were anticipating after receiving the telegram from Long Grove. It was the McLanahan Ford Trimotor, piloted by Jake with Claire as co-pilot and spotter, skimming along just above and off to the left of Rose's train. It drew the attention of Rose's gunmen, who moved two Chauchats over, but Jake skirted out of their range.

The Chauchat in front went silent and we took a peek at our nemesis. Dan pointed out a train about a mile behind Rose's train. Then I almost jumped out of my skin when a large dark boxlike structure glided slowly towards Rose's train on the parallel track to us. It was a boxcar with heavy armor plate on its end facing Rose's train pushed in front of a locomotive.

Dan's trap worked with the blocking of Rose's train from both directions and no switch for them to change tracks. Big Al slowed our train so our end was slightly ahead of the armored boxcar. Twice Rose's thugs tried to fire into our railcar with Chauchats, and both times snipers in the armored boxcar, shooting through firing holes in the armor plate silenced the machine gunners.

The train blocking Rose's train from the rear came to a stop right behind them and Rose's thugs tried to spray it with bullets, but its front was armored and the Chauchat bullets could not penetrate. A loudspeaker called for everyone in Rose's train to throw their guns out and come out with their hands up, but someone with a Chauchat started firing.

The Trimotor moved in with a .50 caliber Browning M2HB machine gun poking out a side door, firing at Rose's train. We saw the side Chauchats pulling in so they could move to the other side to shoot at the aeroplane, but the Trimotor's first pass had already done serious damage to Rose's train. Jake turned in a wide circle for a second pass. The Browning began its heavy throated roar as the stream of bullets concentrated on the Chauchats. The Browning's superior firepower silenced the Chauchats. When they flew by we saw J-P was the shooter, Scott assisting with ammunition belts and loading. After the Browning pounded the Chauchats into scrap, it turned to blast the rifles trying to poke out from the railcars. It looked as if a dragon breathing fire.

Two men jumped out of Rose's train, one waving a white towel. Another of Rose's thugs started shooting at them, but the Trimotor was close by and Dawn took the shooter out with her sniper rifle. There was shouting and a few gunshots from Rose's train, but more gunmen came out and surrendered.

Men from the blocking trains swarmed, Thompsons and shotguns ready. They surrounded Rose's train while the Trimotor flew over watching for anyone trying to come out the roof hatches. Bill said the special task force was Pinkerton agents with railroad and state police. They disarmed the prisoners quickly and not gently as they put them in handcuffs and leg chains.

To my horror, as the Trimotor came around an unseen Chauchat rattled and the right wing engine sputtered and caught fire, then the front engine stopped. With only the left engine operational it did not have sufficient power to fly the aeroplane and Jake would have to crash land. The ground near the river had level spots but they might be soft and there was no way to know which. The aeroplane was descending fast while Jake and Claire continued to wrestle with the controls to keep the wings level and the nose slightly up. "No!" I cried out as the aeroplane was going down too fast as flames consumed the right wing. I started to run down the embankment, Viktor and Dan right behind me.

Jake kept the wings as level as he could but the aeroplane bounced when it struck the ground, the landing gear ripped off when it hit the soft ground a second time and the last running engine stopped when the propeller blades bent from hitting the ground. The fuselage stopped with a forward lean, its tail slightly up in the air. Fire began to consume the body of the aeroplane. I could not see anyone leaving the aeroplane. If they did not get out they would burn to death.

At last I saw Jake running from the Trimotor carrying Claire but I was still afraid for the others. *'My family and friends are in there!'* I screamed. J-P and Dawn appeared, carrying Charles. Scott was slightly behind but catching up to them. He spotted a shallow depression in the ground and yelled for the others to dive into it and hug the earth. They got there just as the Trimotor went up in a fiery explosion. Jake and Claire were farther away from the aeroplane, hugging the ground and the fireball did not reach them. When the fiery blast dissipated, I saw Jake had laid Claire down and was talking to her, but she was not moving. No one in the shallow depression was moving.

We were far enough away that the explosion did not harm us. Everyone from our train except Big Al was now running to the crashed Trimotor. Luigi was carrying our two bags of emergency medical supplies and as Sven ran by he took one of them.

I got to my Pa and Claire first. He was OK but his face and left arm was cut and bloody. Claire was not moving. Dan, Viktor and Evelyn arrived seconds behind me, and Luigi ran to us with a medical bag, Sven running to the others with the second bag.

"Claire! Oh Claire!" Scott was calling as he jumped from the shallow depression and ran with a limp toward her. He dropped to the ground next to Claire. Dan sat next to her checking for a pulse and I was worried she was dead because she did not seem to be breathing. She had a bump on her head, her hair was singed and blood was coming from her nose. Scott was whispering in Claire's ear, which seemed foolish if she were dead, but suddenly her eyes popped open and she gasped. The first person she saw was

Scott, and she tried to pull him to her. She took hold of his shirt, now able to move her arms and legs. Evelyn began to clean Claire's wounds. Claire saw her brother Dan and said she wanted to get up. The two men in her life, her husband Scott and her brother Dan lifted her up and she was able to stand while holding on to Scott.

A railroad work truck arrived and it was fortunate that a doctor was on the truck. He had ordered the driver to go to the aeroplane crash site. The young doctor was closer to Charles and tried to check him out but he told the doctor to see Claire first.

Now that we knew our people would be OK, I wanted to know if Rose was captured. Dan and I went to find the task force commander, a captain of the Illinois State Police. He told us that his men were conducting a thorough search of Rose's train to make sure there were no more gangsters hiding or playing dead, but no one fitting Rose's description was found dead or alive. Dan's plan worked but Rose was still on the loose.

The task force commander came to the crash site with us and finding everything well in hand he went back to supervise securing the train site. Paddy wagons and ambulances were converging on the scene.

Amazingly, everyone in the Trimotor escaped with minor injuries. Scott had a bullet graze his leg. Claire hit the side of the aeroplane when it bounced and had passed out just before Jake shut down the switches and carried her out. J-P, Dawn, Scott and Charles were in the body of the Trimotor but were able to exit the fuselage door and get to the shallow depression before the Trimotor blew up. Scott had saved them by seeing the depression and directing them to it. If they had been in the open the fireball would have caught them. Jake told us that Claire stayed calm, helping him with the Trimotor's controls to land slightly nose high.

Bill came to tell us we needed to leave the area to avoid being pulled into the investigation. Bill and Dawn had considerable influence and I knew that they worked for military and government agencies on secret projects in the past. The doctor asked if we wanted our injured to go to the local hospital, but all said they were well enough to go home after the doctor patched them up. The truck driver pulled up and all of us piled on for the short ride to our train where Big Al and Ole had steam up and ready to go.

Bill told us the railroads and the state governments were enraged that Rose had been stealing locomotives, intimidating railroad dispatchers, shooting people, eluding the railroad cops, leaving dead bodies everywhere they went while they ran all over the country. When Dan's plan was received, authorization was given to provide us with the resources needed and to use deadly force, if necessary, to stop Rose's gangsters.

The M2HB Browning machine gun in the Trimotor had been Jake's idea. He felt that if Rose's train escaped they could track it by air and slow it down until the task force arrived. The main purpose for the Ford aeroplane was air surveillance to co-ordinate the blocking trains. The rear train followed far behind until Charles and Scott identified Rose's train, and they sent a Morse coded radio message to the rear train to speed up to block Rose's train from behind. A radio transmitter and antenna installed in the Trimotor, with receivers on each of the blocking trains, communicated back to the Trimotor by Morse code light signals.

Bill brought us the messages from the railroads, Pinkerton's and the Illinois and Indiana state governments congratulating us on bringing Rose's rampage to a conclusion but the operation was going to be kept quiet and out of the newspapers. Bill told us that Rose's locomotive, a 2-8-0 that her gang had stolen had been left as bait for her gang to steal because it was old and scheduled to be dismantled.

When our train crew had #3447 running as fast as they could, Big Al came back to check on Claire. He always called her Missy and had a special fondness for her from the night she escaped from the siding in Rutherford, Napa Valley last year. Relieved that she was not seriously harmed, he said "I told you Missy, that I would drive this locomotive to the gates of Hell and back for you, and I am happy to report that we are on the way back."

Scott was philosophical about the loss of the McLanahan Ford Trimotor. "A bullet cut a fuel line and it started leaking fuel, the gas reaching the hot engine which started the fire. Losing the Trimotor is the least of my cares. I am grateful that my lovely wife Claire and all of my friends escaped with minor injuries. Everyone on the crew contributed mightily to the success of our mission. I can replace the aeroplane and the railroads have committed to contribute funds for the replacement."

Hidden in the trees on the hill a quarter mile from the bridge, a person wearing a dirty brown monk's hooded robe watched as the plot to kill Laure and Dan went horribly wrong, her gang slaughtered or captured. Some of the captured men would turn states' evidence but they would not be safe from her grasp as they would never live to testify in court. She could handle that through her political and mob connections.

Foster Pell, the idiot who claimed to be an expert on machine guns had advised her that Chauchats were readily available and were superior to anything Laure's gang could get. Rose had ordered the Chauchats from an arms merchant who stole them and shipped the guns at great expense to her financial backers. Rose suspected that Pell profited from recommending Chauchats. *'If Pell were still alive'*, Rose said to herself, *'I would personally strangle him, very slowly'*.

Rose limped to a car where her bodyguards waited behind the trees on a rocky dirt road. She got into the back seat of the big sedan and told the driver to take her to their hideout, an abandoned farmhouse. There was nothing to do but regroup and rebuild her gang. She hired the railroad conductor and his three minions after they were fired from their jobs and they were now her bodyguards and enforcers. When Dan busted them up they had sworn to kill him, and even though their new boss was strange they eagerly joined with her when she told them who they were to kill. They had blood in their eyes and hatred in their hearts for Dan Lindner to match the hatred Rose carried for that lying adulteress whore Laure. Every time she thought of her dear sweet little brother Pádraigh, murdered in cold blood by Laure after she lured him to her bed, Rose promised that next time, as she often told her driver "Laure and Dan will watch each other die slow, painful deaths."

The driver had heard this before and nodded in mock agreement with his strange boss. He was a short young fellow of few words, wore a threadbare brown suit and a flat cap like those worn by messenger boys. Rose had hired him since no one else would work for her after the word was out that the Rose gang was trouble. Rose suspected Capone had something to do with that, and she would deal with him later. The young lad carried letters of recommendation for his driving and other services. They were forged and the messenger boy counted on the fact that The Boss needed a driver when she found her previous driver dead with his throat slit from ear to ear. The Boss made the decision that the young man who could drive so well would do nicely for now, and if he followed instructions, he would have a job in the new gang. If not, she would strangle the boy and leave his body in a burning building.

As he drove, the polite young driver smiled at the thought that he was here because of his ability to use his sharp knife to slit the previous driver's throat, and that he looked forward to finishing the assignment when he slit the throat of The Boss.

A THORNY ROSE PROBLEM

We fixed up the railcar as best we could while moving because I wanted to get to Long Grove as fast as possible. Dan and I were uneasy with Rose still at large.

When we arrived at my parents' home, Vera took us aside and said she received a mysterious telephone call. "I couldn't tell if it was a young man or a woman. Whoever it was said you were in great danger and should be extremely aware of everything around you."

"Did the caller identify himself?" I asked.

"No, the caller only said to tell you 'messenger boy' and that you would understand" Vera replied. "Whatever does that mean?" Dan and I knew who the messenger boy was, but we could not tell anyone else, not even my mother.

Dan and I went to talk privately. "Something is wrong if the messenger boy is active. This sounds like trouble" Dan said. "And I'll bet the name of the trouble is Rose."

"Dan, we should get out of Long Grove. I do not want your mother or my parents, or Scott and Claire to be harmed if Rose comes here. Let's leave, and make it obvious that we have departed."

Dan replied "That should draw Rose away from Long Grove, but Rose might decide to kidnap one or more of them to force us to return."

I thought about it for a few seconds, then replied "Too horrible to contemplate, but it sounds like something she would do. We have to stay here and be obvious about it so she will not grab anyone to get to us. How are we going to stay in Long Grove? If we are using ourselves as bait for Rose we can't stay at a family house or we will endanger them when Rose comes for us" I said.

"We can stay in our railcar. I'll tell Scott we want our privacy and ask him to get us permission to park our railcar on an unused spur track. There are several around here. We can fix the railcar up to make it temporarily livable, and it's not cold here this time of year. We should have Big Al take the locomotive somewhere. We can't keep steam up all the time, and if it were nearby it would be an easy target for Rose to blow up."

Dan arranged to park the railcar about a mile from Long Grove on an abandoned spur track. Scott secured a temporary C&NW contract job for our locomotive to pull an executive train to Green Bay and other northern Wisconsin towns and back to Milwaukee and Chicago. We received a good compensation since we provided a locomotive and crew, since the railroad was short on both. Big Al, Sven and Ole wanted to stay to protect us, but I told them the locomotive would be an attractive target for Rose and we would give them the profit from the job.

To announce our presence in the area, Dan and I frequented the local speakeasies and made ourselves as visible as possible.

A few nights later, a chauffeur drove Rose's Peerless sedan down a dirt track road through a forest. Jerry, one of the ex-cinderdick thugs sat next to him in the front while Rose talked with Teddy, Iggy and their boss Brewster sitting in the back seat and jump seats. It had been a near thing when the chauffeur called Laure's mother to send a warning. Rose had almost caught him but he was sure that he hung up before Rose came into the back of the store where the public telephone was.

But Rose did see the young man hang up the telephone and there was only one reason for him to sneak a call, and that was because he was a spy. Rose needed his driving skills tonight since the other men were lousy drivers. After this job, Rose planned to personally kill the driver.

The dirt track road forded shallow streams and after that the road became two rough parallel tracks in the woods. "Stop here" Rose commanded as she and her goons got out. Rose added "Give me the car key. Stay right here and wait for us. Come quickly if I send for you." But the driver was not going to wait for Rose. He had his own plan to complete his assignment.

Rose thought the driver was a young man, but it was Gina Coniglio in her killer messenger boy persona. Gina was smart, about five feet one inch tall, agile, slender and strong for her size. She killed Joey and her other victims by jumping on their backs and clamping her strong legs around their waists. In the few seconds they had left to live, they were unable to pry her legs loose. With their hands trying to release her legs, they could not stop her when she quickly pulled the victim's hair back to expose their throats. She cut quickly and expertly, severing the tender neck to the vertebrae along with its nerves, blood vessels and windpipe. The victim would lose strength and bleed out. The worst part was the stench as their bowels and bladder eliminated and their blood spurted until the heart stopped.

Rose thought she was smart by taking the car key, not knowing that her driver was an expert auto thief. Gina learned the trade in San Francisco in order to get immediate transportation if she needed to vamoose a crime scene or a failed assassination attempt.

After Rose and her thugs went down a trail, Gina silently got out of the car, careful to close the door quietly. She opened the hood to disable the ignition so Rose and her thugs could not use the automobile. As Rose's chauffeur, Gina had the responsibility of getting maps and she studied the maps that Brewster and his gang used to become familiar with the area where Dan and Laure were living in their railcar.

Gina moved stealthily down the trail to the railcar in time to see Rose and her goons splitting up to attack the dark railcar from each end since they did not know where in the railcar Dan and Laure were sleeping. She saw Brewster and Rose climb onto one end platform while Jerry, Teddy and Iggy went to the other end.

Brewster swung a club to break the door's window, reached in and unlocked the door. Jerry, Teddy and Izzy gained entrance the same way at their end. Gina saw a shape inside the car running to that end, and although she could not tell for sure she thought it was Dan. That meant Laure would be at the other end where Brewster and Rose had gone in. Gina decided to help Laure.

Running to where Rose and Brewster went in, she crept onto the platform, carefully avoided stepping on the broken glass before she got through the doorway and into the shadows inside.

Rose started screaming "Kill her! Kill her!" Now Gina had a smell and a sound to locate her target. It was pitch black inside the railcar with no moon, no lights inside and heavy window curtains drawn shut. Gina could sense movement where she thought Brewster was, but it was Laure. So where was Brewster? Gina wanted to go after Rose. Kill the head of the gang first was her thinking. Gina did not have a gun, only two razor sharp knives. Laure saw movement, probably Brewster and fired a shot. From the muzzle blast Gina saw Rose and committed herself to attack.

Gina made a good jump and landed on Rose's back, but almost passed out from her body odor. She clamped her legs around Rose's waist, but was unable to lock her feet together because of the bulky voice device Rose had attached to a strap of leather around her neck. Gina reached to grab Rose's hair but only got a handful of the rough monk's robe material. She pulled on it but it was tied under her chin. Rose now had a hold on Gina's legs and began to pry them apart. Reaching around with her knife, Gina found the string of the robe's hood and cut it. Rose was almost free of Gina's legs now, and Gina would soon fall to the floor. She grabbed for Rose's hair to pull her head back and expose her throat but to her amazement, Rose had shaved her head.

From the other end of the railcar she heard the sounds of a vicious brawl as Dan fought three thugs in the dark.

Then Laure screamed and her scream was replaced with a choking noise. Brewster was killing her, strangling her. Gina wasn't any help now as her legs came loose from Rose's waist. Rose turned to hit Gina but she was able to drop to the floor and scramble away. On the other side of the compartment, she heard Brewster fumbling with his pants, which gave Laure the break she needed to kick him in the groin. Her kick must not have connected because it did not stop Brewster from choking Laure.

With her moves sharpened as her eyes became accustomed to the darkness, Gina jumped back to where she thought Rose was, and she was there, but now facing Gina. Rose's tinny voice screamed "You!" but the voicebox device was emitting more static than sound. Gina jumped on Rose again, but now on her front. Rose's breath was worse than her body odor and Gina almost threw up.

Rose was strong and Gina felt her legs were being pulled off Rose's waist again, but this time Gina had a better lock on Rose's body. Gina got her arm around Rose's neck and plunged her knife into Rose's back as Rose tried to bite Gina's shoulder. Rose let out the most horrible sound Gina had ever heard in her life. Amplified through the sputtering voice box, Gina was startled and fell, leaving her knife stuck in Rose's back.

Thinking that Rose was incapacitated enough that she could help Laure, Gina crawled across the floor and touched something metallic. It was a gun, Laure's pistol. Gina grabbed it and fired away from Laure, hoping to find Brewster by the flash, but she saw Laure first. Brewster's heavy body pressed Laure hard against the wall and with one hand he was grasping her neck. Brewster's other hand was still fumbling to open his pants. Laure was able to get his grip on her neck loosened temporarily since he was using only one hand, but Brewster rammed his bulky body again to slam Laure on the wall and it took her breath away. Laure was fighting for her life and kicked him in the balls again. Once again it wasn't enough and he was slowly getting Laure under his control so he could finish her off.

Laure kicked again, hitting one of Brewster's kneecaps and he howled in pain but it wasn't enough to make him let go of her throat. Gina fired the gun again, deliberately away from Laure and in the flash got a glimpse of Brewster's backside right in front of her, but she could not shoot him for fear of the bullet going through his body and into Laure.

Gina decided to jump on Brewster to cut his throat but she had ignored Rose for too long and now felt hands grab her ankles, pulling her to the floor. Sensing where Rose was, Gina shot down in that direction and heard another piercing scream from Rose, and in the muzzle flash she saw her knife in Rose's neck but it was in a less dangerous place than she expected and Rose was not dying or incapacitated. Gina grabbed the knife and pulled it from Rose's back while Rose was still pulling at Gina's ankles. She got one ankle loose and kicked Rose, her foot hitting the voice box contraption.

Laure was still fighting, but if Brewster stopped trying to get his pants open and got both his hands on her neck he could finish her off in seconds. Gina kicked herself free of Rose and jumped on Brewster's back, surprising him. He loosened his grip on Laure as he tried to grab Gina's legs, but this time Gina had her legs tightly clamped around his waist. He did not smell good, but he wasn't nearly as awful as Rose.

"Laure, move away!" Gina shouted as she grabbed a handful of Brewster's thick greasy hair, pulled it back hard to expose his neck and quickly sliced his throat with her other hand, a move she had practiced to speed and perfection during her training. Brewster began gurgling as his blood gushed, more stench came as he lost control of his body. Gina dropped from his back and Rose grabbed at her ankles again. This time Rose pulled her down and Laure's gun, which Gina had put in her belt at her back, fell out with a thud to the wood floor. She could hear Rose scrabbling for the gun, but there was another sound – Laure was going for the gun too. Gina did not know which sound to kick so she tried to move away from the fighting women on the floor to get her bearings. Easing around the room, Gina found Brewster's motionless body and her knife. The sounds from the floor told Gina that Laure and Rose were now in a desperate struggle, but she did not know who was who and where to stab or slice.

Suddenly the sounds of fighting from the other end of the car stopped, replaced by the sound of two sets of footsteps coming fast down the corridor. Gina knew Dan would fight to his death for Laure. Three of Rose's thugs had gone into the other end of the railcar, so if two were coming, he must have killed one and Gina hoped that he injured the others sufficiently to give her a chance to kill one and keep the last man and Rose occupied long enough for Laure to escape. Gina pulled herself together for a brutal fight to the finish.

The two sets of footsteps entered the room. Gina tried to analyze the sound to determine where the men were, her knife ready to kill one of the men or Rose, whichever was the closer target.

"Oh Dan!" Gina's heart went to her throat as she heard Laure's voice. The other man lit a match. Gina breathed an even bigger sigh of relief. It was Laure's Uncle Viktor, who must have hidden himself in the railcar to help even the odds when Rose's expected attack came.

Gina's eyes had become accustomed to the darkness in the room and the light of the match almost blinded her. Despite being stabbed in the back, with a furious roar of noise and static Rose suddenly rose up and attacked. Dan and Viktor were too far away to stop her. Gina held her backup knife but could not move fast enough to stab as Rose slammed into her, the bloody metal mask falling off as it struck Gina's left shoulder. Gina got her arm around Rose's neck from behind and held tight so Gina's free right hand could come up. With all her strength, Gina pushed her deadly knife deep into Rose's stomach, sliced downward and twisted it as hard as she could. Rose stopped, cursed and began to gurgle as she fell on top of Gina.

Dan was in front of Laure to defend her if necessary while Viktor got hold of Rose and pulled her off Gina. Rose was still trying to remove Gina's knife from her stomach but Viktor got hold of it first, pulled it from Rose's body and stabbed her again and again until she moved no more. All of us were overwhelmed from the stench in such close quarters and went outside to breathe and throw up. Then we went back in to make a final check to be sure they were really dead.

Once outside, I cleansed my lungs in the cool, fresh night air. Uncle Viktor was next to me and I gave him a hug, thanking him for being there for us. We did not know Viktor was watching at the other end of the railcar from where Dan and I were.

Viktor knew Gina would intervene against Rose because Giuseppe told Bill, who told Viktor that Gina was undercover as Rose's chauffeur and would attack Rose. Without Viktor's help, Dan might have been killed. Despite the many times in his life as he had to do it, Viktor did not like killing, but Izzy, Teddy and Jerry would not stop until they breathed their last. Without Gina, Rose and Brewster would have killed me.

Dan was next to me and I held him close, shivering and putting my head on his shoulder. He had cuts and bruises and a shiner but no serious injuries. I kissed Dan and asked him to wait a minute. I went to Gina and hugged her as though she was my dearest sister, thanking her profusely for all she had done for us.

Gina said "You remember that day in your house in Napa, Dan turned me down when I stripped in his office and tried to seduce him. I knew then that I would never be in his heart, but found that both of you were in mine. That's why I helped last year in Bakersfield even though it was not part of my vendetta. When my godfather Al asked if I wanted to get involved again, I jumped at the chance. I like the excitement and the thrill of danger, but this time it was too close for comfort. If Brewster had killed you, it would have been the end of my life too. I almost died just from Rose's stench."

I hugged her again, all thoughts of jealousy were now vanquished. "You're in our hearts too, Gina. Without your warning and intervention, it might be Dan and me lying on the floor in there."

"Al Capone despised Rose, and gave me a contract to kill her, but first I had to uncover the informants in your crew who were giving information to Rose, and to find out who was funding Rose." Gina told us she could not find all the leaks but learned that Rose and her gang were backed by the political power and wealth of someone named Desmond T. Lincoln in Sacramento. Neither Gina nor I knew the name, but she said Al Capone or Giuseppe would know or would find out.

We couldn't call the police because they might accuse us of ambushing Rose and her goons if they were on the North Side Gang's pad. At the very least we would have to stay around for the investigation. I was getting annoyed from doing so many wrong things to save ourselves.

Gina took care of the problem of the dead bodies when she went back to Rose's automobile, fixed the ignition and drove to a public phone to call her godfather Al Capone, who sent a couple of rough looking fellows in an old truck. Gina led them to our railcar and they took the bodies away. I asked what they were going to do with the bodies and was rudely told "You don't wanna know, dollface." I decided he was right. I didn't want to know.

DANCING TO BIX AT THE GREEN MILL

"Scott's right" said Dan. "We are tough on railcars. I lost track of how many we have destroyed. We will never get the smell out of this one. The way executive railcar design is improving so fast, I'd rather purchase an older car in good condition and refurbish it, then in two or three years order a new one."

I looked at him. "A new executive railcar? Why?"

"Because we have a locomotive but no train. A train needs a locomotive and a locomotive needs a train" Dan looked at me and grinned like a Cheshire cat at his stunning witticism.

My eyes rolled and I muttered "Oh it must be time for a new one." Dan continued in spite of my expression. "We have a movie to film, and a railcar makes a luxurious office and hotel room. Now that we can expect to get the green light for *Road Trip Blues* again, we will need a private room so I can trick you into doing casting couch interviews."

"I was right, you are like all the other producers I've known who expect me to get naked on their couch with merely a hint of a promise of a role in a movie."

"How many producers have offered you a movie role if you got on their casting couch?" Dan asked with a smile.

"Only one before you, and he ran when I showed him my derringer held point blank at his nutmegs. But I am grateful that you are becoming civilized. You know I prefer a nice bed for lovemaking, so if you can produce a comfortable hotel room I might consent to your interview" I replied.

"Who said anything about love? I just want a hot barney-mugging."

"Oh, what am I to do with you?"

"Anything you want my dear" Dan said as he pulled me over for a kiss. "Mmm, yes, I remember now, you're the sexy actress with the cutest little butt who does a devilish sexy Charleston" he said as he put his hand on my ass to pull me closer. I gave my butt a wiggle to encourage him and snuggled closer. I liked my man to be hot for me.

We spent a few days visiting and calming ourselves. We were so relaxed that we had no complaints, even when the Long Grove Village Tavern ran out of Champagne a couple of days later. Dan told them to bring in a supply and Hutfilz thought there was no way we could go through more than two bottles in a week. We called Gina and she sent an emergency supply of Moët & Chandon.

Since J-P and Marie-Laure, along with Charles and Dawn were in the guest rooms at my parents' house, Scott and Claire gave us a guest cottage at their S Bar C bangtail ranch so we lived there in luxury until it came time to go home. We even went for a trail ride with Claire, although Dan did not seem to enjoy riding a horse. That might have been because the animal she gave him was a retired circus horse and even though the gentle mare was past her prime, she still liked to show off her tricks. Dan did not find that as amusing as Claire and I did.

As I expected, my Ma sat me down for a heart-to-heart talk about how she wanted a grandchild to spoil, but I told her we had to make sure Rose was dead or in prison first. I did not want to be trying to escape from a small window in a stone wall while sporting a pregnant belly.

Charles and Dawn were fast becoming more than good friends. Dan said she seemed happier than he had ever seen her before, and Charles walked around with a smile on his face all the time. Charles decided he would like to live in the United States for a year or two because he wanted to study the Chicago style of architecture. Scott was impressed with Charles and gave him a contact through one of his father's business partners to seek employment with a leading architectural design firm, and Charles sent his curriculum vitae. This brought Charles an invitation for an interview with Grant, Anderson, Probst

& White, one of the top architectural firms in Chicago. They were the designers of the Wrigley building and annex in recent years, along with other landmark buildings like the Pittsfield. A few days later, Charles received a letter for a second interview to discuss a potential offer of employment.

As expected, it was a good offer so Charles accepted and signed a two-year employment agreement. Dawn seemed very pleased as well. She told us that this was the sign that he was the right man at the right time for her.

I decided it was the right time to celebrate with a night on the town in Chicago. The celebration party grew into a major event and since it was my idea, by default I took charge of making the arrangements. I made reservations at Pete's Steaks, where Dan and I enjoyed superb dinners twice before. I suggested that after dinner, we should drink and dance at The Green Mill Lounge. Dan agreed.

Dan was unsure if J-P, being a policeman, albeit in France, would be comfortable visiting a well-known mob controlled Chicago speakeasy. I am usually direct so I went to J-P and asked. He and Marie-Laure beamed with joy, since they wanted to do just that but did not want to offend Vera and Jake's sense of propriety. As it turned out, my parents wanted to come too, as did Scott and Claire, who said we should invite Dorothy. I added invitations for Viktor and Evelyn. I felt a thrill at the thought of our families and friends joining us in celebration of Dan and I surviving through the year.

When I called the telephone number for The Green Mill, managed by Al Capone's associate and enforcer Jack McGurn, Jack answered the phone himself. I was surprised that he remembered us, and he told me that he was now a part owner of The Green Mill. Jack was glad to accept our reservation even when I told him Jean-Philippe was a French police colonel. I wanted to avoid any misunderstanding with Capone by bringing a high level

French police commander into The Green Mill, and to make sure there were no problems with guest safety.

"We are happy to entertain our friends from Europe" Jack said. "We wish them to see that serving liquor in the United States can be done safely and with class despite Prohibition, and I will be present to personally ensure your party gets the services of our best wait staff and are served our best wines and spirits. I always stock Canadian Club and Templeton Rye whiskey and we are proud to serve the best uncut whiskey to our friends. We have great entertainment booked for that night Laure, so be sure to wear your dancing shoes."

To complete our night on the town in Chicago I made hotel reservations at The Knickerbocker, a hotel just off Michigan Avenue. It was an unusual recommendation from Jack McGurn, but it had recently opened to great acclaim in Chicago, so I decided to try it.

I asked my Ma what she planned to wear, hoping that she wasn't going to be too old-fashioned, but to my surprise she showed me a contemporary dress, not quite flapper but very stylish with an eye-catching art deco motif. I did not worry about my Pa, he always had a couple of good suits and he was a handsome dapper (a flapper's dad) and he looked sharp when he dressed up. I also did not worry about J-P and Marie-Laure, they dressed fashionably even when my mother took them shopping at the grocers' store. Dawn did not have a modern dancing dress and since she and I were about the same size, I loaned her a sexy flapper dress that looked great on her, although tighter around her breasts. Since our fight she and I had become the best of friends. Dawn said Charles was well prepared with stylish suits. I also knew not to worry about Scott and Claire, they had the wherewithal and Claire had excellent fashion sense. My Uncle Viktor and Evelyn were stylish dressers too, although Viktor in a pinstripe suit looked like a gangster, but he said Evelyn thought the look was sexy on him. I could not argue with her on that.

When I reviewed my party plan with Scott and Claire, Scott said that he and many of his contemporaries were regulars at Pete's and The Green Mill. Then he spilled the beans that he was the one who set Dan up with Pete's and The Green Mill for our first Chicago date when I was at secretarial school and Dan came to Chicago to take me out on the town. Back then, I had wondered how Dan was able to get reservations at The Green Mill because everyone said you had to know someone in the mob to get inside, and it was one of the bits of circumstantial evidence that caused me to incorrectly conclude that Dan was joining the mob, which caused me to break up with him. I looked back on that episode with amazement that I had been so naïve, but all things considered, our relationship was stronger for being tested.

It was almost three years ago when Dan took me out on the town in Chicago for the first time. I had not allowed him to have sex with me, and tested Dan's ability to be a gentleman by telling him that even though it was our first night in a hotel room together, there would be no sex. He surprised me by respecting my wish. I was favorable to him but would not admit that I was in love, although my heart knew it since the day we met. He was so wonderful, especially after my horrible affair with Pádraigh that I could not believe Dan was real and worried that he would turn out to be another loser. It became a standing joke between us that our first night in a hotel room together was a no-sex night, so I told Dan with a straight face that there would be no sex on this Chicago date either. He looked into my eyes with that handsome sexy grin on his face and said "Maybe I wasn't going to allow you have sex with me!" and I broke out laughing. We were married almost a year ago and lived together more than a year before that, yet we still could not keep our hands off one another.

Louise Brooks found out we were going to be in Chicago at the same time she would be on one of her trips from Hollywood to New York to meet with a lover. I gave Louise the rundown of recent events and she wanted to stop in Chicago for a day to see us, then get on the next train to New York. Our friendship with Louise Brooks was complicated because she lived only for the moment. She had an incredibly sexy look in her eyes that easily turned her target into jelly if she desired him. I liked her anyway because she was a smart, independent woman, outrageous and fun. In Hollywood, Louise and I pretended to be cousins and she seemed to pop up in our lives at random times. My guest list was now a party of fourteen:

Charles and Dawn
Jean-Philippe and Marie-Laure
Scott and Claire
Jake and Vera
Viktor and Evelyn
Dorothy Lindner
Louise Brooks
Dan and Laure-Marie

We rode in three limousines with armed chauffeurs courtesy of Scott's father Thomas McLanahan, who also arranged for an escort automobile with four of his best security men tailing us. He was concerned that an unknown Rose gang survivor might make an appearance.

Arriving earlier than planned, The Knickerbocker Hotel did not have our rooms ready but the manager accommodated us in temporary rooms so we could freshen up and change clothes for dinner.

Pete's Steaks owners Bill and Marie Botham welcomed us personally, giving us an upstairs private room because Louise caused so much excitement wherever she went. We all ordered steak and the dinners were the bee's knees. When I made the reservations, I asked for our favorite waiter Phillip who always took excellent care of us. The party was in full swing when Phillip came over with chilled French Champagne and a note:

> *Greetings to our dear friends Laure and Dan –*
> *In remembrance of good times we are sending over three bottles of Champagne and we would like to come by and propose a toast to you.*
> *Bill and Marie Botham*

I happily wrote back:

> *Dear Bill and Marie,*
> *We would love to raise a glass with you. Please join us!*
> *Laure and Dan Lindner*

Bill and Marie arrived with more Champagne. Phillip had the busboys bring more chairs and I introduced Bill and Marie to our group. As could be expected with a group like ours, bottles of Champagne continuously appeared as needed. After a couple of rounds after all our glasses were refilled Bill and Marie Botham stood up to offer their toast to us:

> *"To our dear friends, the lovely Laure and Dan, we always have enjoyed the pleasure of your company in our restaurant. Marie and I were pleased when we met you three years ago. At the time, Marie said to me that she was sure you two would be married soon, and what a beautiful couple you were then and are today. We wish both of you joy in your marriage and that your love for each other grows and goes on forever."*

After that cheerful round Dan and I stood and raised a toast to Bill and Marie. Then Louise gave us a ribald Hollywood toast and it was getting out of hand but we all were delighted with every minute of it.

The evening was not even half over. Dan and I paid for our group's dinners, despite cries to the contrary from

Scott, Jake, J-P and Louise, who was always generous to her friends. As our party got ready to leave, our waiter Phillip told us people were talking about the Brooks Girls being in the restaurant so Louise and I walked out arm in arm as customers stood and applauded us. Louise was prepared with autographed photographs of her and I together on the set of *Rolled Stockings*.

I reminisced back to the first romantic dinner Dan and I enjoyed here and how special it was for me to be treated with respect by my then boyfriend Dan. I never got that feeling when I went to dinner or anywhere with Pádraigh, who liked to belittle me in front of his friends.

At that time I did not know, but had I married Pádraigh I would never have enjoyed a life of my own. I would have been taken out on the town only when he was not with his latest mistress. I would be expected to run his house, bear his children and not have any interest in business, especially his business. Contrast that with Dan, who encouraged me to do what I wanted to do. He supported my efforts when I started The LaureDan Company and did not look over my shoulder, instead leaving me plenty of room to make my own successes and failures. He knew I was competitive and liked to win and told me he had every confidence in me, and he only stepped in to help if I asked. With that kind of backing, I could not fail. The LaureDan Company was profitable from the start, and became the foundation for all our business ventures. When someone pointed out that I had actually built the business, I responded saying that I could not have built the business without Dan's encouragement and confidence in me, and that it was most assuredly a mutual effort.

After a superb dinner, on we went to The Green Mill. Excitement was in the air as our party exited the limousines and walked to the entrance. When Dan gave our name to the doorman, he sent a messenger inside and in a flash "Machine Gun" Jack McGurn and his gorgeous blonde girlfriend Louise Rolfe appeared to greet us. Jack was a spiffy dresser, tonight he wore a well-tailored dark suit that made him look like the world's most elegant gangster. Louise Rolfe looked fabulous as always in a gorgeous red flapper dress. I was wearing a sleek gold dress with black trim, the shortest dress I had ever worn but it had a black fringe that accented my long legs and dance kicks. My mother Vera did not like it at first but everyone else did – especially the men – and she came around when she saw me on the dance floor. Jack escorted us inside and showed us to our tables roped off near the dance floor. Waiters immediately appeared and took our drink orders while I introduced Jack and Louise Rolfe to our party. He and Louise Brooks greeted each other warmly, making it obvious that she had been here before. When Jack saw Viktor, they gave each other a bear hug and Jack said "Viktor, you're looking great. Good to see you again. Let's get in touch soon" which had me wanting to ask what that was all about. For others in our party, this was their first look at an infamous gangster in person.

Jack had done his homework and in his greeting acknowledged J-P as "the most respected lawmen in France" and said "The Green Mill is proud to offer their best hospitality and entertainment so J-P and his wife Marie-Laure could drink, dance and enjoy the show." I glanced over to my Ma because she initially seemed worried about being in a mob speakeasy but Jack had his charm going and everyone felt at ease.

Drinks arrived promptly and soon the band came onstage, starting the show with an up-tempo dance number. Dan pulled me out on the dance floor and soon someone who Louise knew asked her to dance. Soon we were all on the dance floor except Dorothy. Just as I started to tell Dan to go dance with his mother, Jack went over to ask her to dance.

It was a magnificent evening of entertainment. True to his word, Jack provided us with the good stuff. J-P was so pleased with the whiskey he asked Jack what it was, and McGurn replied that it was real Kentucky bourbon made before Prohibition and not some knock-off panther piss. J-P said he wanted to take some back to France and asked if he could buy a couple of bottles. I was stunned, here was a Colonel in the Gendarmerie Nationale, purchasing illegal whiskey to illegally transport home. J-P laughed and told me not to worry, that France would never do anything as silly as to prohibit good whiskey. He said that in France, many people liked Kentucky Bourbon.

When the band played a Charleston, someone called for the Brooks girls to perform their wild and sexy Charleston dance. After a couple minutes Louise waved for the women in our group to join, and Claire, Dawn, Evelyn and Louise Rolfe took up the invitation and we put on a show of female legs to great applause. I liked Louise Rolfe, she had been a wild child before meeting Jack, and she was a lot of fun. Later, we saw Louise Brooks teaching J-P and Marie-Laure the Charleston. They learned quickly and by the end of the evening they looked like professional Charleston dancers. We were not the only dancers, sometimes it seemed like the entire room was up and dancing. Jack told us it was one of the best party nights ever at The Green Mill.

Dan gave each waiter a generous tip and Jake said we should pass a hat around for the band because the bandleader and his musicians were hot tonight and everyone wanted to show their appreciation. From the size of the collection it was obvious that our group liked the band. Dan and J-P took the hat up and gave it to the band at their next break. The bandleader came to our tables and introduced himself as Bix Beiderbecke and his band was called His Gang, a sometime combination of musicians he and friend Frankie Trumbauer had played with in other bands, most recently in the Goldkette Orchestra. J-P surprised us when he said he knew Jean Goldkette from his early days as a musician in France. J-P played the trumpet and might have made it his career, but instead followed his father's footsteps into the Gendarmerie.

Bix graciously thanked our party for the tip money. Later his musicians came over to meet us too, and we asked where else Bix would be playing. Bix told us he was going to join the Paul Whiteman Orchestra in October. Dan and I were impressed with Bix and his cornet solos were the most inventive we had ever heard. He set the bar high with his solo work, and all the musicians delivered. Dan noticed that we had started something. Other men in the room began bringing hats of cash to the band.

I got up and whispered into Bix's ear when the band was coming back onstage after a break. He agreed and gave his band instructions for the next songs while he danced with every woman in our group, beginning with Dorothy and ending with me. Dan and I remembered Bix as we read in the newspapers about his growing and somewhat odd reputation, and before we left Chicago I bought several of his records, many of them featuring Bix in other orchestras. My favorites were the first hot dance number they played that night called *At The Jazz Band Ball* and another number called *Sorry*. I liked just about everything they played that night. I got a laugh out of Bix when I told him that he had just danced with Marie-Laure, and now he was dancing with Laure-Marie. Later on, Bix remembered us every time we saw him perform. Dan's mother Dorothy told me she'd had a wonderful time, her first time at a speakeasy with her son, daughter, son-in-law and daughter-in-law, a Chicago mobster, a movie star and a hot jazz band leader on his way to fame. She commented that it certainly was not her usual night at home in Long Grove.

There were no incidents at The Green Mill that night, no doubt because Jack McGurn had his men on alert to keep trouble away. The police almost never raided The Green Mill and when they did there was advance warning. We learned that if there was trouble, The Green Mill had underground tunnels for Capone and special guests.

When we reluctantly decided it was time to go to our hotel, Jack refused to take our money for the booze, saying it was a direct order from his boss. Although he did not name his boss, everyone knew Jack worked for Al Capone. McGurn had a fearsome reputation as an enforcer, but like his boss, he could be charming when he wanted to be charming. He always treated us very well but his reputation made me a little nervous and I was glad he wanted to be charming that night.

Having chauffeured limousines was a stroke of good luck as we were all at various stages of being sozzled. Louise told me she was invited to stay at The Green Mill to go out later with Bix and his gang. I knew she was going to have a wild night so we said our good-byes. Our limousines delivered us to the front door of The Knickerbocker. Jack McGurn had given Dan a hotel room number to call when we got there. I told him if there was a floozie in the room he had better not go there, because if I could wrestle with Dawn for a couple of rounds I could surely beat down a floozie.

Dan called and found that the number was for a private casino on the 14th floor of the hotel. It was rumored to be operated by Al Capone's brother Ralph, which explained Jack McGurn's recommendation. When Dan told us about it, everyone wanted to go. Answering a question from the doorman, Dan told him we were not big gamblers and the doorman seemed ready to turn us away when Dan gave the doorman Jack's note and with that we were welcomed into the casino. It was very posh and although there was a lot of activity in the room, the luxurious furnishings kept it quieter than I would have expected. Jake and J-P headed over to the craps tables, while most of the others played the roulette wheel except Scott, Claire and Dan and I played at the blackjack tables.

I went to freshen up in the ladies' room and when I returned, Dan got blackjack and won a good-sized pile of chips. Outside, it had started raining and thundering.

I whispered in Dan's ear "There's only two things to do on a rainy night and I don't want to play cards, so I'm inviting you to try your luck with me and the sooner the better to ensure my active participation because I am sozzled."

Dan, who recognized a good invitation when he heard it, picked up his winnings and took my hand to lead me to the elevators. "Your every wish is my command, sweetie" he said in a low sexy voice. In the elevator I told Dan more of my wishes, and I knew the young elevator operator heard them when his ears turned red. Enjoying the effect I was having, I told Dan a couple extra special desires and when the elevator operator called our floor and opened the elevator door his voice was quavering. I gave him a big smile and Dan tipped him. Once in the room Dan acted as if there was not a moment to lose and began removing my clothes, ravenously performing every wish to my complete satisfaction especially after he discovered that when I went to the room earlier I sent for Champagne in an ice bucket. Calling room service would have resulted in a denial that the hotel had any such thing as alcoholic beverages, but Jack had given us the appropriate room number to call.

Dan was up early and used his fingers and lips to awaken me. "Wake up Sweetie. Happy First Anniversary!" My eyes popped open. I was thrilled that he remembered. He went to his suitcase and brought out a box that appeared to be the size of a large book. I told him I had something for him too, and retrieved it from my trunk. Dan told me to open mine first.

It was a book with beautiful deep red leather covers and gold edged pages and trim, the front cover embossed with 'Laure and Dan's Anniversary Memories.' Inside were pages designed to hold photographs and rich textured vellum journal pages to write about our anniversary events. The anniversary journal was an elegant treasure, a beautiful book to be filled with loving memories over the years. "Oh Dan, this is posilutely fabulous! We must get photos of every anniversary and write things to each other every year. I love it Sweetie!" and as I leaned over to kiss him and felt his hand taking possession of my left breast. I told him reluctantly that he had to open his present before we made love.

Dan said "As for photographs, if you recall, it was the same photographer that took photos of us at Pete's and at The Green Mill. The photographer will have the photographs developed and sent to us in Napa. They will probably be there before we get home, and we can set up our first anniversary pages."

Dan surprised me with another beautifully wrapped gift box. "The anniversary journal is an anniversary present to both of us and I wanted to give you a more personal gift" he said.

"Even more personal than the gift you're going to give me when we are done opening these gifts?"

"Yes sweetie, but this is something you can wear any time" and he gave me the box. I opened it to find a most beautiful and probably very expensive art deco style necklace and earring set.

"Oh Dan, this is so beautiful" and I had him put the necklace on me.

"Laure, it is even more beautiful when it is on you" he exclaimed as I looked in the mirror. I gave him my gift. "So what's in the box? Something for me or something for Raider?" Dan asked.

"Silly boy. Raider came to live with you on April 1, so that's his anniversary. This is ours." I worried if he would like it. I had sent for it to be made in Chicago before he was kidnapped and hoped it would fit.

Dan shook the box, trying to guess what was inside. I got an inspiration and told him to go into the bathroom and come out when I called. He was intrigued by my request and when I called he came out to find me on my side in bed wearing nothing but a baseball glove on my right hand clutched over my left breast. I watched the look on his face go from surprise to satisfaction to his happy guy grin. "Look! It fits your breast perfectly. Is this a new bedroom game? Oh Laure, I'm thrilled with your gift and even more the way you gave it to me. Now every time I put it on I will think of what it was holding when I first saw it. I was going to order a baseball glove when we got home because I want to join the baseball league in Napa. When I played last year I had to borrow a glove." He tried it on. "Laure, look. It fits perfectly, the leather is comfortable and it has the modern web and padding style. Oh wait till the guys see this" he said as he fit it over my breast again, making me laugh. "I can't wait to tell the guys what was in the glove when I first saw it."

"You better not. That's our secret and we can grin foolishly when we think of it. Do you really like it?" I asked. "I sent those leather dress gloves I gave you, the ones that you said fit perfectly, to the baseball glove maker to make it to that size."

"Do I like it? No. I love it. Hold on. Put it on like you had it when I came into the room." He went to get our Kodak camera.

"You really want to take my photograph like this?"

"Yes, you said you wanted to do boudoir photographs, and this qualifies as a sports boudoir photograph."

"Dan, there is no such thing as a sports boudoir photograph."

"Yes there is. Our lovemaking is athletic enough to be considered a bedroom sport" he said, trying to be serious.

He took me by surprise with that. "Well... I... oh, OK, you win this time. Take the photo. It can be the first one we put in our Anniversary Memories journal. But then I want to take a photo of you naked except for the glove" I said. "I guess we will never be able to show our Anniversary Memories album to our parents."

"Ready sweetie? Give me a look like you're telling me with your eyes that you are ready to be ravished." The camera clicked as Dan took two more photos from different angles. I remembered the photographer from San Francisco who wanted me to pose for nude photographs but I turned him down even though he offered a lot of money and Dan said it was my choice. I did not want to do that at the time, except now with Dan it felt entirely different. For him I wanted to be sexy and it was easy for me to look at him that way, because now my desire was building for one of my favorite things, great morning sex. We would never get breakfast at this rate.

As if on cue, my Pa knocked on the door. "Laure. Dan. Are you coming down for breakfast?"

"Sorry Pa, Dan and I are celebrating our first wedding anniversary."

"That's funny, I don't hear the bed squeaking" my Pa said as he laughed and turned to go back down the hallway.

Dan laughed himself silly and it got me laughing too, and I said "Now, it's your turn to be photographed nude with the glove. Do not move after I take the photo."

"Why not?"

"Because you are right where I want you" I told him.

Soon after, the bed was squeaking when Dawn knocked on our door and called "Good morning Laure, are you and Dan coming down for breakfast?"

All I was able to say came out as a satisfied moaning sound, and Dawn replied "Now that I know what you're doing, I have to find Charles and we will be late for breakfast too." Dawn said.

J-P and Marie-Laure stayed in Chicago a few more days with Dawn and Charles to help him find and rent a place to live. It was implicitly understood that Dawn would be moving in with Charles. Scott offered to hire Dawn as an investigator based in Chicago, saying that there was plenty of work in the Chicago area. Dawn accepted because she could continue to do the work she enjoyed and not have to be away from Charles for weeks or months on assignments.

ROAD TRIP BLUES GETS A NEW DIRECTOR

We spent a few more days in Long Grove. Dan sent a telegram to Lasky at the studio to tell him the saboteurs were neutralized and he would follow it up with a letter explaining what happened. Dan did not like talking about such things over telephone lines, since they could be listened to by almost anyone. Dan and I agreed that if Lasky wanted to green light the movie again, we would make it; otherwise I was just fine if it didn't go ahead. We had many other things to do.

Josefina and Luigi were waiting for us to return so they could set their wedding date. They wanted us to be best man and maid of honor at their wedding. Vincenzo and Bettina Montanari knew almost everyone in the wine business in Napa and Sonoma counties and they were planning a big traditional Italian wedding. Josefina told me that she and Luigi would be happy to elope and get married at the courthouse, but her parents would never forgive them. Luigi received a letter from his parents in Italy saying that they were coming to California for the wedding. He knew they could not afford it, so he sent money for second class round trip tickets on the Navigazione Generale Italiana steamship liner *SS Roma*.

Major Griffin had followed up on the details of expunging the murder charge against me. He found out that the Navy captain who was the acting base commander that had sent the legal team back to D.C. and declined to terminate the employment of those men who attacked me on the base was linked to a shady lawyer who had a connection to Rose. It was enough to force the deputy base commander to resign when the Marine Commandant learned of it and brought it to the attention of his liaison in the Navy Department.

We received a letter from Captain Tracy of the California State Police telling us he had begun an investigation. So far he found two state senators in the California legislature that were involved. This gave Rose strong political influence, enough to set me up on a false murder charge and almost make it stick. Captain Tracy knew the legislators were up to their necks in it, but he did not yet have the hard evidence he needed to get the attorney general to prosecute. Captain Tracy was investigating if the corruption went all the way up to the attorney general's office, but it was slow going and there was pressure to halt his investigation, which was an indication in itself.

Dan and I sent Big Al, Sven and Ole to check out a couple of used executive railcars. They found not just one, but three railcars owned by a major vendor to the Chicago & North Western. One was an executive railcar with offices and parlors for meetings, the second was a sleeping car with a suite for the owner and rooms for guests and the train crew. The third railcar contained a kitchen and dining room with a baggage and freight compartment at the opposite end. The cars were for the president of the company to travel to major work sites and meetings with C&NW management. The founder of the company passed away – not on the train – and the estate taxes were a burden for his heirs, who decided they were going to have to sell the company.

This started an idea in my mind and Dan agreed. We would purchase the company if the books passed our inspection and other investigations to make sure there were no skeletons in their corporate closet.

"Sweetie, you were so worried about us buying a locomotive, now you're buying an entire company to get a train. You certainly are flexible" Dan aimed a Groucho Marx wink at me as he delivered the double entendre following an especially aggressive romp.

"You're posilutely good at it yourself, big guy" I replied, nearly setting us off on a repeat performance. However, we were right in the middle of making plans and getting ready for our return trip, so I reluctantly told Dan that the bank was closed until our planning was finished.

"You mean I can't even make a quick deposit?" he grinned, making me laugh again.

"I promise you will be able to later, and you know I always keep those promises."

"Yes, you do, and we have a long future together. By the way, apropos of nothing, I heard Moe and Joe stopped by but I did not get to see them. How are they doing?" Dan asked.

"I asked them if they wanted to come out west until things in the east cooled down for them, and we could help them in Hollywood if they wanted to try to break into the movies" I replied, as matter-of-factly as I could.

"And I'm guessing that you asked them to show you how to ride the rails. I know you want to do that. You are crazy, but fun. I only rode the rails to save my ass and get home to you, but you are risking your cute little butt. It's dangerous to ride the rails" Dan said seriously.

"Well maybe I want you to watch my cute little butt and give it a push if necessary. Or is your hand hurting again?" I knew it was, from his fierce fight with Teddy and Jerry and I was making a comparison to back when I surprised Dan by getting off the train with Joey in St. Louis. Dan was so angry at seeing Joey he hit him so hard his hand hurt. At the time, I had decided that Dan and I would become lovers but I wanted Dan to take me dancing at Café Lulu first, and he tried to back off dancing by saying his hand hurt. I shocked him by shamelessly offering myself for him to have his way with me after Café Lulu, telling him that "If you don't dance, no romance." He suddenly decided his hand did not hurt so much after all.

I knew Dan did not like me riding the rails it but he also knew I enjoyed doing things that most women would not even consider, and he would never deny me anything I set my heart on doing. I admit to being called a competitive woman and did not want to become boring, both for his sake as well as my own. I want to keep things interesting in our lives.

Jean-Philippe and Marie-Laure accepted our invitation to travel with us on our train to visit California. They were wine connoisseurs and wanted to taste the best of the American wines. We invited Charles and Dawn to join us, and since they had time before they started their new jobs, they accepted. J-P and Marie-Laure were not concerned with their son sharing a bed with Dawn.

We brought Dan's mother Dorothy, Claire and Scott and his mother Elaine to help us go over the books and company records when we went to Wisconsin to inspect the prospective purchase. Bill was conducting a separate investigation of the company through his railroad contacts.

We inspected the railcars and found them well maintained and with some cosmetic refurbishing they would serve us well so if we bought the company we could return West in our new private train.

The investigation of the company showed it was operating profitably, the books were in good order and there was a nice backlog of work. The company headquarters was in Green Bay in northeastern Wisconsin, and Dan and I at first talked about moving it but we were so impressed with the loyal, hard-working employees and the facilities that we decided to keep it in Green Bay. This went a long way to establish a good reputation with the employees. Except for the late founder, none of the family had been active in the business. A capable and experienced general manager was running the day-to-day operations very well. All we needed was someone to fulfill the former founder's duties, which mostly consisted of being the 'rain man' to sell the company's services to railroads. We bought the company, paying what we considered a fair price. As one of their largest customers, the C&NW Railroad was pleased that the company would continue under stable management. I was already making plans to expand operations to other railroads.

Two days before we were set to begin our return journey, Big Al and the Swedes arrived with our locomotive #3447. Dan noticed that they had a boxcar from the C&NW hooked on as the last car of the consist. I told Dan that Moe and Joe wanted to travel in it but would take their meals with us in the dining car. I had the Swedes set up comfortable beds for Moe and Joe. We offered to purchase passenger train tickets for the vaudeville men, but they told us they preferred riding the rails, and that this would be one of the few times they had management permission to ride in a boxcar.

But Dan knew I was going to ride the rails at least part of the time and he surprised me by saying he would join me. "I am intrigued by the idea you gave me of grabbing your cute little butt to give it a push now and then" he said, but I knew he was being protective of me and tried to do it without being restrictive, which was a careful balancing act for him. I liked that about him and it did make me feel safer. Not to mention being able to snuggle up to him on those cool fall nights in the boxcar. My parents thought I was positulely crazy, but J-P and Marie-Laure said it sounded like fun and they wanted to try it themselves so they could tell their friends in France that they rode the American rails like the hobos did.

Sven and Ole put in another bed large enough for the two of us with a privacy partition at the other end of the boxcar. When they finished it, our boxcar suite was comfortable, if not as luxurious as our room in the executive railcar. And just like children, after the others saw it they wanted to travel in the boxcar too, so we arranged for everyone to have some travel time in the boxcar.

Later that day we received a telegram from Famous Players-Lasky Corporation – West Coast Studios:

```
ROAD  TRIP  BLUES  GREEN  LIGHT  STOP  ADVISE  WHEN  READY  TO
PROCEED STOP HAWKS BUSY STOP CAN YOU DIRECT STOP LASKY
```

"I'll want to do a casting couch audition with you" Dan said as he handed me the telegram.

"I thought that's what we did last night" I said, with mock surprise.

"Yes, that was with me as producer, but now I'm also the director, and I have cast approval rights too."

"Of all the things a young starlet has to do to advance her career" I said as I led him to our new railcar suite "This is my favorite thing, but tomorrow night you have to audition for me. As the associate producer, in the absence of you, the executive producer who seems to be busy every night with casting couch calls, I have to approve you as director. You had better perform to my expectations, and my expectations include exquisite orgasms enhanced by strawberries and French Champagne. Capisce?"

www.ingramcontent.com/pod-product-compliance
Lightning Source LLC
Chambersburg PA
CBHW021304250626
47155CB00002B/372